Lisa Ballantyne is the internationally bestselling author of four novels. Her debut, *The Guilty One*, was a Richard and Judy Book Club bestseller, nominated for an Edgar Award and translated into nearly thirty languages. *Good Bad Love* (previously *Redemption Road*) was a *USA Today* bestseller. She lives in Glasgow, Scotland.

Praise for Lisa Ballantyne:

'Gripping and emotionally charged ... Just brilliant' Clare Mackintosh

'Moving, insightful' *Guardian*

'Sophisticated, suspenseful, unsettling' Lee Child

'Tense' *The Sunday Times*

'Thought-provoking' *Woman & Home*

'Unsettling and compulsive' Rosamund Lupton

'Grips like a vice' *Daily Mail*

'Thought-provoking and clever' Gilly Macmillan

'One of the most readable, emotionally intense novels of the year' Richard Madeley, Richard and Judy's Book Club

'Dark, intelligent, suspenseful' Saskia Sarginson

'Tense and moving' Rachel Abbott

'Subtle, sus

Also by Lisa Ballantyne

The Guilty One
Little Liar
Once Upon a Lie

Good Bad Love

LISA BALLANTYNE

First published as *Redemption Road*

PIATKUS

PIATKUS

First published in Great Britain in 2015 by Piatkus as *Redemption Road*
This paperback edition published in 2021 by Piatkus

A CIP catalogue record for this book
is available from the British Library.

ISBN 978-0-349-43106-2

Typeset in Goudy by M Rules
Printed and bound in Great Britain by
Clays Ltd, Elcograf S.p.A.

Papers used by Piatkus are from well-managed forests
and other responsible sources.

Piatkus
An imprint of
Little, Brown Book Group
Carmelite House
50 Victoria Embankment
London EC4Y 0DZ

An Hachette UK Company
www.hachette.co.uk

www.littlebrown.co.uk

Grateful thanks to Creative Scotland
and Scottish Book Trust, for the gift and inspiration
of the Robert Louis Stevenson Fellowship.

This novel was previously published under the title
Redemption Road

1

Margaret Holloway
Thursday 5 December, 2013

Margaret Holloway wrapped her scarf around her face before she walked out into the school car park. It was not long after four o'clock, but a winter pall had shifted over London. It was dusk already, wary streetlamps casting premature light on to the icy pavements. Snowflakes had begun to swirl and Margaret blinked as one landed on her eyelashes. The first snow of the year always brought a silence, dampening down all sound. She felt gratefully alone, walking out into the new darkness, hers the only footprints on the path. She had been too hot inside and the cold air was welcome.

Her car was on the far side of the car park and she wasn't wearing proper shoes for the weather, although she had on her long, brown eiderdown coat. She had heard on the radio that it was to be the worst winter for fifty years.

It was only a few weeks until her thirty-sixth birthday, which always fell during the school holidays, but she had so much to do before the end of term. She was carrying a large handbag, heavy with documents to read for a meeting tomorrow. She was one of two deputy head teachers at Byron Academy, and the only woman on the senior management team, although one of the four assistant heads below Margaret was female. The day had left her tense and electrified. Her mind was fresh popcorn in hot oil, noisy with all the things she still had to do.

She walked faster than she might have done in such wintry conditions, because she was angry.

'*Don't do this,*' she had just pleaded with the head teacher, Malcolm Harris.

'It's a serious breach,' Malcolm had said, leaning right back in his chair and putting two hands beside his head, as if surrendering, and showing a clear circle of sweat at each armpit. 'I know how you feel about him. I know he's one of your "projects" but—'

'It's not that . . . it's just that permanent exclusion could ruin him. Stephen's come so far.'

'I think you'll find he's known as Trap.'

'And I don't think of him as a project,' Margaret had continued, ignoring Malcolm's remark. She was well aware of Stephen Hardy's gang affiliations – knew him better than most of the teachers. She had joined the school fresh out of college, as an English teacher, but had soon moved into the Learning Support Unit. The unit often worked with children with behavioural problems, who had to be removed from mainstream classes, and she had been shocked by the number of children who couldn't even read or write. She had taught Stephen since his first year, when she discovered that, at the age of thirteen, he still couldn't write his own address. She had tutored him for two years until he was back in normal classes and had been so proud of him when he got his GCSEs.

'He was carrying a knife in school. It's a simple case as far as I can see. He's nearly seventeen years old and—'

'It feels like you're condemning him. This is coming at the worst time – he's started his A Levels and he's making such good progress. This'll shatter his confidence.'

'We can't have knives in school.'

'He wasn't *brandishing* the knife. It was discovered by accident at the gym. You know he carries it for protection, nothing more.'

'No, I don't know that. And that's beside the point. This isn't as dramatic as you're making out. Kids drop out of sixth form all the time . . .'

'But he's not dropping out. You're forcing him out, after all he's overcome. Seven GCSEs with good grades and his teachers say his A Level work has been great. This is just a blip.'

Malcolm laughed lightly. 'A *blip, hardly what I would call it.*'

Margaret swallowed her anger took a deep breath and answered very quietly. 'This decision will have a huge, huge impact on his life. Right now he has a chance and you are about to take it away. There are other options. I want you to take a step back and think very carefully.'

'One of us does need to step back . . .'

'I've said my piece. All I'm asking is that you sleep on it.'

Malcolm's hands fell into his lap. He clasped them and then raised his thumbs at the same time as he raised his eyebrows. Margaret took it as assent.

'Thank you,' she managed, before she slipped on her coat.

'Drive carefully. There's a freeze on.'

Margaret smiled at him, lips tight shut. Malcolm was young for a head teacher: early forties, a keen mountain climber. He was only seven years older than Margaret and they were friends of sorts. They didn't often have differences and he had backed her rise to the school leadership.

'You too,' she had said.

The conversation tossed and turned in Margaret's mind as she walked to the car. She thought about Stephen with his violent older brother and collection of primary school swimming trophies. She thought about Malcolm and his insinuation that her viewpoint was personal, emotional.

The snow had become a blizzard and flakes swarmed. She was thirsty and tired and could feel her hair getting wet. She saw the car, took the key from her pocket and pressed the button to open the doors.

As the headlights flashed on the new snow, she slipped. She was carrying too many things and was unable to stop herself. She fell, hard.

Picking herself up, Margaret realised that she had skinned her knees. Her handbag was disembowelled and the papers for tomorrow's meeting were dampening in the snow.

'Jesus Christ,' she whispered, as her knuckles grazed the tarmac chasing her iPhone.

In the car, she glanced at her face in the rear-view mirror and ran her fingernails through her dark cropped hair. She had worn her hair short since her early twenties. It accentuated her big eyes and the teardrop shape of her face. The snow had wet her lashes, and ruined the eyeliner that ran along her upper lid in a perfect cat's eye. She ran her thumb beneath each lid. The lights from the school illuminated her face in the mirror, making her seem paler, childishly young and lost.

She turned the key in the ignition, but the engine merely whined at her.

'You have got to be kidding,' she said, under her breath. 'Come on. You can do it.'

She waited ten seconds before turning the key again, blowing on to her stinging knuckles and wondering if she might actually self-combust if she couldn't even get out of the *bloody car park*.

Often, she took the Tube to work but there was disruption today and she hadn't wanted to risk being late.

She turned the key again. The engine whined, coughed but then started.

'Thank you,' Margaret whispered, pumping the accelerator, turning on the lights and the radio.

She put on her seatbelt, turned on the heaters, exhaled, then glanced at Ben's text on her iPhone before she turned on to the road. *We need milk, but only if u get a chance xx*

The wipers were on full, the snow gathering at the corners of the windscreen.

She turned right on to Willis Street and then after the Green Man Interchange she took the first exit, signposted *Cambridge and Stansted Airport*. It was just over a half-hour drive from the school to Loughton in good conditions, but because of the snow and the heavy traffic today, Margaret expected it would take her forty minutes or more to get home.

Under her opaque tights, her skinned knees were stinging. The sensation reminded her of being a child. She banged the back of her head gently off the headrest, as if to shake the worries from her mind.

Ben would be making dinner, but as soon as she had eaten it, it would be time to take Paula to her acting class in the local community centre, where Margaret would sit drinking weak machine coffee, preparing for her meeting tomorrow. If they made it home early she would be in time to stop the fight that Ben and Eliot, her seven-year-old, always seemed to have around bedtime, when her son was reluctant to relinquish his iPad.

She was a young parent, or young by today's standards: twenty-five when she married Ben, and twenty-six when Paula was born, with Eliot coming only two years later. Ben was a freelance writer and worked from home and Margaret sometimes felt jealous that he saw more of the children than she did. Often it was Ben who welcomed them home from school, and most days during the week Ben cooked dinner and helped them with their homework.

Heading home, she always felt anxious to see them all again.

At home, on the mantelpiece, there was a black and white photograph of Margaret reading to her children when they were both small. It was her favourite family photograph. Ben had taken it, snapping them unawares. Eliot was tucked under one arm and Paula under the other, and their three rapt faces were pressed close together, the book blurry in the foreground. Not tonight because she had to go out, but most nights Margaret still tried to read to them.

She indicated and then pulled out on to the M11, just in front of a lorry. Both lanes were busy and she kept to the inside. There was a jeep in front of her and a lot of the splashback landed on Margaret's windscreen. The traffic was travelling at sixty miles an hour, and the road was damp with dirty slush.

Margaret slowed down further as visibility was so poor. Caught in her headlights, the blizzard swirled in concentric circles. When she looked to the left of the windscreen, the flakes darted towards her; when she looked to the right they reformed to focus in on her again. The snow building up on the corners of the windscreen was blinkering her. She could see the red of tail lights in front, but not much else except the illuminated, swirling flakes.

Margaret was not aware of what hit her, but she felt a hard jolt from behind and the airbag exploded. She put her foot on the brake, but her car collided with the jeep in front. The noise of metal crushing took her breath away. The bonnet of her car rose up before her and everything went dark. She braced herself for great pain, holding her breath and clenching her fists.

No pain came. When she opened her eyes, there was the sound of car alarms and muffled screams and, underneath it all, the trickle and rush of water. She ran her hands over her face and body and could find no wound, although there was a dull ache in her chest from the airbag. She tried the driver's door, but it wouldn't open, even when she shouldered it. She reached for her handbag but it had spilled onto the floor. Her car was contorted and dark and she couldn't see where her phone had fallen. She leaned over and tried to open the passenger door but the impact had damaged that too.

There was a glow from behind the bonnet as if something in the engine had caught fire.

The snow continued to fall, filling the space between the bonnet and the windscreen, so that it felt as if she was being buried. The lights that remained grew fainter. Margaret rubbed on the side window to clear it of condensation and pressed her face against the glass. She could see shapes moving in the darkness, oscillating in the oily puddles reflected by car lights. The shapes were people, she decided. There was also a wavering yellow, which almost looked like flames.

'It's all right,' she said to herself, out loud. Help would come. All she had to do was wait. She slid over in the seat and searched with open palm on the floor for her phone. She found almost everything else: her lip gloss, a packet of tampons, ticket stubs for an Arcade Fire concert, and two hairbrushes.

While she was bent over, head to the floor, she became aware of the smell of petrol: a noxious whiff. It reminded her of hanging out of the car window at petrol stations as a child. She strained to peer out of the small clear corner of her side window.

7

The grass embankment that ran along the crash barrier had been replaced by a strip of fire.

Margaret's breath suddenly became shallow. It rasped, drying, in her throat.

If she was right, and her fuel tank had been ruptured by the collision and the engine was on fire, then there was a chance that the car would explode.

She wanted to speak to Ben but was now glad that she couldn't find her phone. She wouldn't be able to conceal her fear.

Ben. Just the thought of him brought tears to her eyes. She remembered the smell between his shoulder blades in the middle of the night and the quizzical look in his eyes when she said something he disagreed with; the hunched way he sat over the keyboard in the study when he was working on an article. Then she thought of Paula, impatient to go to drama class, her dinner finished and thinking that Mum was late *again*. She thought of Eliot, lost in a game on his iPad, unaware of the danger she was in, or that his mother might be taken from him.

She looked around for objects that might smash the glass and found a weighted plastic ice scraper down the inside of the driver's door. She used all her strength and succeeded in making a crack in the window.

All she could smell was petrol and her own sweat – her own fear. The car alarms had ceased but had been replaced by the flatline of car horns. She realised that many more cars must have crashed. The flatlining horns would be drivers slumped against their steering wheels. Through the small triangle of cleared window she could see the shape of the fire moving.

'No,' she screamed, pounding her fists and her head and her shoulders at the window. 'NO.' She knew the insulating snow meant that no one would hear her. She twisted round and stamped at the glass, pounding with the soles of her flimsy shoes. It hurt but the window held fast.

She didn't want it to end here. So much was unfinished. There was so much she still needed to know, understand, *do*.

Suddenly there was a man by her door, whom she assumed was a fireman. She could see only his dark body. He was pulling on the door handle, putting his weight behind it.

'Thank you,' she mouthed through the glass, hot tears washing her cheeks. 'Thank you.'

The door wouldn't budge. The man picked up something from the road – a piece of metal – and began to pound her window with it.

'Cover your face,' she heard him say through the glass.

Margaret did as he asked – holding her bag in front of her face – but still watched him, waiting for her chance.

The man tried to wedge the metal into the door mechanism but that did not work, so he returned to the cracked driver's window.

'I can't open it,' she heard him say.

She gazed upwards to see him through one of the larger cracks. He was dressed in a dark sweater, not a fireman.

'I'm sorry,' she heard him say, his voice thickened. 'I can't. We don't have much time.'

She bit her lip and once again placed her palm on the cracked pane. 'It's all right,' she said, loud enough for him to hear. 'Thank you for trying. Go. It's all right.'

The man placed his own palm on the other side of the glass and Margaret was sure she felt its warmth. When he took his palm away, she bowed her head and cried, feeling young, almost infantile, reduced to herself and nothing more.

Shafts of light entered the cramped car space when he took

away his hand. Her throat tightened as she wondered how long it would be and if she would suffer. She hoped for an explosion. The thought of burning alive terrified her so much that she picked up the ice scraper again and bashed it against the window.

'Get back!'

It was the man – his pale face pressed against the glass.

'I'm gonna try and break it, so sit well back.'

She turned towards the passenger seat and covered her face.

There was a dull sound and when Margaret raised her head, the man's bloody fist was inside the car. He had punched the glass in, taking the skin from his hand.

The cold air reached inside and the stench of petrol became stronger. The man was pulling the broken glass from the window with his bare hands.

'I'll pull you through,' he said to her.

'I won't fit.'

'Give me your hands!' As he spoke this time, desperate, authoritative, the scarf he was wearing fell away from his face.

The sight of him was enough to cause her to draw breath, but she did not pull away. It was as if a squid had landed on his face: tentacles grew over his cheeks, forehead and skull and right down his neck. One of the man's eyes was pulled out of shape, to make way for the tentacle's path. His skin shone in the oily fiery light, pale and poreless.

Margaret placed her hands in his. He pulled her through fast, although her hips got caught and she landed on top of him.

She lay breathing on the man's chest, feeling the chill of the snow on her cheeks and scalp and grateful for it. Margaret lifted her face up and saw the gnarled skin of his neck.

He strained to get up, and she could see that he was in pain. He helped her to her feet.

'Hurry, we need to—'

When they were nearly at the embankment, the car blew up. The explosion reverberated through Margaret, expelling all the air from her lungs. Her mind was bright with the horror of it, but the man pulled her into him and back down on to the road, rolling her over and over as debris fell around them. Margaret felt the great weight of his body above her, and then nothing, then the weight again, pinning her down and rolling her forward, a gravitational momentum. She felt safe there, grateful.

Half of Margaret's face was in the snow. The stranger raised himself from her and brushed the snow from his body. He was bleeding badly from his forehead. He knelt, watching the blaze, holding his bloody hand in the other. Margaret rolled over and stood up. Her shoes were gone and the icy snow wet the soles of her feet. She could see paramedics in green rushing towards them. She could hear nothing but her own heartbeats and the roar of the fire.

Her car was engulfed in flames and she saw now that the whole of the M11 was a carnage of crashed cars. The motorway was like a scrapyard: upended vehicles and the stench of burning rubber. The blue lights were so far away because even the emergency services couldn't get close.

Relief flooded into her, warm as a shower. Margaret looked down to the man who had saved her.

'Were you in the crash too?' she asked him. 'You're hurt. Your hand must be broken and your head . . .'

'Fine' was all he said, turning his eyes from her, trying to pull his scarf over his face with his bloodied hand.

'Its all right,' Margaret said, putting a hand on his neck. 'Thank you. I would have died. Now we must get you some help.'

'I'm fine,' he said again, then staggered to his feet and walked away from her, down the lane of concertinaed cars, into the smoke and fire and snow.

'Wait,' Margaret called to him, 'please?'

Paramedics swarmed over the scene. She was wrapped in a space blanket, her pulse was taken and then she was given a tag and instructed where to wait; that she was going to be OK. She gave her details and was told that Ben would be informed.

Margaret shivered on the side of the motorway clutching the foil blanket around her, looking for the burned man who had saved her. She asked the paramedic who tended to her, but he shook his head. 'I'm not sure I've seen him. There's too many injured. You need to rest now. Just take a break and let us look after you.'

She remembered the heat of the stranger's palm against hers, and the sheer size of him crouched in the snow, holding his damaged hand to his chest. He had been hurt, she knew he had; she wanted to find him to make sure he got help.

2

Big George
Friday 27 September, 1985

Big George got up on the table, pint in hand, and began a rendition of 'Sweet Caroline'. He was six foot three with black hair, bright blue eyes, and longer eyelashes than his only sister, Patricia. He was the best looking of all the McLaughlins and had got away with murder for years because of it. He had been his mother's favourite and he could carry a song like her, although it had been years since she had had anything to sing about.

George was on his fourth pint and there was a sheen of glee in his eyes. The whole bar turned to him, clapping in time. The McLaughlins demanded attention, but usually that was enforced with the threat of great violence. Georgie Boy was different. Most people in the East End of Glasgow knew him and were wary of him because of his family, but those who knew him well said that George was a gentle giant. George's father, Brendan, had called him soft, but then they didn't come much harder than Brendan McLaughlin.

George leaned on Tam Driscoll's shoulder as he climbed down

from his impromptu stage. An older man leaving the bar patted George's back: 'Look out, Neil Diamond.'

'Away!' said George over his shoulder, his eyes smiling at the compliment.

'You ready for another, big man?' said Tam.

George nodded, wiping the sweat from his brow with his fore-arm, and put his empty pint glass on the bar. By the time Tam was served, a table had become available at the periphery of the bar and, tired after his performance, George sat down and ran his hands through his hair.

Tam had recently started working with George in the garage the McLaughlins ran, along the Shettleston Road. The garage was semi-legitimate, although cars were 'cleaned' there. It was as close to the family business as George could bear to be. Tam was a mechanic and a good one, but had only taken the job because he had been out of work for nearly a year.

'I don't want to get involved,' he would whisper to George, his face and hands dark with engine grease, when George's elder brother, Peter visited, clasping and unclasping his gloved hands. Peter had taken over, years ago, after their father had disappeared, presumed dead.

'Me neither,' George had reassured him.

In the few weeks they had known each other George had been in the habit of sharing stories with Tam, as a mark of friendship and trust, but Tam had yet to share anything other than his time and his beer money with George.

George understood Tam's fear, and had decided to be patient. His father had made his name as a heavy for the top loan shark in Glasgow. Even now, in this bar, there would be at least two or three people who had been injured by the McLaughlins. One of the people clapping along to George's song had been

Giovanni DeLuca, who owned the chip shop on the corner. Just the sight of DeLuca in the crowd had made George forget a line, although his audience thought it was the beer. He had watched Giovanni's pale, skeletal hand clapping against his other, strong brown one. At fourteen years old George had watched his father force Giovanni's hand into the deep fat fryer.

Tam walked slowly to their table, careful not to spill the beer. He was a full head shorter than George and fifteen years older, thin and wiry with grey hair cut short. He had taught George how to bleed an engine and how to change an exhaust. George, who had never been any good at school, found he loved learning about cars, and picked up quickly what Tam taught him. He had few friends and he had liked Tam instantly. It was as if Tam was a replacement father figure: benevolent, where Brendan, *God rest his soul*, had been a bastard.

'You just can't help yourself, can you, big yin?'

'Nothing like a wee song to raise the spirits.'

'If you say so.'

George took another long drink of beer. 'No, no, not this time,' he said, drunk and patting Tam on the chest. 'Not if I say so. I want . . .' George swallowed a hiccup, 'to hear what you have to say for once. You're the man. The man that can. You're my teacher, my maestro.'

'Och away. You're just haverin' now.'

'I'm serious, by the way. I have serious respect for you. Serious respect. But you never talk about yourself. Tell me about you – YOU – give me your craick.'

'There's not much to say, really,' said Tam.

Even through the blur of beer, George could tell that his friend was worried. George was big like his father had been, but he had his mother's heart. His brothers, and his sister to a large extent, had been inured to the violence. George and his mother had empathy, which they had polished in each other, a pearl in the mud and dirt of their lives. She had died just last year, cruelly, unfairly, dying of a simple infection after surviving a lifetime of violence.

'You have a family,' persisted George. 'You never talk about them.'

'There's not much to say.'

Only Tam's eyes moved on his face.

'You have a daughter. How old is she?'

'Fifteen,' said Tam, his voice faint, as if at confession.

'I'm only asking,' said George, squeezing the older man's arm. 'I just want to know who you are, for Chrissake. If you consider it personal, then just tell me to piss off. I'm not your priest.'

Tam nodded. Once again, George read something in his eyes.

'You're not a Catholic, are you?'

'My mother was a Catholic. I have nothing against—'

'I don't give a shit what you believe in. For Christ's sake, believing in anything at all is hard enough, is it not? You're my man and if you're a Proddy then that's good with me.'

Tam said nothing, nodding. There was a sheen of sweat on his face. George took another sip of beer and decided to return to his old tactics of sharing his own life and hoping that Tam would feel comfortable enough to reciprocate.

'You're lucky,' George said, sitting back and folding his arms. They were side by side on the red pleather bench. George surveyed the oval island of the bar as he spoke, deliberately trying to relax his friend. 'I envy you, having a daughter. Having a daughter changes a man. I mean, it didn't change my father, but he was a special case. It changed me.'

George took a deep breath. Just the word *daughter* took him

16

out of himself. It was like a breach in his drunkenness, a portal to another state of consciousness.

'I didn't know you had a daughter,' said Tam, quietly.

George turned to him again, smiling broadly. 'Have a gander at this,' he said, unbuttoning his shirt and pulling it back to show Tam his chest. There, above his heart, tattooed in red ink, was the name *Moll*.

'Moll was your daughter?' said Tam, taking another sip.

'She *is* my daughter. She's not dead. She's alive.'

Tam licked his lips. George could tell he was interested but afraid to ask more. George took another drink of beer and then told Tam the whole story.

'You won't know Kathleen Jamieson, but I started seeing her soon as I left school, and I told you already that I was chucked out when I was fourteen, so it was early on. She was my first love ... my only love, I suppose. Five, six years we were together, on the sly most of the time, because her family didn't like her hanging around with me. She was a nice girl, you understand. Anyway, we weren't careful and she got pregnant. I was happy when she told me, because I'm not like other guys. I always wanted to be married and have children. I wanted to start my own family since I was six or seven years old ...' George stopped for a long, hearty laugh. 'Probably because my own was such a fucking nightmare, wouldn't you say?'

Tam conceded a smile. He smiled on one side of his face, while the other half remained guarded, almost sad.

'Her family were really devout – you know the types: a Hail Mary every time you fart. Pregnant and unmarried was bad enough, but pregnant *to the likes of me* ... Well, they of course said she would have to have the baby. I was straight round there with the diamond ring and everything, but they were having none of it. They told me she'd had a miscarriage and had gone

17

to visit her aunt to recover. I was sure they'd packed her off to a convent, like they did in the sixties. My mother said as much. She was the only one in my family I told . . . about the baby.'

George put a cigarette between his lips and patted his pockets for his matches until Tam gave him a light. He took a long drag, wincing as he inhaled.

'What happened?' said Tam.

George was encouraged.

'Well, it was just after Christmas and I was thinking of Kathleen and popped round to the Jamiesons' one morning after mass, just to ask for news of her. I thought they'd tell me to piss off, but when I arrived, Kathleen was there and *in labour*. Her father was out, and I think had all but washed his hands of her by that point, and so did I not end up giving her, her mother and her sister a lift to the hospital.

'We were in there for the longest time. I ran out of fags. It was the middle of the night when my daughter was born, and I remember me and this other expectant father were sharing a flask of whisky in the waiting room. Only . . . it was his third, and he knew he was going home with the bairn.' George looked at a spot in the distance as he remembered. 'I can't tell you what it was like when I saw her for the first time.'

'The bairn?'

'She was so beautiful. Did you feel like that . . . ?'

Tam raised his eyebrows.

'Molly. I called her Moll. She has my eyes. Kathleen let me hold her, although her mother and sister were complaining that I stank of whisky and kept shouting at me to mind and not drop her. I don't know how you felt, but there's nothing so humbling for a man. My father'll turn in his grave if he hears me say this, but I just wanted a wee girl.'

'Girls are a lot less trouble, so they say' was all that Tam would concede.

'After I'd seen that bairn, I was in love. I would have done anything for her. When she got out of hospital me and Kathleen went to register the birth and we went for a walk and I proposed to her all over again. On my knees in Glasgow Green ... *on my fucking knees*, but ... she said she was seeing some other guy.'

'How d'you mean?'

'Her family had sorted it all out, I've no doubt. No doubt in my mind at all. Some old bastard that was willing to take on a fallen woman and her child. I mean did these people not know it was nineteen seventy-seven. Nineteen fucking seventy-seven!'

'They married her off?'

'Kathleen was upset, crying. She told me it was the only way ... Her family were angry at her, but over their dead bodies would they let her marry me. She'd changed. She was cold towards me. You know what women are like. "*Forget about her, Georgie*," she told me.'

'I'm sorry,' said Tam, taking a long sip of beer. The bell for last orders sounded.

George nodded, looking at a point far in the distance. 'You for another?' he asked.

'I'm all right,' said Tam, looking into the remainder of his beer.

'Ah, go on, it's payday after all,' said George, slapping his wallet on the table.

Tam nodded his assent. George felt his balance wavering as he stood to return to the bar, but he found it again after a second or two.

'Thanks, big man,' said Tam when George returned, spilling a little beer on the table.

They were silent for a while, watching the other men in the

bar. It was mostly men. The room was tinged blue with smoke and George felt his mind heavy with beer and memories.

'Do you ever think about getting out of here?' said George quietly, but facing the room of people rather than Tam beside him.

'Sometimes,' said Tam, hedging his bets, as always. 'Why?'

'Can I count you as a friend?' said George, turning to look Tam in the eye. Tam's own furtive eyes widened for a moment, under George's gaze.

Tam swallowed and then licked his lips as if in anticipation.

'You need to keep it to yourself.'

Tam nodded.

'I found a bit of money. It would only do you harm to know where, so I won't mention it, but it's enough – enough to totally disappear with – and I'm planning on disappearing. Now you see me . . .' said George, elbowing Tam to coax a smile from him, 'now you don't.'

'Where are you going?' said Tam, his face suddenly grey and drawn.

'North first, then south. I'm not going alone.'

'I . . . Georgie, I have a family. I'm a quiet man . . .'

George allowed another fit of laughter to erupt from his body, although beneath the beer and the joviality he was deadly serious.

'I'm not talking about you, Tam, relax! Christ. I think *I'm* a worrywart, but I've got nothing on you. I mean, I like you and all, but I wasn't planning on running away with you.'

Colour returned to Tam's face. He was too thin-skinned and scrawny for a full blush but he coloured all the same.

George unbuttoned his shirt again and placed his right palm over the tattoo, as if he were making a pledge.

'I found her, you see,' said George, his eyes fixed on a horizon far beyond the walls of the Portland Arms.

'Who, Kathleen?'

'I didn't get to finish my story. Kathleen went north with some old fella and it crushed me, but ... well, I tried to get over her. You've no idea what I was like when I was younger – pissed every night and going with whatever lassie'd have me. I did all that but I couldn't get her and the bairn out of my mind. I couldn't forget how it had felt to hold my own daughter in my arms and to see her face and see my own in hers. It changes a man. Did it not change you?'

Again George looked to Tam for some kind of validation.

'They're bonny when they're young, that's for sure' was all Tam would give.

'Anyway, I didn't care for a few years, or told myself I didn't. I had no idea where they were anyway. Kathleen was gone – not in Glasgow – and she'd basically said that her and the wean were well shot of me. But then I met Wee Malkie. He'd been on the oilrigs and had done work all over the north of Scotland. Did he not run into Kathleen with the wean? He said the wee one was the spit of me.'

'When was that?'

'Two years ago. I've found out where she lives.'

'Two years, people move.'

'People move, but not if you have a big house in Thurso. I know where they are.'

George downed the rest of his pint and wiped his mouth with the back of his hand.

Tam was smiling again – that strange smile he offered when Peter was in the garage. His eyes were scrunched up, which made people think it was a proper smile, but somehow it was out of synch with his mouth. His mouth was wary to commit. When Tam smiled like that, it looked as if he was in pain.

George turned to him, unsmiling, honest, wishing something worthy of Brendan McLaughlin: wishing that Tam was a bigger man. But George was not his father and George was determined to trust small, thin, terrified Tam, who knew an engine as a surgeon knew a body.

'I have the means,' said George slowly, leaning in so close that he could smell the starch on Tam's Friday-night shirt. 'Third time lucky. I'm going up north to ask Kathleen to be mine and then the three of us can go away together – me, Kathleen and my wee girl.'

'Where on earth would you go?'

George leaned in closer to Tam, and spoke to him in a whisper. 'Can I trust you?' he said, squeezing Tam's upper arm.

'Yes.'

'You ever heard of a wee place called Penzance in Cornwall?'

'Cornwall, aye.'

'Well, I want to live there, in peace and quiet, right by the sea. That's where we're gonna be – me and my own wee family.'

'Why would you go there? Who do you know from there?'

'No one. My mother's family were from there. My mum lived there when she was wee and she used to tell me about it – the open spaces and the sea, the tiny wee houses. My mother owned some land there, a cottage on the South West Coast Path, between Sennen and Porthcurno. It's almost a ruin now, I believe. I've never been there although she showed me pictures. My mother left it to me in her will. It was a secret, just between us. My brothers and sister don't know. If my mother could've run away, back to that place, she would've. She told me all about it and that's where I'm gonna be. I'm gonna fix it up – build it from scratch if I have to – and live there with my family. My own family.'

'You're havering, man. If Kathleen's married, what makes you think she'll want back with you?'

'Would you take a look at this face, Tam. Just take a look at this face,' said George, raising his chin, his eyes brightening.

'I know but . . .'

'But what? She loves me. She's always loved me. Plus, I'm that wee girl's father and I think she deserves to know me.'

'What would you do with a baby?'

'She's not a baby any longer, is she?'

'How old is she now?'

'Seven.'

3

Angus Campbell
Friday 27 September, 1985

'I'll come when I'm good and ready,' said Angus, unable even to turn and look at her.

'I was going to serve up.' His wife stood at the door, her hands folded in front of her body.

'I heard you the first time,' he said, hunched over his typewriter, waving at her without turning round, as if she were a bluebottle that was bothering him.

Three days he had been home from his office at the *John o'Groat Journal*, working on the manual typewriter that had belonged to Hazel's father, because Maisie was due to calve. The vet had said she would go into labour in about a week, and Angus was keeping an eye on her for signs. Anxious for her to calve as soon as possible, he was spending his evenings pacing the living room instead of reading, terrified that Maisie would go into labour on the Sabbath. The vet had said the calf was breach, although it could turn. When the time came, Maisie would almost certainly need his help.

'I'm sure that God will turn the calf or that Maisie'll calve before or after the Sabbath and we will help her,' Hazel had said when he told her of his worries.

'Are you stupid, woman? God doesn't rise to our commands.'

All she had were worn phrases of consolation, already stale as the torn pan bread they used at Communion. Every time he cast eyes on the woman he was filled with vitriol. She would test the patience of a saint.

He was working on a story that would run with the head-line ORPHANED OTTER ON THE ROAD TO RECOVERY. He loved animals – more than people, he would sometimes admit – but the story was really *beneath* him. His searing journalistic talent was yet to be discovered, and now, not long after his forty-third birthday, he was beginning to wonder how much longer before he had passed the window of discovery and entered the door of oblivion. Hazel's interruption had just caused him to mistype a word. All she did was keep him back. When the article was done, he would have to drive to the *Journal*'s office in Wick to submit it.

Angus finished the piece and stacked the pages neatly by the side of the typewriter, then placed them in a file. These stories that he was forced to write belittled him: otters, councillors' disgraces and winners of prizes that no one cared about. The Lord intended more for him.

In March, after a full year, the miners' strike had ended, but the *Journal* had put the story on page three. Angus had not been in favour of the strike but he would have valued the chance to write about it. The editor had written the article himself: two hundred words.

Angus could see himself as a reporter, not for the *John o'Groat Journal* but the *The Times*. He dreamed of getting wind of a story that would be syndicated worldwide. The story was out there, but Angus knew he could find it within him, as he had found God.

About six months ago, a researcher from Scottish Television had called the *John o'Groat Journal* scouting for stories. Instead of his colleague Amanda picking up the phone as usual, Angus had answered. The woman from STV was just an intern, but she had said her boss was interested in *any scoop* the *Journal* had.

Apart from Maisie calving, a scoop was now all that Angus thought about. A scoop was his chance of glory.

Finally, Angus went downstairs to dinner. Everyone sat down after Angus sat, and clasped their hands when he held his in prayer.

He closed his eyes and spoke quickly, for he was hungry. 'We thank the Lord for this food before us. Jesus is our best friend. He is our King. He alone can change our hearts to love Him more. We need Him every day. Our church life is empty if we are not dependent on Him. He alone can open the closed hearts of our unbelieving friends. He wants to hear our prayers. He chooses to act in response to them. This is our privilege – and responsibility – for His Kingdom, for our church, for us ... Thank you, God.'

As they had been taught, the children – Rachael, fourteen, and Caleb, twelve – waited until Angus raised his cutlery before touching their own. Rachael was turning into a gawky teenager: spots on her chin. Caleb was small and furtive: sleekit-eyed. As babies, he had had high hopes for them – especially Caleb – but they both still required a lot of guidance.

It was roast lamb, cauliflower cheese and boiled potatoes, and it was *cold*. Angus scooped a spoonful of cauliflower on to his plate and then tested the temperature.

He threw down his cutlery and held on to the table, facing Hazel.

'What is the meaning of this, woman? Are we animals that we should eat cold slops?'

'It . . . it . . . was warm. I- I . . .'

He hated her most when she stammered. It was as if all the weakness in her had welled up into her mouth and prevented the words from being born.

He had given himself a rule: not to hit her in front of the children, and so he merely swiped his plate to the floor and left for the barn.

'I'll be back in an hour and you know that I expect better,' he said, as he pulled on his wellingtons and zipped up his anorak.

As he left, their three faces watched him, blanched and unknowing as uncooked buns.

The walk to Maisie's pen was five minutes at full pelt. The sheer expectation of seeing her brought warmth to Angus's palms, to his whole body. He had raised her since she was six months old. He loved the velvet pink of her nose and the strong tendons on her legs, the curve of her flank, the knowing, loving look that she gave him: passive, adoring, pure. He could see clearly that Maisie loved him, as her master. She trusted him utterly and was devoted to him.

Angus had been brought up in Northbay on the southern tip of the Isle of Barra – the youngest of three boys, born to a fishing family. His father had a small boat, but the Campbells also kept a few animals by their croft: chickens, some sheep and cows and two ponies. As a child, it had been Angus's responsibility to look after the animals.

The Campbells' main business had been fish and the stench of fish guts assumed the house almost as completely as Angus's mother's piety, but the barns had always been the place where he felt safe and most at home. The barns had smelled intimate, warm and alive. Wild kittens scampered among the straw as Angus milked the cows by hand.

His mother had taught him to fear God and the pain of her wooden spoon. His salty-smelling father, with rough palms and face reddened by the sea wind, had done nothing but abandon him, leaving him alone day after day, taking the older boys out to sea with him, while Angus was left at home with his mother.

'*The devil finds work for idle hands,*' she would tell Angus, wagging a forefinger sequinned with fish scales.

The animals had shown him what was right, more than his parents, or else he put more weight on the lessons the animals taught him: Primrose rejecting his cold fingers on her udders, Bolt throwing him the day he tried to make him jump the stream. He had learned to love through loving animals. They had taught him boundaries, but they had also bowed to Angus's will. He had found sanctity at last. Love could not be cast back into his face, like sand.

Maisie was eating when he entered her pen. She chewed her cud with diligence despite the heavy protuberance of her abdomen. Angus entered and ran a palm across the cow's flank.

'There you go, my girl. It'll be soon, I know. I'll help you get it out quick as a flash. As a flash, I tell you. Everything will be just fine. You know that I'll look after you. You know that I'll see you right, my precious girl. By gum, you're looking fine tonight. You're a beauty, that's for sure.'

The cow turned to him, pink-nosed, chewing methodically, submissive. Angus placed a hand on each of her masticating cheeks. Her face was the kindest, gentlest thing he had ever seen. He felt blessed.

4

Margaret Holloway
Monday, 9 December, 2013

It was only three days since the crash, but already Margaret was back at work. She had been absent for only one day – the Friday following – but in that time Stephen Hardy had been expelled. She felt exploited, but had yet to speak to Malcolm about it.

Everyone had been surprised that Margaret returned so quickly. Ben had begged her to take a week off, but she had refused. She had a few scratches still visible on her arms and face, and her ribs hurt when she laughed or twisted, but that was all.

'Why would I take a week off when there's nothing wrong with me?' Margaret had said to Ben, wide-eyed. 'Besides it's nearly the Christmas holidays.'

'You need to listen to what the doctor said.'

The doctor had told her that she was suffering from shock. Margaret had told Ben that she was fine, and finally he yielded.

Her husband was a big bear of a man, with thick black hair and a lopsided smile. Margaret was tall – over five foot eight – but his size still dwarfed her. Love for them had sprung, like mushrooms overnight, sudden but tender, seeming right. They had been together since university in Bristol, when he had sat next to her in an English lecture – knees akimbo because he couldn't fit into the seat – and asked to borrow a pen from her, before putting it behind his ear and not making a single note for the duration. He was from Liverpool with a sing-song accent and a nice smile and she had liked him right away.

Now, in her office on the third floor, Margaret remembered his face when she left for work this morning. He had been tired – fresh from sleep – lines on his cheeks from the pillow.

'I think you're being silly,' he said, again, shrugging, hands in his pockets and a night's stubble on his chin. She had stood on tiptoes to kiss him and told him once again that she was *fine*.

She was attending a deputy head teacher's conference that afternoon and had a presentation to give on behaviour management, so was working through her lunch hour. An uneaten egg sandwich sat by her keyboard.

The crash on the M11 had been a major incident, involving more than thirty vehicles. Most of the injured had been treated at the trauma centre at the Royal London Hospital. Margaret knew that she was lucky to be alive.

She felt on edge and her concentration was worse than usual. Now, at her computer, she searched the internet for news stories of the crash. There were several reports, even in the national papers, because the damage, fatalities and injuries had been extensive. *London's Worst EVER Pile-up*, the *Mail* had called it.

Although she was trying her best to concentrate, her thoughts returned to the crash. The memory which haunted her most was that of the moment when her car had concertinaed around her, the airbag blew up in her chest and the fuel tank burst. Each time she recalled it she could remember more details: the sound of metal rasping against metal, the sweat on her palms against the steering wheel, the precise pattern of snow as it blacked out the windscreen.

She had come close to being burned alive in her car and the thought both petrified and transfixed her. She didn't know why, but the memory was compulsive. She had mentioned it briefly to the doctor and he had said it was a symptom of post-traumatic stress.

She was an atheist and had never been superstitious, but the burned man had appeared like a guardian angel, saving her seconds before a lingering, agonising death. She had barely spoken to him and then he had disappeared into the snow, himself obviously wounded. At the hospital, the waiting room was crowded and Margaret had searched for his face, but she hadn't seen him.

There was a knock on Margaret's office door and Malcolm entered. She pushed up her sleeves.

'I heard you were back. How are you?'

He had phoned the house over the weekend, but Ben had taken the call.

'I'm all right, thanks. Glad to be back.'

'You were so lucky. Absolutely horrendous ...'

'I know.'

'You know it's fine if you take more time ...'

'Thanks. I just wanted to get back and get stuck in. You know how it is.'

Malcolm nodded, frowning.

'Listen, I heard about Stephen,' Margaret said, standing up to face him, leaning against her desk.

'I'm sorry. I knew how you felt,' he said. 'I spoke to Jonathan ...'

Jonathan was the deputy head for curriculum.

'Why did you speak to him? *I'm* the deputy responsible for pastoral. What's Jonathan got to do with it?'

Malcolm smiled and coloured. 'Look, your opinion was the most important, and I took it on board, but ultimately it was my decision.'

'I asked you to consider *Stephen*, and his *life* . . .'

'Margaret, the decision's been made.'

'You had *no right*.'

'I think you'll find—'

'You *knew* how I felt!'

Malcolm closed the door, and it was only then that Margaret realised she had been shouting. Her heart was beating so fast that she could feel it against her ribcage. It was beating as hard as it had the moment when she thought she would die.

'It was my call and it was approved by the chair of governors. I don't exclude pupils lightly, but I think it was the right thing to do. I kept the police out of it.'

'That doesn't make it all right.'

'However valid your arguments, I wasn't convinced it was the best way to go. I'm sure there will be another time when your view will be supported.'

'This isn't *about me*!' said Margaret, feeling the heat in her face. 'It's about him, don't you realise what you've done?'

She began to cry.

Malcolm's lips parted in shock.

She tried to compose herself, immediately embarrassed and confused.

At 3 p.m., Margaret stood before a group of deputy head teachers from across the London boroughs to give her presentation on Byron Academy's behaviour management strategy. The meeting was in a high school in Camden – a 1960s building with low ceilings and strip lighting. Midwinter and the heating was on full blast. She felt sweat at her hairline.

She had spoken to this group many times but today she felt young and vulnerable before them. Her uneaten sandwich was still in her bag and her stomach rumbled. She placed a hand on her midriff to silence it.

Margaret glanced at her rough notes then bent over the laptop to pull up her slides. Her fingers were trembling.

She knew the topic inside and out. Not only had she been in management for more than six years, but she had worked her way up and diversified her fields: head of subject, head of the Learning Support Unit. She was one of the youngest deputies in the room, but knew she was one of the most experienced.

'Thanks for coming, everyone, and thanks to John for providing the cakes,' Margaret began, her voice wavering. She cleared her throat, then reached for a glass of water, noticing again the tremor in her hand. There was a murmur of laughter and quiet conversation.

Margaret beamed a large smile at the group and clasped her hands. 'Today I want to run through not just behaviour management . . .' she was aware of her heart beating, 'but I want to talk about our school drugs and sex education policies and our pastoral approach to . . . to . . .'

The notes shook in her hand and she lost her place.

'You can see here,' she began, turning to the image projected on to the whiteboard. It showed a pupil with his head down on the desk. The words she had planned to say, about disengagement from learning and disenfranchisement, swirled inside her head. She had given this talk so many times before, yet now she struggled to formulate the words to explain the correlation between achievement and behaviour. She knew it all by heart, but there was not enough air in her lungs to complete the sentence. A trickle of sweat coursed between her shoulder blades. She tried to swallow but her mouth was dry.

Her trembling forefinger was too heavy on the button for the next slide and she accidentally shunted too far forward, then fumbled for a moment with the mouse – tremulous cursor on the screen – until she retraced her steps. *Get a hold of yourself*, she thought.

She felt, in this safe, warm staffroom, as she had felt trapped in her burning car.

The air wouldn't go deep inside her lungs when she tried to breathe. She turned to the slide again, full of hope for recovery, but could say nothing more. She thought she was going to faint. Every time she tried to speak, she sounded as if she were running upstairs.

'I'm sorry,' she said finally, touching her face and finding it damp with sweat. Margaret put down her pointer, picked up her coat and left the room.

Outside, the cold air was a deliverance. She was wearing a suit and an open-necked blouse and it was still freezing, but the weather was what she needed. She didn't know what was happening to her. Her heartbeat began to slow as shame filled her. She had actually cried in front of Malcolm and now she had humiliated herself further in front of all her regional colleagues. It wasn't like her. She was passionate but professional. She had never shouted at a colleague, or burst into tears, or broken down in a presentation.

She put on her coat and walked to the Tube, feeling defeated. On the way, she took her phone out of her pocket and scrolled to Ben's name in her contacts, letting her thumb hover over the call sign, but then turned it off. She needed to get things clear in her own head first, before trying to explain to anyone else. Instead, she walked with her hands inside her parka, no longer sure of where she was going or what she was doing.

However much she wished to deny it, it was clear to Margaret that the crash had affected her. She had argued with Ben and forced herself to come straight back to work, but privately she admitted that the doctor might have been right that she was in shock. Yet shock wasn't a clearly defined illness. She had no spots or infection; she could find no wound. Apart from the breakdown at work, the only tangible change was in her mind, with its constant replay of being trapped in a car about to explode and burn. It was as if her mind was a scratched CD, returning and returning to that moment in her life when she nearly died.

At Camden Town, she stood looking at the Tube map, as if she were a tourist discovering it for the first time. She could go back to work, a few stops away, or she could go home. She felt cold and alone, almost disembodied.

Despite herself, her attention focused on Whitechapel station. After a moment's consideration, she pushed through the barrier, descended the stairs and boarded the Northern Line, then changed to the Hammersmith and City. She was walking slowly and found that people jostled her on the escalators and the platform and again climbing the stairs to ascend to street level. When she emerged, she followed the signs for the Royal London Hospital.

As she approached the hospital, she slowed her steps. It was bitterly cold and she turned up her collar, breathing through her nose to try to warm the air. She had been taken to the Royal

London on the night of the crash and she felt at once relieved yet anxious to be returning. She knew why she had been drawn here. She wanted to find the man from the crash: the memory of him walking away haunted her. She needed to know that he had received treatment for his injuries. She wanted to know his name.

When she arrived, she went straight to reception.

'How can I help you, my love?'

'I'm sorry to bother you. I just wanted to ask if you remembered the M11 pile-up a few days ago? I wanted—'

'How can I forget? I worked all night.'

'Oh, great,' said Margaret, smiling suddenly. 'I mean, I'm sorry that must've been a nightmare. It's just, I was one of the casualties ... I was OK, only a few scratches, as you can see, but there was a man that helped me. He was hurt too, and I wondered if he had been admitted. I wanted to visit him and thank him.'

'Well, I can check for you. What's his name?'

Margaret raised her shoulders in apology. 'I *don't know* his name. I wondered if you would be able to help me work out who he is?'

'Oh no, I'm sorry, love. If you don't know his name ...'

'He was quite distinctive. This man, he had been burned – he had significant facial scarring, old scars from some time ago. He was strikingly disfigured.'

'I'm sorry, love, this is a hospital and—'

'He must have broken his hand and he was bleeding from his forehead. He might have been admitted for ...'

'Well, there really is no way to identify him.'

'He *saved my life*.'

'I'm sorry, I can't help you.'

Margaret wanted to explain further, but there was a queue.

38

'I'm sorry,' the woman said again as she turned her attention to the next person in line.

Margaret stood outside the hospital, buttoning her coat and wondering what to do. She was near the smoking shelter and was surprised how many people were crowded inside it to smoke. There were visitors in heavy jackets and patients with coats pulled over pyjamas – smoking with one hand while the other was attached to a drip.

Margaret put on her gloves and was about to leave when a nurse who was smoking near her touched her arm.

'I heard you talking to Carol,' said the woman. She had large brown eyes and a grip that Margaret felt through the sleeve of her parka. 'You were asking about the guy that came in the other night – the one with the scars.'

'Maybe,' said Margaret. 'How did you—'

'He's scarred from the face to the waist . . . terrible. I've never seen anyone as bad and I'm a nurse. Is that the guy you mean?'

'It must be.'

'It was the way you described him. He struck me the first moment I saw him, and you say he helped you?'

'Where is he, do you know? Is he still here?'

'I know it's wrong; I shouldn't say anything, but it was a major incident and it was *crazy* in here that night. I knew the guy you meant right away. You can't miss him, can you, God bless him. He's in my ward. He nearly died and they've put him in a coma. No visitors . . . not a single one. No next of kin on the system, nothing. I know lots of people are lost and looking for loved ones. I shouldn't say anything but . . . everybody needs somebody, don't they? It's not right otherwise.'

'Can I see him?' said Margaret.

39

'He's in the ICU. If you let me finish my ciggie, I'll take you up.'

She extinguished her cigarette, then Margaret followed her inside.

Margaret and the nurse were silent as the lift ascended. The woman wore a badge that read *Tara – Clinical Support Worker*.

For Margaret, it was as if she were seeing herself from another angle and only just recognising who she was.

The lift doors opened and she followed the nurse along the corridor to a locked ward. The nurse punched in a pin code and then held the door open for Margaret.

She put a hand on Margaret's arm. 'He's down at the end, but just let me talk to Harvey – he's the charge nurse looking after him. I'll explain to him why I let you in.'

Margaret waited while Tara spoke to the charge nurse. The ward smelled of antiseptic and reminded her of the Germolene that she pasted on to the children's cuts and grazes. She took a squirt of antiseptic cleanser into her palms and rubbed them together.

When she was called, she followed Tara along the corridor. The nurse opened a door to a room at the end of the hall and then left Margaret alone.

It was the man who had saved her. He was in a room of his own, tubes in his nose and his arms. The sight of him took Margaret's breath away.

This time, it was not the man's appearance that shocked her, but rather his existence itself. The sight of him was gratifying, as proof. She had been involved in a major incident – a multiple motorway pile-up – but had emerged with nothing but a few scratches. It was hard to believe that it had happened at all. It was difficult to fathom that he was real and not a figment of her imagination. But it was true: her car had crashed, and this face-less, friendless stranger had saved her life.

There was a whiteboard above the bed that read *Maxwell Brown, 23-09-55.*

'Maxwell,' Margaret whispered to herself. She stared at his face. If the board was correct then Maxwell was fifty-eight years old. The man's scarred, shiny face defied age.

'Maxwell saved your life, did he?' said Harvey, the charge nurse, coming into the room and flipping through a chart that was hooked to the end of the bed.

Margaret nodded. Harvey replaced the file and then took a pen from his uniform pocket.

'So our Maxwell's a hero then, uh? He's been a mystery to us. If it's all right, I'll take some details from you. We have almost nothing for him on file – just his NHS number and a date of birth, and records of historical treatment. We can't find any next of kin.'

Margaret took the pen and a piece of paper from the nurse and listed her name address and telephone number. 'Is he very ill?' she asked, returning the pen and paper.

'He's in a coma,' said Harvey. 'But you can still talk to him.'

'Thank you.' Margaret folded her arms as she stared at Maxwell, then turned to the nurse again. 'I didn't know he'd been this badly hurt. He helped me out of my car but then he just walked away.'

'I heard he came into A&E as walking wounded – just a broken hand – but then started vomiting and passed out in triage. When they gave him a CT scan they found he had a brain haemorrhage – a slow bleed. He's been put in a coma to try and stop the bleeding. It's easier for us to monitor his blood pressure this way.'

'How long will he be under?'

'Until he stabilises. Might be a couple of weeks or more. We just need to wait and see how he gets on . . .'

The nurse lingered outside the door while Margaret stood looking at the man. The tentacles on his face were extensive and even more shocking illuminated in the harsh hospital light. The scars licked down his throat and on to his chest. Maxwell was connected to a heart monitor, a ventilator and another monitor, which Margaret was unsure about. His left hand was in plaster to the elbow.

As soon as she was alone, Margaret went to the man's side.

'Hello,' she whispered, under her breath.

The ventilator exhaled and inhaled. The tentacled face of the man did not move; his shiny, lashless lids were closed.

'*Thank you*,' said Margaret, again feeling the chasm within herself. Her eyes were dry, her heart was steady yet she felt the breach.

She looked over her shoulder, and saw that the nurse was gone. She was alone with him. There was no sound except the beep-beep of the monitor.

She felt an urge to touch him, and so she gently put a hand on his arm. There was a strange relief in touch. His skin was warm against her cold hands, but he didn't react. Margaret took a deep breath, tasting tears in her throat.

'Thank you,' she said again.

The man's chest was exposed to the lower ribcage and there were pads and electrodes stuck to it. Even the man's chest had been burned and the skin was white, shiny, inhuman.

Margaret took a step forward and placed her palm where she thought his heart might be. She could feel the heat from his skin.

'I'm sorry but it's getting late now,' said the nurse. Margaret withdrew her hand and turned. Harvey was standing at the door. She flushed and her heart began to pound, as if she had been caught doing something wrong.

'Of course,' Margaret said, 'I should get going.'

Harvey smiled and held the door for her.

'Would I be allowed to visit him again?' she asked, turning, swallowing.

'For now, of course. We'll keep looking for his next of kin. I have your details now, so it shouldn't be a problem.'

'Will you let me know if anything changes?'

Harvey nodded. 'Sure thing.'

Margaret took a deep breath as she stepped into the lift. She was alone and she checked her watch and ran a hand over her face. The hospital lift was like a drawer in the morgue. She felt the lurch in her stomach as she descended. Seeing the man had shaken her. *Maxwell Brown*, she repeated silently inside her head, making fists of her hands in her pockets.

She had wanted to know his name, and now she did, but it was not enough. Seeing him had been a relief, but there was a gnawing hunger in her veins to know more. The day had shaken her, and she was exhausted and sore. She felt like a child again – unprotected. The lift jarred in the shaft and then the doors opened. She walked out into the winter air, needing home and needing to be alone in equal measure.

5

Big George
Tuesday 1– Wednesday 2 October, 1985

Big George was in Thurso. He felt taller here than he did in
Glasgow. He felt as if people were watching him in their periph-
eral vision. Being in Thurso cramped him. He was too tall and
his clothes felt wrong. Everyone spoke funny up here, and he
had to keep asking them to repeat themselves, after which they
would say, '*You up from Glasgow, then?*'

It was like being at school again; knowing that the nuns had
his card marked.

It had taken him six hours and he had driven nearly three hundred miles. As he had neared his destination, he had veered off
the A9 and driven up to John o'Groats. Thurso was only half
an hour's drive from 'the start of Britain' and Scotland's north-
eastern tip, and he wanted to see it for himself. He pulled over as
soon as he saw the sea, and smoked a cigarette, looking along the
coast towards Orkney. He reached into his pocket and took out
a small black velvet box. He bit down on the cigarette and then
opened the lid: inside was a sparkling solitaire diamond ring.

It was the same ring that he had used to propose to Kathleen in Glasgow Green, the second time he had asked her to marry him. The first time, he had not had a chance to buy a ring and had offered only himself.

His mother had said he could take her own engagement ring. *'We don't know where your father is, but I hope he's dead. Take this and treat her better than he treated me.'*

George had not wanted his parents' engagement ring to sully his own union. Now, he took the ring he had chosen for Kathleen in forefinger and thumb, and kissed the hard stone.

Kathleen had been right for not wanting him seven years ago when Moll was born. His father had disappeared when he was still winching Kathleen, but his elder brother Peter had eagerly stepped into Brendan's shoes. Even with their father gone, the McLaughlins were still synonymous with fear in Glasgow. George had always dreamed of running away with Kathleen, but it was only his mother's death last year and then the discovery of the money that had made him think that escape could be possible.

George finished his cigarette as he conjured Kathleen in his mind. He found it hard to reconstruct her face, but he remembered the smell of her and the softness of her fine dark hair. He remembered her laugh and black eyelashes and the gap between her front teeth.

He took a deep breath and thought about the weight of Moll in his arms. He had held her whole body in his two hands. He remembered her tiny eyelids opening to reveal blue eyes as sharp as his own, struggling to focus on his face. Everything about her had been fresh and new and perfect.

Standing in the wind, looking along the coast, he felt strange: as if he had shed a skin. He felt free and invincible and full of hope – daring for the first time to think that he could be happy.

It was after three in the afternoon when George drew up before the grey stone villa where Kathleen and Moll lived. He opened the top button of his shirt and leaned back into the seat of the stolen Austin Allegro that had been 'cleaned' at the McLaughlin garage. He sat for over an hour watching the house, amazed by the neatly shaped privet, the tiny flowers on either side of the path, the green-painted garden gate. Even from the road, George could see the large chandelier hanging in the lounge.

He sat in the middle of a row of parked cars, watching for signs of movement inside and out. There was a BMW parked in the red ash drive. A deliveryman came and rang the doorbell but no one answered, so he placed the parcel in the garage at the side of the house.

George smoked another two cigarettes before he saw a woman approach the garden gate and open it. It had been several years since George had seen Kathleen, but even from behind he recognised her. He still knew the way she moved. He had always admired the fluid way that she walked, as if she could hear music. She was still slim, but her hair was longer, hanging between her shoulder blades. He hadn't seen her since that night in Glasgow Green when he had proposed for the second time: the grass wetting the knees of his jeans.

He whispered her name under his breath and, as if she had heard, she turned.

George sat quickly back in his seat, out of sight. Some hot ash fell from his cigarette and burned his trousers. He brushed it off, cursing, but it was too late; it had made a hole in the fabric.

Kathleen turned away again. In the distance, in the direction of Kathleen's gaze, there was a child, running. She had long dark hair and long legs and George peered at her. The child looked older than Moll should have been: nine or even ten, not seven – but she ran up to Kathleen, who held the gate for her, and then together they went towards the house.

'Jesus,' George said again, brushing a hand over the fabric of his trousers. The white of his skin shone through the perfectly circular hole. He glanced over again as the pair went into the house. The girl was wearing the local school uniform, which George had seen when he stopped in the town for a sausage roll.

He lit up again out of annoyance and narrowed his eyes as he stared at the house. In daylight, it was difficult to watch their movements inside. He hadn't expected Moll to be so big. He hadn't been around a lot of seven-year-old girls, but he had expected her to be much smaller.

He took a drag of his cigarette as he contemplated. He had imagined meeting Kathleen again: Kathleen had been willing and the bairn had been tiny, not much taller than his knees, and chubby. In his imagination, both she and the bairn were in thrall to him and he had persuaded them easily to come away with him.

George sat holding on to the steering wheel with sweaty palms. It was as if Thurso was another world, and here he was, a petty criminal from Glasgow, peering through the gate into paradise. He glanced at himself in the rear-view mirror and ran a hand through his hair. It had been a long drive and he felt sticky and unkempt. He fingered the burn hole in his trousers and cursed again.

It was dusk and he watched as lights came on inside the large stone house – the hall, an upstairs bedroom. Through the bay window, George could see the chandelier in the lounge light up and sparkle brighter than the diamond ring in his pocket. After a moment, Kathleen appeared in the window. She reached up and drew the heavy curtains, blocking George's view.

He exhaled into his hands. His daughter and Kathleen were alone inside the big house. He wondered if he should get out of the car, *right now*, walk up the garden path and ring the bell. He sat still, breathing hard. The hopes he had nurtured about meeting Kathleen again, taking her hand and persuading her that she and Moll wanted a life with him, now seemed nothing more than fantasies. The imaginings danced in his mind, light, scorched, insubstantial, like papers up a chimney.

He imagined himself standing on the doorstep with the crease in his trousers gone, a burn hole in his suit and five o'clock shadow on his chin, then ran a palm over his jaw and felt the stubble already breaking through. He and Kathleen had been children together. They had grown up together. George had thought he knew her better than he knew himself. But now, sitting outside her house, he felt beneath her. He felt out of place.

Just then, a long Porsche approached the property and pulled into the drive, tucking itself in beside the BMW with intimate expertise.

A tall, thin man got out of the car: he was suited, sloped shoulders, balding, carrying a briefcase heavy enough to favour his gait to one side. The front door opened, warm light spilled onto the doorstep and the child came out. She hugged the man and carried his briefcase inside with two hands.

George swallowed, feeling sick. He had seen what he needed to see. He turned on the ignition and pulled away.

He spent the night in his car at a northerly point looking out to sea. Autumn, and the wind was up and the waves were wild. He ate a fish supper and drank Tennent's lager.

The money was in a holdall in the boot of the car: nearly one hundred thousand pounds in used notes. He could afford the best hotel Thurso had to offer, but he stuck out like a sore thumb here. Instead, he drank quickly, with the door open and one leg outside, looking out to sea. The dream that had caused him to drive three hundred miles now seemed naive. He was awash with dejection, his body stiff. He knew he should get out and walk around for a bit – stretch his legs – but he didn't have the heart for it, so he shook the tin can in his hands, then drank the remainder of the warm lager.

Now, looking out to sea, he felt stupid, worthless, small. He opened another can, lit another cigarette and tried to smile at his folly. 'Big house in Thurso and a man with a Porsche ... a perfect family and you think she's going to run away with you ... w'you?' he taunted himself. Tears blurred his eyes for a second. He downed the rest of his lager and crushed the can hard, then sat, with his hands between his knees, watching the waves break in the darkness, far out at sea.

The next day, he woke early to the keening of gulls. It was Wednesday. George drove back to the grey stone villa before seven, just in time to see the Porsche backing out of the drive. The metallic shiver of a hangover was upon him but his sense had been restored. There was no way he could go back to Glasgow – not now – but George realised that neither could he face Kathleen. He sat, hunched down in his seat, watching the front door.

It was another hour before the door of the house opened. Kathleen stood on the doorstep in her dressing gown, clutching her arms against the cold. The child came out, uniformed, satchel on her shoulders, and Kathleen fixed her hair and kissed her and then stood at the door with folded arms, watching as she walked down the path and crossed the road. They waved to each other three or four times until Kathleen closed the door.

A thought came to George, insistent as a flame. He felt unworthy before Kathleen, but his daughter needed to know who he was. If he could catch her alone, he would try to speak to her. He only wanted to look into her face again and hear her voice. The thought brightened him and he sat up in his seat.

The little girl walked right past George's car. He peered at her but something startled him about her appearance. Her face seemed strange. Although he only caught a glimpse of her before she passed, it seemed as if she had only one eye.

Getting out of the car, he fell into step behind her, watching the swing of her ponytail, the swish of her grey skirt, and hearing the clatter of the pencils in her pencil box inside her satchel. He drew breath and was about to call to her when she stopped to tie her shoelace, so he hung back, making as if to light a cigarette – not looking at her directly, yet noticing now that the child was not one-eyed after all, but wore a skin-coloured plaster covering her right eye.

When her shoelaces were tied, she pulled her satchel further up her shoulders and walked on. George put away his cigarette, in case the smell distracted her. She was thin: her knees larger than both her thighs and her calves. She walked with two hands on the straps of her satchel and her head down.

He drew breath to call to her again, when a group of three girls ran across the road towards her. The girls seemed Moll's age, but they were shorter, stockier. This time George knelt to tie his shoelaces. Instead of waiting on the girls, Moll quickened her pace, nearly running, and catching her feet so that she stumbled and almost fell.

'Pirate girl,' they called her. 'Pirate! One-eyed freak!'

Moll didn't turn when they called to her, but instead hung her head lower and walked faster.

The girls fell into step behind Moll, in front of George. They swaggered, heavy and loud on the pavement, and George hung back, watching their eyes slanted with malice and their skirted hips swinging in defiance. The other girls' arrival had surprised him, and his first instinct was to return to the car, but he sensed their presence was sinister and he felt an out-of-place urge to protect his daughter. He followed quietly, keeping his distance.

'Are you a pirate?'

'No,' said Moll, to the pavement. She pulled her satchel tighter and George noticed that it rose up her back.

'Well, why do you wear an eyepatch then? Only pirates have patches.'

'It's not only pirates. I need to wear it.'

'Why d'you need to wear it?'

'To make my eyes better.'

'What's wrong with your eyes?'

'None of your business.'

The largest girl – red-haired, freckled and stout as a barrel – nudged Moll. 'Oooo, none of your business,' she whined in imitation, shimmying her shoulders and pouting.

George noticed that Moll's shoulders hunched further, so that she seemed shorter, her spine curved as she walked, eyes to the pavement.

'Why's it none of our business?' said the girl, nudging Moll.

Moll recoiled from her touch, as if electrified.

'It *is so* our business. Did someone poke your eye out and now it's like a big hole in your head, *all bloody and pussie* ...'

The redhead grew louder as she described the horror of Moll's imagined eye, her face reddening and her tongue visible. The other girls laughed but the sound was hollow, lacerating, like breaking glass.

'You've got a big bloody monster eye under that plaster,' the redhead continued. She laughed noisily but without mirth.

George's shoulders were now tense. He wanted to intervene but he didn't know how. He had wanted to meet Moll, not get into a fight with a gang of seven-year-old girls.

'Leave me alone,' said Moll, breaking into a run.

'*Leave me alone,*' all the girls chimed in time, running after her. 'Pirate. Freak,' they called.

The smallest girl, who had seemed to George to be an unwilling participant, suddenly crouched to the ground and then hurled a stone at Moll, which hit her satchel.

Moll began to run faster and the noise of her pencils inside her bag became loud and rhythmic, like a drum. George quickened his pace.

The larger girl ran at Moll suddenly and pushed her to the ground. When she was down, all three girls made a ring around her, calling her names and laughing.

Monster eye

Pirate

What you crying for, crybaby?

'I'm not crying,' Moll screamed, struggling onto all fours to pick up her satchel, which had fallen from her back.

'Are so, crybaby,' screamed the redhead.

George couldn't stand it any longer.

'*Enough*,' he said, taking the redhead by the shoulders. 'What do you think you're doing? Shouldn't you be at school?'

Her face darkened in fear for a moment, then recovered.

'She started it.'

'She started nothing. Get along with you, before I tell your teachers.'

The girls looked down embarrassed, then they turned and ran. George waited until they were round the next corner before he knelt to help Moll to her feet.

'Are you all right? Can you get up?'

'Yes, but I can do it myself,' she said, pulling her arm away from his ready hand. Her knee was grazed and bleeding a little from the fall.

She brushed off her skirt and inspected her knee, then glanced upwards at George. 'Thank you,' she said, very quietly.

'What a shower of eejits. Do you have to deal with that a lot?'

Moll shrugged and looked up at him, her one eye narrowing against the cold autumn sun as she tilted her chin.

'Who needs that crap when you're just going to school?' he said, pushing his hands into his pockets. He shouldn't have sworn, he thought, castigating himself. He felt strangely nervous before her. He still remembered the newborn weight of her in his arms and he wanted to make a good impression.

'Do you know who I am?' said George, offering his most charming smile. It was inappropriate, but it was the one he used when he wanted a lumber.

Moll shielded her face from the sun and shook her head. As she peered up at him, he saw that she was missing her two front teeth.

'I know who *you* are,' he said, rocking back on his heels. He felt pleased with himself. He could always tell when a woman liked him. Fortune was smiling on him today.

She tilted her hips and her chin at the same time, as if to doubt him.

'Are you ... Moll?'

The child pressed her lips together, paused, then nodded once.

'Well, if I know who *you* are, don't you know who *I* am?'

She shook her head, shifting her patent shoes against the pavement.

'I know you, because you've always been in my heart. I can prove it to you.'

George knelt on the pavement and Moll giggled, her head cocked to one side. Slowly he began to unbutton his jacket. Her smile faded a little then froze on her face and her single eye blinked.

'It's all right,' he said to her, 'it's just a surprise. You like surprises don't you?'

Moll nodded warily, but her smile was gone now and he could see her face was washed with worry. He hadn't spent a lot of time around children but he could read a face, and his daughter looked afraid.

'I could give you three guesses,' he said, winking at her and giving her his special smile again, 'but you'd never guess, so I'm just going to show you.'

Moll's lips twitched again into an uncertain smile.

George unbuttoned his shirt. He showed her the name that was written on his chest.

'What does that say?'

'*Moll.* My name.'

'Your name. And you see where it's written? It's right over my heart, see?'

Moll nodded.

'Why would I have *your* name written right above my heart?'

Moll shook her head. The single eye looking back at George was icy blue, yet still not focusing clearly. It unnerved him. He was still kneeling before her, as he would kneel in church. He was penitent, but full of exaltation. She was his wee girl; he was meeting *his wee girl*. He wanted her to know him.

'*Because I'm your daddy*,' he whispered.

'My *real* daddy?'

George inhaled. Kathleen must have told her.

'Yes, your *real daddy*. You're as bonny as the day you were born.'

George smiled another of his best smiles. George's smiles were world renowned, or at least renowned in Glasgow. When he was a wean, George could simply smile and get a free ice cream while his brothers and sister had to stand in line, sweating a coin in their palms.

Only the nuns had been immune to George's charm.

'I like my own daddy,' said Moll, turning on her heels, hitching up her satchel and continuing on her way.

'Don't you want to know about me?'

'Yes, but . . .'

'Yes, but what?'

Moll stopped and looked up at him. She scratched her cheek with her close-clipped nails. Her face was suddenly worried: a neat frown between her eyes. 'My mummy said you're trouble.'

'She's wrong,' said George, surprised by the well of feeling that came with the word *wrong*.

'My mummy said you were nice to her, but not very nice to some other people.'

'She's wrong,' said George again. 'I *am nice*.'

This time, Moll didn't even turn to look at him. He could see the school gates and the cluster of parents and children in the distance. He was now one hundred feet from his car. He knew this was his only chance.

'You're half mine, and *you're* nice. Half of me is in you, and look how lovely you are. I stopped those girls from hurting you,

56

didn't I? Don't you want to decide for yourself? Aren't you even curious to know what I'm *really* like?'

'Maybe,' said Moll. She seemed tired suddenly, rubbing the skin around the plaster covering her eye.

'I could run you the rest of the way to school.'

'It's only over there, I don't need a run.'

George considered. He stood up tall and looked over at the school gates. She was right. There was no need to drive there.

She seemed so small by his side. He wanted to lift her up, so that he could look at her properly, but resisted. At the end of the road, he saw that the three bullies were watching.

'Well ... you want to pull up to school in the coolest car, don't you? Come and I'll take you, m'lady. Ride in my chariot. They'll all be impressed!'

Moll's left eye peered up at George. She bit her lip. 'My mummy said not to go with strangers.'

'Your mummy's right, but I'm not a stranger, am I? I'm your daddy.'

'But I can still walk to school ...'

'I know you can,' said George, throwing his arms out wide. 'You can do whatever you want, but you've already had a bad start to your day. Look at your knee.'

Moll looked down at her grazed and bleeding knee then looked back up at George, her lips shiny with spit.

'Wouldn't you like to get your day back on the right track? Let's have some fun before you start school.'

Moll was still wary, but he could tell that she was coming round to him.

He stooped and held out his arm. Moll considered for a second and then slipped her hand through.

*

George started the car and drove slowly through town. 'Do you want to go to school, or do you want to go on an adventure?' he said, winking at Moll.

'I should go to school,' she said, slipping her hands between her knees.

'I thought maybe we could drive around for a bit – have a chat, get to know each other?'

She shook her head vigorously. She had started to look anxious as soon as he pulled off the school road. As she was staring straight ahead and her right eye was patched, it was hard for George to see her expression without taking his eyes off the road, but he guessed she was nervous from the tension in her long, thin limbs.

'You really like school then?' he asked, driving slowly, smiling at her as he talked. His mother had always told him he could charm the hind legs off a donkey, and so George smiled and carried on, even though Moll had begun to pull and twist the skin on the back of her hands.

'Yes,' she said, her voice brittle. 'Can we go there now? I'm late.'

'School'll be there tomorrow, but this adventure won't.'

'I don't like adventures,' she said.

The skin on the back of her hand was now red. She was a strange eyeless creature, sitting erect beside him. He could almost feel her panic. She was like a bird that had got trapped in their kitchen when he was a boy, which had killed itself battering at the panes of glass to get out, even though they had opened the window.

'OK, OK.' He turned the car and began to drive back to the school gates. There were no more children around, and George assumed she was right about being late. It was not yet nine o'clock, but he had long forgotten what time school started; even when he had attended school, he had rarely been on time.

'When you're at school,' said George, trying another tactic, 'those girls still push you around?'

'Sometimes,' said Moll.

'In class ... the teachers ... they let them pick on you?'

'They don't see it happening.'

'That's not right. How tall are you, do you know? Does your mother measure you?'

'On my birthday, I was four feet ten.'

'That's tall for your age, isn't it?'

'Me and a boy in my class called Stuart are the equal tallest.'

'How old are you now? You must be seven?'

'I'm seven and three-quarters.'

She turned to him, eyebrows raised in emphasis, and he saw that his questions had calmed her down.

'Why don't you tell someone ... tell your teachers what they do to you?'

'Nobody likes people who tell tales,' said Moll, as if by rote.

'Did you not tell your mum?'

'Yes, but ...'

'I reckon you could take them, you know that? I can teach you a few tricks, so that even if they come at you in a three again like that, you can still do them some damage.'

'My mum says to say *Sticks and stones will break my bones, but names'll never hurt me.*'

'Names maybe not, but they laid hands on you; they pushed you to the ground. I saw them.'

Moll sighed. 'I should go anyway. Can you take me back now?' As she turned to him he saw the scorching intensity in her single blue eye.

'We're here,' he said, drawing up outside the school gates. 'No need to get your knickers in a twist. I see you take after your mother, after all.'

He kept the engine running, then turned to her. 'I've got an idea.'

'What?'

'Let's spend the day together.'

'I need to go to school.'

'They won't miss you for one day.'

'I want to go to school.'

'All right, all right.' She opened the passenger door herself, but George jumped out and ran around the other side to hold it open for her.

Her long legs were tangled in the straps of the satchel at her feet. She managed to free one foot, but then tried to get out of the car while the other was still caught.

She fell out of the car before George was able to catch her.

Her knee, face and arms hit the pavement.

'Whoops,' said George, reaching for her too late, not realising that she had hurt herself. For a few silent seconds she lay still on the pavement, silent.

As she looked up, George put two hands over his face. Her nose was bloodied from the fall and she was crying, a string of spit between one lip and the other.

He took her arms and lifted her to her feet, but she pulled away from him. She was crying so loudly, her face smeared with blood and tears and holding her arms out from her body, as if she was a puppet.

'Hush,' he said to her, bending down and trying to thumb a tear from her cheek, but she only cried louder. He looked at his hand and saw a spot of her blood. He glanced around nervously in case anyone was watching. She was making so much noise and he realised that it would look as though he had done it. There was no one in sight.

He knelt on the pavement. 'Hush, I know it hurts, but you're OK.'

She was trying to speak to him through her tears, but he couldn't understand. Above her cries, he heard a single pulse of a siren and looked up to see a police car two hundred yards away at the junction.

'Jesus Christ.' He scooped her up in his arms and put her back in the car, then locked the door and ran around to the driver's seat.

Inside the car her cries seemed louder and George was suddenly full of panic. He tried to keep his speed down on the narrow roads but headed straight for Olrig Street on the A9. He kept his eyes fixed on the mirrors, wondering where the police car had gone. He was driving a stolen car with a bag of used banknotes in the boot and a young, hurt child at his side, and George knew that could only go badly.

She stopped crying suddenly and dabbed at her nose with the fingers of both hands.

'Put your seatbelt on, eh?' said George, preparing to accelerate as soon as they were on the main road.

'Where are we going? Take me back.'

'I can't take you back just now, button.'

She began to cry again. It sounded different this time, no longer the low wail that came after she hit the pavement. Now it was quick gulping sobs. She sat up on her knees and began to slap the window with her palms.

He pulled her back into her seat. The tyres screeched against the tarmac as he turned on to Olrig Street.

'Put your seatbelt on,' said George, but she was crying again and couldn't hear him. She tried to open the button lock on the door once or twice but George reached over and took her hand away, driving one-handed for a while with his left hand pinning her hands in her lap.

'Would you calm down?' he shouted, and she quietened, looking up at him, still crying, her bottom lip curling.

'There's no need to make such a fuss.' It was as if she wasn't listening to him. 'What was I supposed to do?' he said, almost to himself. 'Jesus Christ.' He wiped the sweat from his forehead and ran a hand through his hair.

He had to think what to do, but could think of nothing with the noise she was making.

6

Angus Campbell
Wednesday 2 October, 1985

Angus was sitting in his office typing up a story about a sponsored sing-along by the Caithness choir, which had raised five hundred pounds for the Thurso care home. He had a radio scanner on his desk, which he had tuned in to the police radio frequency. Highlands Police occasionally barked updates on their day as he laboriously typed with two fingers. Angus had bought the scanner a month ago in the hope of discovering a scoop. He had already lost interest. Highlands Police only talked about food and TV, except on the odd occasion when someone shoplifted in Inverness or someone else was glassed in Fort William.

At work, Angus was focused and professional. He didn't make coffee for colleagues or indulge himself from the box of Milk Tray that had been left open after Jennifer's engagement. He was better at his job than most of his contemporaries, because his horizons were wider. He was not merely punching the clock or passing the time. Angus was improving himself and educating the readership of the *John o'Groat Journal*. He wasn't just collecting a pay cheque, he was a journalist: it was a calling of messianic proportions.

He was five foot three but he had always wanted other men to look up to him. There were some in the Free Presbyterian Church of Scotland who considered that Angus's profession was *worldly*, if not blasphemous. Angus was frustrated at the *John o'Groat Journal*, but he felt that the true journalism to which he aspired was fully aligned with his beliefs. Journalism *was* evangelism. He only needed the right story. The right story could bring Angus Campbell's vision to the world.

He pulled the pages from his typewriter and read them with his corrector ready. Suddenly, over the airwaves, Angus heard the sentence that he had been waiting his whole life to hear: it was a soul-completing sentence. Hearing it was like being born: being born again.

'Attention all units: Suspected abduction of a female child from Ravenshill Primary School in Thurso. The suspect is a tall man with dark hair and blue eyes, wearing a dark suit and a light shirt. Car make and number plates are unknown, but it is a dark-coloured hatchback, possibly red, brown or black. The child's name is Molly Henderson, and she is seven years old, with long dark hair, an eyepatch, and was last seen wearing her school uniform.'

Angus submitted his article on the sing-along and then jumped into his car. It whined when he turned the ignition but started on a second try. It was a thirty-minute drive from Wick to Thurso. He drove straight to Ravenshill Primary School, fixed his tie and inspected his teeth in the rear-view mirror, dusted his jacket, slipped it on and then walked into the school, notebook in hand.

Angus knew Betsy Clarke in the school office from church. Her husband, Thomas, often led the hymns. Angus asked for Betsy as soon as he arrived, but she was on her tea break and so he waited, on a chair made for a child, his knees to his chest, considering the questions that he would ask her. He wrote down several points on his notepad and underlined each one heavily in biro.

Betsy came for him the minute her tea break ended. She was wearing a tweed skirt with a Fair Isle jumper. At church, unfailingly, Betsy wore a navy suit with white collar and cuffs and a felt navy hat with net detail.

Betsy took him into the office, made him a cup of tea and offered him a digestive biscuit, which he accepted. He flicked over the pages of his notebook.

'It's a terrible business,' Betsy began, brushing a crumb from her ample bosom. 'You never think it'll happen here. I mean, that wee lassie, just the other day I was talking to her ...'

'You know her and the family?'

'The Hendersons.' Betsy nodded with her mouth closed, dimpling her chin. 'He's the big boss at Dounreay. *They don't want*, that's for sure ... They live in the big detached house on Rose Street.'

Angus's eyebrows shot up. 'Rose Street.'

Betsy nodded.

Angus made a note that Molly's father, Mr Henderson was the managing director at Dounreay nuclear plant, just five miles west of Thurso. Looking back at the notes he had made so far, he said, 'The police have a rough description of the kidnapper ... so there were witnesses?'

'Three girls in Molly's class say they saw Molly go off with him. I think the girls were all walking to school together. The police are questioning each of them and their parents.'

'Do you know who the girls are?'

'I do,' said Betsy, her eyes widening, 'Sandra Tait, Pamela McGowan and Sheila Tanner.'

65

'And do we know the reason he took her and not the other girls?'

'I don't know, maybe the other girls were warier – I heard the girls said that Molly went with him ... arm in arm.'

'And what's Molly like? Is she wild?'

'Oh no, the opposite. She does well at school but she's quiet as a mouse. I'm always telling her to speak up. I think she's shy and she gets picked on a little because of her lazy eye.

'It's a terrible business. I don't know for sure, but there's a rumour a police car was in the area following up a different disturbance. It's like she was snatched right under our noses, but under the police's nose too.'

'And this description of the attacker ...'

'It's from the girls. Silly wee girls, I don't think they were very exact.'

Angus nodded, lips closed.

'What about the Hendersons?' he said. 'Are the family believers?'

'The mother's a lapsed Catholic but I'm not sure about him.'

'And Molly's their only daughter?'

'Their only child.'

By the time Angus pulled up on Rose Street two police cars and three news vans were sitting outside a stone villa set back from the road. A hack with an STV badge was chain-smoking beside the Hendersons' hedge. There was a nip in the autumn air and Angus shivered, zipping up his anorak as he approached the man.

'Are the police still inside?' he asked, straining to read the man's badge.

'Aye. Are you a neighbour?'

'Angus Campbell, *John o'Groat Journal*,' he said, offering a hand, which waited between them until the man took the cigarette from his mouth and exhaled, 'John Burns.'

Angus pursed his lips and put his hand back in his pocket.

'Has anyone spoken to the parents?'

Burns narrowed his eyes and took a drag of his cigarette, as if considering what to tell Angus. 'The police have been in there for hours interviewing the family, but a neighbourhood search has been organised and there's a police plan in place with lookouts on the main junctions leaving town. The word is that there'll be a press conference in an hour or so. A sorry business.'

'Is there any suggestion of a motive?'

'What do you think? Here we go again. I've spent most of my career on these cases. It's only a couple of years since Tracey Begg went missing, and that murder has been linked to Charlotte Martin previous. He takes his time and has a break between killings. It's the Moors murderers all over again. Sick bastard.'

Angus didn't approve of the man's language, but he sympathised with the message. 'I have a daughter myself.'

'Well, keep an eye on her. It doesn't bear thinking about. Molly's father's out there with the search party right now, combing Lady Janet's Wood. Useless if you ask me. If that sick bastard's got her, he'll be long gone. Down south, I expect. The police aren't going to say anything at the press conference, but I have it on the QT that they're already comparing this abduction with the other murdered girls'.'

Standing on the pavement with the damp sea air seeping into his bones, Angus watched the shadow of Molly's mother at the window, pulling her cardigan around her. He went back to the car and drafted details of his story until the police came out and informed the waiting journalists that a press conference would be held in the Royal Hotel.

At the press conference, Angus was three rows from the front but could still feel the heat of the lamps that the television crews had installed. It felt like his time. There was a warm, buoyant feeling in his stomach. The page of his notepad was clean and fresh and waiting for him to mark it. Even although he was in the audience, Angus felt as if he were on stage. The spotlight had finally found him, like the finger of God calling him forward. He loosened his tie as the sweat broke at his hairline. He saw it clearly now: like the crusaders, Angus had been called upon to protect the sacred. A Thurso child had been snatched and his role was to find the person responsible, even if the child was gone. He would not give up; he would be relentless in his quest.

He took a few moments to bask in a fantasy where he was recognised by the Queen for his services to journalism and the public. He imagined himself being knighted, feeling the gentle tap of the sword on each shoulder and a room full of people applauding.

Several people took their seats behind a table covered in a starched white tablecloth. Three microphones had been strategically placed and there were jugs of water and glasses. Detective Inspector Black tapped the microphone three times and noisily cleared his throat.

'At approximately 08.45 hours this morning young Molly Henderson, of 56 Rose Street, Thurso, went missing on her way to school. It's our belief that Molly has been abducted.'

Angus focused his attention on Molly's mother. She was unmistakable; a blur of misery and torment. Her agonised face reminded Angus of a painting by Masaccio, of Eve being cast from the Garden of Eden.

'She is seven years old,' the detective continued. 'A photograph has been circulated. She was witnessed talking to a tall, dark-haired, clean-shaven, blue-eyed man wearing a dark suit shortly before she disappeared. An artist's sketch has been prepared and is also being circulated. A detailed search is already under way, as concerns for Molly's safety increase. Molly's father has prepared the following short statement.'

The detective turned to the tall thin man at the end of the table. He spoke with mouth turned down and eyes focused on a piece of paper before him. 'We miss our little girl very much and are hoping for her safe return. We ask anyone who has seen Molly to get in touch as soon as possible, because we want her home ...' The man's face crumpled and Molly's mother laid a hand on his arm. 'Very much,' the man managed, his voice broken, 'very much indeed.'

'We have one or two minutes for questions,' said the detective, frowning into the audience.

Every hand shot into the air, and Angus's was among them.

'Is there any information on the car the victim was abducted in?'

'As yet we have no clear information on the vehicle.'

'Has this abduction been connected to the earlier abductions of Tracey Begg and Charlotte Martin?'

'No such connections have been made at this time, but we are investigating all possible leads.'

'Are Highlands Police working on the assumption that this is a serial offender?'

'As I said, no connections have been made as yet; we are in the process of collecting information.'

'What is the plan for the next forty-eight hours?'

'A search is under way, including police, dogs and members

of the public; police across the UK have been notified. We urge members of the public to come forward with any information that they may have.'

Angus's hand had been raised for so long that his fingers had begun to lose feeling. The press conference was called to a close before he was able to ask his question.

He got into his car and slammed the door. The engine refused to start until he opened the choke.

'What,' he had wanted to ask, 'is the supposed motive for the abduction?'

'Depravity' was the answer, but Angus had wanted to hear them say it.

Angus put his foot down as he sped home along the Highland roads, headlights on full beam in case a stray deer crossed his path.

He felt different now that the child had been taken. He felt inspired. He had a calling, after all. 'Thank you, dear Lord,' he said, out loud, gripping the steering wheel and allowing a small whoop of joy.

When he reached the farmhouse, it was after eight. Hazel had his dinner in the oven and put his plate under the grill to warm as soon as he entered.

Angus had met Hazel through the church on Barra, at the Bible study group organised for the 'young folk'. Angus had liked her timidity and her piousness. She was just over five feet and Angus felt tall beside her. She had been raised in the church and had always known her place. His mother had passed already when he met Hazel, but his father had approved of the match. Hazel was an only child and her father was an elder at the church. She had been a plain, nervous girl with full hips.

'I didn't think you'd be so late,' Hazel muttered, chin to her chest. 'If the potatoes are too dry I can make some fresh.'

'Fine,' said Angus, brushing past her. He went to the porch and changed out of his work shoes into his wellington boots.

'What do you mean?' said Hazel, suddenly appearing before him, her hands clasped before her.

'What are you talking about, woman?' Angus spat at her.

'Do you mean you'll wait and see what the potatoes are like, or I should boil some fresh ones now?'

'Is that all you care about? Are you gormless?' Angus took a single step towards her and she shrank from him, defensive but accepting, like a dog. 'Boil some fresh potatoes if it pleases you. Day after day the same tripe you serve up; I'm sure I will notice no difference.'

Hazel and Angus's courtship had been pleasant enough, but it was after they were married and the children came that Angus became disheartened by her company. He had enjoyed both of her pregnancies, and liked to put his hands on her stomach to feel the child move. He had urged her to rest and eat well and had been delighted that his second-born was a son. Yet Hazel lacked strength as a mother, and it had fallen upon him to enforce discipline. She was a poor cook, yet had a tendency to put on weight. She failed to learn from the lessons he tried to teach her.

Angus marched out to the barn, striding, his boots leaving large indentations in the mud. The night was quiet and dark, strung with stars, and away from Hazel he felt blessed and chosen.

In the barn, Maisie seemed uncomfortable; off her food and letting out low pitiful moans as soon as Angus entered.

'It can't be long now, my girl,' he said, a hand smoothing her swollen flank. 'Only a few days at most and I'll help you. I'll be with you all the way, and you'll be chasing that calf right across the paddock before you know it.'

Maisie turned to him dolefully, black eyes so large that they could reflect Angus's whole face. He scratched the space between her ears and watched her tail whip in appreciation.

'You're my beautiful girl,' he said, running his hand from her head to her rear.

He put extra feed and fresh water into Maisie's trough, then returned to the house. It was freezing although it was only autumn, and Angus remembered the small Henderson child out alone at the mercy of the demon. It didn't bear thinking about.

Inside, he pulled off his wellingtons and went into the kitchen in his socks, to find Hazel spooning potatoes on to his plate. The sight of her sickened him. She was so proud of herself for those fresh, boiled potatoes, he could tell, and he wanted to let her know that these paltry offerings of hers were nothing to be proud of. He sat, prayed, and then raised his cutlery, ready to pass judgement on her culinary efforts when he heard something . . . forbidden. It was so faint that Angus could not be sure, but it sounded distinctly like music. He threw down his knife and fork and headed for the stairs, but by the time he had reached the banister all he could hear was the sombre tick of the grandmother clock that hung in the hall.

Convinced that he had not misheard, Angus bounded upstairs, his short legs taking the steps two at a time. Rachael was the most obvious culprit. Angus threw open the door of her bedroom to find her standing strangely by her bed, her chin down and a flush on her cheek.

Angus folded his arms as he walked into the room, checking for signs of disarray.

'What are you doing in here, young lady?'

'I was about to do some homework,' she said, avoiding his eyes, and her voice so quiet it was almost inaudible.

'Speak up and look at me when I'm talking to you.'

His daughter's eyes flickered up towards him. She was as sly and weak-willed as her mother. Suddenly he noticed that the frill of the valance around the bed was protruding strangely. He got down on his knees and peered under the bed.

'Well, well,' he said, a flush of vindication filling him. 'What have we here?'

It was the tape recorder, which was normally kept in the loft. In the past, the children had used it to help them recall scripture. There was a tape inside, which Angus removed with forefinger and thumb. It was a self-recorded tape on which someone had written in biro: *Madonna – Like a Virgin*.

'I knew it,' Angus bellowed. 'You brought this filth into our house?'

'I was only, I was only . . .' said Rachael, before her father took her firmly by the upper arm and led her out of the room.

Hazel was fretting at the top of the stairs, whispering his name over and over again: 'Angus, please . . . Angus, Angus?'

'Ach, take a tablet, woman,' he said as he dragged Rachael into the bathroom. The child was whimpering but he paid no notice.

He took a fistful of her hair and forced her down on to her knees so that she was kneeling by the bathroom sink, then took the wooden scrubbing brush that Hazel used to get the mildew off the tiles.

Hazel stepped into the bathroom, her arms rigid at her side and her fists close. 'Please calm down, Angus, you mustn't . . .' Her voice was vibrating in her throat. She was shaking, and he wondered if she was daring to question her lord and master.

'Mustn't what?' said Angus, wide-eyed at Hazel, feeling his daughter's cold fingers at his wrist, asking him to release her.

'You mustn't hurt her.'

'Hurt her?' he shouted. 'I'm *educating* her.'

'Do you like listening to that filth?' said Angus, twisting Rachael's face towards him. She was crying now, without sound, her eyelids fluttering in expectation of violence. 'I-will-not-have-you-listening-to-that-filth,' said Angus, as he rasped the stiff bristles over her ears. She screamed and tried to pull away from him, but he held her fast, rubbing one ear and then the other until he drew blood. The sight of the blood calmed him.

He stood up and let go of her hair, suddenly aware of his wife fretting in the doorway. He held the brush up to Hazel, so that she shrank from him, and then he tossed it behind him on to the bathroom floor and went back downstairs to finish his dinner.

Margaret Holloway
Saturday 14 December, 2013

The Holloways were walking in Epping Forest near their home, taking an easy three-mile circular route that they had done many times before. It was Saturday morning – the last before the school Christmas holidays. They were going to drive up to Rugby to visit Margaret's father in the late morning, and it had been Ben's suggestion to go walking first thing, to get some fresh air before the drive.

It was icy cold and the sky was heavy with snow clouds, but so far it had been dry. The snow on the ground had frozen and crunched under their feet.

The children were running ahead, tagging each other. Paula was fast and would catch her brother quickly, but Eliot was retaliating with hard snowballs.

'Mum!' said Paula, when an icy snowball hit her between the shoulder blades. 'Will you tell him not to do that?'

'The snow's a bit hard for snowballs, Eliot,' Ben called.

Ben and Margaret were walking hand in hand. Her nose was cold and her ribs still ached a little, but physically at least she felt better than she had earlier in the week. The pines were expansive and blue-green against the white snow. Margaret was wearing dark blue skinny jeans and boots, and found that her body and feet felt warm, while her legs were cold. It was the same with her mind: she was functioning as normal, apart from one important part of herself, which felt frozen.

It had been a hard week at work. She was not sure what was happening to her, but things were not *all right*. She had told Ben about shouting at Malcolm and breaking down in her presentation, but she had not mentioned her visit to the hospital and finding the burned man. She had not talked to Ben about what was happening to her because she didn't fully understand it herself. She wasn't sure if she would be able to explain it to him. The doctor's diagnosis didn't seem to explain how she felt inside. It felt as if she was separating, precipitating. Things were rising to the surface that had previously been invisible.

The memory of being in her burning car haunted her. She could still smell the petrol, and hear the roar of flames. For some reason, it was the fire that had shaken her most, and it was the fire that was causing her to reach into herself and sift through fractured memories and feelings she had not considered for a long time.

When she was alone, Margaret found herself alternately ruminating on her childhood then fixating on the burned man: who he was and why he had saved *specifically her*. It was five days since she had visited him at the hospital, but she had called the ICU twice to ask after him. He was stable, but still in a coma.

It had been her suggestion to go up to Rugby to visit her father. Her mother had died fifteen years ago – when Margaret was at university, not long after she met Ben. Her father was in his late sixties, and she wanted to see him before Christmas. The crash had filled her with a strong desire to *go home*. The roads were clearer now, but Ben had still thought the trip could have waited because of the weather. Even if there had been a blizzard, Margaret needed to see her father. Ben had acquiesced – *whatever you want* – and she knew he was worried about her – *you want to see your dad, we'll go.*

There was another reason. She wanted to go to Rugby to get a box from the attic. She couldn't wait until the weather was better. She could visualise exactly where it was, packed in a corner beside her mother's things.

Ben squeezed her hand twice to jolt her from her thoughts. 'You OK sweetheart?' he said, leaning down to speak through the flaps of her woollen hat.

'I'm all right,' she said, looking up at him, her eyebrows raised.

The children ran back towards them and tugged on either side. 'Mum?' Paula asked, breathless, pink-cheeked. 'How's Stephen getting on? He's not been round in ages.'

'Yeah,' said Eliot, using his father's elbow for leverage as he did long jumps in the snow. 'How's Stephen?'

Paula had been just six years old when Margaret had begun to teach Stephen how to read and write. After she had taken the deputy post, Stephen had still visited to tell her of his progress. He had stayed for dinner when he came round to show her his GCSE certificate.

'He's doing not too bad, love,' she said, wincing at her lie, putting a hand on her daughter's face. 'I don't see him so much with my job now.'

The children ran off and Ben took her hand. 'What will happen to him?' he asked.

'I really don't know. Maybe it wouldn't have made any difference, but I think that if I hadn't had the accident I could have stopped Malcolm excluding him. Stephen's whole life's been about exclusion . . . I would have fought it all the way.'

'You never know,' said Ben. 'You helped him get back on track. He might surprise you yet.'

'I hope so, but I don't know.'

'Don't get hung up on this. You've achieved so much. Think of all the kids you've helped, and now you're at the top you're helping the whole school change for the better.'

Margaret sighed and leaned into him gently. 'It's just he was my success story. I get so angry that kids can go to school and leave without even learning the basics. Stephen was another of those kids with so much potential that no one else could see.'

They walked in silence for a while, until Ben squeezed her hand.

'You started to relax yet, after your week from hell?'

'Yeah.' She sighed, taking the cold air into her lungs and then letting it go. 'You were right after all, I suppose. I should've stayed off.'

'Hang on, hang on,' said Ben, breaking free of her hand and patting the pockets of his jacket. 'Can I have that on record?'

'What on record?'

'You saying I *was right*.' He bit his glove off with his front teeth and pulled his phone from his pocket. He flicked to the recording tool and held the phone up to her, his eyes shining. 'Go on, say it again . . . *Ben, you are right*.'

'You're an idiot!' It felt good to be teasing each other again.

'It's OK, I won't cast it up, like. I'll just play it back to myself when you're at work . . . y'know, to build my confidence.'

She laughed despite herself. He had always been able to make her laugh. When she was pregnant with Eliot and her blood pressure was too high, she had been made to stay in bed for a whole month. Only Ben had kept her sane.

'It's all right laughing, but I want it on record.'

The children were quite far ahead now and Margaret smiled at the recognisable shapes of them chasing each other.

'Fine,' she said, stopping and leaning close to the phone's microphone. 'Ben, you are right, on this one occasion ...'

'Oh no no no,' he said, putting the phone away, 'no qualifications are necessary, thank you very much.'

'On this one solitary occasion,' she continued, 'you were right, however you've a way to go before you get to be like me ... right almost all of the time.'

She hadn't finished her sentence before Ben pulled on the strings of her woollen hat, yanking it over her face. While she was blinded, he slipped his hands under her winter jacket and began to tickle her. Margaret shrieked with laughter, and tried to wriggle from his grasp. Together they fell down into the snow. Margaret knocked her hat off and then climbed on top of Ben and pushed lumps of hard snow down his neck.

'Mags, give over.'

When they got up, they had left indentations of themselves in the snow. Ben brushed the snow from her jeans and jacket, kissed her then put her hat back on her head.

They kept on walking and he put his arm round her shoulders. They were both breathing hard. 'You could take the rest of the term off – hardly any time now till Christmas,' said Ben.

'Oh, I'll make it through.'

He stopped again and stood in front of her, hands resting on her shoulders. She felt the weight of them. 'It's not about making it through.' After being so playful, his face was serious. She hated it when he was serious – it was so rare. 'You're my girl. I need you to be OK. I want you to take this seriously and give yourself some time to get over it. I don't know what you went through, but if it happened to me I'd be a mess.'

She nodded and swallowed.

'I mean I'd take *a month off*, at least,' he said, grinning expansively.

Sometimes just looking at his face was enough to comfort her.

'What would that be about for you?' she said. 'Not going into your study . . . you'd never manage it.' It had been hard at first, but Ben had become very successful in the past five years. He regularly wrote for the *New Statesman* and sometimes the *Guardian*. 'You're a bigger workaholic than me.'

'Ah, don't you turn this back on me now,' he said.

They linked hands and started walking again. Paula was a hundred metres up ahead, turning like a ballet dancer.

Margaret couldn't see Eliot. She frowned, but they were near the corner. She quickened her pace and Ben matched it. Around the next bend, she still couldn't see her son.

She let go of Ben's hand.

'Eliot?' Her voice echoed among the trees.

The path was empty of other walkers and he was nowhere to be seen. Margaret jogged to catch up with Paula, hearing the crunch of Ben's feet behind her.

'Where's your brother?'

'Em . . .' Paula lifted up her fringe and looked around. 'He was here a minute ago, he was saying . . .'

'Eliot,' Margaret called, panic rising inside her again. She was panting, her quick breaths visible before her in the cold air.

'It's all right,' said Ben, putting a hand on her arm. 'He'll be here.'

She broke into a run, but couldn't get enough air and her chest was hurting. She tried to call Eliot's name again, but couldn't. Her mouth and throat were so dry she couldn't swallow. Paula and Ben were running too. The sun had come out and every time Margaret blinked she saw a flash of red. Everywhere she looked there were trees and snow – a kaleidoscope of green and white and red before her.

They both saw him at the same time. A man was walking his Labrador on the edge of the park and Eliot was kneeling in the snow, petting the dog. Ben slowed to a walk, but Margaret kept running up to Eliot. The dog turned as she approached and began to bark.

'I've told you not to walk off like that. You have to tell me where you're going.' Margaret took Eliot by the shoulders and shook him lightly as she turned him to face her.

'I was only petting the dog.'

The dog walker smiled at Margaret. 'Don't worry, I know that feeling,' he said, but Margaret did not smile in return.

Ben and Paula arrived, hand in hand.

'He's desperate for a dog,' said Ben to the owner, who nodded and left them. Eliot's face was rueful – brows furrowed and lower lip visible.

'I was just petting the dog,' he said again.

Ben lifted him up and put him over his shoulder. 'Let's go,' he said, swinging his son down to the ground again. 'Back to the car. Let's go see your grandpa.'

As the children walked ahead, Ben put his arm around Margaret and squeezed her.

'I ... I just thought ... I had a bad ...'

'It's all right,' said Ben. 'We found him.'

Margaret was trembling, but she tried to smile.

*

Her father, John, was watching for them out of the lounge window when they arrived in Rugby. He lived in the same detached, Georgian red-bricked house in which Margaret's mother had died. She had developed melanoma and John had nursed her at home for nearly a year. Although she had been gone fifteen years, the decor of the house was still the same, right down to the honesty and catkin bouquet in a vase by the telephone in the hall. Margaret couldn't look at the dried plants without imagining her mother choosing them and sliding the long stems into the vase. Each time she visited, she would thumb the dust from the honesty's shiny dried seed cases, which reminded her of the communion wafers she had placed in her mouth as a child on the rare times her mother had taken her to church.

John threw open the door and his arms. He claimed to be the same height as Ben but he had shrunk a little. He still looked good for his age, but he had grown thinner since her mother died: bones shining through his skin, like fine marble. The children stood on tiptoes to embrace him.

Margaret waited until John and Ben shook hands and the children had taken off their shoes before she hugged her father. The smell of him was a deep comfort, and she was glad that they had made the journey. She held on to him for a moment longer than she might have done, and found that he squeezed her instead of breaking away.

'I'm so glad you made it up here,' he said. 'I just wanted to see you – make sure you were OK.'

'I was lucky.'

Ben had called to tell him about the crash, and Margaret had spoken to her father on the phone when she got out of hospital.

*

John had bought in lunch: sausage rolls and pasties, coconut cookies and strawberry tarts. They sat at the table while he tried to make a pot of tea, opening and closing the cupboards as if unaware of their contents. John still moved around his house with estrangement, as if he didn't belong here, or as if he had recently moved in. He had retired properly only last year and was finding the adjustment difficult. As an engineer he had worked long hours all his life. He played golf and liked looking after his cars, so that although he had stopped work he was seldom home. It was as if retirement forced him to remember, once again, that he had a life to face without her mother.

'Let me help you,' said Margaret, getting to her feet and making the tea as John unwrapped the paper bags containing lunch.

'I should have had this all organised,' he said, smoothing the scant hairs on his scalp.

'You sit down and let me do it,' she said, placing a protective hand on his arm. She was grateful to have a distraction from her own unease.

John settled into a chair at the head of the table as Margaret placed the food on plates. She gave instructions to Eliot and Paula and they laid the table and folded napkins.

'So how's the house-husband thing going?' said John with a smirk, slapping Ben lightly on the shoulder.

It was a joke that John always found more amusing than Ben.

'Hard work,' Ben conceded.

'Only kidding. How's *the writing* going?'

Her engineer and scientist father always gave a grandiose emphasis to the words. Margaret knew that part of her father didn't think what Ben did was *real* work; while another part of him admired Ben, as if his son-in-law were an alchemist.

'Not bad. I'm working on a piece on children and social media at the moment.'

John nodded. 'I read your article on the Organisation for the Prohibition of Chemical Weapons winning the Nobel. That was marvellous. *Marvellous*. I passed it on to a friend of mine.'

'Oh really?' said Ben, and Margaret turned to watch the gentle colour rise in her husband's cheeks. He was bad with praise. 'Yeah ... it's all going well at the moment. There's a chance I might get to go to Brazil next year. I've pitched an article about child footballers in the favelas, to run at the same time as the World Cup.'

'That would be jammy,' said John, winking.

They were all hungry after the drive, and there was silence as they ate. Eliot had red sauce from his strawberry tart dotted on his cheeks and nose. Margaret was suddenly flooded with exhaustion and found it difficult to eat.

'So you're on the mend then?' said John, raising an eyebrow at Margaret as he took a sip of tea.

Margaret nodded. 'Yes, just some bumps and scratches. It was scary but I was ... lucky ...'

'It doesn't bear thinking about what could have happened to you,' said her father, his brown eyes murky with worry. 'It terrified the life out of me ...'

Margaret turned to him and watched the concern gather on his face. He had always had difficulty expressing his emotions. It reminded her of times in her childhood when she had needed him, and he had been unable to comfort her.

'But she's doing well, aren't you, Mags?' said Ben, smiling across the table at her. She could tell from the way her husband spoke that he was trying to protect the children from hearing the details about the accident.

Margaret cleared her throat and took Ben's cue to change the subject.

'Hey, Dad, I wanted to go up in the loft and have another sift through the stuff from the old house – if that's OK?' she said.

'Of course,' said her father, eyebrows raised. 'What's it you're after?'

'It was some stuff of Mum's. I think I know where—'

'I told you I gave away some of her things last year?'

It had taken over a decade, but her father had finally sorted through her mother's possessions and given her clothes to charity.

Margaret smiled at him. 'Yeah, and it's fine if . . .'

'You're welcome to whatever. You'll need to go up yourself if that's OK. My knees are playing up a bit today.'

There was a rope swing attached to the big oak tree at the bottom of the garden, which her father had made when Paula was small. It was almost identical to the one that John had made for Margaret when she was a child. Ben took the children outside to play on it while Margaret stayed in the house with her father. She watched the children push each other on the swing before she turned away to follow him upstairs.

Her father had been a young man – in his early fifties – when her mother died. He had shown no interest in marrying again and had thrown himself into work until retirement.

John used a hooked stick to pull down the stepladder from the hatch that led into the loft. He held the bottom of the ladder to steady it as Margaret climbed.

'The light's on the left-hand side,' he called as she neared the top. 'There's a box of her jewellery that's behind the beams on the far right.'

'Thanks,' she said over her shoulder. 'It wasn't jewellery so much, just some bits and bobs I remembered were up here.' She twisted on the stairs to watch his expression. The skin on his brow wrinkled as he looked up at her. *From that time*, she might have added, but did not.

They had not spoken of it, as a family. Even when her mother was alive it was avoided, brushed over. What had happened to Margaret had sculpted the space between each of them, the way grief sculpts the soul, so that the unspoken took on a tangible shape, defining their family.

She pulled herself up and found the light. She was aware of him standing below, looking up expectantly at the hatch, listening to the creak of the boards as she moved around.

The attic was filled with boxes that were still labelled from the move. Her parents had moved house in the mid-nineties when her father changed jobs. It had been shortly before her mother's diagnosis. Margaret had helped them move into the house and she remembered seeing the box that she was now searching for.

She moved two or three packing crates labelled 'bedding', 'sleeping bags', 'dinner service', then glanced down the hatch to see if her father was still there. He was gone and she was relieved.

It was a large green-cardboard shoebox, she remembered, unlabelled, unlike all the other containers, which her mother had obsessively inventoried. Margaret had only glanced at the box. She had found it during the move and had just opened the lid before her mother took it from her.

'*Don't, love*,' her mother had said, her eyes desperate and misting with tears. '*You don't want to dredge all that up.*'

At the time, she had been confused by her mother's words but had agreed.

Margaret recalled a happy childhood, but she could not

remember much from her lower primary school years. As an adult, she had decided she simply had a poor memory, but there had always been hints of what she had forgotten. She remembered being in hospital but could not remember why. She had asked about it when she was a teenager, but sensed that her parents didn't want to discuss it. Margaret had not pushed for more information. She knew that a portion of her childhood was missing, but there was a sense that she had *chosen* to forget.

The loft space smelled of the un-sanded wood of the beams. The floor was covered in plywood, but it was uneven in places. There were toys from her childhood, which her own children had rejected: dolls that her daughter had considered ugly. An old-fashioned kettle sat beside an electric heater. Near a box of old books were her mother's jam jars, which she would retrieve every summer before she became ill and fill with a fresh batch of gooseberry, redcurrant and raspberry jams.

Margaret recalled the day after her mother's funeral, watching John sit by the fire and thinking how her tall, strong father seemed smaller now. Only a few days since her death yet he seemed shrunken, as if grief had caused part of him to dissipate, like air from a tyre.

She had been young and in love and heartbroken all at once, yet she had said to her father: 'You know when I was little, did something happen to me? Did I nearly die?'

Her father had looked at her, his eyes shining.

Margaret had pressed her lips together, not sure why she had spoken out. 'I was in hospital, wasn't I?' The long service watching her mother's coffin had made her recall all the things she had wanted to ask her mother, which would now go unanswered.

'You had a ... fever,' her father had said, but then his face crumpled and he hid it in his hands.

Now she could hear muffled screams of laughter as her children played outside on the swing. As Margaret grieved for her mother and then got married, became a teacher and had children, the fever had seemed a good enough explanation.

In the warm loft space she smoothed the palms of her hands on her thighs, aware again of the smell of fire: thick black smoke. The fire seemed to have reached further into her mind than she herself had ever been willing to go. She could remember no more than she had before, but for the first time in her life she was fixated on those missing years from her childhood. It felt as if her present self was crumbling and she would only discover why if she could find out what she had forgotten.

It took her some time, but she finally spotted the box she was looking for hidden under a pile of suitcases, wedged in the eaves. The suitcases were filled with sheets and old clothes and were heavy when she shifted them, but she managed to restack them and free the box beneath. Despite the weight that had been stacked above it, the cardboard box had kept its shape because it was packed tight.

She carried it to a space underneath the bare light bulb that hung from the eaves, then sat down on a crate of bedding as she lifted the lid. The box was filled with yellowing newspaper articles, some of which had been carefully cut out, while others had been roughly torn. The box smelled of old books: intimate as skin. She riffled through the papers quickly and saw that there were also several sheets of typed paper and envelopes stuffed with photographs.

She had to work out some way to get the box to the car without anyone seeing what she was taking. She didn't want to discuss it with Ben or her father. It was a box that her mother had always kept private, but Margaret had known that it was somehow related to her.

She touched the rough, yellowed pages at the top of the box. Memories: clean, unearthed as a bone from the ground, came to her, but they did not make any sense on their own.

Margaret picked up the newspaper clipping that sat on top of the pile and read the headline: YOUNG GIRL ABDUCTED BY SUS-PECTED PAEDOPHILE.

She tried to swallow, but her mouth was too dry.

The suitcase tower she had created on the far side of the loft toppled and fell suddenly, making her gasp.

'Are you all right up there?' her father called from below.

8

Kathleen Henderson
Wednesday 2 October, 1985

Kathleen hummed a song as she stood before the hall mirror and pinned up her hair. She put on some pale pink lipstick then went into the kitchen and leaned over the counter to write her list. She had messages to get: eggs, cheese and bananas, steak for dinner; the beds needed changing and she was meeting a friend for lunch.

She skipped up two flights of stairs and stripped the beds, then carried the sheets downstairs and put on a wash. She moved quickly: not rushed but with energy. The radio was on and she sang along in places as she washed the breakfast dishes.

The day was changeable, at once sunny and bright – warm shafts of sunshine catching the soap bubbles in the sink – but then the light would vanish and Kathleen would feel a chill and look up to watch the wind shaking the leaves of the oak tree, as if to remind her that it was autumn after all.

She dried the dishes and put them away, opening cupboards that were covered in Moll's artwork: macaroni collages, self-portraits, still lifes and family paintings. Kathleen's favourite was a large colourful picture which was Blu-Tacked to the fridge. It was a painting of a house with a smoking chimney and green hills in the background and in the foreground were John and Kathleen, with Moll in the middle, holding hands. They all had circle faces and rectangle bodies and stick arms and hands but Moll was the largest figure. Her mother was smaller than her, and John smaller still, which Kathleen found interesting, as he was such a tall, thin man. Below the picture, Moll had painted the words *my family*, choosing a different colour of paint for each letter.

Moll had always been bright. Kathleen had been criticised by the school for it, but she had taught her daughter to read and write before she started primary. Her teachers had worried that she would be bored and cause trouble, but Moll had never needed attention like that. Even at home, she was content to play by herself. She liked to take John's thick hardback books from the bookcase and pretend that she could read them.

Kathleen dried her hands and glanced outside to see if it was raining, just as the telephone rang.

'Hello?'

It was John. He stopped for a tea break at ten and would often call her.

'You're lucky you caught me.'

'You don't have to tell me that. I've always known I'm a lucky man.'

'You know what I mean,' she said, elbows on the bunker, raising her eyes and smiling as if she were talking to him face to face. There was a paperweight by the telephone, which Moll had also crafted: a smooth, heavy stone that she had found on the beach. She had painted *MUMY* in green across it and often told Kathleen that she hated it because it was spelled incorrectly. Her daughter often asked for the gift to be returned so that she could paint over it, but Kathleen wouldn't allow it.

'You can find another stone and paint it with the correct spelling if you want, but I like this one.'

'I won't ever find another stone that flat.'

Kathleen and John talked for a few minutes, low murmurs into the telephone. They had nothing new to say, but simply enjoyed the sound of each other's voices.

'I'm meeting Fiona for lunch.'

'Well, you enjoy your day.'

'When will you be home?'

John sighed. 'After six, I should think. We'll see.'

She could hear the stress returning to his voice.

'See you later, then.'

'Tatty-bye.'

Kathleen put on her jacket and was counting the money in her purse when the phone rang again.

'Are you bored today or something?' she said, laughing, expecting it to be John again.

It was not her husband, but the head teacher of Ravenshill Primary.

'Mrs Henderson, is that you? It's Barbara Wainwright.'

'I'm sorry,' said Kathleen, tossing her bag on to the kitchen bunker. 'I thought it was ... How can I help you? Is everything OK?'

'I don't want to alarm you at all, but I'm just checking that you didn't ask for Molly to be collected from school this morning by a friend or family member?'

Kathleen's lip stiffened. 'Moll? Collected by whom? I saw her off this morning.'

There were a few seconds of silence on the line and Kathleen's thighs began to tremble.

93

'Moll didn't make it to school today, and some classmates witnessed her talking to a strange man and getting into his car. We're going to call the police . . .'

Kathleen hung up the telephone. She had tried so hard to listen as Mrs Wainwright spoke of the next steps, but the only thing she could think about was finding Moll. A notepad hanging on the wall next to the telephone listed important numbers. Kathleen's forefinger shook as she found the one for John's work. She misdialled twice because she was trembling so badly, but finally got through.

His secretary answered.

'I need to speak to John right now.'

'Kathleen, is that you?'

'I need to speak to John.'

'He's at the plant. I can try to get a message passed but it might take some time.'

'*I need to speak to him now. Right now.*'

'Kathleen, love, is everything all right?'

She hung up, her hand over her mouth. It couldn't be true. It couldn't happen to her. She'd read about little girls being taken, but it couldn't happen to Moll. No one would hurt *Moll*.

She felt as if her skin had fallen off; raw, she ran out into the street and towards the school, following the steps her daughter had taken when she waved her off this morning. Kathleen could remember her small wet lips against hers and the uneven strand of hair that had escaped her ponytail which Kathleen had tried to straighten on the doorstep. She could imagine every last pore of her – bone, skin, hair and smell. Tears blinded her as she mentally hugged her, squeezing her tightly, tighter than she ever had, as if she could push her back inside her own body and protect her for ever.

This wasn't happening. It couldn't happen. Moll was never to come to any harm. *She was too loved.*

The streets were a blur of faces and cars and trees. She bumped into one woman and another called after her to watch where she was going.

It was less than a ten-minute walk from the house to the primary school, but Kathleen had been running too hard. By the time she reached the school gates she could hardly breathe. She bent over and had put a hand over her mouth to stop herself from vomiting. Her hair, which she had carefully pinned earlier, was now wild and loose. She ran a hand over her face and hair as she prepared to enter the school.

They had made a mistake, she decided. Moll was inside, in her classroom, stretching up her hand to answer the teacher's question.

In the school car park, she saw two police cars.

9

Big George
Wednesday 2 October, 1985

George put his foot down and crossed the River Thurso, and was about to accelerate out of town on the A9 southbound when an old lady stepped out on to a zebra crossing. George drummed his fingers on the wheel impatiently, glancing to the park on his left and noticing that it was named after him: Sir George's Park.

Moll was turned away from him, still crying, and he was about to speak to her again in an attempt to calm her when she released the lock, threw open the door and fell out right on to the road, such was her rush. She was on her feet before he could reach for her and sprinting back along the road towards the bridge and the town.

'Christ,' said George.

He drove through the zebra crossing, startling the old lady, and parked the car by the side of the road, half on the pavement, before he leaped out and gave chase. Running full pelt, he made up the distance between them in seconds. He caught her by the collar of her jacket and spun her round. She started screaming and twisting away from him and George panicked again. His hand closed around her wrist and he began to drag her back to the car. Up ahead he saw a man and a woman, walking arm in arm, and wondered if he should just let Moll go and make a run for it. The couple both glanced in his direction, but instead of looking alarmed they smiled at him with understanding. Realising that they assumed it was just a young child having a tantrum, George dared to smile at them and shake his head. The couple nodded and walked on.

At the car, George threw open the passenger door and tried to drag her inside, but she leaned over and bit the hand that held her wrist. It wasn't a playful bite; George felt her small teeth break the skin.

He shook her, just to get her off him, but then realised that he had been too rough. She was suddenly very pale, either from shock or terror.

When he pulled his hand away, he saw that she had drawn blood. He lifted her up, put her in the passenger seat and closed the door.

After pushing down the lock and pulling her seatbelt over to secure her, he drove away with a skid, glancing into the mirror to see if the couple were turning back to look in their direction. The speedometer twitched well above the speed limit as they drove out of town on the A9, before George left the main road to take the smaller mountain roads, where he considered he would be less visible.

He needed a cigarette suddenly, but was driving too fast. The chase and the fight with her had shaken him. Two hands on the steering wheel, he glanced at her and noticed that she was crying soundlessly; the tears already breaking through the plaster that covered her left eye.

The blood was trickling from the wound on his hand where

she had bitten him, curling around his wrist. He brought his hand to his lips and instinctively sucked at the wound, tasting the familiar salt of his own blood.

George was seven years old. He was laughing and joking with his sister while they ate their tea of mince and tatties. George liked to mash the tatties into the mince so that it was a huge brown mess, while Patricia liked to keep the mince completely separate from the potatoes, and would complain to her mother if they were touching. She would then eat the mince first and then all of the tatties, leaving stray onions on the plate, which she said were slimy as worms, and which their mother would then cajole her to finish. George never needing cajoling to eat his food. Every time he finished, his mother would tousle his hair and tell him that he was a good boy and he had a good appetite.

'Is not.'
  'Is too.'
  'Is not.'
  'Is sot.'
  'Not, not, not!'
  'Sot, sot, sot, sot!'
The key turned in the lock. George and his sister stopped their chatter and their mother turned off the wireless. His mother focused on the dirty mince pot in the sink and George and his sister looked down at their plates.

Brendan McLaughlin sighed as he closed the front door. George and his sister didn't move, but their mother turned to their father.

'Run a bath,' said their father, without a word of hello. They both knew he was speaking to their mother. She had been washing the mince pot, but she put it down immediately and went to run the bath, wiping her hands on her pinny. She stopped dead at the sight of her husband in the hall. George and his sister followed the direction of their mother's gaze.

They were used to seeing their father roughed up. Often his knuckles would be bloodied and their mother would set a bowl of Dettol on the kitchen table for him to steep his hands. The smell of antiseptic would fill the room, thick as shame, as he made bloody fists into the milky liquid.

But tonight, it was not just his hands: Brendan McLaughlin was covered in blood. His clothes were dark and wet with it; his face was smeared with it and his hair was slick with it. Blood pooled around his black shoes and when he walked to the bathroom, he left dark red footprints on the floorboards.

'Mother of Jesus, a bath? You need the hospital.'

'Run the bath,' said Brendan, his voice slow and menacing.

Not a single person in the household would counter him when he spoke like that, not even Peter. George's mother ran the bath and poured Dettol into it, so that the familiar stink eased through the house like enmity. Patricia brought towels and, with two hands, George put the kettle on the range to top up the bathwater in case it went cold. The children and their mother were like soldiers rushing to their posts.

George hid behind the door, watching his father and mother in the bathroom. He didn't like it when they spoke to each other directly because often it would turn sour, and George would want to protect his mother but be afraid for himself. His father's temper was often sparked by physical pain. If he had been stabbed or beaten badly, it made him angrier. But tonight they stayed calm and his mother passed his father the yellow bar of carbolic soap, so that he could wash himself.

Through the steam in the bathroom, George could just make out that the bathwater had turned red, and he wondered if his father was bleeding to death. The thought brought a small flutter of delight under his ribcage, and he pressed his lips together in hope and expectation.

His mother sat on the toilet seat, preparing dressings.

'Where is it you're hurt?' she whispered. 'If you need stitches then you need stitches; you can't go without like last time . . .'

George held his breath as he strained to get a better look, making sure that he kept out of sight. The water was dark red now, as if all the blood in his father's body was pouring out into the bath.

George rested his head against the door, feeling something akin to happiness.

But then his father pushed his knees forward, leaned back and dunked his head into the bath to wash his hair and George saw the firm muscles of his father's abdomen rising up like a lobster before peeling. Moments later George watched his father's pale, hard body rise from the blood. His father stood naked, dripping in the bath. Brendan McLaughlin was six foot one, and George had to look up to take him in.

His body was clean, hard, faultless as a statue. There was not a single cut on him. At seven years old, he understood that his father had not been bathing his wounds at all: he had been cleaning brutal murder from his skin.

George pressed himself into the crack of the door as he watched, feeling he was invisible. He bit his thumbnail as he watched his father towel himself dry. As his father bent down to dry between his toes, George bit the skin of his thumb right through.

*

George cut off the A9 on to the mountain roads, where he slowed his pace. When he was on the back roads, outside Inverness, he pulled over and turned to speak to her for the first time.

'Are you OK, Moll?'

She turned her face away. The tears had created a gap at the bottom of the plaster covering her right eye.

George stroked it with his finger and she winced slightly at his touch.

'Let's take this off, shall we? Let's see those baby blues.'

She kept her face turned from him, but did not fight him, and he gently peeled away the rest of the plaster. When the patch was removed, he turned her face to his. Her skin was reddened from crying, and George felt guilt gut him, deft as a fisherman's knife. Holding her face in his hand, he realised the reason for the plaster. She had a lazy eye, and so one of her eyes was now fixed on him, unrelenting, accusing, while the other was turned away. The eye that had been covered was her good eye.

Her face was pale, impassive, yet she shrank from his touch. It was not as he had imagined; not as he had wanted.

'I'm sorry if I frightened you, Moll,' he said, rubbing her leg and dropping his chin to look up at her. 'I didn't mean to upset you.'

'I don't forgive you,' she said, almost without moving her lips.

'See what you did to me,' he said, holding up his hand with the tiny, bloody teeth marks on his skin. Because Moll's two front teeth were missing, the marks were like a snakebite on his hand.

'You deserved it,' she said, turning away.

George frowned and stared at the road ahead, hands between his knees. It was not as he had imagined it. He had pictured himself driving this same road, with the money in the boot and Kathleen and Moll singing car songs as they headed south.

Everything had changed overnight. Yesterday he had disappeared from Glasgow, hoping to win back his sweetheart and his little girl. Now, he was on the run with an abducted child, a bag full of dirty money and a stolen car. It was the abducted child part which was the real problem, even if she was his daughter. George wiped a hand across his mouth. Trouble had always clung to him, like summertime sticky willow. Freedom taunted him now but George was determined not to relinquish it.

'You need to do what I say, angel ... We're going on an adventure.'

'You're a *bad man*,' she said, whipping her head round so that her right eye confronted him while the left looked away. 'I want to go home.'

George exhaled, clasping his hands on his lap. 'I'm *not* a bad man,' he whispered, 'I'm your daddy,' speaking as though the two were mutually exclusive – although he himself knew better.

10

Angus Campbell
Friday 4 October, 1985

Two days since Molly Henderson had been taken. Search parties of neighbours, friends and police were still out looking for her, but hope was running out.

The Hendersons had given tearful radio appeals, asking for the return of their daughter, but concern was deepening. In the recent similar cases of abducted children, the little girls had been sexually assaulted and then killed within twenty-four to forty-eight hours of their abduction. Tracey Begg, a little girl taken from Aberdeen just two years earlier, had been assaulted and killed within a day of her disappearance, but her body was found dumped in England, some ten days after her abduction. Angus suspected that the police would have very little to go on, until they found the body.

Highlands Police were now coordinating with the national force, searching for the car and the man who had taken Molly, but the descriptions were imprecise and the witnesses had all been children.

None of the statements that the police made publicly said

anything about searching for a serial offender who had killed before, but Angus knew that this was merely a tactic to avoid panic. His police contacts had told him, confidentially, that they were looking again at the other unsolved child murders.

There were three cases in particular which bore a resemblance to Molly's abduction: Gillian Hardy, 1981, from Ballymena, Northern Ireland; Charlotte Martin, 1982, from Whitby; Tracey Begg, 1983, from Aberdeen. The police suspected these three murders were linked and it had been two years since the last abduction. It was *time* for the killer to abduct another child.

As with the other children, witnesses to Molly's disappearance suggested that she had been tempted away by a stranger. Tracey Begg from Aberdeen, taken only two years ago, had been just five years old. A tall dark man, described as having a scruffy appearance but wearing a suit, was seen paying for Tracey to ride on a merry-go-round, just before she disappeared.

Angus had written a news article for the *John o'Groat Journal* based on the syndicated facts about the Henderson abduction and the ongoing national investigation, but he wanted a feature. He was collating a file on the Hendersons and the abduction and knew that he had it in him to make a breakthrough on the case, if only he could gather enough information. He was still writing his usual articles for the paper, about the petty goings-on in Caithness County, but he was working on the big story. The larger news agencies were still camped outside the Hendersons' house, and Angus knew that the couple had been bombarded with requests for interviews. He wondered if his local connection meant that Kathleen might talk to him.

It was mid-autumn, but the Hendersons' large, walled garden bloomed as if it were still summer: chrysanthemums and fuchsias, roses and clematis. The rowan tree was still dark green but red berries hung heavy from its branches. A large wych elm in the corner of the garden had a makeshift swing attached to one of its branches.

Angus stood on the doorstep and looked through the front window into the cream-furnished lounge before he rang the bell. He peered through the frosted glass of the door. The house seemed desolate: no lights on, and no sound from inside. The bell had an old-fashioned brass bell-pull and sounded loudly in the hallway. He waited a few minutes and was just about to ring again when he saw a shadow behind the glass, and heard the lock turn.

Kathleen Henderson had shrunk into herself. Her collarbone and upper ribs were visible and her eyes were sunk into deeply shadowed sockets. She was well dressed, however, Angus noticed with some disdain. Wearing an expensive, low-cut jumper, she had adorned herself with pearls and long earrings, and swept her hair to one side.

'Can I help you?' she whispered. She held on to the door, not opening it fully. From her accent, Angus could hear immediately that she was an outsider. It had not been so noticeable at the press conference because she had been speaking through tears.

He puffed his chest out. 'Mrs Henderson, Kathleen, my name's Angus – Angus Campbell.' He held out his hand and she quickly gave him her cold fingers.

He had thought carefully about what he would say, should he get the chance to speak to Kathleen Henderson in person. He had heard about journalists who door-stepped bereaved and fraught parents, who cared about the story more than its subject, and Angus did not want to be tarred with that brush. He wanted to win her over; to gain her trust.

Angus was not accustomed to being so ingratiating with women. They were the weaker sex in so many ways, which the Bible helped him to understand. *A woman should learn in quietness and full submission. I do not permit a woman to teach or to assume authority over a man; she must be quiet*, Paul the Apostle had quite rightly said. As a child he had marvelled that when his father came home from sea his mother, with her strong arms and harsh criticism, stopped whatever she was doing to minister to the man of the house. As soon as his father returned she would busy herself cooking and washing, and hanging the fishing nets out to dry in the bitter sea wind. Every Sunday they would sit in church and Angus would suck a large pan drop as he listened to the sermon: '*And unto Adam he said, because thou hast harkened unto the voice of thy wife . . . cursed is the ground for thy sake,*' and of Eve, '*in sorrow thou shalt bring forth children; and thy desire shall be to thy husband, and he shall rule over thee.*'

For thine is the kingdom, Angus would whisper fervently, *the power and the glory*. He was the youngest of three brothers and the smallest. As an adult, he had not grown as tall as his father had been, nor reached the height of his brothers in Barra. Since he had been a very small child, Angus had wanted to be the big man and in his own house he had insisted that he was honoured as such.

Women were infernally weak and he did not like to indulge them, but Kathleen Henderson was a special case that called for delicacy on his part, if only as a means to an end. He remembered his beloved, pregnant Maisie, and imagined that he was speaking to her instead, in the barn filled with warm straw, sweetened with the smell of dung.

'Kathleen, if I may call you that . . .?' Angus paused and raised both eyebrows, and Kathleen nodded once, with a sharp jut to her chin. 'I work at the *Journal* and I worship with the Thurso congregation of the Free Presbyterian Church of Scotland. I wanted to let you know that you are in our prayers, and we are taking a collection to help with ongoing support. *Together* we can find Molly. *We* can bring her home. I truly believe that.'

'Thank you,' Kathleen managed, her eyes glassing with tears, her words clotting in her mouth. 'You're very kind.'

'I know you've been bothered by a lot of press in the last two days, and you look very tired, but I wondered if it might be worthwhile for you to talk to someone like myself, someone local, who understands the area. The police are fantastic, but they're casting their net wide. I just wondered if it would be worth going over the facts once more?'

'You mean, write another story? There's been so many already ... just two days and it seems like every paper, every TV station ...' Kathleen's eyelids fluttered, as if she were on the verge of fainting. 'I don't have anything else to say. I feel as if I've said it all a hundred times.'

'What I'm suggesting is a local take on your story, to bolster awareness and support, and look at things afresh. I'm sure the police have told you they're doing their best, but they don't have much to go on. What's needed is a local campaign focused on jogging people's memories from the day of the abduction. You don't need to sit around waiting for news; we can be proactive. Someone else must've seen *something*. It's Thurso after all: when the streetlamps go on an hour early complaint letters are written, and I should know ... The right *kind* of article ... with the correct approach could mean the difference between ...' the words life and death were on his lips, but he swallowed each of them, like pips in an apple, '... between finding her sooner rather than later.'

Kathleen sniffed and dabbed the end of her nose with her knuckle. She looked down at her feet and Angus wondered if she was indeed faint, and as the moment lingered he thought she might simply close the door on him. Yet Kathleen coughed and pulled open the door, inviting him inside.

The house was immaculate, and smelled of citrus fruits. The fireplace was swept clean and on either side stood tall, thin oriental vases with dried bouquets of honesty and catkins. There were photographs of Molly on the mantelpiece, one taken when she was a baby, and the other a school photograph: posed and turned towards the camera, her glasses on, one side of her fringe sticking up.

Kathleen served him weak tea and offered a plate of chocolate biscuits that rustled as she held them out to him, because her hands were shaking so much. He took a Blue Riband, but dared not taste it until she began to speak. The large, high-ceilinged room had three sofas and a coffee table in the middle. Kathleen sat on one sofa, Angus on the other nearest to her. He took out his notepad and pen, as she sat forward, hugging herself as if she were chilled, chest near her knees.

'I don't know what to say,' she sniffed. 'The words have gone. I've used them all up. I can't tell it any different from what I've said already, and it hurts so much ...' She made a sound that reminded Angus of the noise Maisie made when the vet examined her.

Despite the chill of the autumn air, Angus brushed some beads of sweat from his upper lip before he began his questions. He had already decided that he would not mention the other child murders from the past few years, although he knew the police were working on comparisons with the Thurso abduction. He didn't want to alarm Kathleen; he wanted her to open up to him. 'I want us to take it easy. Nice and relaxed. Let's go over it, not from a police point of view but from a human point of view, a local point of view. Let's think about the details: what has been missed? Let's think about the connections we could make locally or further afield. Let's consider the jigsaw pieces and make a picture.'

Kathleen seemed to be shivering. He considered offering her his jacket, but didn't for fear that it would seem inappropriate.

Angus poised his biro.

'Is there anyone you know that might want to take or harm Molly?'

'No ... not that I can think of. She was just a wee girl. I can't think of anyone that would want to harm her ... take her away from her family.' Kathleen began to break down as she spoke, but she finished her sentence.

Angus took notes in shorthand, marking the paper faster than Kathleen could speak, never taking his eyes off her. In his notes, he also included descriptions of what Kathleen was wearing, how her face looked and whether or not she seemed on the verge of tears.

'What about the girls who witnessed the abduction?' Angus said, 'Did you know them, have you spoken to them about what they saw?'

'They were girls in Moll's class ... When the police told me about the child witnesses, I knew who they were *exactly*, but I hadn't met them in person.'

'What do you mean?' said Angus, his eyes wide and his breathing even and steady, as if he was stroking Maisie's flank. 'Just take your time.'

Kathleen took a deep breath. 'Moll ... told me that some girls in her class called her names, bullied her ...'

'And these were the girls responsible?'

'I'm sure of it, but ...' Kathleen turned to him, two thin lines suddenly appearing between her brows. 'Don't print that ... The important thing is to find Moll, not to start some idiotic thing over name-calling. Their parents would ... I can just imagine ...'

'It's off the record,' said Angus, nodding at Kathleen to reassure her, and he saw that her face and shoulders relaxed. 'Don't worry. You can speak freely.'

'It's just that I know those girls, and they were cruel to her, and I can't get over the fact that ...'

'What names did they call her?' said Angus.

Kathleen was startled by the question and looked at him strangely, but then wiped her nose and continued.

'Och, just names, you know what weans are like. They called her "pirate" because of her eye. My daughter wears an eyepatch – you'll have read in the papers – because she has a lazy eye. And the patch, well, it's supposed to cure it over time. She won't keep it on, that's the problem. She takes it off whenever she can and her eyes are not getting better ... and the name-calling seemed harmless enough at first, but it really affected her. She felt singled out and I think the girls were quite vicious and now I am at the stage of realising that ...' Kathleen inhaled deeply and put a hand over her mouth to stop herself from sobbing. 'They were among the last people to see my daughter alive and could have done something to stop her being taken ... but they were children who tormented her and probably wished her harm. I'm not saying it's their fault, but I don't believe everything those girls say. I don't believe everything they told the police.

'They said that she just went off with a strange man, arm in arm, but Moll is a shy girl. I told the police as much – that those girls *must* be lying. There must be other, more impartial witnesses than the bullies that picked on my daughter each day she went to school.'

Kathleen put her hands to her head. It seemed to Angus as if she was pulling her hair. 'And there was a police car in the area investigating a burglary at one of the houses near the school. Why didn't they see or hear her?' Her eyes were raised towards the ceiling, as if asking God rather than questioning Angus.

She let go of her hair and took a sip of tea for the first time. The cup shook in her grasp.

Angus continued: 'The description that the girls gave was very rough, very general: tall with black hair and blue eyes, dressed in a suit. Did the description sound like anyone you might know?'

Kathleen shook her head.

'Even the sketch?'

Again, Kathleen shook her head. The police had commissioned an artist's sketch based on the schoolgirls' descriptions, which all of the papers had printed. The *Journal* had printed it under the headline, HAVE YOU SEEN THIS MAN?

'Let's concentrate on the local context. You are both local people – your husband has lived here for many years. What has been missed? What should people have seen that the police and the press haven't mentioned?'

Kathleen wiped her hands over her face. 'You're right. The local context is everything. What I find absurd is that my daughter was taken from this small town in broad daylight, before witnesses. I'm from a big city, but here? Thurso? How is it possible?'

Angus sat back an inch. The tendons were standing out on the backs of Kathleen's hands.

'And my daughter's shy but she's not naive. She's sharp as a tack. She just wouldn't be sold on puppies or sweets or all the other things they say these perverts offer a wean. Moll's different...'

Kathleen held her forefinger out, pointing at the coffee table.

'Astute, that's what she is. She's astute.' She turned to look Angus full in the eye and he felt an urge to look away. There was a glare in the woman's pure blue eyes, like looking at the sun. He could only stand it for a second or two.

'Moll's not like some other girls: she's vulnerable but she's not soft, she's accepting but she's not gullible. She has a strength that I have always marvelled at ... She's stubborn, I suppose people would say, and maybe that's true. I didn't ever try to break her spirit. She's a good girl, but she's tough, and, as much as I fear for her, I know she'll fight this man if he tries to subdue her. Every second of every day, I *will* that, and I know that she will find the strength to do it.'

Kathleen was agitated now. Her breath was rasping in her throat. Her eyes were dry, but Angus could tell that she was close to breaking down again. He tore open the wrapper of his chocolate biscuit and took a bite, then turned to her and smiled.

'She does sound like a good girl – and tough,' said Angus, trying to be understanding, 'but she's still wee ... a wee one, just seven years old. It's ...'

'She'll be eight on the twenty-ninth of December,' said Kathleen, whispering. She turned to Angus with a smile. 'It's just after Christmas so it's hard because it seems like all the presents come at once.'

Angus pursed his lips, as he tried to return the smile.

'She wants a blackboard and chalk for Christmas this year,' said Kathleen, sniffing noisily. 'She's told me already.'

'Let's start from the beginning, shall we? You and your husband are from Thurso?'

'No.' Kathleen wiped a palm roughly over her face. She was not wearing any make-up and the action reddened her skin. 'I'm from Glasgow. John's from Aberdeen originally, but he's lived in Thurso for years – long before I moved here. He's been with the plant for over fifteen years. He's the managing director now. Before that he worked in Rosyth.'

'So your husband's a Highlander, but you're from the Lowlands,' said Angus, almost to himself.

'That's right. I moved up here from Glasgow just after we got married.'

'And your full name is . . .'

'It's just Kathleen . . . Kathleen Henderson.'

'And your maiden name was . . .'

'Jamieson.'

'Am I right that there's a reasonable age difference between you and your husband?'

'Nearly fifteen years between us.'

'So you came up here to Thurso when you were how old, twenty-something?'

'I was young – twenty-one years old.'

Angus paused, calculating Kathleen's age. His nose was itchy as he considered and he rubbed it.

'And so now you're twenty-nine, thirty?'

'Twenty-seven,' said Kathleen, coughing.

Twenty-seven.

A warm, sweet shower of revelation shone on Angus in the cream living room. He had always been quick with numbers. He knew he would have to verify it, but it seemed that Molly's age at the time of the abduction, which had been widely publicised as seven and a half, and Kathleen's age at her marriage to John did not tally.

Angus made some casual shorthand markings on his notepad, bracketed with question marks. He noted that Kathleen was perhaps a *fallen woman* and Molly her bastard.

115

Angus felt heat flush his body. He was aware of his fingertips becoming damp and the biro slippery in his hand.

A deep silence filled the room as Angus considered his next question.

'Molly was born in 1977, is that right?'

Kathleen nodded.

'John was your first husband?'

'Yes ...' the skin around Kathleen's eyes had swollen and begun to redden. 'Yes.'

Angus cleared his throat and glanced down at his pad. 'But you ... had Molly before you were married?'

The skin puckered on Kathleen's brow. 'How did you ... What are you asking such questions for? What relevance—' Her face was reddening in anger.

'I'm sorry, I was getting distracted.'

'That's of no consequence and none of your business, quite frankly.'

'Understood. Let's talk about the morning that she left ... tell me what your routine was, and when you saw her last.'

Angus smiled at her penitently, and nodded for her to continue. She took a broken breath to calm herself, then looked out of the window as she recalled the events of 2 October. She talked in detail about brushing Molly's hair into the high ponytail that she liked and the daily argument about the plaster to be worn over her eye. She described how she had waved goodbye to her in her dressing gown, from the front door, and how they waved to each other again, and again and again, before her daughter disappeared behind the hedge, for ever.

Finally, after holding out so long, Kathleen began to weep and Angus passed her the tissue box that lay on the coffee table. He finished scribbling some notes.

'I should leave you. I didn't mean to upset you,' Angus said, standing.

'It's fine,' said Kathleen, getting to her feet and following him to the door. 'You're right, I suppose, that a local take on it might help. I'll try anything.' She tried to laugh, but it looked like someone had just punched her in the stomach.

She opened the door and he stepped out into the crisp Thurso autumn afternoon.

'Thank you very much, Kathleen,' said Angus, touching her arm. 'You and Molly are in our prayers.'

In the car, around the corner from the Henderson villa, Angus looked over his notes, running the tip of his tongue over his upper lip as he deciphered the shorthand. There was something here and he knew it. Kathleen had given him the key to the story he had dreamed of – he only had to discover it.

Angus's interest in finding Molly was sustained, but his image of her had been tarnished. Before she had been a prism of innocence, stolen; now – if he was correct – she was contaminated, a child born out of wedlock. Angus noted down 29 December 1977, Molly's date of birth, and snapped his notebook shut. She had been born nearly two years before Kathleen married and moved north. Angus could not be sure, but he sensed that John Henderson was not Molly's father.

He would still seek Molly out and believed that he had the power to find her, but he noted that human beings were often disappointing, as exemplified by Kathleen Henderson and her bastard child.

11

Margaret Holloway
Sunday 15 December, 2013

It was Sunday afternoon and Ben had taken the children to a
film. Margaret had said that she was going to stay home and
work. It was true that she did have a report to prepare, but when
the car pulled out of the drive, she went upstairs and slid the box
that she had taken from her father's house out from underneath
the bed in the spare bedroom.

As soon as she had opened the box in the attic, she had known it
was the one she was looking for, but her father had been waiting
below the hatch, looking expectantly upwards, and she had had
no time to look through it.

   Margaret knew that her mother had collected the clippings,
photographs and reports and placed them in the green box, but she
knew that her father was also well aware of its contents. It was her
past and her father would have allowed her to take it, but she hadn't
wanted to admit to him that she was being drawn back to that time.
She had taken bedding out of a packing crate and put the shoebox
inside, wrapped in an old sheet, before carrying it downstairs.

'You found what you wanted then?' her father had repeated, fingers smoothing the thin hair on his scalp.

'I always loved this bedspread. We just redecorated the spare bedroom, and I think it would go. You don't mind me taking it?'

'Not at all. If it suits then take it. I need to go up there and go through all that stuff again . . .' He turned away and picked up the hook for the ladder, ready to close everything back up again. 'I still don't have the heart for it. Whatever else you fancy, you're welcome. She would've wanted you to have it, you know that.'

He was reaching upwards, but Margaret noticed tears misting his eyes; a frown between his brows.

'Will you come for a few days at Christmas?' Margaret asked. She had asked him twice already, but he had been reluctant. The house was too big for him and yet he didn't like to leave it. She asked him down every holiday, but he was set in his ways.

Her father used the stick to roll the ladder back up into the loft and nudge the hatch back into place. 'I don't know. It's such a long drive.'

'Don't be silly, we'll come and get you.'

'Well, I don't know. The weather's been so bad, and look what just happened to you . . .'

'It can't happen twice, can it? It's Christmas. Come and let us look after you. The kids would love to spend time with you. What about coming on Boxing Day if you just want a quiet time? You know I'm off for two weeks. It's no bother. I'd love to have you.' She put a hand on his arm and smiled up at him.

'All right then,' said her father. 'Who can resist when you flash your big eyes at me?'

They both laughed and started down the stairs, Margaret carrying the bedding in two hands. Her father reached out to take it from her.

'I'm all right. I've got it, thanks.'

'Independent. You were always so independent.'

Now, in private, alone in her own house as she had wanted, Margaret was ready to open the lid of the box. It was like peeling off layers of her skin. It was compulsive yet harming, satisfying yet disturbing.

Margaret placed her hands on her thighs and took a deep breath. Her memory was fractured. She remembered some things; images came to her in snatches, but apart from that Margaret was in the dark about that time. She had few memories of her early childhood, apart from the stay in hospital. Since the crash, however, she had begun to worry that something much worse than an illness had happened to her when she was small. She couldn't remember specific incidents or scenes, but she was starting to recall feeling very afraid. Maybe she was reliving the crash and imagining childhood memories because the accident had made her feel as vulnerable as a child, but Margaret was not sure, and her uncertainty had driven her to dig deeper. When her mother was alive, she had not wanted Margaret to see whatever was in the box. Her mother's death had come when everything was changing for Margaret. She had buried her mother, then graduated, found work, married and had children. She had focused on the future.

Her mother had not lived to see the person Margaret would become: teacher, mother, wife. Margaret had been on her way to becoming a teacher when her mother died, but all her success had come afterwards. Even now, at the age of thirty-five, whenever she was commended at work Margaret wanted to tell her mother. She still needed her mother to be proud of her.

*

'*Proud*,' said Margaret out loud, as she peered into the box.

The articles, photographs, reports and papers had been carefully collated. When she flicked through them, she had noticed that they were in roughly chronological order, with the oldest dates at the top of the pile. This meant that her mother had not only collected the items but *revisited* and *organised* the box, so that it was like a story waiting to be told, from the beginning to the end. Margaret crossed her legs and touched the sides of the box, imagining her mother rearranging the articles inside. Her pulse quickened, and she put a hand on her chest as she took a deep breath.

She had been at university when her mother's health deteriorated. She remembered the black shadows under her eyes, and the bruises on her arms that appeared after the slightest pressure.

On top of the pile of cuttings was a colour photograph of Margaret as a child. She was in her school uniform, smiling nervously at the camera. She looked scruffy and distracted and Margaret remembered how her mother had been annoyed about the photograph when it arrived, because her hair had been unbrushed.

Margaret placed her hands over her mouth and breathed into them. She felt sick and anxious, but she was not sure why. She flicked quickly, randomly through the pile of papers and photographs. The black, bold printed words seemed to swarm over her hands, like beetles: PAEDOPHILE, MOLESTATION, SEXUAL ASSAULT, SERIAL OFFENDER, GROOMED, INNOCENCE, EVIL, STOLEN, DESTROYED, HEARTBREAK, LOST.

On her knees, Margaret leaned forward, fists on the bedroom floor. She only wished she could remember. She flicked hurriedly through the layers of newspaper articles and found a letter from a doctor addressed to her mother. It was dated 10 January 1986, so Margaret would have been just eight years old. She brushed sweat from her upper lip as she read the letter.

Her vision was blurry and her heart was racing, and she needed a drink of water, and Margaret could read only part of the letter before she was forced to place it back.

> . . . I express my deep regret for the trauma experienced by your family.
>
> I conducted a full examination of your daughter and found no evidence of sexual intercourse or penetration. While that must be gratifying, it is impossible to conclude that sexual assault has not taken place, and the psychological scarring that is currently evident in your daughter may suggest abuse of that nature. I would recommend a full course . . .

Margaret replaced the lid and slid the back under the bed. She was soaked with sweat. She went into the bathroom, washed her face at the basin and stood for a moment, dripping, staring at the drain. She wished that she could remember more.

The hospital, she whispered to herself. She remembered returning from somewhere. She remembered the flowers on either side of the garden path. When she was brought home, she was dumb. She hadn't uttered a word for six months after her return, and she had been taken to see doctor after doctor until she started to speak again, quite naturally and without coercion.

Eliot, Margaret's second child, had not said a word until the age of two and a half, when he had declared, 'It's all right, I'll do it myself.' In the same way, Margaret had returned to the family home unspeaking and unsmiling, until one day at dinner she had said, 'Please can you pass the salt,' and after that everyone thought she was better.

When her voice returned, her mother sat her down and asked her what had happened, but Margaret hadn't wanted to discuss it. Once, her mother had taken her hand and smoothed it, saying, '*Some things are best forgotten*,' and so she had forgotten almost everything.

Margaret dried her face, and felt her pulse steady and her breathing return to normal. This was a private suffering; it was leaning into the deep, dank well of herself, and Margaret knew that she needed to take her time. The crash had literally shaken her, so that she had been forced back to her essence, and things that had once been buried were now coming to the fore. She wanted to carry on as normal for her family, but she couldn't stop what was happening to her.

Margaret Holloway, deputy head teacher, mother, wife, did not know what had happened to her when she was a little girl, and she was terrified to find out.

12

Big George
Wednesday 2 October, 1985

It was nearly dusk when George and Moll crossed the English border. It had taken them almost eight hours from Thurso. He had avoided all the main roads that he could and ensured that he drove under the speed limit.

They had followed the coast until Inverness, with the North Sea to their left and the purple and brown mountains to their right, immutable, timeless. The landscape embraced them as they drove.

They passed through the Cairngorms National Park and the trees darkened the road, stretching up so tall that they almost blacked out the sun. They headed south through Perth and then Kirkcaldy. It was the first time that George had crossed the Forth Road Bridge and he found his steering wavered as he looked at the rail bridge on his left: the bright red girders intricate as capillaries. He bypassed Edinburgh and headed for England.

He had stopped once or twice to smoke or urinate, but had not let Moll out of the car. She had not eaten or drunk a thing since he had taken her. As they approached the border, the

Cheviot Hills came into sight and a full moon slipped early into a still-blue sky. She was asleep, her head resting against the seatbelt and her thin legs akimbo. She had resisted falling asleep, but he had turned on the radio and turned up the heat in the car and finally she had succumbed. He glanced at her as he drove.

He had wanted the three of them to run away together – but he was on the road now with only his daughter. *Daughter. His daughter.* The sleeping child beside him filled him with panic and regret. It was not how he had intended. He remembered the swish of Kathleen's hair and her graceful, rhythmic walk. Years they had been apart, but he could still recall her exact smell and the memory of it cleaved him now, as he realised that he had lost her, for a third and probably final time. Sweat formed at his lip as he considered and he clasped a hand over his mouth.

'*What've you done now, Georgie?*' he whispered to himself. He had taken her baby girl, *their* baby girl. She would never forgive him now.

He was a fugitive. George took a deep breath as he realised. *Fugitive.* In some ways, it didn't feel so different. He had always felt like this. He had always wanted to run, and now, here he was, on the run.

He was strangely grateful that Moll was with him. Seven long years of separation but now here he was, going on a road trip with his little girl. Asleep, she looked awkward but beautiful and he felt a flush of love for her similar to how he had felt when he first held her in his arms. When he found someplace safe to stay, and managed to settle down, he would ask her if she wanted to stay with him. He hoped that she would grow to love him too. He imagined it might be possible.

So much of his life had been like this: a single impulsive

choice mapping out a course of action. Liquid always follows the path of least resistance and so George's life had run away from him in just such a way.

He hunched over the steering wheel as he looked for a place to pull over for the night. He needed to stretch his legs. He had heard on the Scottish news and again on the national news that the police were looking for a tall dark man, wearing a dark suit and driving a dark-coloured car. He knew the police could have more information than they were sharing with the media, but he felt encouraged that the descriptions were so vague. He had brought a few changes of clothes with him.

He was tired and needed to wash, but felt that he couldn't risk a hotel this evening. They were conspicuous: a man travelling alone with a young girl, and he could not yet count on Moll to behave herself. He strained into the dark looking for somewhere to stop for the night.

On the English side of the Cheviot Hills, he found a lay-by near a forest and pulled into it. He kept the car running for a few minutes for fear that the child would wake, but when he turned off the ignition she remained sound asleep. He ran his hands through his hair and then placed them over his mouth. He stared at himself in the rear-view mirror. He was finally *away*. He had done it.

It was five o'clock and the sky was only just starting to bruise, a pale early moon set high in the blue. He opened the door and closed it gently, and then shook a Benson and Hedges cigarette from its packet. The evening was cold and damp, but the air was fresh with the scent of pine needles. He checked that Moll was still asleep, stretched, then lit up, leaning on the roof of his car as he enjoyed the head rush of the welcome cigarette. Deep in the forest was the distant bark of foxes: their voices hoarse screams like the sound of a child in pain. George took another drag of his cigarette, thinking that the foxes reminded him of his childhood.

He was the black sheep in his family. Ever since he was small, he had wanted out of there, and now he dared to hope that he had made it. George had always dreamed of another life. It was partly why he had loved Kathleen. Her family were like the ones you saw on TV: sitting round the dinner table laughing and talking, church on Sundays and holidays in Rothesay. Kathleen's father could do magic tricks and had a beautiful singing voice; George's father only needed a bath to get away with murder and could knock someone out with a single punch. He had loved Kathleen and her family, or at least *the idea* of her family. Losing them all had been like losing his own skin. He had gone crazy for a few years after he split with Kathleen: drink and drugs and women, all of which his own family had tolerated, but George had felt lost.

Back then, Kathleen had been his only chance of escape. He had been *stupid* at school – could barely write his name. All he had ever wanted was *a family of his own*. Now Moll was with him and, at twenty-seven, he had his whole life ahead of him. He felt sure he could win her heart and make a life for them together.

He felt as if he had broken out of prison, only with a suitcase filled with one hundred thousand pounds. The police seemed to have no idea who had taken Moll; and the McLaughlins weren't even looking for the money that George had taken because they thought it was at the bottom of the Clyde. For just a moment, George wondered if he had got the better of everyone. He felt frightened and excited at the same time. He was free at last. He could start a new life away from the garage, which still stank of his dead father's bloody hands.

George remembered it had been a Thursday. He was in the garage with Tam, working on an old Rover. Tam had showed George how to replace a fan belt and give the car a basic service. The instructions from Peter had been to clean the car up and make it roadworthy. Tam had made sure he stayed under the bonnet, saying nothing to George except to ask for tools. The front right tyre had a puncture, and Tam asked George to check in the boot in case there was a spare.

George whistled nervously as he walked around to the back of the car, wiping the car grease on his hands on to his overalls. Cleaning cars was a job that George tried to avoid, but Peter had asked him directly, clasping his gloved hands. The body had been disposed of – weighted down and thrown into the Clyde – but there was still residue and other evidence in the car that needed to be removed. They would fix it up and sell it on. George's jaw was tight as he approached the rear of the vehicle. It seemed as if, all his life, authority had compelled him to do things that he didn't want to do. And after his father had gone, Peter had slipped on their father's shoes without so much as a thought.

A chill sweat on his skin, George laid both hands on the boot and took a deep breath. He wasn't sure what he was going to see, but he opened the boot and peered inside.

It was empty. The carpet lining was dark grey but appeared stained. George put a hand over his mouth. The iron scent of old blood was familiar to him and he took a step back. He was silent and, at the front of the car, Tam was silent also. George knew that Tam would not even speak to him until the boot was closed and the job was done.

He had planned on cleaning the boot with bleach, but the carpet material had soaked up too much blood and would have to be removed altogether and burned. George reached into the recesses of the boot, searching for the mechanism to release the base or at least find the edge of the fabric so that he could peel it back. As his fingers skirted the furthest corner of the boot he felt something soft and cold. When he leaned forward, he saw that it was a portion of a hand: two fingers and a thumb, pressed together, as if to signal 'OK' or as if they were about to snap the beat of a tune. At first George thought the fingers had been trapped, and there was another level of horror waiting for him below the fabric, but then he realised that they had been severed and forgotten in the far recesses of the boot. George scooped them into a plastic bag and then peeled back the fabric. Below, in the space where the spare tyre would have been, there was a black holdall. Again, George paused, fighting a wave of nausea. He knew that sometimes bodies were packed in such holdalls before they were weighted and thrown into the Clyde. Peter had always been threatening to test George's loyalty, and his resolve. George wondered for a moment if this was the test that he had to complete. He took the handles of the bag and felt the weight of it. It seemed as heavy as a small man.

George's fingers began to tremble.

The bag was padlocked, but he used his pocket knife to cut a small hole in the bag. When he pulled back the black material, he did not see what he had imagined: an eye frozen in a death stare, a torn mouth or beaten face. George saw that the bag was tightly packed with used banknotes.

George finished his cigarette, crushed it underfoot then tossed it out of sight into the forest. He saw that Moll had wakened

130

and got into the car beside her. She was rubbing her eyes. The sleep and the tussle with him earlier had messed up her hair. Her ponytail was askew and some of the hair hung loose outside the hairband. George reached out to touch it, but she jerked her head away.

An idea came to him suddenly, and he realised the necessity of it, although he knew now that Moll would fight him. He decided to wait until later.

'Are you hungry, sleepyhead? I've got some rolls, and some Irn Bru. Would you like some?'

George spread the travelling rug over the back seat and set a makeshift table with the bottle of Irn Bru in the middle. They ate, sitting at either side of the back seat, both of the doors open. Midges hung in clouds outside each door. He had ham salad sandwiches and egg rolls and also a sausage roll that he had not finished the evening before. He tore everything into halves and set it on a brown paper bag in front of her. She took the Irn Bru bottle in two hands and raised it to her lips. The glass sounded off her teeth and she put a hand over her mouth as if it had hurt, but then raised it to her lips again and gulped.

'Take your time,' said George, biting into one of the rolls. 'Are you very thirsty?'

The bottle sounded as Moll removed it from her lips. She wiped her mouth with the back of her hand and burped.

'Pardon me,' she said, hand over her mouth.

George grinned at her. 'Eat some food. You need it.'

She ate quietly, but quickly, finishing an egg roll and also the sausage roll. George stopped eating, in case she needed more. He had not made any preparations for looking after a child. He took a swig of Irn Bru, thinking that he should have bought more food along the way: milk, a change of clothes for her, toys for her to play with – but he had only been thinking about evading the police. It occurred to him that he had never looked after anyone before, other than himself.

When she was finished she sat, turned from him, looking at the dark country road. They had been eating for nearly half an hour and not a single car had passed. It was dusk now and the sky was navy blue slashed with red from the sinking sun.

'Where are we?' she asked, her good eye fixed on him, her bad eye staring out into the night.

'We're in England.'

Her eyes filled with tears. 'We're so far away. I want to go home.' She covered her face with her arms and cried and George felt her unhappiness as a sharp pang underneath his ribcage. He had spent his whole childhood crying, it seemed, and he hated to see her cry. When he had imagined running away with her, she had been happy, delighted that her father should return after so long. He hadn't thought that the tall, wealthy old man she called 'Dad' would have won her affection.

How different it would have been, had Kathleen been with them. It seemed naive now, that he had imagined all three of them, happy on the road south, together after all this time.

He reached out and put a hand on her skinned knee. 'Don't cry,' he whispered.

She did not cringe from his touch, but she continued to cry, fists to her eyes.

George didn't know what to do. He was the youngest of four. He didn't have any idea how to console a child, or entertain her. It would have been easier, he thought, had she been younger. Even though Moll was just seven years old, with her long limbs and assertiveness she seemed much older.

He took a deep breath as he considered what to do. She had

132

a strength that reminded him of Kathleen. Even weeping, she seemed stronger than him – Big George had never felt so small. He only wanted her to stop crying.

'Hey, hey,' he said, 'don't do that. You're so pretty and greetin' like that'll just get you all messed up.'

She took her hands away from her face, which was reddened after her tears. A single blue eye focused on him. 'I'm not pretty,' she said, wiping her face with the palms of her hands. 'I'm ugly, so if I cry it doesn't matter.' Her voice was broken, spoken in gasps. 'I just want to go home.' She bit her lip and fat tears rolled silently down her face, dropping off her chin on to her school blouse.

George cleared the picnic space between them. He reached over and took her hand, which felt small and cold in his. 'Sweetheart, don't say that again. You're a princess, I tell you. You're my daughter and you're the most beautiful thing that there is.'

Moll watched him. The lazy eye gave her a duality, so that she was at once a tearful seven-year-old missing her mother, and also a wise, detached older child scrutinising everything that was happening. George felt observed by Moll, even when she was looking away. It was as if he could no longer get away with anything.

'I promise you, you're beautiful and you can't let anyone tell you different.'

Moll put her chin down to her chest. She was shivering and her breaths were unsteady. George was unsure if it was the cold or her tears that caused her to tremble, but nevertheless he dared to touch her again. He reached out and ran a hand through her hair.

'C'm'ere.'

He put his arm out. While she did not pull away, neither did she fold into him, as he had hoped. She didn't resist him, however, and he was able to shelter her under his arm and soothe her.

After a moment, she broke free of him.

'I need the toilet.'

'Have you ever peed outside?'

Moll nodded, her chin up.

George helped her out of the car and indicated towards the trees. The trees were tall pines and it would be dark beneath them. 'There you go. Don't go in too far or the foxes'll bite your arse.'

Moll looked at him strangely, and he was not sure if she was afraid of the foxes or afraid of him.

'I'll wait here for you,' he said, hands in his pockets.

She looked over her shoulder at him, and then disappeared behind the first fir tree. He took out his packet of Benson and Hedges and smoked again, counselling himself to relax, telling himself that it would all be fine. The wean would come round to him and they would be on the road and ready for their new life in no time.

He could glimpse the white of her face from behind the tree as she squatted. He heard again the scalded bark of the fox. They were unlikely to be discovered here, but George conceded that it was an eerie place to spend the night. The pines reached out to him, like limbs of the dead.

George took a drag of his cigarette and called into the forest. 'You all right?'

There was no sound. George took another drag, wincing. 'Moll?' he shouted, exhaling. He waited, butt pinched between forefinger and thumb, then let it fall. 'Moll?' He raised his voice and a fox howled back.

George walked into the darkness of the forest. Sun-deprived, bleached pine needles broke under his feet.

'Moll,' he shouted again, beginning to panic.

There was no sound. He reached the tree which he had seen her crouch behind, but she was gone. He stared into the dark graveyard of trees, not knowing in which direction she had run.

George ran into the forest, calling for her, tasting the sharp tang of the pine trees at the back of his throat. It was like a nightmare, so that as he chased into the forest after her, he had the sensation that he too was being chased.

As a child, he had often dreamed that his father was chasing him, and then sometimes his father caught him and they would fight. It had always been bloody, violent retribution. Yet in real life George had never fought his father. He was the only McLaughlin boy not to have punched Brendan McLaughlin. His father had been dead ten years, yet still he dreamed of confronting him, fighting him man to man.

'Moll-y,' he screamed, with abandon, feeling the tendons in his neck.

After running a few hundred yards he stopped, exhausted, and bent over to put his hands on his knees. George knew that if he didn't find her she would perish. The trees were expansive. There seemed to be no way out – even the sky and the moon were obscured. He began to run again but tripped three times on invisible roots.

The trees organised into a tunnel and George ran down it, looking to either side for Moll. He saw a flash of white on his right-hand side. It was her white school shirt illuminated in the moonless dark of the trees. She saw him too, glanced at him over her shoulder and then began to run harder, and George had to pick up his pace just to keep her in sight.

He was out of breath and felt the fatigue in his body, but he pushed himself, caught up and managed to grab her by the collar.

They both fell on to the soft bleached cushion of pine needles. She was sobbing, struggling, unable to breathe, kicking him away from her.

'Stop,' he whispered, taking both of her arms and pulling her tight into him, 'You're all right.'

'I don't like you,' she was saying. 'I want to go home.'

George pulled her tighter and held her, until she stopped wriggling. When she was still, he got up, pulling them both to their feet. Once again, she was hysterical with tears. He took her by the shoulders.

'I don't want . . . let me go . . . I don't want . . . I want . . .' she sobbed.

He just wanted her to stop.

He considered what to do. They were alone in the forest. There was no call for panic. No need for harsh control. It was just him and Moll.

He knew now that she didn't like to be held or restricted – she had bit him the last time he tried it – but he didn't want her to run off again. She was crying so hard, out of breath, that he thought she might hyperventilate. He thought of hitting her, but couldn't do it. In a moment of inspiration, he got up and lifted her off her feet. He stood tall and raised her up, high above his head.

She stopped crying almost immediately. He turned slowly in the forest with Moll raised above his head.

'I don't want to hurt you,' he said, speaking up to her. The weight of her was almost nothing, although her shoes gently kicked his chest. 'Just don't run away from me.'

'I want to go home. I want my mum,' she said. He didn't know if he would ever be able to win her over.

He lowered her down until he was holding her in his arms, but she sat back, away from his body, so that he had to put a foot forward to support the weight of her and maintain his balance. He sensed the stubborn strength of her and knew that he would have to yield.

'OK,' he said, giving her one of his best smiles. 'I'll take you back, if that is what you want, but I need to get settled first.'

She looked at him, sucking in her lower lip. Her left eye looked askance. Her cheeks were wet with tears.

'We can't go back right away,' he said, looking into her face. 'They'd arrest me. I'd go to jail. But I can take you back when the time's right; when I'm set up. If you really don't want to be with me, I'll let you go back.'

'When will it happen?'

'You come with me till we're sorted, and then I'll let you go. I don't know how but I will.'

'I want to go back now.'

'You can't right now, but in a while it will be OK. Once everything's quietened down. I promise you.' He tossed her in his arms for a second and something resembling a smile appeared on her lips.

'Will you just trust me? I'm your real dad after all!' he said, spinning, so that her hair flew out behind her. Despite the tears, she smiled. He took faith from it, and threw her up in the air and then caught her again. She smiled again and put two hands on his shoulders to support herself.

Out of breath, George put her down. 'It'll just be a while we're away.'

'You promise?'

'I promise. It'll be just like going on holiday – a holiday with your real daddy. Let's go back to the car and get some rest. We have a long day tomorrow.'

It was dark now, and chill. As they walked back, she fell into step beside him and he let his hand fall loose by his side. After a moment, she took it and he was grateful. Her hand felt small and cold in his.

He knew what he had to do when they got back to the car, and he wanted to use this moment, when she was calm, when the roads were quiet and the pall of darkness was upon them.

They had abandoned the car with open doors and George cleaned the back seat of crumbs and rubbish and spread out the travelling rug for her again. He shut the doors to keep the heat in.

George was a city boy and the pure darkness of the countryside unnerved him. Seven o'clock now and it was pitch black. There was not a single streetlamp, and the new darkness was absolute. It reminded George of his childhood home when his father entered – sucking out the light and the chatter, so that all that remained was his father's dark energy and the heaviness of his footfalls.

'You can stretch out and sleep in the back seat. I'll sleep in the front. Tomorrow, we'll go and get you some clothes, something warm to wear.'

She nodded, sniffing, wiping her nose on her cuff. He opened the boot. She was standing by the car door, jumping up and down.

'We'll go to sleep in a minute,' George said, as he opened the bag he had brought with him from Glasgow. 'There's just something I want to do.'

'OK,' she said, still jumping up and down and counting.

In the bag, George found what he was looking for: a hunting knife that he had taken with him in case he got into trouble or his family came looking for him. He took it out of its sheath and tested the blade against the skin of his hand. It would do the trick. He didn't want to frighten her, but he didn't have anything else he could use.

13

Angus Campbell
Saturday 5 October, 1985

It took Angus just over six hours to drive from Thurso to Glasgow. It was a Saturday and he had to leave at four thirty in the morning, to make sure he was there by ten thirty. He could have waited until Monday morning, but as soon as he had checked that the Registrar's office was open on Saturday mornings he had decided to make the journey. The early start had not caused him any difficulty. As a child, his mother had woken him every morning at five and even now Angus rose at that time, waking his own children according to his mother's strict clock and then going out to tend to Maisie.

His appetite had been whetted and he was eager for his scoop. He could taste it. The only thing that worried him as he drove was thoughts of Maisie.

When Angus left Thurso, Maisie was still not in labour, although she was swollen and in obvious discomfort. She had not eaten when Angus tried to feed her just before he left. He had given Hazel strict instructions to call the vet if she should show signs of labour while he was away. The Sabbath was fast approaching. It was a sin to work in any way at all on the Sabbath but calling the vet on a Saturday was not a problem.

Of course, Angus hoped that his heifer would wait for him. He had whispered as much to her, lips to her muzzle before he left her that morning, the cock yet to crow and the moon still high in a sky scattered with stars. Angus wanted to be there to help her. It was difficult to tell if the calf had turned again. Maisie's udder had begun to bag up, and Angus knew that could mean birth was possible in the next twenty-four hours, but he also knew from experience that some cows began to make milk weeks before calving. Maisie's tailhead had not yet sunk, however, and her discomfort seemed minimal. Angus hoped that labour was still a few days away.

He had grown up with cows and had reared a small number on his land in Thurso over the years. He had seen countless calves born. He had been only seven when he had watched his first birth: the calf appearing, pink nose and yellow front hooves, then trembling, sticky-furred, on long thin legs.

He knew from experience how dangerous birth could be. One of the Campbells' neighbours in Barra had killed a newborn calf while assisting a cow in labour. The farmer had pulled on what he had assumed were the calf's back legs protruding from the cow's rear. But it was the front hooves that were presenting and the head had not been manually turned into position. When the farmer pulled, he had broken the calf's neck.

As a teenager, Angus had assisted in one breach birth. He knew that it was not an easy matter. A breach birth was what Angus feared most for Maisie: a calf presenting rump-first could not be born without assistance. Angus had merely studied what to do, but avidly so, and he felt he was ready. He would reach inside Maisie and push the calf back inside her, until he found the feet. It would be hard work: his muscle against Maisie's muscle, but he would get the calf into position so that Maisie could push her calf out.

He parked near Queen Street station and then walked quickly across George Square. The day was dry but the air smelled of rain. A flock of pigeons took flight in his wake and the beating of their wings echoed in the baroque square framed by Glasgow City Chambers and the Chamber of Commerce. Angus felt important, on a mission for the Lord and also for himself. He stopped for a moment on the edge of the square, recalibrating his bearings, then marched down John Street and up the steps of Glasgow City Council Registrars' Office.

Before him in the queue was an old man registering the death of his wife. Despite the mild autumn day, the man wore a long winter coat that smelled faintly of mothballs, his cap folded into the right-hand pocket. As he spoke to the registrar, he dabbed the corners of each eye repeatedly, with a large white handkerchief. Angus felt mild contempt for the man, as he was impatient to be served.

'I'm sorry for your wait,' said the registrar, when Angus reached her. She was a tall woman with jewelled earrings and a wide smile. 'How can I help you?'

Angus was annoyed that he had to look up at her. 'Are you standing on a box behind that counter?' he said. 'Should I get my stepladder out?' but she only smiled at him again and repeated herself.

'How can I help?'

'I would like to request a birth certificate.'

'Certainly . . . name and date of birth?'

'The name is Molly Henderson, twenty-ninth of December 1977.'

'If you take a seat, I'll be back shortly.'

This time Angus did not sit, but paced back and forth on the flagstones, noticing how dirty they were – marked with muddied footprints and scattered with crushed cigarette butts even though the bins were fitted with ashtrays. He paced with his hands in his pockets, his fingers tingling with the prospect of grasping the envelope containing the birth certificate.

The woman came back in a few moments. 'We don't have anything under that name. Could it be registered under another?'

'Oh, of course,' said Angus, twitching with annoyance, 'the mother's name was Kathleen Jamieson, so the child would be under Molly Jamieson.'

'Wait a moment.'

The registrar returned with a piece of paper and Angus opened his eyes wide.

'I have a *Margaret* Jamieson with that date of birth and mother. Is that who you want?'

'Of course,' said Angus, exclaiming. 'It would be; it has to be.'

The registrar cleared her throat. 'We are very busy this morning, with it being a Saturday. Would it be convenient for you to come back and collect it later – nearer lunchtime?'

Angus frowned and stood on his tiptoes to ensure that he was closer to the woman's height. 'It is *not* convenient.'

The registrar pursed her lips. Another three people had joined the queue behind Angus.

'Very well,' she said. 'If you'd like to take a seat, I'll try to get it for you as soon as possible.'

Angus nodded and sat in one of the chairs that lined the room. He sat poker straight with his arms folded, worrying the inside of his lips with his teeth. It was the Sabbath tomorrow and he needed to be back in Thurso before midnight.

*

144

After a twenty-minute wait, the registrar called Angus over. 'Here you go,' she said, smiling thinly and passing him an envelope.

Angus thanked her without meeting her eye, paid for the birth certificate, then tucked it into the inside pocket of his jacket and almost ran down the stairs. He found a dry corner of a bench in George Square and sat down. The envelope had not been sealed. Angus slid the birth certificate out and unfolded it, licking his lips in anticipation. The paper was pale yellow and the form completed in fine ink calligraphy.

He scanned it quickly. Mother's name: Kathleen Jamieson. Maiden Surname: Blank. Date of Marriage: Blank. Name of child: Margaret Jamieson. Date and Time of Birth: 29 December 1977, 5.30 a.m. Place of Birth: Glasgow Royal Maternity Hospital, Rottenrow, Glasgow. Mother's Current Address (if different from above): 1– 2 South Chester Street, Shettleston, Glasgow. Father's Name: George Brendan Thomas McLaughlin. Father's Occupation: Mechanic.

'I knew it,' Angus hissed.

He scattered pigeons once again as he strode back to his car. He was about to turn on the ignition and head back to Thurso when he paused. He realised that he had a rare opportunity – being in Glasgow – to look into this George McLaughlin who had taken advantage of the young Kathleen. The *John o'Groat Journal* had records and backlisted papers, but it was mainly local news. Angus decided that here, in Glasgow, was the best place to find out more. He checked his watch. It was just after eleven.

He found a telephone box near the station and called Hazel. It rang out and Angus was about to hang up when she answered.

'Hello?'

'I nearly hung up. Where were you?'

'I was checking on Maisie.'

'Good,' said Angus, nodding in the phone box as if Hazel could see his approval. 'That's why I was calling. How is she doing?'

'There's still no sign . . .'

'Did she eat her breakfast?'

'Yes, she must have eaten what you gave her this morning.'

'Did you notice any discharge?'

'No, nothing. I looked for all the signs you told me about. I would think not today . . . But p-possibly . . . Mmmm-Mmm—'

'Yes, yes. I think Monday too. Very well. I have further business. I will be back late tonight.'

He hung up.

Reassured, Angus drove to the Mitchell Library, muttering about the inefficiency of the one-way system in Glasgow, as he was sent on futile loops of the city centre before arriving at his destination.

In the warm silence of the library, Angus searched through the electoral register and found there was only one George Brendan Thomas McLaughlin in Glasgow and, sure enough, he was from the East End, 578 Shettleston Road, not far from Kathleen's 1977 residence. He was listed as living with Peter and Richard McLaughlin, who Angus assumed were family members.

He skipped lunch and instead spent the time painstakingly searching through microfilm copies of the *Glasgow Herald* from 1977 to 1979. His stomach rumbled as he checked the film, scanning for anything on Jamieson or McLaughlin.

He was just about to give up and begin the drive north, resentful of the one pound fifty he had paid for parking, when he turned to the more recent newspapers and spotted something in the *Herald*'s local news section. Near the fold of the paper, the story bore a picture of a man smiling, surrounded by his family, and punching the air in victory.

Peter McLaughlin (pictured) outside Glasgow High Court after walking free from his second murder charge. The jury returned a 'not proven' verdict for murdering James Banks in what was believed to be a gangland murder in November 1983. The jury acquitted on the basis that there was insufficient evidence that McLaughlin had not acted in self-defence. McLaughlin, who was known to police for his gang affiliations, was acquitted in 1980 for the murder of Tommy Gordon (25), who was found decapitated and folded into a barrel dredged from the Clyde.

McLaughlin, of 578 Shettleston Road, was also the victim in an attempted murder case in 1978. The accused, Branx Murphy, was sentenced to ten years for inflicting grievous bodily harm on McLaughlin. McLaughlin had been severely wounded in the knife attack, in which his assailants attempted to amputate his arms and legs, but made a full recovery. McLaughlin commented after the 1978 verdict, 'I don't do dying well. I leave that to others.'

McLaughlin, who has a large visible scar on his neck, attributed to a bar fight in his youth, said after Tuesday's hearing that he was 'delighted and overwhelmed' by the not-proven verdict. He was joined in court today by his sister, Patricia McLaughlin, and brothers, Richard and George.

Asked what he was going to do to celebrate, Peter McLaughlin said, 'I'm going to get drunk and forget all about it.'

Angus crouched forward in his chair, so that his nose was less than an inch from the monitor. Reading the article had brought a bitter taste to his tongue. He despised Peter McLaughlin and his kind so much that he could have spat his distaste on to the short-pile library carpet. Instead, Angus leaned in to get an even closer look at George. He leaned so close that George's face became nothing more than grey and white dots.

Angus thanked the librarian, shook on his jacket and left. In the lobby, he saw a row of public telephones and decided to make a call.

He had an acquaintance at the *Glasgow Evening Times*, who was also a member of the congregation of the Free Presbyterian Church of Scotland, worshipping in the Partick area of Glasgow, if Angus was not mistaken.

He cleared his throat as the phone rang, holding a ten-pence piece near the slot, ready to feed it in if his friend answered.

'Don Balfour,' said a gruff voice.

'Don,' said Angus, gesticulating in his phone booth as if he were face to face with his friend. 'So good to hear your voice. You might not remember me. It's Angus Campbell from the *John o'Groat Journal*, we met at the, the . . .'

'Angus, of course. How are you, wee man?'

Angus pursed his lips. He disliked it when people referred to his physical stature but Glaswegians seemed to make a habit of it. In the background, he could hear the punch of electric typewriters in Don's office. It was the sound of a real newsroom, unlike the room he shared at the *Journal*, with Amanda and Jennifer. He put another ten-pence piece into the slot.

'I'm well. I'm in Glasgow . . . working on a story. I didn't know if you wanted to have a bite to eat . . .' Angus checked his watch. It was just after one o'clock.

'That sounds great.'

They met in the café in British Home Stores. Angus ordered a pot of tea with two teabags and a ham sandwich, while Don just ordered a scone and a coffee.

'The thing is,' Angus said, after they had exchanged pleas-antries about each other's families and church congregations, 'I wanted to ask what you knew about Peter McLaughlin.'

'The Hammer?'

'Excuse me?'

'You mean Peter "The Hammer" McLaughlin, the East End heavy, son of Brendan?'

Angus cleared his throat and then nodded warily, pushing a corner of sandwich into his mouth. He watched Don's face carefully.

'He's a gangster?'

'I'm sure you don't have anyone like him up in Thurso.'

'The family?'

'They're all in the business, loan sharks, heavies ... Brendan, the dad, he was the big man, but he died ... probably murdered but no one has ever found his body. They had a funeral for him not long before Peter's last trial.'

'*All* the brothers, they're *all* in the family business?'

'And don't forget Patricia. Some would say she's the most dangerous. I've interviewed people who said if Patricia asks for the money, you're as good as dead.'

'The sister's a killer?'

'She's ... how can I put it ... the angel of death. When she calls, it won't be far away.'

'How on earth do they get away with it?'

'Well, they have their legitimate businesses. They run a garage on the Shettleston Road: Fix It, I believe it's called.'

'What about George?' said Angus bitterly. 'What do you know about him?'

'Big George?' said Don, looking at Angus for the first time. 'He's the baby McLaughlin. He's in it up to his neck but only by

149

association. I never heard of George laying a finger on anyone. Some people say he's not all there. He dropped out of school when he was twelve or thirteen or something ... even before it was allowed.'

'What else do you know about him?'

'George? Not much. I know where he drinks. I know he likes to do a turn – fancies himself as a singer. But he's just one of those laddies that like a drink and an easy life.'

'There's no news on him of late?'

'None? Why do you ask?'

'Well, it's just we had a girl kidnapped up in Thurso.'

'I saw ... Molly Henderson? They say it could be linked to those other girls, Begg, Martin and Hardy?'

'Well ...' Angus licked his lips, ensuring he did not give any-thing away. 'That's the current school of thought.'

'You think the McLaughlins are linked somehow? Believe me, abducting kids is not their business. They're far too busy with extortion and murder to be bothered with something as risky and niche as child abduction.'

'Of course I don't think they're involved,' said Angus. 'It was just I was at the Mitchell while I was waiting for you ... You know, looking through the Glasgow news, and I saw that family featured quite a lot. It was just out of interest.'

'Aye,' said Don, shaking his head and downing his coffee. 'The McLaughlins have had their fair share of infamy.'

'Indeed. I'm always on the lookout for something big, you know?'

'You getting bored at the *Journal* then?'

'Not at all,' said Angus, sitting back with an expansive smile. 'We're just always on the hunt for news. You never know where the next scoop is coming from.'

'They're laying off folks at the *Herald*,' said Don, staring into his empty coffee cup and stroking the edges of his moustache.

'Really?'

'Be a laugh if I was applying for a job at the *Journal* soon!'

They both laughed nervously and shook their heads and then made movements to go – Don reaching for his umbrella, Angus folding up the sugar sachets he had used and placing them carefully on his saucer.

'Nice to see you again,' said Don, taking Angus's hand and squeezing it.

Angus walked in the fine, soaking rain to his car, feeling a well of excitement burgeoning inside him. He wanted back to Thurso immediately, so that he could view again the artist's sketch of the abductor. He wanted to cross-check it with the picture he had copied of George McLaughlin, Glasgow gangster and, Angus now knew, ex-boyfriend of Kathleen Henderson. He had known there was something wanton about Kathleen from the moment she opened the door in her low-cut jumper and pearls. He saw now that Kathleen had invited the devil into her life, some time ago, and now the devil had taken her child. *Hell mend ye*, as Angus's mother might have said.

Angus got to his car just before his parking ticket expired. Everything he had heard reinforced his private thought, that *this* was his scoop. The abduction of Molly Henderson was a story meant for Angus Campbell.

Angus checked his map. It was a straight road from Queen Street station: right along George Street and on to Duke Street. Just ten or fifteen minutes and Angus could be at the McLaughlin garage.

He checked his watch: just before three. He needed to leave

Glasgow by five o'clock, six at the latest, if he was to arrive home before the Sabbath.

His stomach tightened with what in a lesser man might have been fear, but Angus knew that true investigative journalists had sometimes to put themselves in danger.

It was his calling. Angus put the car into gear and headed east.

On the Shettleston Road, after a supermarket and a dark, bleak stretch of tenement housing, Angus saw what looked like a garage on the left-hand side. It was set far back from the road and fenced in with wire mesh rimmed with barbed wire. He pulled over and strained through the windscreen to read the sign: Fix It.

Angus got out of his car and squatted on the kerb, unscrewing the cap on his back right tyre then pinching the nozzle to let the air escape. He let the tyre sink on to the pavement a little, then replaced the cap. He got back in the car and pulled into the garage.

The sun had gone down and Angus felt a chill in the air. He pulled on his cuffs as he walked into the yard. Broken-down cars were parked on either side but there were no lights on inside the garage, no signs of life, and Angus wondered if they were closing. A large wooden sign read *Tyres, Repairs, MOTs, Cars Bought for Cash*.

He heard the rasp of metal against metal and turned to see a small man in a boiler suit pulling down roller shutters covered in swirls of graffiti. The man looked over his shoulder as Angus approached but said nothing.

'Hello there,' said Angus, putting his hands in his pockets. 'I was wondering if you could help me out? I have a long drive ahead and think I might have a slow puncture.'

The man padlocked one of the shutters and turned to Angus, saying something that he couldn't catch.

'I beg your pardon?'

'We're closing,' said the man; his skin was translucent, wrinkled on the forehead.

'Well, I need to get up north. I just wondered if you could take a look? I have a six-hour drive ahead. It was just to put my mind at rest, y'know?'

The man hesitated, then motioned for Angus to come inside.

'This is your garage?'

'McLaughlins',' said the man, turning to go back inside the shop. He was thin inside his boiler suit.

'And you are?'

'Tam,' the man said, turning.

'Tam McLaughlin?'

'Driscoll.'

Angus followed Tam Driscoll inside.

The garage was small, but there was a ramp and a cupboard-sized office and a display of oils, antifreeze and car polish. The walls were stacked with spare parts and old tyres, all blackened with car grease.

'All right, bring the car in,' Tam said, without even looking at Angus.

Angus reversed into the garage, then watched as Tam jacked up the car.

'How long do you think it'll take?'

'Shouldn't take long.'

'It's just I have a long drive up north.'

'You said.'

'I came all the way from Thurso.'

'Where's that?' said Tam.

Angus was shocked at Tam's lack of knowledge, but also

encouraged. This was the first part of the conversation that Tam had initiated.

'It's right at the very top of Scotland. Have you heard of John o'Groats?'

'Of course, John o'Groats to Lands End.'

'Well, Thurso's only half an hour along the coast from John o'Groats. So I have a fair drive ahead if I want home this evening, and of course ... tomorrow's the Sabbath.'

Tam raised an eyebrow, glancing up at Angus.

'It's just I'd noticed the tyre going down, and ... just between you and me ... my spare's bald,' Angus said, putting his hands in his pockets and shifting his weight from one foot to the other.

Tam blinked but said nothing. Another worker came in and went straight into the office. Angus nodded at him, and he nodded back. The man had very blue eyes that Angus found chilling.

After a moment, he hunkered down beside Tam as he pulled the tyre off.

'So ... this place is the McLaughlins' garage?'

Tam nodded, rolling the tyre on the garage floor, not looking at Angus.

'*The* McLaughlins ... as in Brendan, Peter, Richard and George?'

Tam's nod was imperceptible. Angus was sure that he had assented but it was too small a movement to be sure.

Angus asked again, 'As in Brendan, Peter, Richard and George?'

'Keep your voice down. What's your fucking problem?' said Tam, dropping the wrench on to the floor of the garage. The sound of metal against concrete echoed in the corrugated iron space.

Angus noticed that the man in the office looked over at them.

He had *smelled* this story since the moment he heard about Molly's abduction on his police radio. Now, he sensed how potent it was: how far the spores had been dispersed.

Angus crouched down beside Tam again. He wished that he was a smoker and had a cigarette to offer him. Up close, the man smelled of stale tobacco and Angus knew that a cigarette would have cemented their new relationship as hack and informant. Instead, he used bravado: 'What can you tell me about George?'

'What's George to you?'

'You know him?'

'What if I do?'

'Where is he?'

Tam wiped his hands on his trousers and then lifted the tyre up, ready to take it out back for checking. 'Where is George!' he said, laughing lightly.

Angus did not know Tam, yet his laugh was surprising.

'Where is Georgie Boy?' Tam repeated, grinning and showing his straight but yellowed teeth. Smiling, Tam was almost handsome. '*That* is the magic question.'

'You know him then?'

'I went for drink with him now and then . . .'

'He works here?'

'When he sees fit.' Tam spoke under his breath. 'I'll be back in a bit,' he said, very loudly, as if wanting the man in the office to hear. He took the tyre out back.

Angus stood stooped with hands in pockets. He dared not approach the man in the office. Instead he stood waiting for Tam in the open garage, shuffling his feet on the oil-stained concrete.

Tam returned with the tyre and then dropped down on his

knees to replace it. 'Your tyre's fine. There's no puncture. I'll blow it up for you. It'll last you the drive no problem and then just keep an eye on it ..."

Angus bit his lip. The time had passed so quickly and he had not yet got what he needed from Tam.

'I wonder ...' said Angus, clasping his hands as Tam got to his feet. 'Now that I'm here I may as well ... The car hesitates starting. Saying that, it's been fine for the last few days, but with the drive ahead ... would you check it?'

'What do you mean, hesitates starting?' said Tam, with wrinkled forehead.

'The engine keeps turning but then finally starts ...'

'Could be the spark plugs.'

Without another word, Tam opened up the bonnet of the car and leaned over it, black hands spread over the engine. Angus ducked under the bonnet to speak to him.

'I detect from your tone that George is not around at the moment. Has he skipped town?'

'You seem to know more than I do,' said Tam, pulling out and inspecting each of the spark plugs.

'You used to work with him but he's no longer here, correct?'

Again Tam nodded imperceptibly.

'You say you used to drink with him. Did he say where he was going?'

'How would I know? Why would he tell me?'

'Did he say anything about a child?'

Tam's face was perhaps the most inscrutable that Angus had ever set eyes upon, but – as a parent, and a husband – he had learned to tell when people were lying. He had learned to read the sly lick of light that caught the eye of the liar. He saw that wink of deception in Tam's eyes, just as he said: 'No, nothing

156

about a child ... This spark plug is pretty bad. Do you want it changed?'

'Please.'

Angus felt a dry hunger at the back of his throat: knowing that he was in Glasgow, having his car fixed by someone who might know where Molly Henderson had been taken and by whom.

He was not a tactile person – not a *toucher* – yet as Tam leaned over the bonnet again, Angus reached out and took his arm and squeezed it. 'Are you a father?'

As if commanded by Angus, Tam nodded.

'Do you think it possible that George McLaughlin would have taken a young girl?'

'No,' said Tam, avoiding Angus's eye and continuing with his work.

'You seem uncertain?'

'I'm not uncertain, maybe you are?'

'No, I'm just interested in the facts.'

'Is everything OK, Tam?' the man in the office called out. Angus looked over at him. It wasn't Peter, he was sure, but there was something about the man that made him wary: the tilt of his chin, the cut of his suit, the way he forced his hips forward when he put his hands in his pockets.

'All fine,' said Tam, wiping his hands and raising his voice so that it carried over his shoulder to the man in the office.

'If you know anything ...' Angus pressed again.

'I know that's you sorted to drive up to Thurso,' said Tam, with a one-sided smile, letting the bonnet slam closed.

Angus took a deep breath. 'What do I owe you?'

'I won't charge you for the tyre ... give us a fiver for the plug?'

157

'Very well,' said Angus, opening his wallet and taking out a twenty-pound note.

'Pay over there,' said Tam, walking away.

Angus approached the cash desk and gave his twenty-pound note to the man behind the counter. He found it hard to look the man in the face, but he was sure that this was the other McLaughlin brother – Richard. He recognised him from the photograph taken on the steps of the High Court.

The man placed fifteen pounds' change on the counter in front of Angus.

'Can I have a receipt?' said Angus, raising his eyes, swallowing and then looking straight at the man.

Richard stared at Angus for a moment or two then slapped a receipt book on the counter. He leaned so heavily on the page that the biro tore through to the carbon paper beneath.

Tam had returned to rolling down the shutters when Angus moved to leave.

'Thanks for seeing me when you were shutting up,' said Angus, loudly and for effect. 'I'm very grateful to you.'

Tam nodded and then Angus leaned over and passed him his business card. 'If you need to get in touch with me ...'

Tam glanced at the card then slipped it into his pocket. 'Why would I want to do that?'

'In case you remember anything more. I have reason to believe that George McLaughlin has abducted a small girl. As a father, you might—'

'I told you I know nothing,' said Tam, nodding goodbye to Angus and turning away.

*

In the car, Angus checked the clock. It was just after six. Even if he drove continuously, it would be midnight before he was home. Glasgow was heavy. He sensed the weight of its Baroque red sandstone and felt the leaden energy of the garage still surrounding him. He was a newspaperman and he knew it was his calling to mingle with the filth of the earth, but sometimes he felt besmirched by it. It was like gutting out the barn: one way or the other, it got under your fingernails.

The sun set as he drove, and his thoughts returned to Maisie and the discomfort that he knew she would be feeling. The thought of the heifer suffering caused him deep pain. He considered the characters from the garage earlier: shifty Tam and his nameless boss, who Angus was sure was part of a crime family.

Animals were so much purer than most of the human race. Angus remembered the barn when he was a child, and the comfort that the animals offered him: taking him into their fold and nurturing him. He had wrapped his arms around the warm necks of ponies and nuzzled their faces, taking the smell of them down into the deepest part of him. The animals had healed him. They had shown him love outside the coldness of his family: his father's indifference, his mother's criticism and the house that stank of gutted fish.

It had been the animals that had shown him the beauty of God's love and God's forgiveness.

He leaned forward and accelerated so that he was driving just below the speed limit, in order to get home as soon as possible. Saturday evening and he had expected the roads to be clear, but he got stuck in a traffic jam before Dunfermline, and then there was an accident after Perth and again just before Inverness. By the time Angus pulled into Thurso, it was eight minutes to midnight. He was glad he had made it home in time. Technically he had been working, and it was immoral to do *any kind* of work, or indeed play, on the Sabbath.

The Sabbath was *only* for worship.

As he passed through the town, then turned off the main road and drove down the farm track to his house, Angus felt a heavy, sick feeling in his stomach. It was time for bed, but there was a minute or so left to put his mind at rest. He had to check on Maisie. He felt an anxious joy at the thought of seeing her again, but also a strange panic, a premonition that things were not well.

He got out of the car and opened the door to the house. All the lights were on, but there was no sign of Hazel. He pulled on his wellingtons and walked down the path to the barn.

He heard Maisie before he saw her: long, agonised cries, deep and stirring as the low note on a viola. He broke into a run.

He was out of breath when he arrived at the barn, not because the distance was far but because he had run too fast. The familiar smell of the barn, sweet hay and dung, was laced with the bitter, iron smell of blood. When he went to Maisie's pen he saw she was on her side, her large eyes wide with panic. Hazel was kneeling, red-handed, at Maisie's tail. The concrete floor was splashed wet with her waters, and the straw was blackened with blood.

Angus looked at his watch. It was two minutes to midnight. Sometimes the Lord's grand design eluded him, yet he knew that it was not his place to question God's will.

'Get up,' he shouted to Hazel. '*Get away from her.*'

Hazel stood. Her arms, the front of her cooking apron, her knees and the toes of her rubber boots were all covered in blood, so that she seemed a strange communion of homemaker and butcher.

'You're not to touch her.'

'You were away and she's in such pain. It's stuck. It's breach.

160

I can feel its rear end. She needs the . . . the v-vet. Will you help her, Angus?'

'Did you do this? Did you interfere before her waters broke, out of your *ignorance* and your . . . *impulsiveness?*'

'I did nothing.'

'This morning you told me she was fine and now look at her . . .'

'She needs you . . . she needs a vet. Will you call?'

'*It's the Sabbath,*' Angus whispered so quietly that the words were only felt leaving his tongue, not audible.

'Will you help her though?' said Hazel.

Angus struck her across the face with the back of his hand. She stumbled under the blow and turned away from him, cowering against the barn wall. He was filled with pain and fear for Maisie and could think of nothing else. He didn't want Hazel in here. He didn't want her anywhere near the barn. It was the Sabbath and she had no right.

'You had *no right,*' he shouted, taking her by the neck and then driving her face into the wall. She buckled under the blow and put a hand to her nose.

A shovel, used for mucking out the barn, stood near the door. Angus picked it up with two hands. Hazel made no sound but ran for the door. He caught her before she got there, once between the shoulder blades and again in the small of her back. She fell under the blow, then curled up in the mud outside the barn.

Exhausted, chest heaving, Angus threw down the shovel and looked up at the moon.

He blinked and remembered being a child, locking himself in the barn on their farm. The barn was a place for exaltation and love, not pain and death. It had been the place where he felt safe.

'Why?' he screamed, a single, long, diaphragm-aching syllable that emptied him of air and hope.

Hazel began to crawl, in the mud, back to the farmhouse. Angus looked down at his hands and the shovel at his feet. He felt a shiver of shame. The force of the blows had jarred his shoulder and he realised that he had gone too far. Nevertheless he turned his back on her and re-entered the barn.

He could see that Hazel was right for once and that Maisie was in trouble. Angus looked at his watch – midnight – and then removed it. He turned his hand to the side and flattened his palm, fingers tight together like a swimmer, and then entered the heifer. He could feel the calf's rear before he was elbow deep. It was breach and it was stuck.

If it had been Monday, Angus would have called the vet and paid the emergency call-out fee; then, as he waited, he would have got down on his knees and slipped his hands inside her, pushing the calf further inside in the hope of turning it. Maybe he would have been able to turn the calf and find its feet, allowing him to slide it out of her, timing his actions with her own muscular push. She would be silent, breathing heavily through flared nostrils, knowing that he was caring for her. The calf would slip out, blue and yellow, stuck with the gel and slime of the birthing.

Angus stood before Maisie and looked into her face, his right hand slick with her insides.

'It is the Sabbath,' he told her. 'And the Sabbath is sacred. I have to leave you. I know that you can do this by yourself. It is God's will.'

Maisie let her head fall against the hay, her mouth open and her eyes half closed. Angus got down on his knees.

'You understand, my girl,' he said, making long, flat-palmed strokes on her velvet neck, 'that I love you, but I also love God.'

She jerked away from him. He wondered if a contraction had taken hold or the calf had shifted, or if she had heard and understood every word he had said and was, now, appalled by him.

There was a tremor in her abdomen and Angus could see the angle of the calf under her flank. Maisie bent her front leg, as if preparing to stand, but could not. She moaned again, so loudly that it caused the water in the metal trough to ripple.

Angus got up and ran outside. He ran towards the farmhouse, two hands pressed over his ears. By the time he arrived at the house, he was in tears. He covered his face and sank down on his knees into the mud.

'Dear God, give me strength,' he said, putting a hand to his face that smelled of Maisie.

It was God's will, but he had never felt so damned.

14

Big George
Wednesday 2 October, 1985

George gave Moll a big smile. 'C'mon back here till I show you something,' he said, offering his hand.

She folded her arms.

George exhaled: she was hard work.

He offered his hand to her and after a moment's consideration she took it. He led her to the back of the car. The boot was open and the hunting knife was lying where he had left it. The blade of the knife reflected the moonlight. When she saw it, she bucked away from him. He held her wrist and pulled her into him.

He hunkered down and took her by the shoulders. 'Listen to me. I'm not going to hurt you. I said I'd take you back and I will, but there's something I need to do, and you need to trust me.'

She dug her heels in, leaning against him, but when he looked into her good eye he saw that she might yield to him.

'You have to know that I won't hurt you. You *have* to understand that, but this has to be done before tomorrow, and we may as well do it now.'

'What?' she asked, blanching with fear. 'What are you going to do to me?'

He let her go. 'Turn around. Trust me.'

She hesitated for a moment, her good eye searching his face. 'Go on,' he whispered.

She watched him intently for seconds that seemed like minutes, then slowly turned around.

Her shoulders were raised in anxious expectation, as if a kitten might jump on her back.

He picked up the knife.

She rolled away from him and crawled backwards, her mouth set and her brows lowered. 'No,' she said. 'What are you going to do?'

'I'm not going to hurt you. I just need to cut your hair a bit.'

Moll sat up on the moss she was sitting in and stroked her long ponytail. 'Cut my hair, why?'

'It's a wee bit long.'

'I like it that way.'

George stood up. It was as if, with every step, he had to reach deep inside himself to find the right way to charm her. In that sense, she was the most challenging girl he had ever met, apart from the nuns.

'Short hair's all the rage,' he tried, raising his eyebrows. 'It's *very* with it. I'm just talking about a trim, mind, a wee shaving off, just to make you a bit more fashionable.'

Still sitting on the ground, Moll hugged her knees and stared at him.

'You know you want to.'

She was still reticent.

'Listen to me,' he said, bending over so that he could look her in the eye. 'I'm going to take you back, but right now there are people looking for you and looking for me, and so I just want to change the way you look a wee bit, so we're not so . . . obvious.'

'I don't want to change the way I look.'

'How long have you had that haircut?'

'Always.'

'Well, always is a long time. A change is as good as a rest, they say. Help me out. Shorter hair'll show off your pretty face.'

She clasped her hands and looked up at him, as if considering.

George turned around, scanning the scene for inspiration. There was a dirty cloth in the boot of the car that George used for the windows or to get rid of excess grease. He picked it up and flapped it gallantly, like a barber's towel.

'If madam would like to sit on this fine chair,' he said, bowing and motioning to the hatchback, 'I will be glad to give her a grand bouffant worthy of the greatest film star.'

Moll smiled, showing the gap between her teeth. George held out his hand and she got to her feet.

He lifted her up and set her on the boot of the car, then fussily tucked the greasy cloth around her neck as if it were a hairdresser's cape. 'There we go. Is madam comfortable? Would madam like a glass of Irn Bru while she gets her hair cut?'

Moll giggled and nodded.

George retrieved the bottle from the back seat and set it between her knees. She was about to open it and drink when he stopped her.

'Careful now,' he said, picking up the knife. 'You can take a drink when I've done this, but now you need to stay still. You can't move an inch or it'll cut you.'

She heard the serious note in his voice and froze. He took her ponytail in his right hand. Her face was pale, and he worried again that he was frightening her.

'Nearly done now, madam.'

He knew he didn't have long. He cut her ponytail right

through – cutting close to the nape of her neck. He handed the hair to her.

'Hold on to that. You can keep it as a souvenir.'

He had expected her to cry again, or try to fight him, but she merely looked at the hair in her hands and said, 'Why?'

'You'll see when I'm finished.' He used the knife to cut off the remaining long strands of hair. 'Hold still. Hold really still, OK?' he said, with the knife against the nape of her neck.

She nodded her head.

'*Dear God, I said don't move. Pretend you're a statue.*'

She did as he had asked, straightening her spine and sitting tall and still, arms at her side. He cut as close to the scalp as he could, shaving through the hairs.

'Ow,' she said, but did not pull away.

'Does it hurt?'

'You're pulling my hair.'

'Sorry.'

'I like my long hair,' she whined.

'You know the great thing about hair?' he said as he worked. She shook her head and he tutted at her because of the movement, but she kept still and so he answered, 'It always grows back. Hair's the easiest thing in your life to change. Hair's your chance to change without doing anything drastic, and why would anyone not want to change if they could?'

She looked up at him, brows raised quizzically.

When he was finished, he put the knife away and spun her around to inspect her. He lifted up her chin. Shorn, he could see the shape of her face better. It was the shape of her mother's face: high cheekbones and a pointed chin.

'You look great,' he said, smiling at her. 'Do you wanna see?'

She nodded and he led her around the car to the side mirror, which he twisted towards her. She peered into it, smoothing the hair over her forehead.

'I look like a boy.'

George leaned down to peer into the mirror beside her. He wanted her to look like a boy, and he planned to buy her an outfit tomorrow to complete the look. The police didn't know who they were looking for, but they were looking for a tall man with a seven-year-old girl.

'I don't think you look like a boy. I think you look cool. I think you look like a dark-haired Annie Lennox.'

'Who's that?'

'A cool lady with very short hair.'

Moll looked back to the mirror and turned her head this way and that. 'I suppose it doesn't matter. I'm ugly anyway.'

'Hey,' said George, sitting down in the back seat, taking her by the wrist and dragging her gently into the space between his long legs. 'You mustn't say that.'

'It's true. I have a weird eye and I'm ...'

George pulled her into him and spoke close to her ear. 'Nothing about you is weird or ugly, do you hear me? You're my wee lassie.'

She looked up at him. Her hair was spiky, uneven and longer along the back of her neck and George thought she looked like an otter, although he would never have told her. 'You're cool, and you're strong, and I think you look great. You're just the way I always knew you would be ... I used to imagine meeting you. Did you ever think about me? About what I would be like?'

Moll considered for a moment, then nodded.

'What did you think I'd be like?'

'Taller.'

'I'm six foot three!'

'I thought you'd be taller, and thinner, more like my dad.'

'I'm taller than your new Dad. I saw him; I'm sure.'

'But you're not thinner.'

'Not many men are.'

She was leaning against his thigh, looking at her thumbnail, making a teardrop shape with her forefinger and thumb. He put his arm around her.

'You're better than I ever imagined. I mean it. I told your mum when you were born I always wanted a wee girl, and I did. I didn't want for you to be taken away from me. I asked your mother to marry me, you know, *twice*. Did she ever tell you that?'

Moll shook her head, not looking at him.

'I got her a diamond ring and everything. I still have it.' George reached into the pocket of his jacket and opened the box. Moll stroked the diamond with her forefinger. 'I asked her once in front of her parents, and a second time I got down on my knee in a park in Glasgow. That's pretty romantic, don't you think?'

She nodded again, and bit down on a yawn. He snapped the ring box shut and glanced at his watch. It was nearly nine.

He spread the travelling rug across the back seat and told her that she could lie down. He told her to take off her school jumper and use it as a pillow. When she was lying down, he took off her shoes and laid them at her side, noticing how long and thin her feet were. He shook off his jacket and covered her. He closed the doors, then reached into the front seat for his lighter and packet of Benson and Hedges.

He smoked a cigarette, leaning against the car and wondering what would happen now. As a child, his sister had told him that the way to succeed was to surrender. 'Just do what they say,' she had counselled him, referring to their older siblings, their father or the nuns, but George had not been able. His sister's sympathy for him had waned as he was repeatedly belted by the nuns, beaten by their father and taunted and exploited by their brothers. In the end, even Patricia had turned against him. George's inability to listen to her had confounded him.

In the McLaughlin family he took his share, but being the youngest and his mother's favourite he had seemed able to coast below the main violence, although his mother had never been able to protect him fully. Nevertheless, he remembered the day when his sister gave up counselling him, his father broke his spirit and he decided to run away one day where no one would ever know him; somewhere no one would recognise his face or know the family he had belonged to. He had decided to start a new family, to raise children who loved him. Even now, it was this that George wished more than anything else: he wanted someone to love who would not kick him in the teeth. The money in the boot had never been an end in itself to George. It was his escape, nothing else.

George used his wrists to pick up his lunch box and started to walk home. His hands were swollen from a belting Sister Agatha had given him because he had been unable to write with his right hand. He was seven years old and had been punished from the beginning at school, because of his left-handedness, but this year Sister Agatha had taken it on herself to cure him of the bad habit. George walked with his head down, feeling his knees cold beneath his grey school shorts.

The brief space between home and school was usually when George felt most comfortable. The hours between three thirty and five were always his happiest. He would play football among the tenements, or he and the other boys would tease the girls who were playing peever, drawn roughly on the pavement with stones.

Sometimes the girls would chant at him:

'Georgie Porgie, Puddin' Pie,
Kissed the girls and made them cry,
When the boys came out to play
Georgie Porgie ran away.'

George would mimic a dance as the girls sang, and then, as they finished, he would rush in and upset one of them. Sometimes he would steal a bow from a ponytail, or lift up a skirt, or take their skipping rope and run off with it.

Arriving at school and coming home were always the worst points of the day. He hated being at home, the dread of his father's return, and then the hours when his father was there, when George felt as if he were holding his breath, as if he might explode. Every act required so much concentration and it was only a matter of time before George let go, and drew attention to himself.

But then, he hated school too: the nuns, like black jellyfish floating around the classroom, ready to sting him at a moment's notice.

Now George struggled with the lock to the close door, the key awkward in his purpled hands. He dropped his lunch box in the hall, but managed to pick it up and take it into the kitchen, where his mother was staring into the fire, smoking.

He sniffed and she turned to him.

'There's a loaf there, take a slice with a pickled egg.'

His mother pickled her own eggs, which were kept in a pail at the bottom of the wardrobe. He used to love touching them with his forefinger, ducking their cold bald scalps and smelling the acrid vinegar from his fingertips.

But today his hands had been beaten into gloves. He knew he was unable even to cut himself a slice of bread, let alone eat a slippery egg.

'I'm all right.'

'What d'ya mean?' said his mother, turning. 'You're always half starved.'

George stood at the door, sniffing. His nose was running and he licked it with the tip of his tongue.

'Do you want me to do it for you?' she said, exhaling and casting her cigarette into the fire. There was an opened pack of Woodbines on the table.

George sniffed again and his mother got to her feet. The kitchen smelled of stewed beef and turnip and he knew that they would have mince for their tea. She was in a kitchen overall, her arms blanched white as she took the knife and cut him a piece of bread.

Most of his friends' mothers had strong arms and fat, pink fingers. His own mother was thin and small and when she cut through the loaf the sinews showed on her lower arm. George was not sure why, but her thinness always made him feel sad.

She put the slice of bread on to a plate and passed it to him. He kept his hands at his side.

'Are you handless?' she said, holding the plate in mid-air.

'I got belted,' he said finally.

His mother put the plate on the table and turned over each of his palms. 'That's a bloody disgrace. How many times?'

'Twenty-six.'

'Twenty-six! What on earth for?'

'Writing wrong.'

His mother pursed her lips. Today was the worst belting he had had at school, but George knew that it counted as a small injury at home.

173

She took his palms in hers and raised them to her lips. 'Kiss it better, shall I?'

He still couldn't eat the bread or grasp an egg from the pail, but he felt better when her warm, thin lips touched his bruised palms.

Sometimes his mother was days in her room after Brendan had been at her. George wouldn't hear her or see her, yet would be told to empty the basin of bloodied water. So much of his relationship with his mother was physical, unspoken: a kiss, fingers through his hair, a bowl of bloodied water. Neither of them ever needed to say a word.

George took a seat at the table. 'Tell me about when you lived with your granny.'

His mother smiled and lit another cigarette and settled back in her chair, staring at the fire. She had told him the story so many times, but only when they were alone. She would whisper to him when he was in bed at night, or when he had been younger she had sat him on her knee and rocked him.

'When I lived with my granny,' his mother began, 'that was when I remember being happy. She lived in a cottage by the sea close to Penzance, in Cornwall, near Land's End, right at the bottom of the country, far away from everything. The cottage was all on one floor, no stairs, and there was no electricity and no running water, and the old place smelled of peat and the ocean. It was so cold in the winter that your hands would swell up until the fires were lit. There was a well out the back and sometimes my granny would ask me to get a pail of water and I was a wee skinny thing but I would carry it with two hands back to her, and then she would make breakfast: porridge and hot tea and sometimes eggs or a kipper ...'

'Tell me about the oil lamps,' said George.

'Well, there was no electricity in the house and so when it got dark, my granny would light the candles. But she had a big oil lamp that she would carry around the house and light my way to bed. I loved the smell of it and the golden light that came out of it. When I was tucked up in bed I was always warm, with a crocheted blanket on top that my granny had made herself. Some of the patches were made of the softest wool and I would stroke those patches while she sat in the light of the oil lamp and sang to me.'

'Tell me about the morning.'

'In the morning, we would get up at daybreak, just after the cockerel crowed, and we would light the fires and clean the house, and we would listen to the waves crashing on to the shore, and we would decide what to do with our day after the work was done. Sometimes we would knit or crochet, or sometimes we would look for stones on the beach, and if the weather was bad we would just sit by the fire and tell stories ...'

George closed his eyes. He could imagine the whole cottage almost as if the memory was his own. His mother had lived there until her grandmother died, and then she had come to Glasgow to live with an aunt and find work, and it was then that she had met his father. But it was only the Cornwall piece of the story that George liked to hear. In his mind, the cottage was heaven: peaceful, distant, safe.

He was smiling at the bread on his plate, when his brothers and sister burst into the room, tearing into the bread and butter and trading insults like marbles. His mother put her ashtray away and started to prepare dinner. She never tended to the others as she tended to George. She didn't ask them about their day, or cut them a slice of bread, or tell them to help themselves from the pail of pickled eggs in the bedroom.

'Patricia, will you do my maths homework for me?' said

George, pushing the bread to the side of his plate and lowering his mouth to take a bite.

'What'll you give me?'

'A big smile,' said George, giving her one anyway. He had more than maths homework to do, but the teachers would think he had done his own maths. He couldn't ask anyone to do his other homework, as his ugly, backward letters were too distinctive. There was talk of him being held back a year or put in a class just for idiots.

'If you do everything I say from now till bedtime, I might help you out,' said Patricia, leaning back in the chair and looking down at him as she ate her bread. Patricia looked like her mother, but she was similar to their father in that she enjoyed power and control. George looked like his father, so everyone said; he couldn't see it himself, but his character was unlike him in every respect.

'Awright,' agreed George.

'Kneel down on the floor to eat your bread.'

George leaned forward on to the plate to take a bite then got down on to the floor as his sister requested.

'Eat your bread down there. Take it in your hands and eat down there.'

'I can't,' said George, laughing, showing her his palms.

'Wow. How many did you get?'

'Twenty-six.'

'That's unheard of,' said Patricia, raising her voice to her mother, who was stirring mince. 'Wouldn't you say, for the primary, like?'

Their mother sighed and nodded.

'Well, just stay down there. I can feed you.' Patricia swiped his piece of bread and then forced a piece into his mouth, so that George had to twist away.

'You're my little puppy dog.'

George crossed his legs and accepted it. He liked his sister best and he needed his maths homework done.

The McLaughlins owned two flats side by side on the second floor of a tenement on the Shettleston Road. They had two bathrooms and two kitchens and four bedrooms, but one of the kitchens was unused. Each of the children was carefully conditioned to know the sound of their father's footfall on the stairs. Brendan did not follow regular patterns, so there was no particular time to expect him. Often he came home for dinner, but sometimes he did not. When his father was not yet home, George felt that his whole body, every inch of his skin, was listening for the sound of his hard heels against the stone steps.

While George and his sister were fooling around, everyone heard Brendan's footsteps.

'Get up off the floor and sit down at the table,' said his mother, but George was already getting up, using his stomach muscles as it was too painful to press his palms against the floor.

His brothers, who had been fighting underneath the pulley – mock-stabbing each other below the drying sheets – stopped without being asked and sat down at the table. Patricia, with her sharp mouth, was silent. She got up and began to set the table, taking extra care over her father's place setting, seeing that the cutlery lined up and the glass was clean.

Only Patricia was allowed to pour him a glass of lager and, as she heard his key in the lock, she took the can from the fridge. In their neighbourhood, the McLaughlins were the only people with a fridge. Patricia took her father's glass and tilted it the way that Brendan had taught her. The can had a picture on one side of a blonde woman in white underwear and a negligee.

Brendan closed the door, and George slipped his hands under the table and cast his eyes to the floor. The kitchen, which had been so noisy – Patricia bossing him, his mother frying and boiling and sighing, his brothers punching and scratching and shouting – was suddenly so silent that George could hear the bubbles burst in his father's lager.

All the children sat; his mother wiped her hands on her apron. 'When do you want it served up?'

'When I've drunk this,' said his father, throwing off his coat and winking at Patricia for the carefully poured beer.

George had never been winked at by his father, nor had he been aware of his father winking at his brothers. Patricia preened silently.

George loved his sister, second to his mother (he only loved his brothers a little, and his father not at all), but his sister's callousness seemed to be directly related to affirmation from her father. George had noticed on more than one occasion that Patricia could be vicious for the sake of Brendan's approval.

His father smoked and read the paper, and drank his beer in silence, and they all waited in silence for him. His father didn't really read the paper; he merely glanced at it, hunting for stories on people he knew. When he was finished, he folded it and tossed it aside.

After the newspaper fell to the floor, the kitchen was filled by the scorching sound of his father's last inhalation of a cigarette. The smoke appeared down his nose, like a dragon, and then he crushed the butt in the glass ashtray. There was half a glass of lager left, and Brendan sipped it.

George suddenly began to feel very itchy. His palms itched most and he remembered his mother telling him that wounds itch when they heal and that made sense after the belting, but then his back began to itch, and his scalp. It was not nits. One or two children at school had nits at the moment, but George's mother insisted he, his brothers and sister were dooked and combed every Sunday. The itch was all his childish energy, trapped inside his still body.

George wriggled slightly to ease the itch, but then realised that his movement was gently rocking the table. Cutlery sounded off plates.

'Would you sit still?' said his father, putting his glass down, hard, on the table.

George nodded. His father rarely focused attention on him. He was five years younger than his sister Patricia and his place in the family was very much that of an afterthought.

'Sit still, I said.'

George looked his father in the eye. He was not sure if he had ever done it before, and after this moment he would never do it again, but they looked across at each other, each at either end of the table, like two opponents.

Brendan left his half-glass of beer and stood up. The furniture in the room seemed to shrink before his height. It was as if even the chairs and the table were afraid of him. Every object in the room, even his mother and his brothers and his sister, became smaller, while Brendan's presence swelled.

George tried to make himself smaller too, so that he couldn't be seen. He put his hands between his knees and hunched his shoulders and looked at the placemat in front of him, which bore a picture of a primrose. He stared straight at the yellow flower, wishing that he were two-dimensional like the primrose, or indeed possessed no dimensions at all: invisible.

George felt his father's vice-grip lock on to his shoulder, and turned to him only then.

'I'm talking to you, sir.'

'I'm being still,' said George, his whole body wincing, aware of how weak he sounded.

'Not still enough,' said Brendan. His eyes were filled with that same watery rage as when he beat their mother. There was a sheen over his too-blue eyes, like the clear eyelid of a crocodile when it submerges its prey. George knew the look, but would always, for years to come, be unable to articulate it. There were times when the look in his father's eyes changed and it meant murder.

'It's all right, love, he's just had a hard day. He'll stop his fidgeting,' said his mother, sealing his fate.

George's mother never spoke up for *any* of them, and George knew that the fact that she spoke up now meant that he was in for it, and probably she was too. It meant that his mother had calculated in her head the damage to him against the damage to herself. Her words were always meaningless: they were like spores of dandelions on a lawn. She had power in her nurturing, but her words were nothing at all.

'Hard day?' said Brendan hoarsely, gritting his teeth. Their father never raised his voice.

'*People are either shouters or thumpers, one or the other,*' George's mother had told him.

'Hard day? What kind of hard day can you have when you're seven?'

George was silent, staring at the primrose on his mat until it started to blur and morph into tumorous monsters.

'I'm talking to you,' said Brendan, pulling George to his feet by the shoulder of his jumper.

George stared straight ahead, at his father's brown tie and cream shirt. He could feel every pore in his body: the roots of his hair, the soles of his feet.

Brendan lowered his voice to a whisper. 'What kind of bad day did you have?' He spoke leaning down so that he could look George in the face. George could smell aftershave on his father's skin and lager on his breath.

'He got belted,' said Patricia.

If his brothers had spoken then, Brendan would certainly have slapped them because they were not being addressed, but Patricia had certain privileges.

'What for?' said Brendan, still addressing George, not Patricia, standing up but staring at George, his hands on his hips.

George took a deep breath. 'Writing with my left hand.'

'And were you?'

George panicked. 'What?'

'Were you writing with your left hand?'

'Yes.'

George blinked in quick succession, expecting a blow. His father threw back his head and laughed. He laughed for a long time: long enough for Peter and Richard to start sniggering too. Suddenly, Brendan stopped laughing. As a conductor silences an orchestra, so Brendan silenced the room. No one wanted to be caught out laughing when he was not.

Brendan grabbed George's sweater and shirt with two hands and lifted him off his feet. George closed his eyes.

Brendan set George down on the table, so that his brothers and sister were looking up at him. Stood on the table, he was almost eye to eye with Brendan, but George chose not to look him in the face. He stared at his father's Adam's apple instead. Brendan began to pace back and forth.

'Only *you* could get belted for writing with the wrong hand. There's a lot of good reasons to get belted at school, but that's the most ridiculous I ever heard.'

George felt tears prick in his eyes but held his breath and forced them to bide their time. Even during the belting at school he had not cried, which was why Sister Agatha had been so harsh.

Brendan began to circle the table. 'Which hand do you write with? Show me.'

George held up his left hand.

'NO!' Brendan shouted so loud that George almost fell off the table. 'That's the hand you *did* write with. What's the hand you write with?'

George held up his right hand.

'What's the hand you did write with?'

Swallowing, George held up his left.

'What hand is that?'

'Left.'

'Right.'

George bit his lip.

'Show me the hand you write with?'

George took a breath, then held up his right hand.

'Which hand is that?'

'Right.'

'Right.'

'Show me the hand you did write with . . .'

George again raised his left hand.

'What hand is that?'

Remembering the lesson from the last time, George answered, 'Right?'

'Wrong. What are you, an idiot? You think you have two right hands?'

George swallowed. 'Left?'

'Right!'

George began to cry. Brendan put a fist in front of his face. 'No son of mine cries.'

George took a deep breath, wiped the tears from his cheeks and somehow managed to stand up straight.

'Let's start again.'

It continued, until the mince was cold on their plates, small globules of fat hardening on top of it. Richard actually fell asleep at the table, his cheek pressed against the placemat, his lips pursed like a fish and saliva drooling. His mother and sister were both crying silently.

'Show me the hand you write with . . .'

George raised his right hand.

'What hand is that?'

'Right.'

'Right.'

'Show me the hand you did write with . . .'

George raised his left hand.

'Which hand is that?'

'Left, no right, right . . . no left.'

Finally, his father slapped him. He hit him with the back of his hand and sent him toppling off the table and on to the range, where he burned his newly belted left hand, if only for a second, before he fell to the floor.

As soon as he landed, Richard woke up and dragged his chair out, so that he could see him more clearly, on the floor.

George swallowed, holding his burned hand in the other. His mother was a white-faced statue, arms at her sides. His sister was holding her knife and fork in two hands as if she was bored and only wanted her dinner. His brothers were smirking.

Brendan walked around the table and stood next to George. George sat on the floor, knees up to his chest, looking at the white bubble of skin on his purpled palm. The skin of his newly burned hand was tighter now, as if the palm was pulling the fingers in on itself. From his position on the floor, George could smell the leather of his father's good shoes.

'Get up.'

George got up and stood, arms at his sides, accepting his fate. He wondered if his mother would carry a bowl of bloody water from his room in the morning.

'What you've proved,' said Brendan, hands in his pockets, 'is that you're an idiot. You can't write, you can barely read and you're not ever likely to be able to write because you can't even figure out what hand you're supposed to write with. Right?'

George nodded.

'Right?'

'Right,' George whispered.

'The nun that belted you's an idiot too, if she thinks there's any point in trying to knock some sense into *you*. If I were her, I wouldn't even bother.'

George nodded and turned for the door.

'Where do you think you're going?' said Brendan, taking off his tan jacket and putting it over the back of the chair.

George hesitated.

Brendan sat down, loosened his tie and downed the rest of his lager. 'You'll sit and eat your dinner.'

George turned and took his seat again at the table. He felt a strange itch near his temple and nudged it with his knuckle. When he lowered his hand there was blood. He had knocked his head when he fell on the range, but not noticed because of the burn. George sat with both hands under the table, each of them throbbing and feeling twice their normal size. He wondered how on earth he was supposed to hold a fork, in either his left or his right hand.

Brendan's chair creaked as he sat down. He raised his fork to eat and the family also raised their cutlery. Brendan touched the food to his lips and then threw it down, the fork clattering against his plate.

'What the hell is this? Are we animals, that we eat cold slops now?'

'I'll heat it up,' said George's mother, gathering in the plates, while Brendan narrowed his eyes and lit another cigarette.

The cigarette was finished before George wanted it to be. He smoked it down to the butt then tossed it into the brush. He turned to the car, expecting Moll to be asleep, but she was tossing and turning in the back seat, curled in a ball alternately on her left and right, then sitting up to smooth his jacket over her.

'Can't you sleep?' he whispered to her, through the car window.

'I'm too cold. I can't get comfy.'

He opened the back door and rearranged everything, so that she was sleeping on half of the travelling rug with the other half pulled over her, and his jacket on top. After a few moments she said she was still cold.

'You'll be fine when we get you some new clothes tomorrow. I'll buy really warm ones.'

'My head's cold too.'

He peered into the car at her; her shorn head was almost bald in places where he had cut too close to the scalp.

'When I go to sleep I have my hot-water bottle,' she said. 'My mum wraps it in a towel.'

George sighed, closed the door and turned away from her. He placed another cigarette between his lips. Even though the windows were shut and the car doors were closed, he was still aware of her tossing and turning as he smoked. The car rocked gently against the base of his spine.

Finally, he opened the back door again.

'What is it?' he said, accidentally exhaling smoke into the car.

'I'm cold.'

'Still cold?'

She nodded, clutching her arms.

George turned his back on her. He pinched the cigarette between forefinger and thumb and took a long drag, before tossing it away. 'For Christ's sake,' he said, exhaling into the blue-black pine of the forest.

He leaned into the car, whipped the travelling rug from her, then climbed into the back beside her.

Her eyes were large shiny pebbles. Each time he looked at her, George could not fail to be disconcerted by her squint eye. It was as if she could see all sides of him, as if he were transparent.

He took the rug and wrapped it around her shoulders. 'C'm'ere,' he said, pulling her into him.

At first she was just leaning against him, but after a while she tired and shifted, so that he was cradling her, swaddled in her travelling rug, like a baby. 'Are you warm now?' he whispered to her, trying not to breathe in her face because he knew he would smell of cigarettes. Briefly, he remembered his mother kissing him good night, with the smell of the Woodbines on her lips and in her hair, and her soft whispered stories of a cottage by the sea.

'Warm,' she replied.

He could feel the weight of her in his arms. It was a precious weight. He pulled her tighter into him.

'Will you read me a story?'

'What do you mean?'

'My mum always reads me a story before I go to sleep.'

186

'We don't have any storybooks. I can get you some tomorrow.'

'Just read anything to me, even the paper.'

'I don't have a paper.'

'There's one on the front seat.'

It was true. George had bought it for the football scores.

'Who reads the newspaper as a bedtime story?'

'We have nothing else.'

'I could tell you a story . . .'

'OK.'

George hugged her tighter. The closeness with her resolved something within him, but he was not sure where or why.

'Once upon a time, there was a . . . little girl and she went to school one day . . .'

'I don't want to hear that story.'

'What d'ya mean?'

'That's real, that's me . . . I want a story.'

'A story . . .' George heaved a sigh. 'Once upon a time, there were three bears. There was a little girl bear and she . . .'

Moll sat back in his arms to look up into his face, so that he felt the weight of her.

'You're rubbish at stories. Just read the paper. I like being read to. It makes me go to sleep.'

'I could sing to you.'

'I like to be read to. Read the paper.'

Holding her in his left arm, George reached into the front seat to pick up the paper. It was the *Daily Record*.

He settled into the back again, with Moll cuddled into him. He chose an article on page six with a picture of a polar bear. He folded the paper over and began to read:

'The polar bear at Glasgow zoo is very unhappy. The keepers have stopped giving him Irn Bru on the grounds that it is turning his fur orange, but now campaigners say the bear has a right to choose his own beverage . . .'

Moll threw back her head and laughed and he rocked in the back seat with her. Her eyes were turning coins of mirth and her long limbs moved against his as she giggled. George saw again the sheer beauty of her: his own daughter.

'Stop it,' Moll said. 'It doesn't say that. Read the real thing.'

'How do you know what it says?' George asked her, tilting her downwards so he was looking right into her face.

'Because I can read it,' she said, still giggling at him.

George took a deep breath.

Years since he had ever admitted it to anyone. 'I can't,' he said, tossing the newspaper on to the floor, then hugging her close.

'What do you mean?' She was looking up into his face.

'I can't read.'

15

Angus Campbell
Monday 7 October, 1985

It was still dark, but it was, finally, Monday morning.

Angus slipped his bare feet into his wellington boots, feeling them like cold, hard porridge against his toes. He was in his pyjamas. He was planning on going back to bed after he had seen to Maisie.

With the passing of the Sabbath, Angus now crept out to the barn where Maisie had calved, to check on her. His legs felt cold in his cotton pyjamas and his wellingtons stuck in the mud. The day was just opening its eyelid. The Sabbath had passed and now he could tend to her.

After Angus returned from Glasgow, he had spent a sleepless night worrying about Maisie. He imagined he had heard her moaning deep into the early hours of the Sabbath, but he had to strain over the noises that Hazel was making. Eventually Hazel had locked herself in the bathroom, and Angus had been grateful.

The Sabbath morning, Angus had been sick with worry for

Maisie and the calf. The Campbells always fed and watered the animals on Saturdays, so that Sunday was reserved for God.

Hazel was grunting as she put on her tights and attempted to zip up her dress. Angus assumed she was doing it just to spite him. She was pretending that he had hit her too hard, and her back pain was so severe that she could no longer reach the zip. She didn't ask for his assistance but simply struggled, then left it gaping as she sat to put on her shoes.

'Would you have the folk at church think you're a strumpet?' said Angus, marching across the room to pull up her zip. She threw up her hands in defence and the action both annoyed and saddened Angus. Sometimes his wife behaved as if he were a cruel and pernicious man, when he was merely a husband who was trying to educate his wife.

'Calm yourself, woman,' he said as he zipped her up. He noticed that the area between her shoulder blades was bruised. He knew it was his job to teach her, but sometimes he didn't like to see the evidence.

'I don't think I'm able to go to church,' she said, standing and turning in front of the mirror.

Angus followed her gaze and noticed that, although she was wearing a long-sleeved dress that fell below the knee, her lower legs were bruised. He wondered how that could have happened. Had the shovel slipped? Had she knocked herself as she fell? She would need to wear trousers to cover the marks. Angus disapproved of trousers on a woman and forbade his wife and daughter to wear them, but in any case trousers were unsuitable for church.

'Nonsense,' said Angus, looping his tie and scoffing. 'You *have* to go. If you don't, folk'll be turning up at the door with currant cakes and sponges.'

Hazel had nodded once and slipped her heels into her shoes.

Straightening his tie in the mirror, Angus had glanced at her as she pulled her heavy camel coat from the back of the wardrobe.

He had been unnecessarily severe, he admitted silently to his reflection, pursing his lips. But he had been concerned for Maisie and Hazel infuriated him because she never seemed to *learn*.

Now, finally on his way to the barn, Angus noticed that the thistles were blooming. They glowed white instead of purple in the waning moonlight. He slowed his pace as he approached, his mouth dry and his eyes wide.

Returning from Glasgow, Angus had been inside the barn at the very onset of the Sabbath – as Saturday turned into Sunday – and he still considered this sinful. He had witnessed Maisie's plight but left and returned to bed, where he had barely slept a wink. It had been twenty-eight hours since he had last checked on her.

Although he thought he had been awake, he remembered a dream from the Sabbath night and wondered if he had in fact slept, or if the dream had been a vision from God sent to comfort him. He had dreamed of the birth and the calf:

The calf was male, large-eyed and watchful, sitting on the straw with the sheen of birth still on him. He stood and suckled within an hour. Maisie was tired, but Angus could tell from the reflection in her large eyes that she was happy; that she had not felt deserted by him, that she had been happy to give birth alone.

Now, as he approached the barn, taking his time, he remembered the dream. He didn't care about the calf, he realised. The most important thing to him was Maisie. He was well prepared for the calf to be dead.

By the time he reached the barn door, his wellingtons were

dirty to the ankles with mud. Heavy rain had fallen while he was in Glasgow, softening the ground.

Everything about the slowly opening day was *too clean*, and made him nervous: the fresh tilth of the soil, the alertness of the thistles, the neat stack of feed by the barn door. Angus's head hurt. There was the brain-harrowing chirp of songbirds against the death crash of the sea.

His mother had been a fisherman's daughter and had known the sea as if it were a relative. It was his mother who had talked to him about waves travelling for miles and then dying on the shore. He had never been able to look at the ocean since without thinking of death.

Now, turning the latch and opening the door to the barn, Angus remembered his mother's funeral. The coldness of the memory, bone clean, made him pause.

Angus's mother, Annabel, had been a devout woman, but someone who was pathologically claustrophobic. She had been terrified of small spaces since a young age, when she had been locked in a cupboard for stealing apples. Growing up, Angus had known never to close a door on a room, as his mother always liked to see her potential escape. Their home had been cold, with open doors and open windows, which his father never condemned, no matter the weather or complaints from the children.

His mother had been a worker: when Angus was a boy, she had gutted fish for six hours a day, hung the nets out to dry and looked after the family as well. Her palms had been coarse and she had been short and fat with bulging biceps that even now, at the age of forty-three, Angus could not equal. She had died suddenly after a virus, when he was only fourteen years old.

Angus could only remember his mother criticising him. He couldn't remember a single word of praise.

When he had stood at her grave, in his black, itchy wool trousers and too-tight tie, he had imagined her fighting and struggling in the coffin that was lowered to the ground. Cremation would have been fairer for someone as claustrophobic as his mother, but his father had insisted on a burial. His father and two of his uncles tossed a handful of earth on to her coffin and Angus and his brothers each threw a carnation over the lip of the grave. But all the while, Angus imagined that she was alive inside that box. He knew this was the worst thing that could ever happen to her. He felt the horror of her panic deep inside him, in buried places: under his fingernails, in the roots of his hair, in his gums, in the strange-feeling skin of his navel. He had dreamed about her for months afterwards, fighting to get out of that coffin, under yards of tightly packed earth. Even now, in his forties, Angus would sometimes dream about her fervent quest to escape from underneath the earth.

But at her funeral all he did was toss the pink carnation on to the box, wait for the words, and watch as the earth was thrown over her.

The door of the barn creaked as Angus opened it. Before he entered, two fat flies flew in his face. He swatted them away. As he stepped inside, he inhaled the desperate smell of stagnation, of abortive hope.

Maisie was spread across the rank, bloodied straw of the barn, her tongue hanging out, white beads of evaporated sweat on her flank, and a dead, unbirthed calf between her haunches. The rear end of the calf was visible: a slick black tumour, but Maisie looked as she always had: pink-nosed and smiling, save from the protuberance of her tongue, and the strange glaze of her eyes, like unset jam.

Angus left the barn and walked straight back to the house, the back of his hand over his mouth. He vomited at the front steps, then almost immediately brushed it away with the yard brush and scoured it with bleach. Inside, he called the vet with the acid taste of vomit in his mouth, leaving an answer message asking that he come to remove animal corpses from the farm.

Angus stepped back inside the barn. He put a hand to Maisie's rear, as if preparing to do what he would have done: slid his hand inside and pushed the calf to turn it. He wanted to do it. He wanted to help her, but he knew that Maisie was dead and the calf was dead.

Instead, Angus knelt, smoothed a hand over Maisie's flank and took her tail in the other. He whispered words of prayer: 'God of hope, we thank you that not even death can separate us from your love . . .'

When his prayer was finished, Angus staggered outside, his eyes wet. Day had not yet broken but dew had formed on blades of grass, the skies were loud with birdsong, and an army of flies was now forming at the barn door.

Angus went back inside the house, washed his hands and forearms with disinfectant, then went upstairs. Hazel was asleep: curled as a cashew nut. The children's alarms were set for six.

It was only four twenty-two in the morning when Angus entered his study. He felt no tiredness, only immense sorrow for Maisie. It seeped into him, like the cold on a wet night, right into his bones.

'You have to get on with it,' Angus said to himself, out loud.

He rolled a fresh piece of paper into his typewriter.

It was all he had been thinking of since he returned from Glasgow. He hadn't wanted Maisie to die but she had, and now that she was dead Angus felt sharper, angrier, ready to write his story: the story of George McLaughlin stealing Molly Henderson from Kathleen, his former lover and the mother of his child. It was like no other story Angus had tried to write. But he saw it clearly and he was willing to report it truthfully, as he saw fit.

Pushing the image of Maisie's death-frozen muzzle out of his mind, he began to type. He typed angrily. Angus was often angry, and there were many targets for his anger, but today his anger was clearly focused on one person: George McLaughlin.

George was a depraved criminal, who had kidnapped a young girl for God knows what perverse purpose. George was part of a Glasgow crime family who were familiar with torture, extortion and murder. George was the tallest in the family: six foot three and big-built and Angus could imagine that he used his size to intimidate others, to help him to carry out acts of violence. It was George McLaughlin who had caused Angus to take a trip to Glasgow to discover the sinister links to the Thurso abduction, coming home too late to save his heifer.

It was therefore possible to consider that George McLaughlin had caused Maisie's death, and Angus didn't know how long it would be before he hurt the young girl who was now in his charge, if she was not already dead, as Angus well expected.

He typed faster than he knew he was capable of typing: he could only type with his forefingers but he generated a sound worthy of a seasoned touch-typist. He referenced the court picture he had found in Glasgow, with the McLaughlins standing on the steps of the High Court after Peter's acquittal, and also referenced Brendan and Peter's criminal convictions. He had not found any note of George's criminal convictions, but he was sure that George was sly and evasive of the law, and that his clean record belied the gravity of his crimes.

Before the children's alarms sounded and before Hazel got up to make their porridge, Angus left the house. He drove into Wick and placed his newly written article on his editor's desk with a note: *Exclusive from Angus Campbell. This HAS TO BE in tomorrow's paper. The nationals will be all over it.*

Angus returned to the farm, just in time to meet the vet, who arrived in his Land Rover, wearing dungarees and long green boots. They shook hands and Angus led him out to the barn.

The barn door was now swarming with flies, and inside, Maisie's corpse had begun to smell. The barn was well ventilated, but the scent of rotting flesh was heavy in the air.

When he saw the sight, the vet, Branx Conlan, a young man with an old man's face, shook his head.

'It's been a while,' said Branx, stepping forward to touch Maisie's corpse. 'I'd say she's been dead thirty-odd hours or so – rigor mortis is starting to wear off. What happened? Were you all away? You were so anxious about being here for her . . .'

'I know,' said Angus, pinching the corners of his eyes, to stave off tears. 'I was in Glasgow. I hoped to make it back in time. It was only my wife and she didn't know what to do. She thought Maisie would be able to do it by herself, and just left her to it.'

'Did she not think to call me?'

'If Hazel thought of anything, it would be a miracle,' said Angus, forgetting himself.

Branx Conlan was a quiet man, and he was a heathen. When he had vaccinated Maisie he had told Angus, 'I've been

196

an atheist as long as I can remember, but some days I envy you believers. I envy your certainty.'

Angus had said nothing, but had privately sneered at him. There was no need to envy, because he had it in his power to believe!

Branx went back and forth to the van, getting animal body bags and laying out chemicals in the barn. He put on a plastic suit as he waited for his assistant.

'Is Maisie that dangerous?' Angus asked.

'It's just a precaution. She's passing out of rigor mortis, so decomposition is setting in, and the added aspect of labour and the trauma of birth ...'

Mortis. Labour. Birth.

Again, Angus felt the horror and sickness of grief.

He wanted to ask that she be treated carefully, respectfully, but as soon as Branx's assistant arrived, Maisie was hauled into the body bag and lifted by crane on to Branx's lorry. She was lifted like butcher's meat, by the hook, the calf still inside her. Angus wondered about her burial, and if there would be one, and if the calf would be buried inside her.

For a moment, as the midday sun warmed the skin on his brow and the last whiff of Maisie left the farm, Angus thought of Kathleen. As he watched the truck pull away, and the tremor of the black body bag, Angus wondered what Kathleen would think when she read his newspaper article the next morning.

16

Kathleen Henderson
Tuesday 8 October, 1985

Kathleen had not slept all night. She had not been conscious of sleeping since Moll was taken, but John had told her that she had slept a little.

She got up when she heard the velvet thump of the newspaper against the doormat, pulled her dressing gown on and went downstairs. She opened the door and took inside the two glass bottles of milk that were set on the doorstep, then picked up the *Journal* and tucked it under her arm. Every second there was a pain in her throat; every moment, a horror – on her skin – like a shiver she couldn't shake.

When she was putting the milk into the fridge, Kathleen began to cry, silently. Pouring a glass of milk for Moll was one of the first things Kathleen did each day. Since Moll had been taken, Kathleen cried often, and so did not stop to experience the tears, but simply continued putting away the milk and filling the kettle as she wept. She cried with sharp intakes of breath, so that it sounded as if she were being stabbed. When she stopped crying the kettle was boiling and her face was completely wet.

She seemed to have so many tears. She placed two hands over her face, took a deep breath and then wiped her cheeks and eyes.

She had noticed that she cried more fitfully when she was alone. She had heard John breaking his heart locked in the bathroom, but in front of her he had been strong. Kathleen found it hard that they didn't share their grief, anger, impatience and, most of all, fear.

John had adopted Moll when she was a baby, just after they were married. He loved Moll like his own, yet Kathleen had always felt that her daughter was hers first and foremost. There was a sense that she and John were each afloat and separated in their suffering. They tried to comfort each other, but ineffectually. The other night John had tried to rub her neck and she had told him he was hurting her. She cooked for him but he had no appetite.

She poured a cup of tea, heavily, mechanically, not sugaring it although she liked two sugars, and not adding milk because milk made her cry.

She sat down with her weak, unmilked, unsugared tea and the local newspaper. She checked the clock. It was nearly 7 a.m.. She would normally be busy at this hour, supervising school uniform and making packed lunches and listening to the news while her tea went cold on the counter.

Now she had the time to prepare and drink a hot cup of tea, but this luxury broke her heart.

When she was alone, the worst fear consumed Kathleen. She would sit and imagine where her daughter was and how she was feeling. She wondered if she was bound; if she had been molested or hurt in some other way. When her thoughts turned to this horror, desperation would fill her and she would tremble with the desire to run to Moll, to physically save her, to protect her. But there was nowhere to run to, no way to know where she was and nothing, *nothing at all*, that Kathleen could do.

They hadn't said so in the news, but the police had told John that they were comparing the scant facts that were known about Moll's abduction with those of other young girls from across the country who had been abducted and later found sexually assaulted and murdered. Even though John was part of a large group of volunteers searching the local area, the police had told them that they believed Moll would have been driven far away from Thurso soon after she was taken. With each day passing, the belief that Moll was still alive waned.

The child abductions of the past few years bore similarities to Moll's. All the children had been snatched in a public place. Nine-year-old Gillian Hardy had been taken while cycling to a nearby friend's house, eleven-year-old Charlotte Martin was abducted crossing a bridge over the River Tweed, five-year-old Tracey Begg was snatched while playing outside near her home. All three of the victims had been dumped long distances from where they were abducted, but found within the same twenty-six-mile radius in England.

The witnesses to all three abductions had been weak, but rough descriptions matched and were not dissimilar to those of Moll's attacker: tall, dark, unkempt.

The suspect for the Aberdeen abduction had been described by two separate witnesses as 'scruffily dressed' yet the three girls from Ravenshill Primary had said the man who took Moll had been wearing a suit. The girls had proved poor witnesses but each girl had separately remarked on the suit worn by the man. Because of the previous crimes and the bulk of accumulated evidence, police suspected a lorry driver or someone who drove for work and knew the network of national B roads. The suit was an anomaly, although the police were following up all leads.

With a shaky hand, Kathleen took a sip of tea and turned over the newspaper. There was a photograph of her face on the front cover. It was the picture from the news conference she had given on the evening of Moll's abduction. The police had told her it was best that she ask for the public's help in finding Moll, and in their fraught state John and Kathleen had complied. It was the worst picture, but Kathleen was now used to seeing it: her hair was sticking up and her eyes were red and glassed with tears and her mouth was turned down at the corners. There was no place for vanity at the press conference on your daughter's abduction by a suspected serial killer and paedophile.

She glanced at the headline and by-line: I JUST WANT MY BABY BACK by Angus Campbell. Kathleen shook the paper in her hands to straighten it and took another sip of tea.

She remembered Angus Campbell turning up at the door, unannounced, and persuading her to speak to him. She had disliked him intensely; thought him furtive. He had smelled like the inside of an old wardrobe. He had small eyes, and extremely small hands with bitten-down fingernails, and had a strange habit of constantly wiping his nose with the knuckle of his forefinger. She disliked how he took all his notes in shorthand, so that they were like a foreign language she had no hope of deciphering. She hadn't liked him or trusted him, but she had decided to talk to him because of what he had said about community support and keeping Moll in the public eye. Newspaper interviews were the last thing she wanted to do, but she had forced herself for Moll's sake.

Not even a week since Moll's disappearance, yet Kathleen was already becoming numb to the newspaper articles. She had been on television, and in the national press. Each teller regurgitated what the last had said; mistakes were made and then repeated. Kathleen was a Thurso local, then from Aberdeen. Some of the journalists wrote about the Moors murderers, as if these comparisons were helpful, when Kathleen knew they were just thrilling speculations to feed their readership. She didn't know if she blamed the journalists, or the Madame Defarge appetite they fed.

Kathleen took another sip of tea, steeling herself as she began to read.

Six days since the abduction of seven-year-old Molly Henderson, her mother, Kathleen, talks of her heartache and desperation as she waits for news of her daughter. Exclusive to the *John o'Groat Journal*, KATHLEEN HENDERSON talks about their family, and how she and Molly's stepfather, John Henderson, are coping with her disappearance.

Kathleen frowned, leaning closer to the newspaper. This was the first time that John had been referred to as Moll's *step*father.

The article correctly summarised events on 2 October, stating the time that Moll was taken and repeating the rough description of the man and his car given by 'three classmates'. The article gave a detailed description of Moll and stated her age and also that she was a 'bright, dedicated pupil at Ravenshill Primary'. There was a picture of Moll, and a reproduction of the artist's sketch of the abductor.

Before she read on, Kathleen jumped to another picture further down the page. She recognised it from somewhere, and stared at the black and white photo of a group of men in suits.

'What on earth?' Kathleen spread the paper out over the kitchen table and bent over it.

She had not seen a picture of him for years: it was Big George McLaughlin on the steps of the High Court in Glasgow, with his brothers. Kathleen could not be sure, but she thought it was one of the times when Peter had escaped conviction.

She could not understand what the McLaughlin family were doing in the *John o'Groat Journal*'s article on Molly's disappearance. She flicked back to the beginning of the article and skimmed back and forth until she found the explanation.

John Henderson has lived in Thurso for over fifteen years, moving to the town in 1970, and now has a management position at Dounreay. Molly Henderson was illegitimate, born to Kathleen Henderson nee Jamieson and George McLaughlin, in Glasgow in 1977. George McLaughlin is part of a notorious crime family from Glasgow, who collectively have stood trial for extortion, torture, moneylending and murder. George McLaughlin is pictured celebrating below on the steps of Glasgow High Court following his brother's second murder trial, which was concluded with a not-proven verdict.

While John Henderson married Kathleen Jamieson in 1979, and has acted since then as Molly's father, the story of her real family background has only just come to light. George McLaughlin is not an official suspect at this time, yet Highlands Police are aware of the link and he is wanted for questioning in relation to his daughter's disappearance.

The search continues for young Molly Henderson who has now been missing for nearly a week. The investigation has swollen to 40 police officers and another 40 trained mountain rescue personnel, according to Detective Inspector Pat Black. Police are thought to have accepted a large contingent of 200 volunteers, who continue to search the Highlands.

Volunteers have said their search is being hampered by difficult terrain, which includes mountain areas, forest, rivers and farmland. 'There's a lot of us here and we want to just do what we can to help and support,' one female volunteer said.

'The terrain is very difficult, there are acres and acres of forest, we've all got a bit of local knowledge but I don't know how good that's going to be.'

'It feels like a needle in a haystack at times,' another volunteer said.

Highlands Police are coordinating with the national force, comparing details of this abduction with other open child murder cases.

The Caithness community continues to offer staunch support for the family, as the desperate search for Molly continues.

Kathleen pushed the newspaper away from her with such force that she spilled a little of her tea. She stood up and paced the kitchen, the back of her hand against her lips. She was furious at Angus Campbell for his intrusion into their lives. She considered calling the *Journal* to complain about him. *Illegitimate*, he had called Moll, as if it mattered a damn who her father was, or wasn't, or if Kathleen had been married or not – when Moll was *missing*. Kathleen bit her lip.

There was no great revelation in the article and she did not worry about others reading its contents. John knew about Moll's father, and Kathleen had even told Moll herself, so that the child had a vague notion of who her father was. But the article was insinuating that George McLaughlin had played some part in Moll's disappearance.

Kathleen held on to the back of her kitchen chair. *Would George have taken Moll?* Kathleen considered for a moment, incredulous. George was incorrigible. He wasn't as dangerous as her parents made out, but they had been right about one thing: he was no *father*, no *husband*. He would be twenty-seven years old now, and probably still a bigger wean than Moll.

Big George. Georgie Boy. She had loved him like no other. He was tall and heavy, with the blackest hair and the bluest eyes, and a smile that had made her heart skip the first time she saw it.

They had started seeing each other when they were just thirteen years old, not long before George got kicked out of school. By the time they were sixteen he had persuaded the good Catholic girl that she was to sleep with him, and he had told her all his secrets.

Even now, Kathleen could still remember the weight of George's head on her chest, feeling blessed that his mind and his thoughts had chosen her as a place to rest.

He was beautiful and everyone agreed, but he was also *bad* and everyone seemed to be in agreement about that too. But Kathleen knew that George was as afraid of his family as everyone else. He was guilty by association, but she knew the kind, beautiful person that he was inside.

'Are you glaikit?' Kathleen's mother had said, pinning her to the wall with the sleeve of her jumper, when Kathleen admitted she was pregnant with George's child. 'You'd have no life and your child would have no life either. It's death you've chosen, *death.*'

Kathleen had not chosen anything at all, because the pregnancy had been an accident.

Even now, at the age of twenty-seven, standing in her thick cotton bathrobe, in her four-bedroomed stone house in Thurso, Kathleen could still remember, exactly, how it had felt to be nineteen and in love, and pregnant, to Big Georgie Boy McLaughlin.

There had been no one else she had wanted. He had been everything to her, and she knew that he had been sincere in his affections towards her. She had never felt so needed as when she and George were together. They had been deep, deep in love, so that leaving him had hurt her physically, as a rip or a tear, and then a scar, as time passed. She still remembered him walking into the room and kissing her, and how time had stopped and stretched out, so that *now* was an elongated sweetness, like soft toffee pulled. He had taken her into adulthood. He had taught her about herself. They had taught each other how to love.

Kathleen remembered grave family meetings in her family's tenement, talking about adoption and single parenthood, and – God *forbid*, *abortion* – over countless cups of strong tea. She remembered George getting down on his knees in Glasgow Green, after the hardest rain, so that she could almost feel the cold wet that must have soaked through his jeans as he proposed to her, and was refused by her, again.

'You might love him, but let me tell you,' her mother had said, pursing her lips as she always did in moments of truth, 'the McLaughlins come as a package and believe you me, you don't want that package!'

Kathleen had been grateful that Georgie had been there for the birth but she remembered being exhausted, watching George take Moll into his arms and sing to the baby with his whisky breath, twirling her around the room. Her daughter was newborn and so small and yet he was spinning her as if he couldn't understand how fragile she was and how precious.

Walking away from George had broken her heart, but her mother had been right.

John had loved Moll and Kathleen had grown to love him and life had been so *easy* and so without grief, she had thought that the possibility of loss had been evaded. Yet no one escapes loss, and Kathleen knew that now, as she had always known it. In the beginning she had often thought of George and how her life would have been different if she had said yes to him.

John had been a widower, known to her parents and their friends. At a family dinner he had taken a shine to Kathleen right away. She had found him kind.

Over time, she had come to admire many things about John Henderson: his calmness and methodical approach to life, his love of industry and his generosity of spirit, his leanness, the fine sinews of his body. He had a weakness for soft-centred chocolates and she loved to buy him violet creams, which he would eat on a Saturday night if they were watching a film. He liked solid gold or silver cufflinks and Rolex watches and good-quality umbrellas and tweed caps. He liked to brush Moll's long hair after a bath, before Kathleen tied it back for bed. He liked reading stories to her: *Peter Rabbit*, *Blackberry Farm* and Aesop's *Fables*. He would lie on top of the covers and Moll would tuck herself into the crook of his arm.

More than once Kathleen had found him asleep in the child's bed with a storybook in his hands. 'Don't wake him up, Mum,' Moll had whispered, suddenly wide-awake. 'I like him here.'

John ... John was wonderful, and Kathleen was grateful.

But George, *George*, Georgie Boy, he was still special in her heart. She could only whisper his name to herself, it was such an admission. It was as if he had whittled out a little place for himself, etching the detail of their young, intense love. It was memorable because it had been unfinished. It had not been destroyed, but had merely ended. Sometimes Kathleen wondered if it still lived on in some uncharted psychic space between them both.

As if it were yesterday, Kathleen could still remember looking down at him, on his knees before her, and seeing all the love and hope in his eyes. Saying no to him had been the hardest thing that she had ever done. Walking away from him hurt her more than anything else she had ever experienced. Being without him had been like living without her skin. She had been raw with the sorrow of it, and had it not been for her daughter and the need to make a good life for her, Kathleen was not sure that she could have done it.

At first George wouldn't accept it, but when they finally said goodbye they had held each other, crying. The noises they made were like the noises of wounded animals. Parting was a violence to them both – an intense insufferable pain.

They didn't stay in touch.

Kathleen remembered that she'd lost over a stone in weight after she parted from George and the doctor was worried that it would affect the baby. Kathleen was eating but it was as if nothing could nourish her now that George's love was gone.

For years afterwards, when she visited Glasgow, she would find herself unconsciously scanning the streets for his face. Sometimes when the doorbell rang unexpectedly she would wonder if it was him. She hadn't told him where she had gone but she knew that he could have found her if he had wanted; *if he had wanted.*

Would *George* have taken Moll? Kathleen didn't believe it. He had loved her, Kathleen knew, and he had said how much he loved Moll when she was born. Seven years, but Kathleen still felt that she knew him well. In the early years of her marriage, she had wondered if George would reappear and try to win her back, but taking her daughter was not something he would do. The act was too violent and spiteful for him. George might have come to the door begging for her hand, but he would never have taken her child.

Nonetheless, a flicker of anger licked her gullet and the brief change of chord in her emotions was a small relief. *If George had* taken her, Kathleen would *have* him. But the whole idea was ridiculous. What would George do with Moll? He could barely look after himself.

After it had been confirmed that Moll was missing, two police officers had interviewed Kathleen and John at length, asking about relatives and friends who might have taken her or posed a threat. In the artist's sketch based on the young girls' description of the man who took her, he looked wild and malicious – blank eyes and a wide, thin mouth. It looked like no one they knew, and John had asked what the police were planning to do. Moll's disappearance fitted the profile of a stranger abduction, but even in those cases the man was often known in the community. Both she and John had said they could think of no one who would take their little girl.

During that first interview, Kathleen had thought of George but knew *in her bones* that he wouldn't have taken Moll. She had pressed her lips together instead of speaking his name. She hadn't wanted time wasted on her George. Perhaps she had also wanted to protect him.

The phone rang and Kathleen was startled by it. She picked it up quickly.

'Kathleen?' said Detective Inspector Black.

'Yes,' she replied. They were already on first-name terms. She could hear John upstairs in the shower.

'I'm sorry to disturb you so early, but I knew ...'

'Yes, I've been awake for hours. Is there news?'

'I'm afraid not. I only called because last night a journalist from the—'

'I know, that *ridiculous* article.'

'There's an article?'

'This morning, the *Journal* has a front page on Molly, and reveals her real father and suggests but doesn't say that he might have taken her.'

'I wanted to discuss it with you ...'

'Why?' said Kathleen, a fist of worry under her ribcage. 'What do you know?'

'Well, a writer from the *Journal* called me last night with information on Molly's natural father ... You hadn't mentioned him.'

Kathleen swallowed, considering her answer.

'I never thought. He's had no contact with her. He's had no contact with me. George is ... George *wouldn't* take Molly. To be honest, I wouldn't have been surprised to see George at my door one day, but the thought that he would take Molly when he hasn't seen her for seven years ... it makes no sense.'

The detective inspector cleared his throat. 'It sounded improbable to me too, and for all we know he's on holiday, but I had one of my officers look into it just out of interest and sure enough, George McLaughlin is not at home.'

'That means nothing. George doesn't have a real home. He'll be with whatever girl he's with right now. If I went to the East End of Glasgow, I could probably find him for you in five minutes, but he won't answer his phone or his door, that's if he even has a door ... I know him well.'

'So you think this is not worth following up ...'

'Oh God, if only,' said Kathleen, unable to keep the grief from returning to her voice. 'If she's with George ...' The tears came again and she put a hand over her mouth to stop them but had to take a hard gasp of air before she was able to control herself, 'Then she's OK.'

'I checked his record. His family are rather colourful, but he seems only to have been cautioned for being drunk and disorderly five years ago. He's clean, but that might be ...'

'He's not like the rest of them,' said Kathleen, relaxed again, heavy with sheer exhaustion. 'He's a tearaway and he always has been, but that's all.'

'Well, I just thought I'd run it past you ...'

'Thank you and we should look into it. I want everything investigated – every lead, every single tiny detail, but ... I know George and he wouldn't take her. He wouldn't do it *to me*.'

'Well, rest assured, we're checking it out. We'll leave no stone unturned.'

'Thank you.'

The detective inspector rang off and Kathleen drank the rest of her now cold tea. As she washed her cup, she listened to the creak of John's feet on the upper floorboards, as he got ready for work.

Kathleen wondered if all this would have been easier, or harder, if she had had another child to look after. In one sense she needed the distraction. John was gone all day, although he had taken two days off to look for Moll himself, combing the woods from dawn to dusk.

After they had married, she and John had tried for a child, but without success. She had become pregnant so easily with George – just that one night of carelessness – but there had been years of consciously trying with John; taking her temperature and watching the calendar, and elevating her hips on a pillow afterwards. She had not even had a single false alarm. It hadn't mattered. John had talked abstractly about wanting a son, but he was smitten with Moll, and Kathleen had never been sure that she was ready for another child.

Moll had been their world, and now that she was gone, their world was empty.

Kathleen dried her hands on a dishtowel and stood staring out of the kitchen window at the back garden. The trees had begun to shed their leaves and the grass was strewn with them. There was a makeshift swing strung to the tree at the back of the garden. John had hung it there for Moll and Kathleen watched it moving gently in the wind. Sometimes when she was in the garden by herself, Moll would lie on the swing, so that it was resting against her stomach and use her feet to push off from the ground.

Taking a deep breath, Kathleen forced herself to look away. She washed the kitchen surfaces and put on a load of washing. She put bread under the grill for John's breakfast and placed two eggs in a pot of water, ready for the boil when he came downstairs.

It didn't matter what she did or how fast Kathleen moved, Moll was still there, the panic of separation was still there and the fear that she was being hurt.

She heard John's footsteps above her and knew that he would be fixing his tie in the long mirror. She turned on the gas and lit it. She stared at the two eggs in the pan, remembering things which had gone before. She was no longer religious, but just then, before the boiling eggs, she crossed herself.

'Georgie, if you have her, look after her,' she whispered.

As she heard John's feet on the stairs, Kathleen bit her lip. She wasn't sure what had come over her. George wouldn't have taken her, but the sheer thought that Moll might be with him gave her a strange desperate hope. He was a wild man, and Kathleen was grateful that they were no longer together. But there was no other wild man she would trust her daughter to.

17

Margaret Holloway
Thursday 19 December, 2013

It was the first day of the Christmas holidays and Ben had gone to central London to interview a contact for his latest article. It was the afternoon and Margaret was wrapping Christmas presents in the lounge with the children.

The term was now over, but she had left without attending the glut of Christmas dinners and parties. Normally the two deputy head teachers, the four assistant heads and Malcolm would go out for dinner, and then there was the big staff party, which was held in the school canteen with lethal punch and a secret Santa. Margaret also usually went out with her old team from the Learning Support Unit. This year she couldn't face any of it. She had gone into work every day until the break, but told Malcolm that she was not feeling able to socialise and he had told her he understood.

Margaret was wrapping the presents and Paula was decorating them – curling ribbons and sticking on golden-leafed holly. Eliot was supposed to be helping too, but had already lost interest.

When Margaret was in the middle of wrapping a shirt for her

father, Eliot stood up and put his arms around her neck. She kissed and nuzzled his hands, but he stayed where he was and she could feel his quick hot breaths against her neck.

She had been an only child. As a young mother, she had been fascinated by the differences between her children. Her son had always asked for more affection than her daughter, from Ben too, but particularly from her.

When Margaret was Eliot's age, she had been a shy and with-drawn child. Her parents were kind and loving, but she had been left with a sensation that they were unable to give her all the love she needed – that they were *not enough*. She lacked clear memories of her childhood, but she remembered loneliness. It was not that her parents' love had been sparing, but that their love had not been able to reach the place inside Margaret that needed love.

As a parent, Margaret tried to give her children all the love she had in her. She was compensating, but she didn't know for what. She didn't want them to feel the ache, which was almost all that Margaret could remember from being small.

Paula knelt before the couch to change the music on the laptop that was open on the sofa. She was wearing leggings and a sweatshirt with sequins on it. Her nails were painted dark glittery blue. She looked older than nine. Margaret smiled at her, remembering the baby she had been. Paula put on some Christmas tunes and then jived to them, spinning around with her long hair swishing back and forth.

'Dance, Mum, this is a good one.'

'In a minute, sweet,' said Margaret, feeling a twinge of guilt that she did not feel able to rise and dance as her daughter expected. 'Good moves, darlin'.'

When the song ended, Paula collapsed on the floor beside her mother, midriff showing, her face full of glee. Margaret reached over and tickled her belly.

When Paula was born, Margaret's mother had been dead six years. She had grieved for her mother anew, shuggling the colicky infant back and forth across the living-room floor, not knowing what to do.

Margaret opened a tin of sweets that she had been given by her old colleagues in the Learning Support Unit. She and the children each chose a chocolate before they continued wrapping. The doorbell rang and Margaret went to answer it.

They lived in a terraced house off Oakwood Hill, with a painted awning above the doorstep. It was dark already and Margaret could not see clearly the young, hooded man who stood scuffing the garden path with the tips of his trainers.

'Hello?' said Margaret, swallowing her chocolate and straining into the darkness.

The young man looked up and she recognised him instantly. He pushed down the hood of his sports top.

'Mrs H,' he said, his breath clouding in the cold air.

Margaret held the door open and motioned him inside.

'Stephen! Are you all right?'

'I got expelled, miss,' he said, hunched. He had never been able to keep still and now he jived in her hallway, shifting from one foot to the other.

Both Paula and Eliot appeared at the living-room door. 'Hey, Stephen,' said Paula, blushing shyly. He raised his head in greeting to them both and drove his hands into the pockets of his hoodie.

'You guys take a break for a bit,' said Margaret, running her fingers through her daughter's hair. 'D'you want to put a film on for you and your brother? I might be a little while . . .'

Paula raised her eyes heavenwards and turned into the living room, with exaggeratedly heavy footfalls.

In the kitchen, Stephen stood pulling the cuffs of his sweatshirt over his hands, as if he were cold. Instinctively, as she would have done for her own, Margaret poured crisps into a bowl and shook biscuits on to a plate.

'Do you want something to drink? I've got Coke or ...'

'Coke, thanks.'

He crunched the crisps hungrily while she poured Coca-Cola into a glass.

'I can make you a sandwich?' she said, placing the glass before him.

He tucked his hands under the table as if merely showing hunger was an admission of guilt.

Stephen grinned at her. ' 'Member that first time I came round, miss, and you made me spag' bol' and everything ...'

'I can make you spag' bol' again.' Margaret turned to him, one eyebrow raised. It was so good to see him, but she worried he would ask her to try to get him back into school.

She was wearing an old pair of jeans and one of Ben's sweatshirts. Before other students, she would have felt underdressed, but Stephen had been at the house many times and she was comfortable to be herself. 'Are you hungry?' she pressed.

'Nah, 'm'all right, I was just saying, like. You're just always so nice to me.' He pulled his hands underneath his cuffs again, and looked down at the table, suddenly shy.

'I wasn't responsible for that decision to expel you,' said Margaret, sitting down opposite him. 'I didn't support it.' She spoke very clearly and calmly so that nothing could be misconstrued.

'I know, miss.'

Stephen met her eyes. His large brown eyes seemed hunted, making him look older than seventeen.

Margaret had taught Stephen how to read and write. She still remembered the day he appeared in her Learning Support classroom, covered in bruises, yet seemingly feared. It was his second year at high school but he had failed to meet any learning objectives. He had been removed from normal classes and kept in the classroom at breaks and lunchtime for the safety of other pupils. At the beginning he had been disruptive in Margaret's classes – once trying to throw a chair through the window, although the window was plastic and the chair just bounced back into the room, hitting another student on the shoulder.

It was weeks before Margaret had been able to reach him. She had been to his home, met his bullying elder brother who was his only family, and seen his swimming trophies before she knew that Stephen could barely write his own name. His father was in prison and his mother had died.

He was bright but had been ignored and punished. Once she'd taught him to read and write he had changed completely. She had risen to management by the time he got his GCSEs, but she had cried with pride.

Margaret took one of the crisps. 'I don't know if you heard, but I was in a car accident and the decision to expel you was taken on the day I was off. It's not what I would have wanted.'

'I know. I don't blame you or nothing . . .'

Margaret sighed and ran her hands through her hair. 'There was nothing I could do. Even if I *had* been at school, there's no saying I could've stopped it happening.'

Stephen sniffed.

'You shouldn't have had a knife in school, Stephen. You shouldn't carry a knife at all.'

'I know, miss.'

Margaret put her hands on the table. 'I wanted to see you get your A Levels.'

'One day, maybe.'

'God, Stephen . . .'

'That's why I came, like. I just wanted to come and see you, 'cause . . . it was just, like, y'know, what you said to me about trying my 'ardest. Well, after I got expelled, I thought I could give up or I could 'ave another go—'

'You can; it's not over,' she interrupted.

'I'm applying to college. I thought you could be my reference, like.' Stephen pulled course information from his pocket, and an application that had been printed from the internet and was dog-eared from its journeys.

Margaret exhaled with relief and smiled. 'Good for you, Stephen. *Good for you.*' Tears sprang to her eyes and she pressed her lips together.

'It's just a practice, like. I'll do it online.'

Margaret unfolded the form and smoothed the creases. Out of habit, she looked it over for spelling and other errors. Stephen had neatly printed each line and everything was correct. He was applying to do three A Levels.

'Are you all right now?'

'I'm fine.'

'You were in that really big pile-up on the M11?'

Margaret nodded.

'And you were all right. Figure you're a pretty good driver, huh, miss?' He smiled, showing his perfect white teeth.

'It wasn't skill, it was luck.'

Margaret brushed a hand over the application form on the kitchen table. She did it to signal a change of subject and also to steady herself. The talk of the crash had brought a tremor to her fingers again. 'I'm proud of you for doing this ... and all by yourself. It's just what I would've wanted you to do. You get knocked down, but you get up again, remember.'

Stephen shrugged. 'Only 'cause of you. You're the best teacher ever.'

When Stephen left, Margaret went upstairs and splashed cold water on her face. She leaned on the basin and stared at herself in the mirror. It had been easier to sit and talk to Stephen, who expected her to behave professionally, than it was to face her husband each night. It was a strain to hide how she was feeling from Ben and the children.

She went downstairs slowly. She could hear the children laughing at the film they were watching. She went into the kitchen and opened Ben's laptop, then Googled *nervous breakdown*.

She read the text, biting her lip: *Severe stress-induced depression, anxiety or dissociation in a previously functional individual. The disorder will mean that the individual can no longer function on a daily basis. A nervous breakdown bears great similarities to Post Traumatic Stress Disorder.*

She hadn't been able to go through the box that she had taken from her father's house. When she started to look at the collected articles and pictures she felt physically sick – yet the contents of the box, the burned man and the memory of being trapped inside her burning car were Margaret's constant present. Whatever she did, those feelings were inescapable.

She had called the hospital every day to check on Maxwell and now she thought of him again, alone and friendless, no loved ones knowing that he was hurt. She wanted to go and see him again. She *needed* to see him.

Before she closed the computer, she checked her Facebook account. Ben had sent her a message to say he was bored waiting to meet his interviewee and would be late home. She sent a message back although she knew that he was no longer online. She took long slow breaths as she left the kitchen and returned to the living room. The film credits were rolling; Paula was practising her gymnastics and Eliot was trying to copy her.

'Can we go outside?' said Eliot.

'Not now, it's too dark.'

'But I can take my torch.'

'No. It's too dark. It'll be time for dinner soon.' Margaret glanced at her watch, wondering when Ben would come home. She didn't feel up to an argument. 'Come on,' she said, sitting down and patting the couch beside her. 'Come on, we'll read another chapter of your Roald Dahl book.'

She had been reading *George's Marvellous Medicine* to Eliot.

Eliot leaned into her as she broke the spine of the book and struggled to focus. Paula was trying to do headstands, then looking up at her mother intermittently, red-faced with effort. Reading to her children was what Margaret loved most, and yet even this precious time was no escape. Her heart was beating so hard that she thought it might break through her chest.

'Mum, stop it,' said Eliot, elbowing her in the stomach.

'Stop what?'

'Your hands are all shaky. I can't follow the words.'

18

Big George
Thursday 3 October, 1985

In the morning, they set off again. There was only an inch of Irn Bru left in the bottle, and George let Moll finish it. He looked down at her as they left the Cheviot Hills. With her newly cut hair, there was a chance that she might not be recognised, but she was still a little girl in a crumpled school uniform with spots of blood on her collar and skinned knees scabbed over.

They left Northumberland National Park and headed south. There were farms on either side of the road and signs for deer and cattle. The car was running low on petrol, but George thought he could make it to Newcastle, which was only an hour away. They drove through towns like Longframlington and as they neared residential areas, an idea came to George.

At Morpeth, he veered off the road and drove into the town, rolling his window down and weaving through the housing schemes.

'Where are we?' said Moll. 'Are we going to visit someone?'

He didn't answer her. It was a quiet scheme of red-brick council houses with small fenced gardens. George hunched over the steering wheel as he peered out on either side, scanning the yards. It was another clear day – dry and bright although there was a chill in the air. He turned into another street and sure enough there were three different yards strung with washing. He crawled along the kerb inspecting the clothes on offer until he saw what looked like a boy's green tracksuit.

'Wait here,' said George.

'Where are you going?'

'I'm gonna borrow something.'

He narrowed his eyes and scanned the street but there was no one around. It was after nine and people would be at work and at school. He vaulted over a wall into the garden and was startled by the sound of a dog barking inside the house. He yanked the tracksuit off the line, sending the pegs flying, jumped the wall again and slipped back into the car, throwing the tracksuit into the back seat. He drove out of Morpeth slowly, looking into the rear-view mirror until he was sure that they had not been seen.

'I'm hungry,' said Moll, as he turned on the radio.

'As soon as I see a shop, we'll stop and we'll go and get something hot for lunch, I promise. Can you hold on?'

He turned to her, and she nodded, and he winked at her.

It was late morning when they arrived in Newcastle and George parked in a multi-storey car park near the high street.

'Take your shoes off,' he said.

'Why?'

'Because we need to get this on you.'

'Why? I don't like it.'

'We'll get you something you like. It's just ... so you'll be warm when we're walking on the street. It'll do for now.' He bit his lip, watching her, but she kicked off her shoes and so he leaned over and fed one foot and then the other into the tracksuit bottoms.

'Pull them up and take off your skirt.'

She did as he asked. The skirt was a pleated kilt and he helped her undo the second button.

'They're all wet.' Her face was peaked.

'It's only for a wee while, till we get you something better.' He held out the tracksuit top and she fed her arm through.

'It doesn't smell nice.'

'I promise we'll get rid of this as soon as we can.'

'I'm hungry,' said Moll again, when they got out of the car. The tracksuit was oversized and he could see patches of dark green where the fabric was wet. The white of her school blouse was still visible and so he zipped her up and pushed the collar inside.

'Where will we go to eat?'

'I'll find some place. Maybe we should get you some proper clothes first, then we'll go get something to eat.'

The car park smelled of dank, wet concrete. It was only half full of cars, but there were no people around and George was relieved. He offered Moll his hand as they descended the stairs to the street and she took it and kept hold of it all the way to the high street, where he took her into C&A.

As soon as they walked into the department store, it seemed as if every shop assistant turned to stare at them. George realised what a sight Moll was, with her shorn hair and damp, oversized tracksuit. He was nervous and almost left the store, but instead he pulled Moll in the direction of the escalator and they ascended towards Men and Boys.

'Your hand's all sweaty,' she said, pulling away from him.

'Well, stay close to me,' he said. 'We need to be in and out of here, quick smart. You're hungry, aren't you? We need to get out of here and get you something to eat.'

She was quiet but sullen, following him around, looking at the clothes.

He picked out a pair of jeans and a sweatshirt, several T-shirts, socks and pants for boys aged seven to eight, and then they went for shoes. She chose a pair of Batman trainers.

'Do they fit you?' he asked.

'Yes,' jumping up and down. 'They're bouncy.'

As an afterthought, he bought her an anorak and wellington boots and a pair of thick gloves, a baseball cap and a scarf.

Moll curled her fingers over the checkout desk and put her lips to them. The man folding and bagging her clothes winked at her. George risked tapping Moll on the shoulder. 'Stand up properly,' he whispered.

He didn't know how to predict her, had no idea what she would do. She looked up at him and he held his breath, but then she did as he asked. He smiled at her, and touched her head. She blinked slowly and shrugged at his appreciation.

He wondered if she knew that he had kidnapped her. All she had to do was tell the shop assistant that he had taken her, and it would all be over. He couldn't remember being a child. He had only snatches of memories, mostly bad. He couldn't remember how children thought and processed things.

'I'm *hungry*,' she said, whining now, when they got outside.

He hunkered down beside her and straightened the tracksuit on her shoulders. She was pale and wearying and he knew she needed to eat, but even though she looked almost like a boy now, she was still attracting glances in her damp, oversized clothes.

'Let's go back to the car and change and then we can get lunch,' he said.

'No, now,' she whined.

There was a little shop off the high street and he bought her a packet of crisps and a can of Coke. She walked slowly, crunching the crisps and spilling little dribbles of Coke down the green tracksuit. By the time they got back to the car, the Coke and the crisps were finished.

The car park was still deserted. George pulled the tags off the jeans and T-shirt and asked her to change.

'Can you manage by yourself?' he asked.

She nodded, and so he walked ten feet away and smoked at the edge of the car park, looking down at the city. He was finished with his cigarette before she was done struggling into the new clothes. Finally, he went to help her: shaking her into the jeans and buttoning them up and wrestling the sweater on to her. She put on her Batman trainers and he knelt to lace them.

'I can tie my own laces,' she said.

He stood back to let her, but she took an age, and his own stomach rumbled as he waited. She made a big loop and a small loop, whispering instructions to herself.

'You sure you don't need me to help you?'

'No!'

He sighed, looking over his shoulder. He put her school uniform into one of the carrier bags and put it in the boot. Finally, she stood up, her laces tied.

'You look good.' He placed the baseball cap on her head and led her to the wing mirror so that she could look at herself.

'I look like a boy.'

'You look cool.'

'I look like a boy.'

'Let's go get something to eat.'

The streets were busy and he held her wrist as they navigated people on the pavement. She stopped and dug her heels in and pulled against him until he released her.

'What is it?'

'I don't like getting my wrist held.'

'It's busy. You could get lost.'

She had her hands pushed into her anorak pockets and was glaring up at him, fixing him with her good eye. The pavement was dirty with litter, and the street smelled of car exhausts. The sharp scent of vinegar and the sweet smell of potato wafted from a chip shop across the street, and George felt hunger again cramp his stomach.

She pushed past him, hands still in her pockets, so that she seemed to shimmy as she walked. He didn't want to argue, so he let her walk a pace in front of him, tugging at her jacket when he needed her to turn a corner. At the main road, George took a pinch of her jacket and tried to take her across when the traffic had stopped.

'No,' she said, scowling at him again. 'You can't just walk across. You have to wait for the green man.' She reached up to press the pedestrian button.

George sighed deeply and put his hands in his pockets, then found that she slid her hand through his arm as they waited, as she had when he took her from school.

'If you'd gone when I said, we'd be across by now.'

'But it's not allowed,' she said, pressing her lips together as she looked up at him.

Across the road there were shops and department stores and

she was distracted by a busker with a guitar, cymbals between his knees and a drum on his back, singing out of tune, and then by a street vendor selling small battery-powered dogs that yelped and wagged their tails. She crouched down to look at them, pointing and smiling up at George. He asked her if she wanted one, but she shook her head. When they left the toys, she continued to walk slowly, her head turned by Goths with flowing purple skirts, an old man asking for spare change, and a Sheik with a long black beard.

'Have you ever been to a big city before?' he asked her.

'I've been to Inverness.'

'I told you I'd take you on an adventure.'

'Where are we now?'

'We're in Newcastle. I've not been here before, either.'

'Why did we come, then?'

'We're just passing through.'

They ate at a café off Northumberland Street, a booth in the back corner. George and Moll both had fish and chips with tomato sauce and vinegar. The waitress was Italian, wearing a pink apron and a lipsticked smile.

'Can I get you boys anything else?' she said, wiping their table with a dirty cloth.

Moll's eyes opened wide when she heard but her mouth was still full of chips, and George was grateful.

'Just the bill.'

'Just the bill?' she said, her accent blended with Geordie. 'The little man doesn't want some ice cream?'

'OK,' said George, 'the bill and . . . strawberry ice cream,' so pleased that Moll had passed for a boy.

'Chocolate,' Moll corrected him.

'He'll have a chocolate ice cream, then,' said George, nodding.

'SHE will have an ice cream,' Moll said, almost shouting. 'I'm a girl, not a boy, even though you want me to be.'

The waitress smiled and nodded, pulling crumbs to the edge of the table with her cloth.

George gave the waitress one of his special smiles, but as soon as her back was turned he placed a ten-pound note on the table.

'Get up right now,' he hissed at Moll. 'You just blew your chance of a chocolate ice cream.'

Moll got up with him, but he didn't touch her until they were outside the restaurant. As soon as they were round the corner, George lifted her into his arms. He felt her pulling against him and broke into a run. The movement and his own urgency meant that she couried into him and he held her close, but as soon as he stopped running and they neared the street where the car was parked, Moll began to fight him.

'Let me *down*,' she said and he felt her kicking him, her small fists pushing back against his chest. Her face was once more full of the anger and fear he had seen when he tried to drag her to the car in Thurso.

He could feel his heart beating and sweat on his upper lip. Not for the first time he wondered how it was all going to end. At the entrance to the multi-storey car park, he set her down. She pulled away from him, and leaned against one of the metallic, graffitied walls – her arms folded and her chin down. Despite the large skip of her cap, George could tell that she was glaring at him.

'I'm sorry,' he said, squatting down in front of her. 'We had to get out of there. I didn't mean to grab you like that. Come on – let's go back to the car.'

He got up and took a couple of steps from her, and found that she followed; arms still folded and chin down. There were one or two people walking to their cars, and so George walked slightly in front of her, not daring to speak in case she made a fuss. He kept her just in sight and returned to the car, unlocking her door first and holding it open for her.

He was still learning about her, and did not yet know how to behave around her. He remembered how she had allowed him to rock her to sleep the night before, and thought that if he were to win her trust he would have to woo her. Confrontation only seemed to harden her to him, and he could understand why.

He stood, waiting beside the open door, watching her dark face and folded arms and the criss-cross steps she made, willing her to come to him. To his great relief she got inside the car, but awkwardly, refusing to unfold her arms.

He got into the driver's seat, put the key in the ignition, then turned to her, both hands pressed between his knees.

'I'll get you another ice cream when we get to the hotel,' he tried.

'I don't want any ice cream. I want to go home.' She wasn't looking at him, but rather speaking down into her folded arms.

George ran his hands through his hair. Bribery wasn't working and he didn't want to frighten her again. His only option was to talk to her, although he didn't know if she would understand. He took her cap off, so that he could see her face properly. He saw that she was on the verge of crying again. She was turned away from him, her arms still folded, looking out of the window with her lower lip quivering.

He took a deep breath, wondering how to phrase what he wanted to say. She seemed so little suddenly and her vulnerability made him feel wretched. He decided it was no time to be serious.

'Are you in the cream puff?' he said, grinning and poking her gently in the side. He had spent his whole life teasing girls, it seemed. It was what he knew best.

She elbowed his hand away from her.

'You are too, admit it. You're in the cream puff.'

'I am *not* in the cream puff,' she said, frowning at him, her mouth pinched and her voice haughty. It reminded him of the night he proposed to Kathleen in Glasgow Green and her mother's coldness towards him. He took heart from the fact that Moll's eyes were no longer threatening tears and that her piqued anger seemed to have stopped her lip quivering.

'Do you know what the cream puff means?'

'Yes,' she said, still frowning.

'What's it mean then?'

'In the huff, but I'm not.'

'Who told you about the cream puff?'

'My mummy,' she said, lips wet, swallowing.

George smiled, remembering Kathleen riled. 'Your mum's a good one for the cream puff too, believe me, I remember.'

George poked her again, on her right side, just below her ribcage, leaning down to whisper into her neck, knowing that his words and breath would tickle. 'You're in the huff, admit it; you're in the cream puff.'

She twisted away from him, touching her neck and smiling, but quickly correcting herself.

'Am *not*,' she said, facing him, her chin forward and the gap in her teeth showing.

'Are sot!'

'Not!'

'Sot!'

'Not, not, not.'

232

'Sot, sot, sot.'

He tweaked her side again, and she smiled but then turned around in her seat and knelt, facing him, so that they were eye to eye. He knew that the game was over. She was sitting back on her heels in the front seat, and he noticed that, like him, she not only had long legs but a long back too. He faced her, letting his chin drop a little so that he had to look up at her. In a bar, that worked with girls: they seemed to like his submission.

'I want to go home *now*,' she said.

'I can't take you back just yet.'

Her face darkened again, her good eye considering him and the corners of her mouth turned down. He had broken one of the most basic rules. He had left school at fourteen but he had watched smarter men than him fail with women. Positivity was the first rule of flirtation. *Can't, won't, never, no*, were words not to be uttered in the early stages.

He pressed his palms together, as if in prayer.

'Listen to me,' he said, very gently. 'I know you want to go home, and I said I'd let you go when it's time, didn't I?'

'*When* will it be time?'

'Soon,' and then, 'I *promise* . . .'

'But *when*?'

'Soon.'

George put two hands on the wheel and stared straight ahead at the bare concrete walls of the car park, wondering how to negotiate this with her – or how to distract her.

'I'm as good as my word,' he told her.

She folded herself back down into her seat, so that she was facing straight ahead, her long limbs tucked underneath her. She rubbed her eyes.

'Do you trust me?' he asked, and she turned to him, her eyes quizzical or confused, and he wondered if he had heard or understood her, but he did not have the courage to ask her again.

'Tell you what,' he said. 'We've got another drive ahead – couple of hours or so before we stop. Let's play a game. A car game.'

He hadn't expected it to be this easy, but she turned to him, the gap in her teeth showing and nodding her head eagerly.

'What game?'

George placed two hands on the steering wheel. Suddenly he couldn't remember any games – or none that could help him now. He remembered playing football in the street with his socks at his ankles and his nose running; he remembered conkers and marbles and the games the girls played: elastics and peever and complicated hand-clapping games. His sister had tried to teach him once, asking him to hold up his palms while she sang and slapped the rhythm, but he had forgotten even the song.

'Let's play I spy,' she said, clasping her hands together.

George winced and let his head fall back against the headrest, but before he could say a word in protest, she had begun.

'I spy with my little eye, something beginning with ... G.'

'George,' he said hopefully, grateful that it was a letter he was familiar with.

'No, that's too easy,' she said. 'I never say easy ones.'

The Irn Bru bottle was almost empty on the floor by her feet and so George pointed at it. 'Juice.'

She turned to him, frowning and with her lips pressed together. 'That begins with a J, not a G. Don't you know the difference?'

George turned on the engine and rolled out of the car park.

He lit a cigarette as he waited for the barrier to rise. He had suggested it and so couldn't complain but he just wanted the game to end.

'Put your seatbelt on,' he said, hearing the sharpness in his voice.

19

Tam Driscoll
Sunday 6 October, 1985

It was the kind of place that Tam had imagined when he thought of all the atrocities the McLaughlins committed. He sat alone on a chair in the middle of the empty warehouse by the Clyde. He wasn't tied down, but he had been told to sit and wait, and so he did, a pain in his bladder because he needed to urinate, his mouth dry and his throat tight.

He worked for them because he needed the money, and no matter how hard he tried *not to know* what they did, he knew all too well.

His father had been a miner, spending his daylight hours underground, fighting against gas and coal dust, cramped in a cage with other men. He had died of Black Lung before Tam's daughter was born. Tam had never been down the pits, but working for the McLaughlins felt, psychologically, how he imagined his father felt every day at work. He was trapped; filthy dirty by association and endangering his own life.

It was only a few minutes before Peter and Richard came into the room, Richard walking in front and Peter hanging back, one hand in his pocket and another cupped around a cigarette. Peter's silence made Tam most nervous.

It had been nearly three o'clock on Sunday afternoon when Richard had called him and asked Tam to come to the garage. With George gone, Tam had felt sick at the thought of being asked to come in when normal business was closed. He wasn't sure what he would be asked to do.

When he arrived at the garage, Richard had indicated a white van and asked Tam to get inside.

Tam had wondered about making a run for it, but knew that was futile. He forced himself to look Richard in the eye and ask, in as deep a voice as he could manage, *why?*

'There's a car needing seen to ... Peter told me to come and get you.'

'It can't be brought here? We have the ramp and all the tools.'

'No,' said Peter, his face devoid of emotion, 'it can't.'

Tam had nodded, fear making his arms so heavy as to feel paralysed. When he tried to get into the front of the van, Richard had opened the back door and asked him to get in there.

'We don't want anyone to see you, do we?'

Alone in the back of the van, beside tools that Tam imagined were used for other purposes, he wondered if the McLaughlins had a car from a crime scene that needed cleaned. George had done that for them, but now he was gone.

George had always cleaned the cars at the garage. Tam had a deeper worry: that it was not simply a dirty job that awaited him at his destination. He had no idea where they were going, but he sensed from the movement of the van that they were headed south-west of the city. His wife had been concerned when he was called into work on a Sunday, but he had made light of it, for her sake. He had told her that there was a car that urgently needed fixed. He didn't want her to worry about him.

They had arrived at a warehouse. The perimeter walls were stacked with oil drums and old machinery, and Tam could not be sure but he thought he could smell the black, oily water of the Clyde. He looked around for a car that might need fixing, but saw only Peter's black Ford Escort by the warehouse doors. Richard had led Tam inside to a cavernous space with a single chair in the middle. It looked like the setting for an urban existentialist play.

'Take a seat,' Richard had said, and left, and so Tam had walked to the centre of the warehouse, and sat down on the chair.

October, but it had been a warm day with sunshine. The metal walls of the building had absorbed the heat so that the room felt muggy and airless. There was no sound apart from the metal sheets of the warehouse walls creaking and shifting in the breeze.

Peter and Richard entered together, but Richard spoke first, while Peter finished his cigarette.

'We heard that you might know something that we want to know,' he began, one hand in his pocket and one foot resting on top of a plastic packing crate.

'What would that be?' said Tam, feeling the hot itch of sweat break at his hairline.

'That's what we hope you'll tell us.'

There was a deep relaxation in the younger McLaughlin's limbs, which seemed so unnatural that Tam was suddenly shot with terror. Richard's eyes were fixed on Tam, his mouth loose so that he seemed half asleep or drugged. Tam decided immediately that if he did know something the brothers wanted to know, then he would tell them. He nodded, quickly, feeling the tension in his jaw and his neck as he waited for more information.

'Correct me if I'm wrong, but you and my baby brother were pretty pally, were you not?'

'We went for the odd pint, that was all.'

'Nah, I could tell George liked you, and when Georgie likes someone, he talks. He's always been the same.'

'What do you mean? What is it you need to know? If I know anything, I'm happy to help.' Tam was taciturn at best, and he knew that his sudden willingness to talk only communicated his fear.

'Good,' said Peter, his voice so quiet that Tam could barely hear him. 'Good, good. You see . . .' Peter undid the button of his jacket and put one hand in his pocket. 'We think that George has something that doesn't belong to him – something *precious* – which doesn't belong to us either, but it does belong to *somebody* we know, and that somebody wants it back very, very much.'

When Tam opened his mouth to speak, it was so dry that it made a sound like a boot leaving mud. His eyes felt hot, and his T-shirt was damp underneath his boiler suit. He wiped a hand across his mouth, remembering George unbuttoning his shirt in the Portland Arms to show him his tattoo.

'Now, you understand, this person thought that the precious item was gone for ever, but has now realised that it's only missing, and can therefore . . . be returned. It's this matter we want help with. Richard tells me even the press know you know something. Journalist turns up at the garage to talk to you yesterday. To *you* . . . asking *you* where George is.'

Tam managed a smile, licked his lips and began to speak. All his breath was in his throat and he knew he sounded terrified, but he continued as best he could.

'You understand George and I are not friends, but you're right he can talk, and the last time we were out for a pint he told me he was leaving.'

'Where did he say he was going?'

'Up north to Thurso, and then south, he said he didn't know where, but he didn't sound as if he was in any hurry to come back.'

'Thurso?' spat Peter and Richard, almost in unison.

'Where the hell is that, anyway?' said Richard.

'What's in Thurso?' said Peter, frowning, looking at Tam. 'Why would he go there?'

'Well ... the precious thing you were talking about ... His daughter.'

'What?'

Richard took one step back but Peter continued to frown at Tam.

'*His daughter?*' said Richard.

'Aye,' said Tam, looking from one brother to the other.

'Which daughter is this?' said Peter. 'I didn't hear about him knocking up someone else, although I wouldn't put it past him.'

'Em ... I remember, her name was Moll,' said Tam, recalling the bright red tattoo above George's heart. 'Moll, yes, that was it.'

'And how did he knock up someone in Thurso?' said Richard.

'It was a while ago, a girl from Glasgow. I can't remember her name, but she moved north and—'

'Kathleen Jamieson,' Peter spat. 'You're joking. I heard talk that there was a wean, but ... there's no way.'

'He was fond of Kathleen,' said Richard, turning to Peter.

'Ach, Georgie's fond of anything in a skirt.'

'That's where he told me he was going. He was going to ask Kathleen to marry him again and then the three of them would be together,' said Tam, hope buoying under his ribs that this was the information needed and now that it was given, he would be free. 'That was what the journalist was asking me about the other day. He was from up north. Sure enough that little girl's gone missing and somehow he'd clocked on George.'

Peter nodded, both hands in his pockets. 'Are we talking about that kid that's on the news? Is she not called Molly?'

Tam shrugged.

'I'll be damned,' said Peter, and shook his head at Richard, whereupon both of the brothers burst out laughing. They laughed for well over a minute, Peter reaching out to lean on Richard's shoulder when the mirth began to hurt his stomach muscles.

Tam watched, confused, and then deeply relieved, and he began to laugh too: not a hearty genuine laugh, but a laugh of empathy, as when a joke is cracked that one doesn't understand, but wants to, for the sake of being accepted.

Both brothers stopped laughing at the same time, and suddenly the warehouse was silent and creaking as it had been when Tam was alone. The smile slipped from his lips.

'Nice story. I wouldn't put it past my crazy wee brother, but now cut the crap and tell us ... *where's the fucking money?*'

Peter was leaning forward, hissing in Tam's face, so that he could smell the elder McLaughlin's quintessence of cigarettes, aftershave and malice.

'What money?' said Tam, swallowing. 'I don't know anything about money.'

'Do you expect me to believe that?' said Peter, still close to Tam's face so that Tam could barely breathe. 'He told you his life story and forgot the bit about nicking the Watt brothers' hundred grand?'

Tam closed his eyes. He struggled to recollect the night at the bar. He had been drinking, and he hadn't wanted to hear what

George was saying anyway, but he did remember George saying he had '*enough to disappear*' and that he had '*found a bit of money*' but that it would be harmful to Tam if he knew where.

Tam's heart was beating so hard that he thought he might have a heart attack – and he began to wish for it. The stress of being taken, and then the relief that had flooded his veins, and now the deep, thickening dread were all hitting him in waves from inside. He felt sick and his vision was blurring and sweat from his forehead had begun to sting his eyes.

Richard reached out and grabbed Tam by the scruff of the neck. Tam shouted out, and recoiled, as if he had been struck. 'What did he do with the money? Did he take it with him?'

'I think he might've,' Tam whispered.

'So you *do* know,' said Peter, so quietly that he was almost inaudible. '"*I know nothing about money*" you said a moment ago, but in fact ... you do.' He spoke very slowly, so that each word seemed separated by seconds.

'All right, all right,' said Tam, out of breath, his chest heaving. 'He told me he had found some money, enough to run away with, but that it was best I didn't know about it, and so he told me no more. That's the truth, I swear to God.'

'And did he find it somewhere in that car you both worked on in the garage? The Watt brothers are now convinced it was there, instead of at the bottom of the Clyde. They switched cars. Was it in the tyres? Where was it?'

'He told me no more. He said it was best I didn't know. That's the truth, I swear to God.'

'You keep saying it's the truth, Tam, but you have already lied to us, and so that makes me suspicious.' Peter was smiling, teeth bared, his eyes fixed on Tam.

'I swear. I promise that's all I know. That's everything I know.'

'I don't think you realise how serious this is. If our baby brother has taken the Watts' money then they'll be coming to get it back ... from us, if they can't get their hands on him.'

'I understand, but, please ... I've told you all I know.'

Peter nodded at Richard, and again Tam thought that they had believed him and it was all over. Peter folded his arms and turned his back on Tam while Richard walked to the side of the room and returned with a plastic container, which as he drew nearer Tam realised was full of petrol.

'Dear God, no,' Tam whispered. He felt his bladder contract and then the warmth of his own urine down his left leg. 'Please ... please, I told you all I know.'

'I'm not sure that I do believe you, Tam,' said Peter, as Richard took the cap from the container.

The familiar, heady, heavy scent of petrol wafted over to Tam. He had worked with engines since he was a boy, and had always loved the smell of petrol. Now the scent choked him. He tried to get up, but Peter put a hand on his shoulder and pressed him back into the chair.

'I wonder if you need your memory jogged?' said Peter. 'I mean, you were drinking and all. I wonder if you can remember something else? Should we have a go? Maybe I should light a cigarette and consider it.'

'No, please,' Tam whispered, his voice raw and hoarse – no moisture left in his mouth at all. He remembered again the Portland Arms with George singing on the table top, and the sight of Giovanni DeLuca's wasted hand.

Richard stood with the cap in one hand and the canister of petrol in the other. He looked to Peter for instruction. Peter shrugged at his brother and held out his hand for the canister.

As Peter took the plastic container and stepped towards him,

Tam began to cry. He thought about his wife and his daughter, and if he would see them again.

Peter put a hand on Tam's shoulder. 'There now. Pull yourself together, man. I'm not going to hurt you. We just want to make you understand the seriousness of this. You should have come to us about it from the start. You need to remember who you work for ... and you certainly shouldn't have *lied* to us just then. We need to know the truth. This is a *very serious* matter.'

Tam nodded, hands over his face, taking a long slow breath in. He looked up at Peter. 'I'm sorry.'

'Apology accepted,' said Peter, with the same bared-teeth smile he had used earlier. 'Now, I want you to drink this. All of it.'

Tam looked up at Peter. He considered asking him for mercy. 'Peter, I-I ...'

'Do you remember when you were wee, Tam?'

Tam looked at him, unblinking.

'Do you?' Peter raised his voice, just slightly, and the sudden inflection echoed in the large metal space.

'Aye.'

'So do I. Do you remember what the punishment was for lying?'

Tam swallowed, the urine cold on his leg, and now he felt that he was shivering all over; his muscles shaking with fear.

'In our house it was washing your mouth out with soap, wasn't it, Rich?'

'Lying or profanity ...'

'Lying or profanity ... wash your mouth out with soap. Well, Tam, here we are. This is the next best thing. Go on – drink it.'

Tam had accidentally drunk sips of petrol in the past – once a large gulp – while siphoning fuel. He had sucked on a rubber tube and it had come too fast and he had gulped it down. He had been fine. His wife had called the doctor, who had told him to drink a glass of milk.

'Drink it,' said Peter, again his voice unusually loud and echoing as if his pernicious authority had grown larger.

Tam took hold of the plastic canister with two hands. It trembled a little in his grasp. It was only about one-quarter full. Tam felt his chin drop, and he nodded. He raised the canister to his lips, his eyes and nose stinging with the smell. He screwed his eyes tight shut, took a mouthful and swallowed, gasping and coughing at the burn in his throat.

When the spasms of coughing subsided, Tam opened his eyes and looked up at Peter, pleading for it to end.

'Go on.'

'It . . . Peter, it's too much, please, I . . .'

'You've only had one sip. You'll drink at least half. Imagine it was that dram you had when Georgie Boy spilled his beans . . .' Peter showed his lower teeth. 'Now drink it.'

Resigned, Tam gulped and gulped again. The fumes made his eyes stream and his throat burned with it and his stomach tightened and lurched, so that twice he retched dry before he was able to continue. He took one more gulp and then Peter swiped it from his lips, spilling some petrol on his cheek and his trousers. He handed the canister to Richard, who slowly and carefully screwed the cap back on.

'There now,' said Peter, brushing imaginary dust from the sleeves of his jacket and buttoning up. 'All over. That wasn't so hard, was it?'

Tam shook his head. His teeth were chattering and he could hear the rattle in his skull.

'Now you remembered your manners, but have you remembered anything else?' said Peter.

Tam could barely speak, but he managed: 'P-Penzance.'

'Penzance?'

Tam tried to swallow. His nose and his mouth were filled with the oily burn of the petrol. 'That's where he told me he was headed.'

'Penzance? Why there? Whereabouts?'

'A cottage ... it was in the family or something,' Tam gasped.

'I don't know of any cottage.'

'He said ...' Tam screwed his eyes tight shut as he tried to remember George's words in the bar. 'Between Sennen and Porthcurno ... It's all I know, I swear, *I swear.*'

'Very well,' said Peter. 'You relax now.'

Tam felt ill and weak. He sat back in the chair, watching the brothers.

'You did well,' said Peter.

Richard returned the canister to the side of the room, turned and walked towards the door. Peter buttoned up his jacket, and put a hand in his pocket.

'You take care now, Tam,' he said, turning.

When he saw each of their backs walking towards the door, Tam buckled over and cupped his face in his hands, feeling hot new tears of relief against his palm.

From inside his fingers, he was aware of the smallest sound: *scrape, scrape, scrape* ... like a blade sharpening against stone.

He opened his eyes just in time to see Peter frowning into his fingertips, as if trying without success to click his fingers. The flame of his lighter finally took and he tossed it down on to the floor.

20

Margaret Holloway
Saturday 21 December, 2013

It was visiting time on the Saturday before Christmas, and Margaret had returned to Ward 19 at the Royal London Hospital. The children were both at friends' houses, Ben was working on an article and Margaret found herself at the hospital once again.

It had been twelve days since she had seen Maxwell: nearly a fortnight, yet she had called almost daily to ask about his progress. Walking to the ward, she wondered if he would be awake when she arrived – if the doctors had brought him out of his coma. The thought of talking to him – meeting him properly – filled her with excited trepidation.

Maxwell Brown was still unconscious, in a private room and, according to the nurses, he had had no visitors apart from Margaret since he had been admitted.

She sat down at his bedside. Christmas was only a few days away, yet already she felt deadly tired. The kids were both excited but Margaret's temper had been shorter than usual. She had snapped at the children once or twice since they had been off school – filling the house with mess and noise. She had also been distant and withdrawn from Ben. It was as if she couldn't contain what was happening inside her and now the ones she loved were starting to suffer for it.

Margaret leaned over the bed and took Maxwell's hand. It was surprisingly smooth. She had been sitting staring at him for some time, wondering who he was and if his family were missing him. He wore no jewellery; he had no watch, nor a ring on his finger, unless the medical staff had removed it.

A nurse Margaret was unfamiliar with came in to change Maxwell's urine bag and she stood aside as the nurse drew the curtain and slipped behind it. The nurse talked to Margaret from behind the curtain as she worked.

'Nice to see he has a visitor. I know he'll appreciate it. Are you family?'

'Em . . . just a friend,' said Margaret. She found that she could no longer talk about the crash to others.

'Well, you may not think it, but I'm sure he's grateful.' The nurse's voice sounded as if she were bending and then stretching. Margaret could see the shape of her body move along the inside of the curtain.

'He's technically in a coma?'

'That's right.' The nurse dragged the curtain back on its rail, and smiled at Margaret. 'He was put in a medically induced coma. He seems to be stabilising now though, so the doctors will likely bring him back in a week or so . . .'

'Really?' said Margaret.

'I think that's the plan.'

'Can he hear me?'

'Well, we don't really know, but I'm sure on some level he can. You could read to him or something. I'm sure he'll be happy to hear your voice.'

'Thank you,' said Margaret. 'I will. I read to my kids all the time. I have a book in my bag.' She took the novel she was reading from her handbag and placed it on the bed.

The nurse left and closed the door. Once again, Margaret took Maxwell's hand. The room was warm, and he was stripped to the waist as he had been the last time she visited. She could see his ribs underneath his scarred skin as his chest rose and fell. He looked thinner, his head turned away from her and his chin down, making him seem vulnerable and alone. Looking at him now, it was difficult to believe that *this* was the powerful man who had saved her.

Margaret cleared her throat and spoke in a low voice. 'I just popped in to see you before Christmas. It's good to hear that you'll be waking up soon. I'd love to meet you properly. I'm so, so grateful to you. I think you're an angel.' Margaret smiled and let go of his fingers. She felt silly, talking to an unconscious man as if he could hear her.

There was no blind on the window that looked out on to the nurses' station, but when Margaret peered through it, she could see that the nurse was seated at her desk with her back to Maxwell's room, doing paperwork.

She bit her lip. She was desperate to know more about *who Maxwell was*. No one had come forward to claim him. He had to have a history, and a life that was waiting for him.

There was a long cupboard beside the bed and Margaret opened it. It was a wardrobe with shelves at the bottom. On the bottom shelf were the brown boots that Maxwell had been wearing in the crash – dirty and unpolished. Above were the clothes he had been wearing, neatly folded: brown corduroy trousers, a T-shirt and a checked shirt; and hanging – a heavy brown jacket.

Margaret peered through the window at the nurse again, but

she was still bent over her desk. Instinctively, she reached into the pocket of the jacket. She was not sure what she was looking for, but the pocket was empty. She slid her hand into the other pocket. She felt a coin and then a piece of paper, which might have been a receipt.

She glanced over her shoulder and saw that the nurse was now on her feet, talking to one of the doctors.

Margaret took the piece of paper out of the pocket. Before she was able to inspect it, she saw the doctor and nurse walking together towards Maxwell's room. She crushed the paper in her palm and closed the cupboard door. She knew nothing about Maxwell other than his name and his date of birth. She was desperate to learn anything she could about him. The flap of the cupboard sounded loudly as it closed, and the room door opened. Margaret swallowed, feeling embarrassed and guilty, but the doctor, a tall Asian woman with dark-rimmed glasses, only smiled at her.

'I'm sorry to disturb you,' the doctor said. 'We're going to send Mr Brown up for another MRI. Visiting hour's nearly over anyway, but I'm sorry to rush you off.'

'Not at all,' said Margaret, picking up her coat and her bag. 'I was just leaving. You're thinking that you might bring him out of the coma soon?'

'We'll know more after the MRI.'

'He had bleeding in his brain?' Margaret frowned, trying to understand the extent of Maxwell's injuries. She wondered if he might have sustained brain damage.

'That's right, an extradural haematoma.'

'It sounds so serious, but I was with him on the motorway. I knew he had hurt his head, but he had so much strength. He saved my life.'

The doctor adjusted her glasses on her nose. 'That's right. With EDH, patients can be lucid for periods of time – sometimes days – before they lose consciousness. He did the right thing to come in.'

'He broke his hand saving me. He smashed the window of my car.'

'Yes, we heard Mr Brown is a hero. But that broken hand maybe saved his life.'

Margaret touched Maxwell's arm before she left the room, then watched through the window as the doctor checked his chart and the nurse began to lower his bed in preparation for moving him to the MRI scanner.

Margaret put on her coat and walked down the corridor. The hospital was too warm and she was looking forward to being outside.

There were few visitors in this critical ward and Margaret was alone in the corridor as she moved towards the lift. As she walked, she slowly unfolded the note she had clutched in her palm. It was not a receipt but a telephone number handwritten in thick, bold felt pen.

Margaret stopped still in the corridor as she realised that it was the main office telephone number for her school: Byron Academy.

21

Big George
Thursday 3 October, 1985

Leaving Newcastle, George chose not to follow the A1 south but cut west, on to the smaller roads, passing through Consett, Crook and Bishop Auckland. Moll sat looking out of the window at the passing fields, villages, houses. He kept the radio on and drummed his fingers on the wheel to the beat of the tunes that were played, but turned it off when the news came on.

They had stopped their game half an hour or so ago. George had said he needed to concentrate on driving.

When the radio was turned off, the car seemed too quiet – all of the sound lost to Moll's sad eyes. The day was waning and the sun cast sharp shadows on the harvested fields. Cylindrical haystacks were spaced around the corn stubble, random yet deliberate, like pagan standing stones. The horizon was pink and bloodied by the sinking sun, and George flipped the visor down to shield his eyes from the glare.

He took one hand off the wheel and reached inside his right pocket, taking out a coin. 'Penny for your thoughts,' he said, offering it to her and winking at her when she turned.

She took the coin from him, smiling thinly and clasping it in two hands, as if holding something alive, a beetle or a butterfly. The smile stayed on her lips and yet she didn't share her thoughts with him.

He knew he had it in him to win her.

He wished he had thought to buy sweets for the journey and decided that he would get some when they stopped. Was he possibly the only man to kidnap a child and forget them. George had smoked cigarettes since he was eleven years old and could now barely taste sweet food, but he remembered being Moll's age and loving it – elbowing his way to the front of the queue when the ice cream van came.

'Right,' he said, rolling down the window and lighting a cigarette. 'Don't you know any car songs?' The friction of the air against his window was awakening. The smell of his cigarette blended with the smell of manure off the fields.

'I know "Row the Boat",' she said, eyebrows raised.

'So do I.'

They sang 'Row, Row, Row Your Boat' overlapping verses, each trying to sing louder than the other.

George had no idea where he was going, but he ended up in York at six thirty at night. The wean was starving again and tired and they both needed a bath. He wanted a big hotel, where people wouldn't ask too many questions, and so settled on the Queen's Hotel, which looked on to the banks of the River Ouse. He was apprehensive about taking her inside after the incident in Newcastle, but they needed real food and a bath and a bed and he believed that he had begun to win her over.

George turned off the engine then turned to look at her. He could see that she was weary.

'This is a hotel. I'll get us a room here and we can have something nice to eat.'

She turned to him, nodding.

He took a deep breath. 'The truth is people are looking for you. They're looking for a little girl. I know you don't like your hair short or those clothes I bought you, but you can grow your hair again. It's kind of a disguise, like I said ... like dressing up.'

She watched his face.

'It's just like pretending. Do you ever pretend when you're playing?'

She nodded vigorously.

'Well, that's what this is like. I need you to help me out. You just *pretend* that you're a little boy. It's a game we can play, and only you and me know we're playing it. You can even choose a boy's name. What name do you think you'd like?'

The thought brightened her. She put a finger to her lips, considering, her body suddenly tense with the thrill of it.

'Come on,' said George, getting out of the car and taking their bags from the boot. He looked down at her and smiled. She was convincing with her Batman trainers and her jeans. He touched the skip of her cap. 'Well, Batman, did you come up with a name?'

'Batman?'

'Your shoes, I was meaning. What name do you choose for yourself? Your pretend boy name.'

'Batman.'

'You can't be Batman, that's a bit weird, but you could be Robin. That OK?'

'OK, are you Batman, then?'

George grinned at her. 'No, I'm George Harrison, like in The Beatles.'

Moll smiled and George felt grateful.

'Come on then ... Robin.'

She giggled.

The receptionist was a young woman who wore bright red lipstick. George put a hand on Moll's shoulder and smiled at the young woman, making sure that he made eye contact.

'I wondered if you had a twin room free?'

'Certainly,' she said, blushing as she checked the register, so that George knew that she liked him. 'We have a twin available for sixty pounds, and the suite for one hundred.'

George paused to consider. He had the money for three suites, but experience had taught him only to throw money around when you wanted to be noticed. Where he came from, the only people with money were doctors, lawyers and gangsters, and it would be obvious which one George was.

'I think the smaller room will be fine,' he said.

'Very well, I just need you to fill this in, and then it will be sixty for the room and a ten-pound deposit.'

George stared at the form, feeling a desolate sickness that he remembered feeling every day at school. He opened his wallet and counted out sixty pounds and placed it on the counter. 'Here you go.' He took another five-pound note out of his pocket and placed it near the woman's long, pale hand. 'And this is for you, for that beautiful smile.'

'I can't really,' she said, blushing deeply, and passing the note back to him.

'What do you mean? I could give it to the guy who'll carry our bag, but I can guarantee that he won't have a smile that beautiful.'

'Hardly.'

'What do you mean?' said George, warming to her already. 'Don't underestimate your beauty.'

The woman laughed, and gently pushed the form towards him. 'If you could just fill this in.'

'I tell you what,' he said, winking, 'you'll not believe it, but I sprained my right hand only last week. Even driving's difficult. If you need it completed *desperately*, could you do it for me and I'll sign it?'

The receptionist frowned in confusion but then agreed.

'Your name?'

'George Harrison.'

The woman glanced up, smiling.

'I know. That guy from The Beatles is mistaken for me all the time.'

The receptionist printed his name. 'And your son is ...'

'Batman,' said George, winking at Moll, who grinned and corrected him.

'Robin!'

'Address?'

George gave the address that he had had printed on his fake driving licence, which he had arranged before he left. It was an address in Edinburgh.

'You're just in York for the weekend?' the woman asked.

'Just passing through. We're on our way back up north.'

'Well, enjoy your stay.'

'Thank you.'

The woman took their key from the slot and then smiled down at Moll, before passing the key to her. 'He has your eyes,' said the receptionist, and George winked at her.

'Lucky him.'

Their room was large with its own bathroom and there was a view of the river and the car park, which George thought was useful, although he was trying not to get too paranoid. As soon as they were inside, he gave Moll the room service menu and asked her what she wanted to eat, then began to run the bathwater.

'Do you like bubbles in your bath, Robin?' George said, raising an eyebrow at her.

'Yes,' Moll said, reading with her forefinger pressed against each word. 'I want steak pie.'

'That sounds great. I'll get one for me too.'

While the bath filled and the bubbles frothed, George made the call and asked for two steak pies, a pint of lager, an orange juice, and a chocolate ice cream sundae.

'There you go,' he said, hanging up. 'You get your ice cream after all. I told you I always keep my promises.'

Moll smiled at him, but it was a wary smile and he wondered what she was thinking.

'Come on,' he said, kneeling on the bathroom floor to test the water. 'I think this is cool enough for you. You get in there, wash your hair, mind, and then we'll eat our tea and watch the telly.'

He left the bathroom door ajar and fetched her fresh clothes. When he returned she was deep in bubbles and trying to open a small bottle of shampoo.

'Will you be all right?'

'Yes.'

'Well, you'll shout if you have any trouble.'

He turned on the television, then saw the mini-bar and poured himself a whisky. He drank it straight as he changed the channel. It was the six o'clock news and Moll's school picture flashed on to the screen.

And now to our top story, said the suited male reporter. *Police continue their search for young Molly Henderson, who was abducted from her home in Thurso in the Scottish Highlands yes-terday. The seven-year-old, who was last seen wearing the school uniform pictured, was witnessed getting into a dark-coloured car with a tall, dark man, wearing a suit. Highlands Police are coordin-ating with the national force but have asked for the public to report any suspected sightings.*

George turned the volume down a little and stepped closer to the television to hear the report. When Moll had been asleep, he had listened to the news about her on the radio. One of the radio stations had suggested that the abduction could be linked to other child murders, and this had pleased George. He wanted the police to waste time comparing Moll's disappearance with other crimes by other criminals.

Yesterday evening, Molly's mother Kathleen gave the following address . . .

The camera cut to a recording of a press conference, where Kathleen was sitting with her husband at her side. They were both grey with grief, and Kathleen's lip trembled, her eyes searching with confusion, not sure where to look. She had pre-pared something to say and now looked down at the piece of paper which shook in her hands.

Molly's very little and I know she'll be frightened. Kathleen's voice trembled and broke, but then she regained composure. *If anyone has any information, I urge them to come forward so that I can have her back. Please. Please. We . . . miss her very much.*

George cleaved at the sight of Kathleen in such pain. He took a large sip of his whisky, wincing.

Just then, Moll screamed in the bathroom.

'Shit,' he said, assuming that she had heard and spilling some of his drink as he rushed to change the channel.

*

He went to her, cringing at the bathroom door before he entered.

She had soap in her eyes. Her hair was covered in white foam and she was screaming with her knuckles pressed into her eyes.

George rinsed a facecloth and wiped her face, then got a fresh towel and dried it off.

'Are you all right?'

She nodded, blinking. Wet, her eyelashes seemed impossibly long.

'You've got too much soap in your hair, you daftie. Do you want me to help you rinse it?'

She nodded silently, so he took down the shower hose and ran the water until it was the right temperature.

'Lean your head back.'

She did as he asked and he washed all the soap out of her hair, noticing some areas where he had almost shaved it to the scalp. When her hair was clean, he picked up one of the big towels and lifted her out of the bath, wrapping her in it. He rubbed her a little, and then told her to get dressed.

Their dinner came, on a trolley and hidden under silver serving dishes. George paid and tipped the waiter and then set the table up for her, and changed the TV channel to cartoons. They ate in silence, watching *Bugs Bunny*.

She ate almost all of her dinner and he let her sit on the bed with the ice cream to watch the television better, while he took a shower.

The water was hot and the jet was strong, and he felt relief as he washed. He hadn't bathed since he left Glasgow and he felt the dirt and stress of the journey rinsing off his skin. He thought about Kathleen and the brave way she had fought back tears at the press conference and he thought about Moll and her strange shorn head that made her seem like an urchin.

He had started this, and he didn't know what was next, but he hoped to find some place where they could be at peace, and then he would try to persuade Moll to stay with him. There was no going back now, he thought, as he rinsed his hair and turned off the shower.

George roughly towelled himself dry, put on one of the hotel robes, wiped a clear spot on the steamy mirror and shaved. When he opened the bathroom door, he found her asleep on the bed with an empty dish of ice cream beside her. He looked at the clock: it was nearly eight.

He put the ice cream dish on the trolley, then folded her limp sleeping body under the covers. He was exhausted himself, so he lay on the bed opposite, drinking his lager and watching a war film with the sound turned down low. He was about to light a cigarette when he became aware that she was whimpering. Her eyes were rolling under her eyelids and her hands were clutching the bedcovers.

'Wheeesht,' he whispered in an attempt to soothe her.

She became more restless and just as he was about to go to her, she sat up in bed and burst into tears.

'Hey, what's the matter?' he asked, leaning over.

She didn't seem to hear him, and so he sat on the edge of her bed and put his arm around her.

'Hey, Moll, what's the matter? Why are you crying?'

She looked into his face, her lashes wet and her eyes full of confusion.

'Were you dreaming?'

She nodded, once.

'What were you dreaming about?'

'A monster was ... was coming to get me,' she said, between stolen breaths.

'A monster? I wouldn't let any monsters near you, would I?'

She looked at him, the same wariness in her eyes as earlier, but then shook her head. He got a tissue for her and she dried her eyes then looked around at the hotel room, as if she had forgotten where she was.

The film he was watching was full of guns and fighting, so he changed channels, but only found the news again, or a soap opera. He turned the television off.

'Settle down now,' he said to her. 'Lie down and try to get back to sleep. We have another long day of driving ahead of us tomorrow.'

She lay down, her big eyes open.

'Try and sleep.'

'I like to be read to, but you said you can't.'

'I could sing to you.'

'OK.'

He sat on the bed opposite, facing her, and began a quiet rendition of 'Sweet Caroline'. She giggled and turned on to her side to face him, two hands tucked under her cheek. When he finished, she asked him to sing it again. He sang instead, 'Song Sung Blue', which she thought she knew and tried to sing along at the chorus.

When he was finished, he tucked her in and pulled the covers up to her chin, the way he remembered his mother doing when he was little. He bent and kissed her forehead. She smelled of lemon shampoo. The skin of her cheek was clear and perfect, and he touched it briefly with his thumb, which seemed rough and old and dark in comparison. He thought he had never felt anything so soft and smooth as the skin of her cheek.

'Why can't you read?' she asked him.

'I dunno, I just can't.'

'Can you write?'

'I can write my signature: GM.'

'But why can't you read and write? *I* can read and write.'

'I just . . . was never good at school.'

'You mean you weren't clever?'

'No, I was the dunce.'

'What's a dunce?'

'Someone who's stupid.'

'Why were you the dunce?'

'I don't know why. I just . . . was never able to do the lessons.'

'But even people who're not good at school can read. Everyone can read and write even if they're not good at it.'

'Can they?'

Moll nodded, her mouth hidden under the edge of the bed sheet, making her blue eyes seem bigger. As always when she was facing him, he found that he spoke to the eye that looked straight at him and not the eye which turned away, so that after a while he was unaware of her squint.

'Well, when I was wee, I used to write with my left hand.'

'So do I,' said Moll suddenly, raising her face up off the pillow and smiling at him. She held her left palm outstretched towards him, and he touched it with his.

'And that's OK now, is it? The teachers allow that?'

Moll shrugged and nodded.

'When I was wee, the teachers would belt me when I used my left hand. Do they have the belt at your school?'

Moll shook her head.

'Well, it was the nuns, you see . . . They wanted me to use my right hand and so every time I picked up a pencil with my left, I got it. Sister Agatha was the worst. I still remember her. She was tall and fat and in her habit she looked like a big, giant . . . penguin.'

Moll giggled. 'Giant penguin.'

'Aye, but you wouldn't laugh if you saw her. I remember one day, she told me to come forward and hold my hands out for the belt. And I got up and went to the front of the class and did as she asked. You had to hold your hands like this, one hand under the other, so it was harder for you to pull away.' George demonstrated, sitting on the edge of the bed and holding out his hands towards Moll. She was rapt, listening to him. 'One day, I remember, there was a hair on my hand. It might have been my own, or one of the girls', I don't know,' he said, winking at her. 'But anyway, when Sister Agatha belted me she caught the hair, and it cut the palm of my hand so that it was bleeding. The class saw the blood after that first crack, and I remember they all just gasped …' George paused again to mime the shock of his classmates. Moll was frowning now, her small mouth pursed together. 'But it didn't stop Sister Agatha. All she did was ask me to change hands, then she kept on till she'd finished.'

'Did your mum and dad not complain?'

George grinned and pinched her cheek. 'My mother had a lot to complain about, believe me, but her whole life I never heard her utter a word of complaint and my father, well …' George looked away, 'well no, he wasn't bothered.'

Moll was silent and serious, looking down at her fingernails, and George was sorry that he'd told her the story. She had been frightened already, and now he had scared her again. He sighed and looked away, and was about to suggest another Neil Diamond song when she put her hand on his.

'*I* can teach you to read and write,' she said, licking her lips and sitting up suddenly.

'Don't be silly,' he told her. 'I'm a lost cause.'

She climbed out of bed and padded barefoot to the desk, and brought back a sheaf of hotel paper and a pencil. There was a large black Bible on the bedside table and she opened it, and for a moment George thought this was to be his reading book, but she only placed it on the bed as a hard surface for them to write upon.

She smoothed the paper over the Bible, took the pencil in her left hand and wrote, *Aa, Bb, Cc.*

'You try,' she said, giving him the pencil.

'I'm tired, can we do it tomorrow? You need your sleep.'

'It's only *three letters*, we can do the rest of the alphabet tomorrow.'

George sighed and picked up the pencil in his right hand. He held the pencil the way his brother Peter held a knife.

'*No*,' she whispered to him, opening his large palm with her small fingers and prising the pencil from his grasp. 'Use your left hand, if you're like me and you're left-handed.'

He put the pencil into his left hand and she tried to move it into position, but then pulled the pencil from him again.

'Look at me,' she said, kneeling on the bed. 'Look how I hold it. Can you do this?'

She handed George the pencil and he copied how she had held it.

'Good,' she said, 'well done. Now try and do the A.'

He made an attempt, but it was messy and not joined together. 'I can do a G,' he said, shrugging nonchalantly.

Moll bounced from the bed again and took another pencil from the desk.

'Let's do it together,' she insisted, writing slowly beside him each of the three strokes of the letter A, waiting for him to finish. She wrote on her stomach, propped on her elbows, with the tip of her tongue between her lips and her face very close to the page.

Nevertheless he watched her and made the three strokes when she did. To his surprise, the letter looked good.

'See, you *can* do it,' she said, smiling at him, up close to his face, so that he could see the pink of her gums where her baby teeth had been.

'That's only one letter,' he said. 'I'll have a problem with the others.'

She leaned in close to him and put her forefinger against his lips to silence him. 'There's only twenty-six of them, and you'll learn them in no time. I'm a good teacher. I want to be a teacher when I grow up.'

'You are a good teacher,' he said, replacing the Bible and putting the pencils and paper away, then tucking her back in. 'I tell you what, you're better than any teacher I ever had.'

She smiled at him, and from this angle he could see the tip of a new tooth breaking her gum. He bent to kiss her forehead again.

'Good night, Batman.'

'Robin!'

22

Angus Campbell
Tuesday 8 October, 1985

It was the middle of the night, but Angus was lying with his hands behind his head and his eyes wide open. The light of the full moon strained through the thin bedroom curtains. Hazel was sound asleep and still beside him, curled as she always was, away from him on her right side.

He got up, put on his trousers and a pullover and went downstairs. In the kitchen, he poured some milk into a pan and turned on the stove. He watched the ring turn red, and stared at the circle of milk for a few moments. He went to the window and looked out at the barn. Unable to help himself, Angus slipped on his boots and wandered down the dirty path, rubbing his arms against the chill of the night. The moon was bright and lit his way.

At the barn, he stepped inside Maisie's pen. It had been scrubbed clean and stank of disinfectant. There was no straw covering the floor on which she had lain, no grain in her feeding trough, no water in her bucket. He cupped his hand the way he used to when he touched her cheek. He could almost still feel her.

Angus placed his cupped hand over his eyes and began to cry. He wept with abandon, spit stretching from his mouth to the floor and his shoulders heaving. After a few moments, he had to lean against the wall to catch his breath. He wiped his face with the sleeve of his jerkin, and whispered small prayers of apology and forgiveness, moving his lips without sound, as if whispering to a lover.

Finally, he turned towards the door and stood staring up at the night sky. The loss filled him, as the spirit of God filled a believer. Being filled with loss was like being full of darkness and Angus had never felt so empty. In the midst of his grief, nothing seemed to matter any more: he had no interest in prayer or worship, no motivation to guide his wife and his children, no interest in the farm. He knew that God was testing him, as he had tested Jesus in the desert. During the day, Angus was fatigued and sullen and at night he could not sleep. Whenever he drifted off, he would dream of Maisie moaning in labour.

The only thing that still inspired and motivated Angus was his quest to find out the truth about the criminal who had taken Molly Henderson. Now, standing in the moonlight, his tears chilling on his cheeks, Angus chewed the inside of his mouth, twisting his lips one way and then the other, as he contemplated that, in a few hours' time, Kathleen would read his article. He had reported his findings about George to the superintendent in charge of the Molly Henderson investigation while he was writing the article.

Detective Inspector Black had not realised the great importance of the information Angus had given him. He had merely muttered, 'We'll look into it,' when told about George McLaughlin. Angus remembered that the Yorkshire Ripper had been questioned *several times* before he was finally caught and Angus saw Black's lack of interest as another example of police incompetence.

It was now six days since Molly had been taken, but her body had not yet been discovered. Angus hoped that his article would be picked up by the national press and the police would confirm that George was wanted for questioning.

The similarity of Molly's abduction to those of the murdered children meant that Highlands and Islands Police were coordinating with police teams nationwide working on the other open cases. Black had taken note of Angus's information about George, but it seemed as if the team's attention was focused on the danger that Molly's abductor was a serial child murderer.

Angus was certain that there was a way to track George McLaughlin down, and prove that *he* had taken the Henderson child. Angus was bitter that the police could not see the light. Blinking in the moonlight, Angus imagined the heat of flashbulbs, as he was interviewed by an audience of the national press, all asking how he had solved one of the most pressing cases of child abduction in recent years.

Angus was smiling, formulating a response in his mind, when he became aware of a dark shape in the kitchen window, watching him.

Clarity returned to Angus and he saw that Hazel was staring at him from inside the house. He marched back to the farmhouse to find the kitchen blackened with smoke and Hazel scrubbing the cooker, pink rubber gloves pulled over the sleeves of her nightie.

'What are you doing, woman?'

'I woke up. There was smoke. Did you p-put some milk on?'

She was hunched over, turned from him and watching him with downcast eyes.

'Oh, yes,' he said. 'I must've. Now that you're up, you can put on some fresh. I'm having trouble sleeping.'

He left her with the hazy smell of burned milk and climbed the stairs to his study.

Angus's study smelled of mothballs and old hymnbooks, but he found the smell comforting. He sat down at his rickety mahogany desk, which needed sanding and varnishing. The top of the desk had been scored by the legs of the typewriter and one of the knobs had fallen off the drawers, so that his pencil drawer was perpetually open for ease of access.

He had been avidly collecting articles by other journalists on the Molly Henderson kidnapping, and these were stacked to the right of his typewriter. Because the police had not communicated any real leads, there was a tendency for the newspapers to repeat details over and over again, possibly adding one new piece of information. The others speculated on similarities between the Henderson abduction and the abduction of other children who had been found dead and linked to a single killer who was still at large. This speculation allowed the newspapers to reprint details of the previous abductions and murders, thereby creating a feature when nothing new had been discovered.

Angus knew that he was different from the other writers. He was an *investigative journalist* and as such he was committed to discovering the truth. He would stop at nothing until he found it.

He remembered Tam at the McLaughlin garage and the way he had laughed when Angus asked where George was: 'That is the magic question,' Tam had said. Whatever the police or the other newspapers thought, Angus felt that Tam was right. Finding George was the key to finding Molly, dead or alive.

He looked through his notes and decided that it was worthwhile trying to speak to the three girls who had witnessed Molly's abduction. He would have to go through their parents, but there was a chance at least one of them would talk to him. It was still early, but Angus decided to shower and dress and call his contact from church at the primary school, Betsy, to see if she would give him the addresses for the girl witnesses.

At eight o'clock, as soon as he had finished his porridge, Angus called Betsy Clarke at home. He was now full of passion and energy and ready to act. He wanted to avoid visiting the school and having to wait for Betsy's tea break.

'Good morning, Angus. Are you well?'

'Very well, and yourself?'

'Grand. Just about to go to work . . .'

'I don't want to hold you back. It was just about those three names you gave me last time.' Angus consulted his notebook, pressing the point of the pen underneath each name as he spoke, 'Tait, McGowan and Tanner.'

'The girls that witnessed . . .'

'That's right. You don't happen to have their addresses? I wanted to talk to their parents – see if anything's been missed.'

'Well, not on me, but you can look them up. Sandra's father works in the post office in town, Pamela's mother runs the café-gallery on Main Street and Sheila lives next door to Gordon and Jeanette who cover the Sunday school when David is unavailable.'

'Perfect,' said Angus, making careful notes. 'That's enough to go on. I'm sure I'll find them, no problem.'

'You will. I'll have to dash now.'

'You've been a great help once again, Betsy. You're in my prayers.'

'And you mine. You heard, of course, about the other witnesses?'

Angus swallowed and hunched over the telephone, as if someone was listening to him. 'Others?' he whispered.

'My next-door neighbours – you might not know them – an old couple, the Stirlings – they're heathens but they've paid the price for it; a hard life, lost a child to leukaemia, poor souls. You might know Sue, of course, she was the one . . .'

Angus pressed his teeth together in irritation. The minutiae that women thought relevant or even interesting made his soul white hot with rage. It was all he could do not to scream at Betsy to *shut up* and tell him *what they saw*.

He took a deep breath and interrupted as politely as he could. 'I think I know who you mean. What did they see? Do the police know?'

'Oh, yes. I was talking to Sue just yesterday. They were in the police station for some hours the other day. After all the newspaper articles, they decided to come forward – thought that what they had seen might be relevant . . .'

'And what did they see?'

'A little girl that matched Molly's description being dragged screaming into a car near Sir George's Park.'

'My goodness,' said Angus, almost to himself.

'Anyway, I really must dash. I did like your prayer of repentance on Sunday. You can tell you're a writer, because you do have a way with words.'

Angus blushed at the compliment, and hung up the phone, his mouth twisted into a sneer. *When the Lord closes a door, somehow He opens a window.*

The Stirlings were retired and Angus had thought they would be at home so early in the morning, but no one answered when he

274

pressed the doorbell. He peered through the letterbox and saw that there was no build-up of mail on the doormat to suggest they were away on holiday. He went around the back of the property. There was no letterbox on the kitchen door, but there was a cat flap, so Angus got down on his knees on the step and pushed his nose inside. He picked up a distinct smell of toast in the kitchen.

'Can we help you?'

Angus heard himself being addressed by a very properly spoken man and scrambled to his feet. Mr Stirling and his wife, Sue, were standing arm in arm, frowning at him. Mr Stirling was a tall man, so Angus chose to stay on their doorstep as he threw out his hands in welcome and gave them a large smile.

'Hello. What a surprise. I'm so glad you came back. My name's Angus, Angus Campbell, from the *John o'Groat Journal*. I was very keen to speak to you.'

'So I can see,' said Mr Stirling, watching Angus's outstretched hand wavering in the space between them, before he finally took it.

Angus tried to compensate for his behaviour by giving Mr Stirling's hand a manly squeeze, but found that the older man tugged his hand away.

'What is it you want to speak to us about?' said Sue.

She was a thin-boned woman wearing bright lipstick.

Angus made sure his smile remained in place as he addressed her. 'Forgive me for the interruption, but I'm working on the Molly Henderson story – I met with Kathleen, bless her, just a week ago. I heard that you had information.'

The couple looked at each other. 'We spoke to the police. We're not sure if what we told them is relevant,' said Mr Stirling.

'When a young girl goes missing, every detail is important,' said Angus.

'You'd best come in then,' said Sue, as her husband took the house keys out of his pocket.

Mr Stirling stood pointing the key at Angus, as if it were a knife of some sort. 'You'll need to move away from the door so that I can open it,' he said, and Angus detected a note of irritation in his voice.

As he was bid, Angus climbed down from their doorstep and waited for the door to be opened.

The Stirlings' home was traditionally furnished and cluttered. There was an old globe on its axis, a collection of blown glass animals, several bookcases with glass fronts and a considerable stack of records beside an old turntable. Two crystal decanters were filled with what Angus presumed to be whisky and sherry. He turned down his lips in distaste as he waited for Mr Stirling to return from the bathroom and Sue to bring the tea she had offered.

When they were settled, Angus took out his pad and pen. 'I am working on the bigger story. What you tell me won't be printed any time soon and possibly not at all, but I am working on finding who has taken Molly and what you tell me may well be useful in tracing her abductor. Ultimately, I am hoping to write a good news story when she is found. Although some others believe she is already dead, I am hopeful that she is still alive.'

'Oh, we hope so too,' said Sue, placing a plate of buttered scones on a small table in front of Angus.

'So, if you could tell me what you saw?'

Mr Stirling cleared his throat and looked at his wife, as if to ask for her permission to proceed. Angus opened his eyes wide in anticipation.

'It was only after reading the article in the *Journal* ... your interview with Kathleen Henderson in fact, that the two of us thought again about the incident and then we reported it. It may be that it is still of no consequence . . . However, we were on our morning walk – our usual route by the park – and we saw a car stop at the pelican crossing. A young girl jumped out, possibly not as young as seven . . . to me she looked older – nine or ten years old, but she did have long hair like Molly . . .'

'Did you notice an eyepatch?' asked Angus.

'No, neither of us did,' interjected Sue, lifting her tea, which rattled on the saucer. 'But that doesn't necessarily mean she didn't have one. At the time neither of us thought any of this was untoward.'

'However, after the young girl jumped out of the car, she started to run,' continued Mr Stirling, 'and a tall man got out and gave chase. He was very tall, I would say a good few inches taller than me, and I am hardly short . . .'

Angus twitched at the mention of height, but nodded.

'He was heavy too,' said Mr Stirling, 'not fat at all, but large built and it seemed that the run was taxing for him, and he was wearing a suit and so he caught your eye so to speak – a man of his size in a suit, running at full pelt. He caught up with the girl and took her by the arm and began to pull her back to the car. As we approached, we saw that the girl was crying and shouting, but we assumed it was his daughter . . .'

'Yes, some sort of tantrum,' said Sue, sipping her tea. 'And they could have been father and daughter, not that we looked closely, but they both had dark hair. He smiled at us, though. He seemed . . . nice.'

Angus had brought with him a copy of the photograph of George and his family on the steps of the High Court in Glasgow. He slipped it from the back of his pad and passed it to the couple. 'Do you know if this was the man you saw?'

Mr Stirling sighed, one hand over his mouth. 'In truth it could have been any of the men in this photo. Do you agree, Sue?'

'Yes,' she said, nodding. 'We didn't get a good enough look at his face, but the car . . .'

'Oh, yes, we told the police . . .'

'You got a number plate?' said Angus, feeling a flutter of pre-emptive joy.

'No, but the car was definitely dark red, and it was an Allegro. I only remember because we used to have one. And when they drove off we noticed there was a bumper sticker on the car that said *Glasgow's miles better*.'

Angus felt a flush of vindication. It *was* George McLaughlin; he knew it in his bones.

'And where were they headed?'

'They were headed out of town, on the A9.'

Angus returned to the office, where he made notes on the McLaughlin case and called Inspector Black, who said that there were no new leads at this time.

'I'm aware of what the Stirlings said about the Glasgow sticker, but that means nothing. We can hardly arrest everyone in Glasgow, I'm sure you'll agree, Angus,' said the detective.

'But you *still* haven't managed to question George McLaughlin?'

'We haven't managed to locate him, but he is not an actual suspect at this time.'

'The Stirlings' description matches George . . .'

'Yet they failed to identify him. I thank you for your efforts, but I have nothing more for you at this time.'

That afternoon, Angus wrote two articles: one on the Thurso autumn fair and another on the Caithness boat race, and then, at three o'clock, he got into his car and drove to Sheila Tanner's home, a council house with a well-kept front lawn.

He waited outside for the child to return from school – hoping to catch both her and a parent on the doorstep and persuade them to give him a few moments. If he had no success with Sheila, he was planning to go to the post office to speak to Sandra's father and then to the café to speak to Pamela's mother.

Sheila was a heavyset child, with red shoulder-length hair. Angus got out of the car as soon as he realised who she was and lightly jogged along the pavement towards her, then followed her down the path to her front door.

The girl turned at the sound of his footfalls, just as her mother opened the door. Mrs Tanner had the same build and colouring as her daughter and a similar hardened expression: deep-set eyes and pinched, thin lips.

'Hello,' said Angus, giving them both a wide smile. 'How fortuitous to see you both together. My name's Angus, Angus Campbell, from the *Journal*. I wanted to talk to you about Molly Henderson.'

Sheila's mother put a hand on her daughter's shoulders to usher her inside.

'She's said her piece.' Sheila disappeared and her mother stood at the door, arms folded above her stomach and the corners of her mouth turned down. 'It's only just this week she's back at school. All that business was far too upsetting: a classmate taken right before her eyes. She's hardly slept since.'

Mrs Tanner was frowning down at Angus. He found her abhorrent. He hated excess flesh on a woman; when the female nature of indulgence and weakness was visible on the outside.

He blinked slowly, remembering Eve taking the apple into her eager palm: *The woman saw how beautiful the tree was and how good its fruit would be to eat, and she thought how wonderful it would be to become wise. So she took some of the fruit and ate it.* Angus struggled to maintain his façade before Mrs Tanner.

'I understand that this is a very distressing subject. I would be quick. Also, I am not going to write this up immediately. I am investigating the kidnapping itself and, as I think we all are, I am intent on tracking down Molly's abductor.'

'Isn't that what the police are for?'

Angus narrowed his eyes at Mrs Tanner. 'I just want to go over a few facts – make sure that nothing has been missed . . .'

'She's not speaking to any journalists and that's that,' said Mrs Tanner, as she closed the door in his face.

Disheartened, Angus returned to his office to consider his next move. There was both the post office and the café to try next, in an attempt to speak to Sandra Tait and Pamela McGowan's parents, but Angus felt he had better plan his visit more carefully, for fear of frightening off all the families.

While he was working, the editor told him that another press conference had been scheduled at the Royal Hotel in an hour's time. Angus glanced at his watch and knew he would need to hurry in order to get a good seat.

He transposed his notes from the meeting with the Stirlings from shorthand into longhand, while the police radio crackled quietly on his desk. He had grown used to the radio's background noise both at work and in the car and often had to remind himself to maintain vigilant of its content. It was nearly five o'clock and Angus was just putting on his jacket to leave when his telephone rang.

'Angus Campbell,' he said, still standing, exasperated at the thought of someone calling with what he fully expected would be trivialities, when he was on his way to a press conference about an investigation into a missing girl.

It was a woman with a very quiet voice. He listened, frowning, as he put his pad, pencils and Dictaphone into his briefcase. He snapped his briefcase shut and then barked:

'Will you please speak up? I can barely hear a word you're saying.'

The woman cleared her throat and started again. 'I'm very sorry to bother you. My name's May Driscoll. I'm not sure if you can help me at all. It was just on the off chance. You see ... my husband's missing and ... well, I think you might know him. I found your business card in his work overalls.'

'Your husband? Who might he be?' Angus stood looking at the ceiling, frowning.

'He's Thomas Driscoll.'

'I don't recall anyone of that name. What does he do? In what capacity would we have met?'

'I don't know how you met. He's just a mechanic but I'm very worried—'

'Tam!' said Angus, sitting back down on his chair and leaning forward, elbows on the desk, so that he could hear more clearly.

'Yes, that's right. You remember him? Do you know where he is?'

'Eh ... I had ... no idea he was *missing*. He works at the McLaughlin garage in the East End?'

The woman began to sob and Angus waited for her to stop. He pulled his pad out of his briefcase again and flicked back to the day when he met Tam, scanning the minimal notes he had made on the meeting.

'You know him?'

'I ... met him briefly on Saturday. He did some work on my car and I spoke to him about a case I'm working on ... You say he is missing ... When did you last see him?'

'Sunday. He never works on Sundays, but they called him in.'

'Well, you should contact the police.'

'I did, but ...' she sniffed, 'he's not a priority. It's only been forty-eight hours and I told them he doesn't enjoy work, and we've had ... money worries and ... we've been under a lot of strain. I get the impression that the police think he's just run off, but I *know* him, and I also know he's been worried sick working in that place. They're not good people. They're the kind of people who could make a man ... disappear.'

'Hold on one minute,' said Angus, putting his hand over the receiver. His colleagues were all leaving the office and he waved them goodbye.

He switched off his police scanner and gave May his full attention.

'Let me get this straight,' said Angus. 'Are you ... are you still there?'

'Yes,' said May. Angus could hear the tears in her throat.

'You have reported Tam's disappearance to the police but you believe that he has come to some harm ... from the McLaughlins?'

'Do you know something? Oh dear God, I begged him not to take that job. We were desperate, but I told him not to take it. They're cruel, violent people and ... Tam not even being a Catholic, it just ...'

'Not a Catholic?' said Angus, purely out of interest. 'What faith does he follow?'

'We're Protestant, Church of Scotland,' said May, very quickly, then quietly blew her nose.

'And you called me because?'

'Like I said, I found your card in Tam's pocket. Do you know anything ... anything at all that might help?'

'I don't know anything,' said Angus, then, more cautiously, 'but I do know what you mean when you say the McLaughlins are not good people.'

'They're *evil*,' said May, her voice becoming stronger and louder. 'I begged him not to work there when they offered him a job, but he promised me it would be OK. He said he would just do his work and come home, not get involved, but I could see the pressure of just being there was *making him ill*. He was *sick* with it ... and I told that to the police and now I think they think he's just upped and left me, deserted me ... but I know Tam and he wouldn't, he just wouldn't leave me, *ever*.'

Angus bit his lip as he considered.

'You're saying that you think the McLaughlins are involved in your husband's disappearance?'

'Oh, God, I hope not. It's my worst fear. It's what I've feared since he took the job ... but they asked him to come in to work and now he's missing.'

'What reason would the McLaughlins have for taking Tam?'

'I don't know. I called because I thought you might know something, I don't ... I just don't have any idea. And you don't know him? He just worked on your car? But why would he have your card?'

Angus felt an icy dread in his veins. It felt like yesterday morning when he had gone out to the shed, hoping for a newborn calf but finding Maisie's dead body.

'I ... I was speaking to him about a story I'm working on.'

'For the *John o'Groat Journal*? But we've never been further north than Oban! What story?'

'I don't know if you've seen the news? A little girl from Thurso was abducted a week ago ... Molly Henderson.'

'Molly? What does Tam have to do with that?'

May, who had been so inaudible at the beginning of the call, was now almost shouting, and Angus had to hold the earpiece an inch from his ear.

'I was talking to Tam, not about Molly but about George McLaughlin, who I understand has skipped town. I wondered if Tam knew where he was.'

'George *has* skipped town.'

'You know about it?'

'Tam tells me everything. We're very close. We have our troubles, but we share everything, we always have, which is why I know that he wouldn't have just left ... abandoned me. He's a proud man, a quiet man, a strong man ... but he wouldn't just disappear, no matter what pressure he was under. Tam and I ...'

May broke down again; as she sobbed, Angus took the time to turn over a new leaf in his pad and draft some questions for her.

'I understand how very difficult this must be for you, he said. I see two issues here: you want to know what happened to your husband, and I might have been one of the last people to speak to him, outside of close family, before he disappeared. Secondly, I am trying to find George McLaughlin, and you might know where he is?'

The line went quiet, and then there was the muffled sound of May talking to a child. The office light was waning, and he turned on his desk lamp.

'I'm sorry, I can't talk now. May I ask ... can you call me back?'

'Certainly,' said Angus, 'give me your number.'

*

Angus made a note of the number, hung up, stretched over to Amanda's desk to steal one of her Turkish delights, then dialled May Driscoll.

May picked up right away. Her voice sounded different and there was an echo.

'I'm in the front bedroom, so we won't be disturbed. My daughter's home, you see. I don't want her to worry . . . Tam did tell me something about George.'

'What did he tell you?'

'It was payday, a Friday, and Tam came home drunker than usual. He often went to the pub on payday but he's a quiet man; he can take or leave the drink, and so I was surprised. I remember I made him a cup of tea and he accidentally dropped it. It wasn't like him to get so drunk.

'In the morning, I spoke to him. He was full of worry, and he made me promise not to tell anyone, but he said that George McLaughlin had found some money, and was going to run away to Penzance in Cornwall with it. I asked him why Penzance and Tam said it was a family cottage down there. I know the area and I asked him where – it was between Sennen and Porthcurno. I asked him about this money and he said he didn't know whose it was, or where he'd found it, but that George was going to leave all the same and Tam wasn't sure he could keep on working at the garage once George was gone.'

'Why was that?' said Angus, making notes so fast that his hand was cramping.

'He told me George wasn't like the others. I'm not saying George McLaughlin was a saint, but Tam had a sense that George was keeping him safe.'

'He and George were friends then?'

'Only in the loosest terms. I guarded him against it, and Tam agreed. They worked together and went for the odd pint, but that was all. I gather George is quite a character.'

'Really?'

'I haven't met him but Tam tells me he's quite the performer. A joker. Big tall man.'

Angus made a note: *performer*, not sure what to make of it.

'Did your husband say if George had mentioned anything about a girl?'

'No, only the money and Penzance. He swore me to secrecy. But I gather George always has a girl in tow.'

'No, I mean a child. Did he mention anything about a child?'

'Not that I recall.'

'But you told the police?'

'I told the police Tam was missing, but not about George's money and Penzance.'

'Why didn't you tell them about the money and George?'

'Is there a wee want about you? *Why do you think?* Anyone would think twice mentioning the McLaughlins to the police. That family have ears everywhere.'

Angus made another note on his pad: *McLaughlin – Police?*

May was quiet and so was Angus, and they listened to the measured sounds of each other's breathing for a minute or so. His mind was racing, the biro slippery in his hand.

'Oh my God,' said May, suddenly. 'Do you think they've gone away together?'

'Who?'

'George and Tam.'

'I don't know,' said Angus, cautiously. 'How much money did George find, do you know?'

'I've no idea.'

'And would your husband be tempted by wealth, if ... the money found ... was significant?'

There was quiet on the line for a moment, then May spoke. 'No, definitely not. We need money. We're skint. We have been since Tam lost his job last year; it was the whole reason he took the McLaughlin job ... but do I think he would leave us for money? Not for a second.'

Angus took down May Driscoll's address and telephone number, and promised to keep in touch. He sat back in his chair, eyes and mouth wide open as he considered the information she had given him. He realised that there was no other option than for him to give chase. He knew now where George McLaughlin was headed, and despite what the police seemed to think and what May had said, Angus knew in his gut that Molly was with him.

He wasn't sure that he now had time for the press conference, but he stopped at the Royal Hotel and ran inside. The room was crowded and hot with lamps and flashes. There were no seats left and Angus stood at the back.

Inspector Black was just finishing his address. 'We are coordinating with national forces and can reveal that we are looking into links with other young girls who have gone missing in the past few years.'

'Does that mean you are looking for a serial killer?' asked a journalist near the front.

DI Black's red cheeks puffed in annoyance. 'Molly has been missing for several days, but a murder investigation will only begin if we find a body. At the moment we are still hoping to find her alive.'

'But the suggestion is that it could be a serial abductor?'

'We are following up all leads.'

'Do the police think that Molly's disappearance is connected to the murder of Tracey Begg?'

Angus stood on his tiptoes, straining to spot the journalist who was asking the questions, but he could not see over the heads of the people standing before him.

'All leads are being followed up, but no definite link has been made at this time.'

'Tracey Begg was found dead in England ten days after her abduction and Molly has now been missing for nearly a week. Is there—'

Inspector Black interrupted and raised his voice. Angus could see that he was exasperated with the journalist. He lifted a hand to silence further questions.

'To repeat: this is not presently a murder investigation. We are coordinating with the national force on the assumption that Molly is now no longer in the local area. We are following up a number of leads. Her natural father, George McLaughlin from Glasgow, is wanted for questioning and should go to a police station in case he has any information related to Molly's disappearance. Similarly, we urge those who know McLaughlin to help us identify his whereabouts . . .'

There was another rowdy wave of questions, but Inspector Black held up his hand again to silence them. 'We are also following up links about a vehicle spotted leaving Thurso.'

Before further questions could be asked, DI Black stood up and left the table with his colleagues, and the microphones were switched off.

Because he was at the back of the room, Angus got out before the swell of other journalists. He went straight back to the farm, ate the dinner that Hazel had prepared for him, and then packed his suitcase.

'Where are you going?' Hazel managed, as he opened the stiff drawer under the wardrobes to pull out one of his winter sweaters. The anaesthetising scent of mothballs filled the room.

'You don't need to know,' said Angus, snapping shut the fastenings on his suitcase. 'Suffice to say I am going south on business and will be gone for some time.'

'When will you be home?'

'That is none of your concern, but I will call you once a week and tomorrow, before I leave, I will take out sufficient money to feed you and the children for the period of my absence.'

'What are you doing, Angus? Where are you going in the south?'

'That,' said Angus, heaving his suitcase to the floor and straightening his collar and cuffs, 'is none of your concern. Suffice to say that I am being sent on very important business ... business of national, if not international importance. I leave first thing in the morning.'

He was intoxicated at the thought of being on his way. George McLaughlin was on the run, but Angus Campbell was going to catch him.

23

Margaret Holloway
Monday 23 December, 2013

'Harry, I'm so sorry to bother you at home,' said Margaret. 'I need to get into the school. I have a presentation to prepare for the in-service day in January and I need something off my computer.'

It was the 23rd of December and Margaret was sitting in her car in the school car park, calling the janitor, who lived a block away.

She hadn't set out to drive to school. Their car had recently been returned from the garage. Ben was looking after the children and she had decided that she needed to get behind the wheel again. She hadn't driven since the crash but knew she had to. Before she knew what she was doing, she had found herself on her familiar commute.

'Why don't you wait until I can come with you?' Ben had said.

'I need to do it on my own. I can't have you drive me everywhere.'

'I'm not saying drive you. I'm just saying be with you.'

'It's something I need to do by myself. I need to get over it.'

'Well, we'll come with you,' he said, meaning him and the

children. 'I'll give them a shout. We'll come right now if you're in the mood.'

'As if I'd take that risk,' she had said, putting on her coat. 'The last time I was behind a wheel I was in a pile-up. I'm better off alone.'

It had been the wrong thing to say. Ben was the most easy-going man she had ever met, but his face had been full of worry for her when she drew away from the house.

She had felt all right until she got on to the motorway. Now, sitting in the school car park calling Harry the janitor, she was sweating and thirsty. After she had found herself on the road to school, she had decided to try to get in to cross-reference Maxwell's name with those on the databases.

'Ah, Mrs H, you work too hard, you do,' said Harry. 'It's Christmas, remember?'

'I know, I know, and once I have this file I'm sure I'll procrastinate the whole holiday. It's just I really need it ... otherwise I wouldn't trouble you to let me in.'

'Ah, you don't trouble me, Mrs H. Anything for you. I'll be along in a jiffy.'

Margaret sat watching ice crystals form on the windscreen. She had been unable to sleep last night, wondering why Maxwell Brown had the telephone number for *her school* in his pocket. She wondered if he was a parent of a child in the school, or if he was on the supply teacher list. She wondered if she had met him before.

Harry arrived within ten minutes. He had a bad leg and his gait favoured one side. Margaret got out of the car to meet him.

'I'm so sorry to call you out on a night like this,' she said, a hand on his upper arm.

'Anything for you, Mrs H. To tell the truth if anyone else'd asked I'd've told them to get to ...' he nodded instead of swearing, 'but seeing as it's you.'

Margaret waited until Harry went inside and switched off the alarm. The lights came on in the lobby and then he held the door open for her.

'I'll be as quick as I can,' said Margaret.

'You take all the time you like. I'm here if you need me.'

Margaret took the stairs to her office and switched on her computer before she shrugged off her coat. She stared at the photograph of Ben and the children on her desk. Ben was at home, wrapping more Christmas presents. *Stop shutting me out,* he had said to her last night. Margaret had not known what to say to him. She was not aware of shutting him out. She felt as if she were falling, into herself, into her own past, as if down a well, and Ben was simply becoming further and further away from where she was. He thought that he was losing her, but that was only because she felt lost.

Margaret opened up the database and searched for pupils named Brown. Out of eight hundred and ninety-five pupils there were thirty-two with the surname Brown. As quickly as she could, Margaret checked each record for a parent called Maxwell, but there were no matches. Finally, she checked the supply list, but there were no male teachers with Brown as a surname. Considering, Margaret also checked pending applicants to the school and the list of visiting specialists, such as drama teachers and speakers. She could find no mention of Maxwell Brown.

'Bugger,' she said, out loud, then turned off her computer as she heard Harry's footsteps at the bottom of the staircase, jangling his keys.

*

When Margaret returned to Loughton, she stayed sitting in the car outside her house. She was dispirited that she had not found any matches for Maxwell on the school computer.

The darkness of the car was a relief. She was glad to be alone. She didn't want to go inside yet. It was such an effort to pretend that she wasn't falling apart. If only she could find some answers, she felt she would begin to recover. What she had found in the box suggested that she had been abducted and molested as a child. She had been sexually assaulted, and that was the reason her parents had encouraged her to forget.

The memories that had been unearthed were dreamlike and defined by fear. She remembered running, out of breath, in a forest of dark trees. She remembered her mother shaking her, to make her speak. She remembered feeling empty and wordless and, beyond that, a potent, unfathomable *ache* inside her that no one could assuage. She remembered crying in bed once the light had gone out, making sure that no one heard her.

Tears wet her face.

Ben knocked on the side window and Margaret was startled. She wiped two hands over her face. He opened the door and got into the front seat.

'Well? How'd you get on?'

'It was good. I made it,' said Margaret, trying not to sniff, putting her hands back on the steering wheel and staring straight ahead, as if she might drive off again.

He didn't reply and after a moment she turned to him. He was looking at her, his brow wrinkled and his right eyebrow raised. Through the living-room window she could see the Christmas tree lights.

'Have you been crying?' he said.

She put a hand over her mouth.

'C'm'ere.'

He pulled her into him. The gear lever was sticking into her side and it hurt because he was pressing her so tightly. She cried hard in his arms, as she had after her mother died. She had met Ben and then lost her mother; grieved and fallen in love at the same time.

'It's OK. You're all right. I'm here,' he was whispering, smoothing her hair and kissing the top of her head.

She broke away from him, gulping, trying to catch her breath. 'The kids, we should . . . The kids . . .'

He pulled her into him again. 'They're fine. It's you I'm worried about.'

'I'm OK,' she said, into the wool of his sweater.

'You're so not.'

When she caught her breath, they sat in silence for a few minutes. She knew she owed him an explanation. The smell of him relaxed her.

'The crash,' she started, haltingly, not sure what she was going to say, 'it's had a big effect on me, but not just . . . driving . . . or . . . dealing with school or . . . It's made me remember things.'

'What things?' He reached across and took her hand.

'I'm sorry I've been so grumpy . . .'

'You have, but you know I love you even when you're grumpy, so . . .'

She tried to smile. 'It's just my head hurts with it all. I'm trying to work it all out. There's memories and there's this . . .'

He turned to her. 'What do you mean, remembering? About your mum? Is that why you wanted that box from your dad's?'

She and Ben had spoken often about her mother in the early

295

days of their relationship. '*I wish you could have met her,*' Margaret had said to him. '*I feel like I know her,*' he had said.

'I don't know,' Margaret said, resting her head against the window. 'Not just her – a lot of things. Things that happened when I was small.'

He squeezed her hand. 'Things you've not told me about?'

'Things I don't even know.' She turned to him. 'That's the thing. And then there's ... you know I told you there was that man who saved me, who was very badly ...'

'Burned, yeah.'

'Well, I don't know what it is, but he saved me and I keep going back to visit him. I found him, and ... he's in a coma and ... I want to know who he is.'

'He's in a coma?'

'Yeah. He had a head injury from the crash. He was hurt himself but he managed to save me. The hospital put him in a coma to try and stop the bleeding. *His life's* in danger now ... and no one visits him. I've been going and sitting with him. I don't know why, but that's what I've been doing. He saved my life and I don't know who he is. Maybe I want to know why he saved me? Why I was worth saving.'

Ben reached over and put a hand on her face and took hold of the back of her head. 'Of course you're worth saving. You are the most important thing in the world to me.'

There were tears in his eyes. She put a hand on his thigh.

'I drove to the school. I was checking the computers. The man ... Maxwell is his name ... he had the school's phone number in his coat pocket. There could be a million reasons for it, but I wanted to check that he wasn't a parent or a supply teacher or ...'

'And was he?'

'No. I can't find him on any of the databases. I mean it's a public number – there's no reason why he wouldn't have the phone number … It's just that it was *my* school's number and he saved *me*. I convinced myself that I must know him … that I had met him before, but now I don't know.'

'What do the doctors say? Is he going to make it?'

She sniffed and shook her head.

'He *saved my life*, when my car was going to … explode. It was dangerous. He didn't just save me. He risked his life. He broke his hand punching through the car window. And now he's in a coma and he …' Margaret let her voice drop to a whisper, 'might die.'

Ben held her. Tears burned her eyes again and she pressed her face into his neck.

'You'll get through this,' Ben said. 'Just give yourself time.'

Margaret nodded into his chest. He was right, but she still didn't know *what it was* that she needed to get through.

24

Big George
Friday 4 October, 1985

They drove through South Yorkshire and Derbyshire before George stopped.

They had left the hotel in York just after eight. Moll had eaten well: porridge and fruit, toast and eggs. George had enjoyed just watching her eat. With her lazy eye and her lips smeared with jam and fruit, she had seemed like a goblin. Now they had been on the road again for over two hours and she had fallen asleep. Her head lolled against the seatbelt, her small soft palms turned upwards, resting on her thighs.

George rolled the window down an inch and smoked a cigarette. It was his first nicotine of the day and he enjoyed the hit, leaning back against the headrest. He turned on the radio, keeping the volume down low. The Beach Boys played and George tapped the beat on the steering wheel. It was Friday and the day felt new and free, the sky a sheer cloudless blue, the roads clear of traffic. It was easy to speed in such conditions, but George made sure that he kept under the speed limit. The Derbyshire hedgerows were full of berries and the fields with cylindrical bales of hay. Moll slept right through the Peak District – they drove past a majestic-sweep of bare mountain on one side and fertile lowland on the other. George might have stopped here. The place felt good – felt as if it could be home – but he was set on Penzance. He wanted to be as far away from Glasgow as he could get before falling off the edge.

He felt hopeful for the first time. He was almost halfway there already. Moll was getting used to him; they were almost friends. A few things worried him, such as the incident in Newcastle when she told the waitress she wasn't a boy, but there had been few real concerns since then and they had attracted less attention than he had expected. He was keeping a low profile, but those people they had met seemed to accept them as father and son. He had expected to feel more hunted. He had stolen one hundred thousand pounds and got away with it and then, two days ago, he had taken his daughter from her school. He was glad that Moll was with him, but he still wondered what it would have been like had Kathleen come away with him too. He had dreamed of the three of them together again – the family he had always wanted. He was with his wee Moll now and that felt precious, but if Kathleen were with them it would have been perfect.

The Beach Boys ended and the national news came on. The hills meant that reception was patchy and the station scratched into and out of frequency as George drove. He finished his cigarette and flicked it out of the window.

A national manhunt is on for the abductor of seven-year-old Molly Henderson, who was taken from the northern town of Thurso in Scotland on 2 October. The man witnessed abducting Molly was tall with dark hair and blue eyes and was wearing a suit. He was driving a dark-coloured vehicle. Molly has long dark hair, often wears an eyepatch and was last seen wearing her school uniform.

The report paused to play the tape of Kathleen begging for her daughter's return. George winced as he listened to it again and reached for another cigarette.

There have been no sightings of Molly since her disappearance and police are urging members of the public to come forward if they have any information.

Despite his hopeful thoughts earlier, the report unnerved George. He exhaled, accidentally letting his foot rest more heavily on the accelerator. He thought about the people they had encountered. There had been the couple by the park who had seen him and Moll fighting before they left Thurso, and then the schoolgirls who had taunted Moll before she rode in his car, but George felt that none of these witnesses would have been able to identify him.

Nevertheless, he was uneasy. He felt exposed and wondered if he and the bairn would do better to hide away somewhere for a few days. The hotel had worked in York but it was too dangerous to keep going out together in public. Moll needed a good rest and a chance to play and George had no idea what state the Penzance cottage would be in when they got there.

There was a girl he knew from Glasgow. They had been close for a while and then she had moved to England. She lived in Hanley in Stoke-on-Trent and had asked George to visit many times. She had told him she loved him, and he knew that he could trust her. George took a deep breath and held it. They were only one hour from Stoke.

He turned the dial on the radio to find some music, then tried to put the worries from his mind as he thought about whether or not to drop in on Bernie.

He was close to finding happiness, and he didn't want to let go of that dream just yet. He turned to the sleeping Moll and smiled to himself, remembering her patient teaching from the night before.

'George McLaughlin, stand up and face the class,' said Sister Agatha, gently slapping the leather strap against her palm.

George's desk legs sounded loudly against the floor as he pushed it away and got to his feet. He felt the familiar sense of the whole class looking at him: their attention a singular blaze, like a bonfire. His cheeks burned and he made fists with both hands. It wasn't the belt that he feared so much as the humiliation. Sister Agatha seemed to want to break his spirit and in that sense she was like his father: it was not about the pain she would inflict but the bad thoughts she would put in his head. Long after the welts had healed George would still feel the sense of worthlessness she had bestowed swelling up inside of him.

George walked to the front of the class and looked down at his fingernails.

'Stand up straight,' said Sister Agatha, whacking the strap across his shoulder blades.

George did as she asked.

'Now, I want you to say the alphabet. You're in primary three, you should know it back to front.'

Breathing heavily, accented, unable to breathe through his nose, George said the alphabet: 'Abcdefghijklmnopqrstuvwxyz.'

The heavy strap flapping impotently at her side, Sister Agatha took a fresh piece of chalk and gave it to George.

'Now, write that on the blackboard.'

George took the chalk into his right hand. The sweat of his palm immediately mixed with the chalk powder so that the stick was pasty and slippery in his hand. He turned towards the blackboard, which had been wiped clean.

'Hurry,' said Sister Agatha. 'This should come naturally to you. This is baby stuff. Anyone in this class could do it with their eyes closed. If we went to the nursery school I could find you children who could do this . . . so go ahead, write the letters. I want the whole alphabet written on the blackboard.'

George turned to her, knowing that he couldn't do it, feeling the fear of failure thick in his throat. He licked his lips to speak.

'You do it,' she whispered to him, the spit stretching between her lips, 'and be clear you'll get one stroke of the belt for each incorrect letter.'

George swallowed and turned to the blackboard. He took the chalk in his right hand and managed to form a shaky *a*, *b* and then *c*. He felt cold and hot at the same time, as if there was a layer of frost on his skin that was burning him. He tried to form the letter *d*, but it looked strange, like a wheelbarrow. He changed the chalk over into his left hand, but Sister Agatha intervened:

'No! You will do it properly.'

George tried again. He made a circle but couldn't close it up and then his downward stroke did not meet the circle. When he looked at it, he wondered if it was back to front.

He tried for an *e* but could only manage a squiggle on the blackboard. The figure of *f* he couldn't recall, but tried all the same, sure that it resembled a bird or a cross in some way. When he had finished, he turned to Sister Agatha.

'Well, that's three incorrect letters already but we won't stop there, George. Let's proceed. We know you're going to get more than twenty but let's find out for sure.'

George swallowed and moved closer to the board. His right hand felt as if it didn't belong to him. He made marks on the board, knowing that they were wrong but unable to control them, and knowing full well that whatever he did he would be punished for; x, y and z were mere slashes on the board. He turned towards Sister Agatha, his face burning. The class was a sea of faces, and he could hear the hiss of their whispers.

'Well, George,' she said when the class was quiet. 'This is for your own good. We have to jog that memory somehow. I will teach you to write if it kills me. You may be stupid but you can learn the basics, one way or another. You're stubborn and you're not trying.'

Sister Agatha straightened and raised the belt to her shoulder.

'Is this what you wanted, George?' Sister Agatha said, smiling, her plump cheeks puckering like old dough.

'Sure,' said George, smiling at the class and holding out his hands.

Sister Agatha pursed her lips. Her lips had a mean tilt. George knew she was going to hurt him, but he also knew that he could take it. There was, he thought, only one positive in having Brendan McLaughlin as your father: it increased your stamina for pain. George would never be able to say he got used to it, but, yes, after a fashion, he did get used to it.

Sister Agatha began her lashes and George counted, blinking each time but never pulling his hands away.

The mountain roads had tight bends and blind summits, but George cornered each bend at sixty miles an hour, his mood dark despite the scenery. When they left Derbyshire, George continued to drive at full pelt through Staffordshire and the West Midlands.

When they reached the Black Country, George saw blue lights behind him. He checked his speed. He had let his concentration drift and was just over the limit. He slowed down, hoping that the police car would pass them, but instead it tailed them and then sounded the siren. As soon as the siren started, Moll woke up.

'What is it?' she said, rubbing her eyes at the noise. 'What's the matter?'

'Nothing's the matter.'

'Is it the police?' she said, turning round in her seat, kneeling and peeping behind the headrest.

'Sit down,' said George, sharply. 'Put your seatbelt back on right now.'

Her face darkened at his command but she did as he asked. George flicked his cigarette out of the window. The police car tucked in behind them, lights flashing, urging him to pull over. He slowed down, eyes to the rear-view mirror as he watched the dark-suited men inside the police car. George had never been good with authority. Whatever the reason they wanted to stop him – speeding, child abduction or the abnormality of his licence plates – he knew that it could not go well. He indicated to pull up at the next lay-by. He watched the police car do the same. He drew to a stop then waited as they both got out of the car to approach him. He kept his eyes on the rear-view mirror as he checked that Moll's seatbelt was tightly fastened.

She began to speak but he shushed her. 'Hold on to your hat, little lady,' he said as he put the car into first gear and set both hands on the steering wheel. One policeman bent to examine the licence plates as the second walked around to the driver's side.

George pulled out so fast that dirt spun from the wheels. He took his foot off the clutch and floored the accelerator so hard that Moll squealed beside him. He watched in the mirror as the police at first started, then ran back to their vehicle. There was a car in front of him on the narrow mountain road, but after he tailgated it for a few moments it pulled over and allowed George to overtake. The police car was over two hundred yards back and then got caught behind the same car, as George sped right through Castleton, startling a woman with shopping who was about to cross the road.

The peak of Mam Tor, a sloping breast of a mountain, disappeared from view as George continued driving south. The Allegro was an old car and wouldn't go much over sixty, but the tight roads and George's skill meant that he was able to keep ahead of the police car. He knew that he didn't have long to lose them. It was not merely a question of driving faster – he knew that they would be radioing ahead for assistance and the only thing saving him was the clear country roads.

'Slow down,' Moll whined, her legs straight out in front of her and her hands clinging to the edge of the seat.

'We need to drive fast now,' he said, accelerating on the bends to carry them round. There were signs for deer and cattle, but George did not slow down. They were far enough ahead that the siren was faint. His hands sweated on the wheel. At his side, Moll began to whimper. He tried to comfort her, a hand on her knee, but swerved and so returned to concentrating on driving. His eyes scanned the road ahead. It was still bright daylight and they needed to hide and then get rid of the car.

The road was straight and downhill, and the Allegro managed over seventy miles an hour. It was a stretch of road famous for the British Cycle Race, with the hills of the Roaches shimmering green in the distance. Ahead was the town of Leek. George had never been there, but he knew from the map that it was a market town and would be cramped and busy, and he was sure to get caught in traffic or worse. There might even be police in the town waiting for him.

He glanced in the mirror and saw the flashing lights on the top of the last hill. About a mile away, George could see a tractor trailing a wagon. There was no other option.

'Hang on tight,' he said, as much to himself as to Moll.

There was an opening in the field at the bottom of the hill and George cut off the road on to the Staffordshire Moorlands. There had been little rain in the autumn and the land was dry so there was sufficient traction in the wheels to take them forward. George cut right across the field, behind a barn and towards the tree-lined river. Moll squealed as the car jumped up and down on the rough grass. George drove in second and third gear, feeling sweat break at his hairline.

The moorland was uneven and he put the car into first gear to climb a small ridge. The car's undercarriage got stuck on the mud and grass, and George swore, reversed then tried again, this time making it over. On the other side, he drove down the hill slowly, breathing through his teeth, aware that they would no longer be visible from the road. Moll was pitched forward, both hands on the dashboard and her eyes screwed shut.

He drove alongside the River Churnet until he found a spot hidden by tall ash trees that cast the bank into shadow.

George parked the car and looked around. There was no sign of anyone. He rolled down the window and heard the thin whine of the siren above the sound of the river.

'Why did you do that? What . . .?'

'Whssht,' said George, a finger on his lips and his left hand on Moll's head. 'You gotta be very quiet, angel, just a moment longer.'

Moll wiped her cheeks and turned to look in the direction of George's gaze. The whine of the siren grew louder and George sat holding the key in the ignition. The police car slowed and turned off its siren, and George reached out to take Moll's hand. She squeezed it and he squeezed back, coursing his thumb across her soft skin. It was close and he knew it. If the police car had seen them branch off, they might not be able to get away. George turned to peer out of the window. The police car kept on driving on the A53 into Leek.

George put both hands on the steering wheel and exhaled.

'Are you OK, pet?' he said, wiping sweat from his forehead with the back of his hand.

'I don't like it when you drive that fast.'

'Well, you're in charge. I'm not going to drive that fast again. Matter of fact, I think we need to leave the car here.'

'What do you mean?'

George got out of the car, went round and opened Moll's door. He helped her out and then lifted her right up so that she was sitting on the roof of the car, looking him straight in the face. She was smiling again, all blue eyes and eyelashes and gapped teeth.

'How was the first part of our adventure?'

'I don't like fast driving,' she said, frowning.

He tickled her and she squealed and wriggled. 'I told you, I'm done with driving just now. We're going to leave the car and I need to figure out what to do. We maybe need to catch a bus. You remember your name, Batman?'

'Robin.'

'That's right. I want you just to hold my hand and let me do the talking. We're going to walk into town and we'll catch the bus and then I'll get us another nice place to sleep and a new car to drive, OK?'

Moll nodded. 'And when will we start to go home?'

George lifted her down quickly, to avoid her eyes. 'We'll

go home after we've finished our adventure ... after we've got where we're going. Penzance.'

'Where's that?'

'It's a bit further south, not far now.'

She seemed satisfied with that. George took her satchel out of the back seat and his bag of money out of the boot and tucked his change of clothes and Moll's new clothes inside, along with his knife and a torch. He took off his jacket and draped it over the hold-all. Moll was crouched in the grass picking daisies and dandelions, feet apart and knees together, sucking her lip in concentration. George checked inside the car, and took out his cigarettes.

'Button, get over here,' he said suddenly.

She looked up at him, coy; chin over her shoulder.

'Come and sit over here.'

She went to him and presented him with the posy, standing on her tiptoes and holding the flowers up to him.

'They're gorgeous,' he said, smiling and getting down on one knee to take them. 'No one's ever given me flowers before. Really.'

She was pleased, hands clasped behind her back and swinging side to side. George put the flowers into his shirt pocket.

'How does that look?'

'Good.'

He lifted her up to the first low, thick branch of the ash tree. 'I want you to sit tight there and don't move.'

'Where are you going?' she said, her face suddenly shot with concern.

'I'm going nowhere, but our car's going for a swim and I want you safe and out of the way.'

She giggled, one hand over her mouth. 'Cars don't swim.'

'Well, this one does.'

He had done it several times before – tipped cars into the River Clyde to get rid of evidence. But he was a stranger to this place and he felt alien in the countryside. The quiet and the sweet smell of dung unnerved him. He hoped that the river was deep enough. The Clyde was deeper and darker than all hell. It had been a dry week, but he remembered that there had been rain in the north the week before.

George took a screwdriver from the boot and removed the number plates front and back and then tossed them into the river upstream. He rolled down each of the windows, then put the car into neutral, took off the handbrake and pushed it to the edge. He glanced at Moll for a second, sitting on the branch wide-eyed like an owl. He pushed with all his strength and stood back as the car tipped over the edge and splashed into the river.

Moll wriggled off her branch and shimmied down the tree then ran to the bank beside him. He was standing with his hands on his hips, but she reached for his hand, and they stood side by side watching as the body of the car disappeared from view and sank further, until only the top of the roof could be seen.

'Damn it,' said George, letting go of her hand for a second to shake a cigarette from his pack and light it. When his cigarette was lit, he took her hand again.

'Why are you saying "damn it"?'

'Because I want it to sink.'

'It has.'

'Not all the way. I want it to sink right down.'

The river emitted a gulping sound, there was a creak of metal and the car sank further. George exhaled. It was enough. If the water stayed at that level, the car could go weeks or longer without being discovered, but if the river level dropped, even by a few inches, the car would be obvious.

'Come on, button,' he said.

He put her satchel back on her shoulders, picked up the holdall, took her hand and then together they walked towards the town. The grass was soft and Moll jumped from one mound to the other, the pencils rattling inside her satchel. As soon as they hit the road, George slowed his pace. There would be police here. He was sure that the police who had chased him had not seen his face, but he still did not know why they had asked him to pull over. They might have been looking for him, and knew the make of car. He needed to get to Stoke-on-Trent and see if Bernie would take them in.

'I'm hungry,' said Moll.

'I know, precious,' he said, 'but I need to sort something out. Hold on if you can and then I'll get you the best dinner ever.'

She sighed and he squeezed her hand.

'What's your favourite thing for tea?'

'Macaroni cheese.'

'Good choice.'

'Is that your favourite too?'

'Well, it's up there in my top five.'

'What's your number one?'

'Stovies.'

'They're in my top five,' she said, and he smiled, realising that she was trying to please him.

He was doing his best to stay calm and cheerful for her, but his stomach was now tight with tension. He stuck out and he knew it. He needed to steal a car and get somewhere safe, where they had food and she could rest. Without the car, they were a long way from Penzance and the danger of being recognised was high.

The bus station in Leek was on Ashbourne Road and George found it quickly. A woman stopped him to ask the time and two other men wished him a good afternoon. He hated small towns. It reminded him of how he had felt when he arrived in Thurso: tall and conspicuous. He smiled and rushed his words to try to disguise his accent. He kept Moll close to him as he looked at the timetables. The numbers made sense, but the names of the towns were just letters swarming at him. He felt a pain in his throat, remembering the failure he had felt as a child.

George crouched down beside her. 'I don't know if you can do this,' he said to her, 'but if I lift you up, can you read the names of the towns to me? I have a friend lives near here. I'll lift you up and you tell me if you see a timetable for a bus going to Hanley. Can you do that?'

She nodded gravely and held out her arms to be lifted. He held her into his hip, pointing at the town names listed at the top of the timetables.

'Here,' she said, pointing after a few moments.

'Are you sure?' said George, shifting her weight so that he could peer at the word.

'Yes . . . Ashbourne, Buxton and then Hanley.'

He looked at the bus number on the timetable Moll had indicated.

'X18,' he said, under his breath. 'Today's Friday. Can you find the right day on the timetable?'

Moll leaned forward, sucking in her lower lip and letting both palms rest on the noticeboard. 'Maybe this one,' she said, looking worried and unsure. 'It says Monday and Friday.'

He let her down then took her hand.

'OK, good job. Now we need to find a phone box.'

There was one at the other end of the station and George pulled Moll inside. He felt safer inside the call box. It smelled damp like a cellar. He reached into his pocket and took out his change and placed all the silver on the metal tray inside the box. There had been a phone book but now only the outer pages remained. George knew that he would be unable to read a phone book anyway, and he wasn't sure if Moll could either. She leaned against the booth and looked up at him as he picked up the telephone and dialled. He wanted a cigarette very badly.

George had kept in touch with Bernadette after she moved south and they still got together for a cuddle when she went back to Glasgow to see her family. They had even talked about Moll once or twice. The first time he had slept with Bernie, she had thought the name tattooed above his heart had been a lover, and he had told her the story.

It had been nearly six months since George had seen her in Glasgow. If Bernie was home, he could trust her and she would help him out.

'Directory Enquiries,' said a woman's voice.

George cleared his throat. 'Hello, I wonder if you have a number for Bernadette Shaw in Hanley, Stoke-on-Trent.'

'I have two listings for a B. Shaw in Hanley. One is B. P. Shaw on Rawlins Street and another B. Shaw on Cavendish Street.'

'Rawlins Street,' George exclaimed, remembering. His inability to read and write had honed his memory.

'Very well, the number is—'

'Hold on a minute ... Moll, pen and paper, please?'

Moll crouched on the floor of the booth as she took out her exercise book and selected a pencil from a tin box that bore an image of Scooby Doo.

George wrote the number on the back of Moll's exercise book. He fed a fifty-pence piece into the slot and dialled. He checked his watch: just after four o'clock. He expected Bernadette to be at work. He stared through a small pane of glass in the phone box, thinking that he could get the wean some food and they could wait and call later when she returned.

After the fifth ring, to George's surprise, Bernadette answered. He recognised her voice.

'Bernie? It's George ... How are you?'

Sweating with anxiety in the cramped call box with Moll, George still flashed his smile, as if Bernadette was before him.

'Georgie!' she said. 'This is a surprise. I thought you were allergic to phones?'

'I am indeed, but the thought of hearing your dulcet tones again drove me to it.'

She laughed.

'How are you, beautiful?'

'I'm very well,' she said and George could tell from her tone that she was also smiling. 'I'm kind of rushing at the moment. I'm about to go away for a week's holiday and you know what I'm like. So bloody disorganised. I can't find my passport.'

'You're leaving the country?' George put a hand against the phone box and leaned against it. He was the unluckiest person he knew.

'I am indeed. I'm going *abroad* with a girlfriend.'

'Abroad? Get you! And here was I coming to visit you.' George leaned his forehead against the glass.

'Where are you?'

'I'm eh, I'm passing through ... in Leek just now, would you believe – bloody Leek – and I thought to myself, I can't pass Stoke-on-Trent and not say hello to wee Bernie.'

'God, your timing's always off. I need to go in half an hour ... unless I really have lost my passport and then I suppose I can't go anywhere.'

Pips began to sound and George hurriedly fed more coins into the slot.

'And here was me thinking you'd give me a bed for the night, but you're right, I should've warned you.'

'You're welcome to stay if you need a place …'

'Is it a trouble, Bern'? How would I …?'

'I can leave a key under the mat for you. If the key's not there, it means I'm still home because I couldn't find my passport.'

'You're a sweetheart, Bernie, do you know that?'

'And you're the bane of my life. How long will you stay? Will you be here when I get back? I'm back on the eleventh …'

'How could I not wait for you, gorgeous?'

'Where are you off to anyway?'

'I'm headed to London, but I can hang about a few days if it means seeing your pretty face again.'

'I'll look forward to it.'

The bus to Hanley was every half-hour, and George bought a newspaper for himself to hide behind, and crisps and juice for the bairn.

The bus came just as she had opened her crisps. They waited in line and then George lifted her up on board. He took her almost to the back of the bus, setting the holdall on the floor at her feet and helping her into the window seat.

'Why are we going to Hanley?' she said as the bus pulled away.

'Hush,' he said, leaning down towards her. The bus was almost full, mostly elderly people, but they had not been in such an enclosed public space since he left Scotland. 'We're going to stay at a friend of mine's house. I'll tell you all about it when we get there.'

He helped Moll open her can of juice. The crack and fizz

sounded and the woman in front turned around at the noise. She had grey hair twisted into a neat knot at the nape of her neck, and small pink lips. George smiled at her broadly, and she returned the smile and then turned back.

'Drink it carefully and don't spill it,' said George as he passed it to Moll, who took it into two hands as the bus left the station. He felt a flicker of nerves after the woman's attention, so he risked saying, 'There's a good boy.'

Moll turned to him and George held his breath, but she only said, 'Robin,' and smiled. He tapped the skip of her cap.

Trying to relax, he opened his newspaper. There was a photograph of Rock Hudson. George had heard on the news that he had died. There was also a picture of rioters in London. He looked at the photographs and turned the pages, working his way slowly to the back where he would be able to read the cartoons. He took his time, his eyes scanning the pages, as if he were able to read. He had practised the art. Suddenly he stopped and folded the paper over, drawing it closer to him. There, on page seven, near the fold, was the picture of Moll. Her photo was at the top of the article: the same school picture that had been circulated before.

George felt his throat dry. The bus was full. He looked at Moll. The squint had been mentioned on the radio reports and now, he thought, even in her boy's clothes, it was obvious who she was.

He needed a cigarette, but daren't light up on the bus for fear of irritating someone and drawing further attention to himself. He wanted to ask Moll what the article said, but he didn't want to upset her.

He sat hunched on the seat, sweat in his armpits, glancing up and down the bus to see if anyone was watching him.

*

316

When they pulled into Hanley, George helped Moll out of her seat before the bus had come to a stop. He prodded her gently forward, one hand on the back of her T-shirt to stop her from falling as the bus rolled into its stop. They were first in line to exit. The holdall was heavy and George could feel his hands sweating. There was no air and he just wanted off the bus.

The doors opened, and Moll skipped down the steps. George was just about to follow her when he felt a man's hand on his arm.

George turned, his smile slippery, to see an old man with watery blue irises looking up at him. George swallowed, looking down at the man, whose lips twisted downwards. George tightened his fist in panic.

'You forgot the lad's hat,' the old man said, handing him Moll's baseball cap.

George buckled with relief. 'Thank you,' he whispered, got off the bus, took Moll by the hand and strode out of the station.

Bernadette lived in a tiny one-bedroom terraced house that had been painted pale yellow. There was a thick brush doormat on the step and underneath George found a key. He unlocked the door for Moll and followed her inside.

George lit a cigarette, feeling the relief of the nicotine and the safe empty house all at once. Bernadette had left a note for him on the kitchen table. He handed it to Moll as he settled into a kitchen chair. He was exhausted.

'What does that say, button?'

Moll stood with her feet together and her back straight, holding the piece of paper in two hands, frowning. '*Enjoy Hanley, Georgie. Help yourself to anything. You better be here when I come back, or I'll come up to Shet . . . Shettle—*'

'Shettleston,' George guessed.

'Shettleston and kick your . . .' Moll placed the paper on the table with her eyes wide and her lips pursed. 'A bad word.'

George blew a smoke ring at her, and she poked a finger through to break the circle.

25

Kathleen Henderson
Tuesday 8 October, 1985

She did it several times a day, usually when John was out of the house, but once again, Kathleen entered Moll's bedroom.

She sat down on the bed and smoothed the cover. It was a cream bedspread decorated with forget-me-nots. Moll had always liked it, and all of the blue items in the room – the lampshade and the rug and the curtains – had been chosen to coordinate with it.

It was three in the afternoon and Kathleen was fully dressed, yet she lay down on the bed and pulled the cover over her. She held the duvet over her face and inhaled the smell. She had changed the sheets a week before Moll was taken, yet still, if Kathleen concentrated very hard, she could *smell her*. It brought her momentary comfort and the deepest pain.

Alone in the big house, curled up in Moll's bed, Kathleen wept. She cried, pressing the duvet into her face to suppress the noise, and wetting it with her tears and her spit. She pulled it into her, tugging it into her stomach and breasts.

When her tears subsided, she was exhausted. She lay on her side, watching the bedside Minnie Mouse alarm clock. The hands of the clock were Minnie's gloved arms. Moll had liked it because the arms were glow-in-the-dark. She had learned to tell the time early – when she was five or six – and now she liked to test herself if she woke up and it was still dark.

'*I can still tell the time – even though I can't see the numbers*, Mum,' she had announced proudly to Kathleen.

Each second was measured by the twitch and turn of the ribbon bow on Minnie Mouse's head. Kathleen sat up and swung her legs out of bed. Hot tears flashed over her face. Her eyes still had tears even though she had exhausted herself with crying.

It was *the time* that was killing her, slowly. Every second without Moll was agony. It was like being burned from the feet up, like Joan of Arc.

Kathleen got to her feet and went to the jewellery box on the dressing table. She opened it and a ballerina began to twirl, haltingly, dancing mechanically to a high-pitched plucked melody. Kathleen raked among the jewels: her old strings of sixties beads, plastic children's rings from Christmas crackers and old ladies' clip-on earrings.

Kathleen chose one of the rings and slipped it on to her finger. It was made of cheap metal, painted yellow gold and set with a piece of shiny plastic, but it was meant to look like a diamond ring. Kathleen wiggled the ring on her finger. It was too small to pass her knuckle. She sat down on the low stool before the dressing table and looked down at the ring finger of her left hand, now bearing two diamond rings.

'I *do* love you,' John said, whispering across the table at her.

They were in a posh restaurant in the city centre of Glasgow and Kathleen felt as stiff as the table linen. Her shoulders had been aching since she arrived, just from the effort of sitting up straight.

Moll was just a month old, and Kathleen was anxious to get back home to her.

She had started going out with John, at her parents' urging, before she had begun to show. The last time they had been out for dinner, Kathleen had been eight months pregnant and she had felt uncomfortable, constantly excusing herself because of heartburn or the need to pee. The baby had been kicking and she had just wanted to go home, to the sofa.

John's first wife had been young and in good health, but had died tragically after a fall. She had slipped on the ice and banged her head, but refused to go to the hospital and had died in her sleep at his side. He had been friends with Kathleen's parents for some time, and her mother said that – before he was introduced to her – he had been resigned to spending the rest of his life alone.

He was bright and funny and kind. Kathleen liked John and she knew that he loved her, but she was not sure she could ever feel anything more than that. Her heart still belonged to George; nevertheless, she had made her mind up early on that her daughter needed a father more than she needed a lover.

It was just two weeks since she and George had registered Moll's birth and he had proposed to her in Glasgow Green. Now Kathleen sat smiling at John, feeling a husk of herself but trying to remember what was important.

I do love you.

Kathleen took his hand and squeezed it tightly because she did not feel able to say that she loved him too. She didn't even know if she was capable of loving anyone other than George McLaughlin.

They had finished their main courses and the waiter cleared

their table as John held her hand. They asked for the menu for dessert and coffee and when it came John put it to one side, then reached into his jacket pocket. He said nothing, but opened the ring box and placed it beside the candle on the table.

Kathleen looked straight at the ring, feeling sick. It was not dissimilar to the ring which George had chosen for her: a solitaire diamond, set in gold. John's ring was larger, and, Kathleen imagined, significantly more expensive. She would have been with George, ring or no ring, house or no house, but things with John had to be navigated more formally. Her parents approved and she had Moll to consider.

They spoke of Moll often. John talked about the good schools up north and *how safe* Thurso was, and close to the sea, so they could take Moll to the beach when the weather was fine.

John smoothed the hair over his head. At thirty-four years old he was thinning and greying already, yet his cheeks, especially above the line of his stubble, seemed young as a boy's, and flushed when he drank or was overcome with emotion.

They flushed now, as he clasped his hands and looked at the ring on the table.

'You would do me a great honour,' he said, without meeting her eye. Kathleen swallowed, but finally he met her gaze. 'I can sense that you have been through a lot, and I know that is something you may never wish to discuss with me ... but I love you and I will love Moll and I think that we can be happy together.'

He blinked, waiting for her response.

Kathleen inhaled.

'I know you don't feel as strongly as I do, but sometimes that can come with time.'

'I will marry you,' said Kathleen, snapping the ring box shut, taking it and clasping it in her palm. 'There's a lot that we need to work out, but . . . I would love to marry you.'

She had managed this. It was as close to *I love you* as she could get. Her soul was a wasteland. Apart from Moll and her strong need to care for her, Kathleen was no longer sure of anything.

Kathleen slid the cheap metal ring from her finger and closed Moll's jewellery box. She remembered John from those days: hesitant, insecure, asking for her love. She had been wrong about him. It had taken time. Moll had been a toddler, at least two or three, before it hit her, but she and John had finally fallen passionately in love.

She had always loved his smell and even now, in these dark days, she felt comforted when he was close.

They had come to Thurso before Moll's first birthday and John had the house ready for them. It was a small town at the very top of the country and Kathleen was lonely initially. She missed Glasgow and all her friends and family, but she made new friends at the children's playgroup and was soon drawn into a community of young families.

These were the early walls that she built for herself. She moved away and started a new life and tried her best not to think of George.

Her tears spent, Kathleen looked at her face in the mirror. Moll had her shape of face and she had her temper and strength, but the child's blue eyes had always been George's. Moll's squint had become more noticeable when she was due to go to nursery. When she was a baby, they had hoped it would correct itself. Fighting with her daughter over the need to wear her eyepatch, Kathleen had sometimes wistfully wondered if one of Moll's eyes was looking at her and the other was looking behind in search of her father.

It had upset John, but Kathleen had needed to tell her the truth about her father.

'We loved each other very much, but not as much as we loved you.'

'But did my real daddy not want to visit me, even?' Kathleen still remembered the loud whisper and Moll raising her head off the pillow.

'He knew John was your daddy now, and he was happy for you. He knew we'd all be happy here and he gave us his blessing.'

She had reached the point where even she believed it. It had been another version of herself who had loved George, and she would not now be able. She could only love John now, and was grateful for him.

Kathleen smoothed the hair back from her face and stared at her reflection in the mirror. Her daughter had been her meaning for so long, and now that Moll was gone she was not sure where her meaning lay. One day since the newspaper article naming George McLaughlin, and Kathleen felt pummelled by her own memories.

It was too much. No one should have to endure it. Kathleen opened the bedroom window to let in the air then went downstairs to call Inspector Black, in case there was some news.

26

Big George
Friday 4– Wednesday 9 October, 1985

George opened up the cupboards in Bernadette's kitchen. There was no bread or cereal, but he saw rice and pasta, tomato sauce, brown sauce, vinegar and a bottle of sherry. George was not the best of cooks, so he focused his attention on the tinned goods: chopped tomatoes and several cans of beans, plus tinned pork and meatballs and a couple of tinned steak and kidney pies. There was tea and coffee and an opened packet of dark chocolate digestive biscuits, and George ate one and gave one to the bairn as he considered.

In the fridge he found some eggs and three onions.

He knew there were the makings of a good meal in the house, but he didn't have the foggiest idea how that would come together.

He turned on the radio that sat on a shelf by the window, poured himself a mugful of sherry and began to cook to Otis Redding singing 'I've Been Loving You Too Long'.

'Will you set the table?' he said to her.

'I don't know where things are.'

'Neither do I,' he said as he lit the gas and raked in the cutlery drawer for a tin opener.

He gave her sliced pork with beans and he ate a steak and kidney pie. When they finished, George found a packet of Angel Delight and Moll helped him follow the instructions so that he could make her pudding.

'Why are we in Bernie's house?' she asked, putting a dessert-spoon of chocolate Angel Delight into her mouth.

George poured himself a little more sherry as he considered how to answer her.

'Well, Bernie's a good friend, and it's a nice wee place to have a holiday. Also I need to spend some time looking for a new car for us.'

'What kind of car are you going to buy?'

He was going to steal it, not buy it. 'What kind would you like?'

'A pale blue one.'

'Well, I'll see what I can do.'

They were both tired when the meal was over. He turned on the television and they sat side by side in separate armchairs, watching a western. There was a telephone on the table beside Moll's chair and halfway through the film she turned, kneeling on the chair, and picked up the receiver.

'What are you doing?' he asked, frowning.

'I'm going to call my mummy and daddy.'

'You can't,' George said, checking the sternness in his voice. He couldn't have her making phone calls, but at the same time he knew how wilful she was and he didn't want to cause another argument.

'I think the phone's broken,' he tried.

She put the phone to her ear and looked over her shoulder

at him, round-eyed. 'There's a dialling tone. When you hear the dialling tone that means it's working.'

George clasped his palms. His fingertips were sweaty and the gunfire on the television put him on edge. He got up and turned the volume down.

'Well, I don't know the number,' George said, biting the inside of his lip.

'It's OK, I know it. It's 94712 . . .'

She turned her attention back to the phone and leaned over the arm of the chair to dial. George took a step towards her, ready to take the phone from her and risk her tears and anger, but then he saw what she was doing and stopped.

Her tongue protruding between her lips, her small forefinger hooked and pulled on the dial, 9-4-7-1-2.

He exhaled through his teeth and ran a hand through his hair. She didn't know the area code.

She turned to him, frowning. 'It's not working.'

'That's not possible,' said George, taking the phone from her. There was a recording of a posh lady's voice saying, *you have dialled an incorrect number*.

'Try it again,' said George, handing the phone back to her. 'Maybe you accidentally dialled the wrong number.'

Moll tried again, to no success. Her face crumpled with dismay.

'Hey, button,' said George, lifting her up and setting her on his lap. 'We'll try again another time. Maybe the phone's just having a bad day. Don't worry.'

She rested her head against his chest. 'I wanted to tell my mummy about Bernie's house.'

'You will tell her. You can tell her all about it once we get to where we're going.'

By the time the film finished, she had fallen asleep, squashed beside him on the armchair. It was eight o'clock. He carried her upstairs and put her to bed in Bernadette's double bed. He pulled off her trainers and set them at the side of the bed and then drew the pink frilly curtains.

Upstairs there was only the small bedroom and the bathroom. The ceilings were low, and George had to hunch up. He ran a bath and peered at his reflection in the tiny bathroom mirror, before it steamed up and his face disappeared.

'What the hell are you gonna do now, Georgie?' he asked himself.

George was asleep on the couch in Bernadette's living room. He was lying on his back with his feet raised on the arm of the chair. When Moll leaned over and lifted one of his eyelids he was startled awake.

He looked around the room, confused. The living room was dark but it was cast in a blue light from the television, which showed a static picture of a young girl at a blackboard with a clown. A high-pitched noise pierced the room, signalling the end of TV programming.

'What is it, button?' he asked, focusing on Moll's face and glancing at his watch. It was just after three in the morning.

'I woke up. I don't like it up there. Can I sleep down here with you?'

'Em . . .' George ran a hand over his face, still dazed with sleep.

She didn't wait for him to reply, but instead curled up on the couch beside him. He was too tired to argue, so he shifted on to his side and put his arm around her.

'You don't have a cover or anything,' she said, in a deafening whisper.

'Are you cold?' he mumbled, yawning.

'Not any more,' she said, curling into a ball. 'Night night.'

In the morning, George made tea and drank it peering out of the net curtains on to the street. It was a grey day, but he could see that the sun was trying to shine through the clouds. He had big plans for today. He wanted to go out and scout the area for a car to steal, and buy them some food for the next few days. He had decided that if they lay low for a while, then things might calm down, although he wanted to be gone before Bernie got back. He could trust her but he didn't know what he would say to her about the wean.

They were eating boiled eggs for breakfast.

'My mummy makes me toast soldiers so I can dip them,' she said, her brows gathered.

'Well, I'm going to go out and get some shopping, so I'll be sure to pick up some bread and then you can get toast soldiers tomorrow. You can stay here and watch the fort.'

'No!' she exclaimed suddenly, throwing down her spoon and jumping out of the chair. 'I don't want to be by myself.'

'I'll only be gone an hour or so. You can watch telly.'

'No.' Her lip curled, and George took an intake of breath, knowing that tears were soon to follow.

'OK, OK, you win.' He pushed his plate away. 'C'm'ere.'

He pulled her into the space between his legs, and brushed what hair she had left off her face.

'If I take you with me, you must remember to be very quiet and not talk to anyone.'

She nodded slowly.

'Tell you what ... I bet Bernie has some scissors. We could try and sort your hair and that would be a start.'

He set newspapers on the floor and a stool on top of them and got her to sit on it. Bernie had a mixing bowl in the cupboard and George set it over her head.

'What are you doing?'

'I want to make sure I cut it straight this time . . . You need to sit still now. Hear me?'

She nodded.

He tutted loudly. 'Sit still means sit still. You can speak instead of nodding your head.'

'OK.'

When he was finished, she looked a lot better. There was a mirror on the kitchen wall and George held her up to see.

She said nothing, pulling at the hairs on her fringe.

It was a twenty-minute walk from Bernie's flat into town. George was wearing a T-shirt and a sweatshirt and Moll had her baseball cap on. They walked hand in hand through the terraced streets. It was Saturday morning and the streets were busier as they approached the shops, but George felt more confident than he had when they had taken the bus. He was not wearing his suit, and he had shaved his stubble last night. He had considered growing a beard, but one of the radio reports had described the abductor as *scruffy*. It had offended George. Moll, with her hair cut, was a more convincing boy.

'I'm hungry,' she said, lagging behind. The weight of her on his hand was slowing him down.

'Have you got hollow legs?'

'No.'

'Well, you just had breakfast.'

'Only two eggs and no soldiers.'

He glanced at his watch. It was nearly eleven o'clock. He felt her hand tug away from him. He turned and she was crouched on the street, her head in her hands.

'We need to keep going, Moll,' he whispered to her.

'When are we going to get to the shop? I don't want to walk any more.'

He regretted telling her about the shop. It was not his top priority.

He had thought about going to a parking lot to find a suitable car to steal, but there were none nearby. He would have time in a parking lot to work on the locks. He turned round and looked down at her. She was rubbing her lazy eye, and looking up at him with her good eye, now standing with her feet turned in and her stomach thrust forward. She was too big to carry, and yet he knew he wasn't going to get very far unless he offered.

'Tell you what, you want a piggyback?'

Moll blinked and then smiled. He turned round and took her arms around his neck, tilted forward and caught her feet.

'You'll need to hold on tight.'

She curled her long legs around his waist as they walked down Eaton Street. There was a park and George turned on to Baskerville Street, noticing that there was a line of parked cars opposite the red-brick terraced houses. He walked with the park on his left side, peering into cars to see if they were unlocked. He would have tried a few doors just in case, but he was sure that she would comment.

He decided that it would be best to find a suitable vehicle and then come back at night, when she was asleep.

Her lithe limbs were tight around his neck and waist and he almost didn't feel the weight of her. After fifty yards or so he felt her bury her face in his neck.

'You smell nice,' she said, so close to his ear that it tickled.

'I find that hard to believe, but thank you anyway.'

'You smell like crisps.'

George smiled and put a hand on her wrist at his collarbone. Just then, ten feet from him, he saw a gift from God.

Until that moment, he thought every ounce of religion had been beaten out of him. His father had been a staunch Catholic and yet George had never known a more sinful man. The nuns had been his religious instructors, yet all they had really taught him was pain and humiliation. George had not considered it carefully – he had given up God like some people give up cigarettes – but he supposed he was an *atheist*.

He was an atheist until he saw the gift from God before him.

Parked opposite the next house in the terrace was an eight-year-old Volkswagen caravanette in powder blue, with a *For Sale: £300 or nearest offer* sign inked on to cardboard and taped to the inside of the windscreen.

George tapped on Moll's arm before lowering her to the ground.

'What is it?' she asked, peering up at him, her lips pulled back, exposing the gum where her front teeth had been.

George wiped his mouth with his hand, unbelieving, as if it were a mirage in the desert. He almost crossed himself, and then, as he took her hand and crossed the road to the house in question, he *did* cross himself. A sign on the gate that said *Beware of the Dog*.

'Remember you're Robin and don't speak unless you're spoken to,' he said, finger pointing at her, then lifting up the skip of her cap until she nodded assent. He opened the garden gate and walked up the path.

As soon as he pressed the buzzer, he heard the sound of a dog barking. George pulled Moll behind him.

He prepared his best smile.

When the door opened, an ungroomed standard poodle leaped on to the doorstep and licked Moll in the face and then knocked her off her feet.

'Beware of the dog indeed,' said George, helping Moll up and thrusting a hand at the small, corpulent man in shorts and T-shirt who stood behind the door. 'Affection is the best defence, so it seems.'

'*Dudley*,' the man said sharply, and George thought for a second it was an introduction until he realised that he was calling the poodle inside. The house smelled of sausages and George guessed that he had interrupted Saturday brunch.

'Is it about the van?' said the man, frowning.

'It is. Does it go?'

'It goes, but I promised it to someone last night. I meant to take the sign off. I'm sorry.'

George turned to look at the van, hands in his pockets.

'You promised it last night and they're still not here?' he said, turning to face the man. 'Maybe they're not that keen?'

'They were keen enough. We've agreed a price.'

'I can match it,' said George, smiling again, wishing that the man was a woman.

Moll stood on her tiptoes and leaned into George, like a sunflower against a fence, and he thought briefly that the action might seem strange for a supposed ten-year-old boy and his father. Certainly George had never leaned against his own father without consequence.

'Well, I'm sure you can, but he said he'd be round midday and I don't like to say no – it was a done deal, after all – fanks all the same.'

The man tried to close the door, but George held out his hand.

'I *really* like the look of it,' he said, persisting with his smile although it was difficult, looking down on the pale hairless-legged man who barely reached George's chin. 'How about you fire it up and let me hear it, just for the hell of it, like? Me and the missus were looking for something similar.' George placed a hand on Moll's shoulder. 'He's one of five and how else are we to get a holiday? If the engine sounds OK, I can throw in an extra twenty or so ...'

The man's face crumpled, as if George had suggested a huge inconvenience, but he picked up a set of keys from the telephone table, slipped on a pair of slippers and followed George out to the VW, the poodle in tow, sniffing at Moll and causing her to cling to George even more.

'It's George, by the way,' he said, through the open van door, as the man tried to start it.

'John,' said the small man, shaking the gearstick.

The camper van sounded throaty, as if there was a small hole in the exhaust, but otherwise started without trouble. George took a look at the engine, which was at the rear of the van, casting an eye over it that Tam Driscoll had bestowed on him after many days of patient teaching. The engine was old and dirty, but George thought not too bad. The van had over eighty thousand miles on the clock.

'You got around in this baby, then?' said George to the man.

'Oh, we've had it for years. Been all over the country in it. Wales mostly we'd go to, but we even took it to France a couple of times.'

'I'll take it,' said George, hands in his pockets and chin up.

The small man ran his fingers through the curly grey hair on the poodle's head. 'She's a beauty, but like I said, I made a deal. The guy'll be here any minute.'

'How much d'you want?' said George, taking out his wallet.

Moll let go of George's hand and, with some effort, opened the back door of the van, exposing the small camper kitchen with its cooker and tiny sink. 'It smells like cabbage,' she said, turning to them both with her head cocked to one side.

George peered inside. It was perfect. Moll was opening and shutting the cupboards. It was all set up with utensils: plates, knives and forks, even blankets.

He poked his head out and sat down in the doorway, so that he was looking up at John in his sandals and shorts.

'He's right, it does smell a bit of cabbage.'

John leaned down towards Moll, who was squatting at the van door. 'I'm sorry, are you a lad? I thought you were a little girl.'

'Robin!' said Moll, folding her arms.

'*Sensitive*,' said George, whispering sarcastically to John. 'So now you've offended my child, are you prepared to sell me this cabbage-smelling rust bucket with a dodgy exhaust for three twenty?'

'It *does* smell of cabbage,' said Moll, pursing her lips to hold in a smile.

'An astute judge,' said George, offering up one of his best smiles. 'What can I say?'

'Oh, to hell,' said John, pulling the waistband of his shorts over the curve of his abdomen. 'Never know, he might not come back. Bird in the 'and, I always say . . .'

'Bird in the hand indeed,' said George, placing three hundred and twenty pounds in John's outstretched palm.

They shook hands.

'You 'ad one before? The roof goes up to give you more space and I can show you how to put the table up and put down the bed.'

'Don't you worry, we'll work it out,' said George.

George helped Moll up into the passenger seat, rolled down the window and waved at the man.

'Do you know what this is, Moll?' said George as he lit a cigarette. 'A van.'

He tutted. 'Don't be daft. This isn't just a van. This is a hotel on wheels! Do you like it?'

She smiled up at him, her head cocked to one side. 'You got a pale blue one just like I said.'

'What can I say, button? What the lady wants, the lady gets.'

George felt better once they had the van. The VW had no link to the abduction and the police would not be looking for it. It wasn't stolen. The van would allow them to drive to Penzance, camping when they felt like it and driving when it was safe. When they arrived in Penzance, the van would give them somewhere to live until he got the cottage set up. While he lived in Hanley, there was no need to draw attention to themselves by driving to the supermarket. It was perfect.

He spent the next few days working on the engine and getting supplies for their journey. His hands and arms blackened with car grease, George squinted at the wiring in the old engine. He wished he had listened more carefully to Tam. George had spent his life around cars, but he had no interest in them. He was no more a mechanic than his mother had been.

When the van was as ready as he could make it, George began to stock up on food and necessities to last them for their journey and the time in Penzance before the cottage was ready. He had no idea how long that would be. His mother had inherited the house, but had never had a chance to return. The way she had spoken of it, it might be a ruin by now.

In Hanley, they were only five and a half hours' drive from

Penzance if they took the motorway, but George had decided to stick to the quieter roads. It meant that the drive might take them eight hours. He had checked the calendar and hoped to set off in the afternoon or evening of Wednesday 9 October. Bernie was due home on the Saturday. George had the idea of spending the night halfway down, somewhere between Swindon and Bath, and completing the journey the following day.

Moll was content while they were at the house. Bernie had teddy bears in her bedroom and Moll gave them all names and lined them up on the couch, where she would stand facing them, pointing at the wall and lecturing them as if they were her pupils. The largest teddy was continually given punishment exercises for not listening, and George wondered if this was supposed to be him. She was creative in her play and he admired her for it. When he had been little, he had been lost without his brothers and sister and the other children in the neighbourhood, but Moll was an only child.

On their last evening, they ate a special dinner of fish and chips from the local chip shop. When they were finished, Moll sat licking the vinegar off each of her fingers. George kicked his feet up on the end of the sofa again, but soon became aware that she was staring at him.

He looked over at her. She was kneeling on the floor, her hands on her hips and her head cocked to one side. She had a smile on her face; her good eye was fixed on him while her left her looking out of the window.

'We should practise your reading and writing,' she said to him.

'Not now, button.' He was tired.

'We have to. If you don't practise, you won't get any better.'

'I think I'm a lost cause.'

'You're not a lost cause but you need to do a little bit every day. I'm the best reader in my class and that's because I always do my reading when I first get home. In fact, I read ahead . . .' she frowned and pursed her lips, 'although you're not supposed to do that.'

George sighed deeply. He could have argued with her but he knew that she would win, so he swung his feet back on to the floor and surrendered to her teaching.

She was thrilled with the idea, so much more so than George. She pulled the largest of a nest of tables over and set it in front of him like a desk. She stormed up the stairs and came thundering back down with her satchel.

'Dear God, you're like a fairy elephant,' he said.

She stooped over the wastepaper basket and sharpened two pencils for him and placed them on the desk with her exercise book – carefully folded to a fresh page.

'Hmm,' she said, head in her satchel, her voice muffled by the leather. 'I think we should do *reading* tonight. We only did writing last time.' She fished a book out of her bag, then stood, a finger on her lips, looking upwards. 'I can't remember, but I think I learned to read before I learned to write . . .'

'Well, you're the teacher,' he said. 'I'm in your hands.'

She placed the book on the table in front of him and slid a fringed leather bookmark from the margin. It looked not unlike the belt Sister Agatha had used on him.

'It's called *Charlotte's Web*,' she said, then looking worried, sucking in her lower lip, 'but it's for the group-one readers, so it might be a bit hard for you.'

'I'm sure it will be,' said George, furrowing his forehead, trying to smile.

*

Moll came to his side, and pointed to the first word. 'We can take our time and spell them out,' she said, sounding suddenly older than seven, 'but unfortunately the first word is a hard one.'

George raised his eyebrows at her.

'It's OK.' She was speaking very close to his face, so that he could smell the sweetness of the chips she had eaten and the vinegar from her lips. 'I'll help you.'

Her skin was so flawless and soft, and for a moment he couldn't believe he had made something so beautiful.

She pointed at the first word, and so George made an attempt.

'I don't know,' he said, beginning to feel impatience, no longer so keen to indulge her.

'It's all right,' she said. 'It is a hard word. What is the first letter, do you know?'

George did. It was a W.

'Good, and what is the next letter, do you know?'

'N?'

'Nearly. It's an H. Now, an important thing to learn is that when W comes before an H it makes a special sound, not a *wuh* sound like normal . . .'

George frowned.

'It makes a *whhh* sound, for words like *where* and *what* and . . .' she screwed her face up as she considered, ' . . . *when*. So this,' she said to George, 'is *where*.'

'*Where*,' he repeated, nodding, feeling fatigued already.

'The next word you can manage, I'm pretty sure,' said Moll. Again, her voice was strange, as if she was mimicking someone else. George wondered if it was her teacher, or Kathleen.

He surrendered to her once again and tried to read the word she was pointing at.

'Puh, puh, pa-pa.' He had barely finished when she exclaimed with joy.

'You're right.' She flashed him a gummy smile. '*Papa* ... like you.' She kissed his cheek and George felt strange, humbled before her.

She curled up on the sofa beside him, book in hand.

'I think it's a bit too hard for you,' she said, nodding. 'Do you want me to read you a bit of it? I'm a good reader.'

'I know. You've proved that already,' he said, putting an arm over her shoulder.

She read quickly and with confidence, her elbow digging into his stomach.

'Where's Papa going with that axe?' said Fern to her mother as they were setting the table for breakfast.
'Out to the hoghouse,' replied Mrs Arable. 'Some pigs were born last night.'

'You see,' said Moll, looking up at him, 'the daddy is going to kill the little pig, 'cause it's a *runt*. That means it's not as good as the other piglets.'

'Aye, I think I've heard this story,' said George, standing up and stretching. 'It sounds like my house.'

Bernie had a guitar in the corner, and just to halt the onslaught of letters George picked it up. He settled down on the armchair with it and strummed. It was almost in tune. He wasn't a skilled player, but he had learned a song or two. Bernie had taught him how to play. He had met her in a bar when she was doing a turn on an open-mic night and getting heckled because she was the only woman. He still called her Joan Bernie Baez for a joke sometimes.

'It's nearly time for bed,' said George, strumming, as she curled up on the sofa and put two hands under her face. 'Maybe you should have a bath and get to bed. We're going to hit the road in our hotel on wheels tomorrow, and we won't have a bath handy for a while.'

'Where are we going tomorrow?'

'We'll travel south and then camp somewhere that we fancy on the way. When we get halfway to Penzance I'll tell you and then you can choose where we camp.'

'What will happen when we get to Penzance?' she said, frowning. 'After that, will you take me back home?'

'I said I'd take you back when we were settled, and I always keep my promises.'

Her face was serious, and just to distract her, he began to sing, strumming the tune he had learned but getting some of the chords wrong.

And I love you so
The people ask me how . . .

When he glanced over to her, she had fallen asleep, curled up like a kitten.

They took baths in the morning after breakfast and then tidied up the house together, before taking their things out to the van. They made a big box of sandwiches and filled flasks of sweet tea and coffee and put them in a bag under the seat behind the driver's.

George dictated, and Moll wrote a letter to Bernadette.

'*Dear Bernie*,' said George.

'I can do joined-up writing if you want?' said Moll, her face deadly serious. 'I can do it and that's how grown-ups write.'

'However you want to write it will be fine.'

George locked the door, slipped the key back under the mat, and they were on their way.

Wednesday 9th October

Dear Barnee

Thank you very much for your lovly house. We had a nice holliday here. I am sorry that we had to leef before you got back but we were in a huree. I hope you had good fun abrod and that you got a good sun tan.

Lots of love and kisses
George

PS. I am sorry that we ate all the Angel Deelite

27

Angus Campbell
Wednesday 9 October, 1985

It was to be an epic trip – Thurso to Penzance – almost John o'Groats to Land's End; the tip of the country to the bottom and thirteen long hours of driving. Angus was glad that he had popped into the McLaughlin garage after all. It had just been an excuse, but after Tam's work the car now started quicker than it had in years.

Considering how much better the engine sounded, Angus vaguely wondered what had happened to Tam, and if he had been murdered as his wife feared, although she had not explicitly said so.

It would have been more comfortable to take the train, but Angus reasoned that he should make the journey by car because George was travelling by car and Angus could always change his route if he got a new lead. He planned to drive down as fast as he could and wait in Penzance for George, if he was not there already. He guessed that Penzance was not that big: about fifteen thousand people. Angus felt in his gut that he would be able to find George McLaughlin and take Molly safely home with him to Thurso. This was his calling.

The article he had written had been syndicated as he hoped but the national press had not put the same emphasis on the McLaughlin link. Angus's editor had been hesitant to publish the story at first – doubting its relevance – but Angus had been vindicated and his boss had grudgingly praised him.

Last night's press conference had infuriated Angus. After failing to locate George, the police had merely confirmed to the media that McLaughlin was wanted for questioning. They had failed to say that he was an actual suspect. Angus knew that they had issued a national call-out on the dark-red Allegro (the car hadn't been identified at the press conference in case the driver was alerted) but it seemed to Angus that the police were still not convinced that *George* had been driving the Allegro, and that *George* had Molly. Angus was exasperated that others were so slow to listen to him – it was like trying to convert heathens.

Angus looked at the map and chose a west coast route, passing Inverness, Glasgow, Liverpool, Birmingham and Bristol – the A9 initially, then M5 motorway. George would be unlikely to use the main roads, Angus reasoned, but he was behind and had to catch up. It had been seven days since the abduction. He wondered if George had settled in Penzance, or if he had left already. There was no time to waste.

The police were seeking George *and* the dark Allegro with the Glasgow sticker, but Angus felt certain that if the police could track the vehicle, they would also find George. It was possible that, before he disappeared, Tam had told the McLaughlin brothers whatever George had told him; this meant that the gangsters were also chasing George down the country to retrieve the money May had mentioned. He must have stolen it.

All of this Angus considered as he drove down the A9

towards Inverness. He sat leaning forward in his seat, two hands on the steering wheel and his chin jutting. He was a knight charging into battle against the forces of evil. He kept the radio on to listen to the news bulletins, but turned the volume down when the music started. It was some time since he had taken a trip. He had told Hazel to expect him gone for a week or more. He had taken out three hundred pounds for food, fuel and accommodation but hoped to spend only half of that. It wasn't just the expense that bothered him: Angus didn't like hotels or bed and breakfast establishments, as they were often places of sin and he felt sullied lying on the improperly cleaned sheets and eating the lukewarm slops they served as food.

It occurred to him that such a journey would have been better undertaken in some sort of camper van – so that he could rest and eat when he needed and drive when he wanted and the roads were clear.

Hazel had packed him a picnic bag of sandwiches and two flasks of hot sweet tea. He pulled into a service station around twelve to eat. Halfway through his salmon sandwiches, Angus decided to call his contact at the *Evening Times* again. He washed down his sandwiches with a mug of lukewarm tea, and left the car in search of a phone box.

There was a public telephone within the service station and Angus hunched inside the booth, a palmful of coins in his hand, and dialled Don Balfour's number. He smelled the sweet dough of burger buns and heard the shrieks of young children as he listened to the phone ringing.

Don's answer message kicked in and Angus pursed his lips in annoyance, about to hang up without leaving a message, when Don answered, clearing his throat loudly. 'Don Balfour.'

'Don! Hello,' said Angus, one hand in his pocket, raising his eyebrows and a smile, as if Don were actually before him. 'It's Angus Campbell here. How are you?'

'Not so bad. How goes it, wee man?'

'Fine, fine,' said Angus, frowning, 'I just wanted to call you about the McLaughlins – follow up on a conversation we had last time I was in Glasgow.'

'Sure, no probs. I see they still haven't found that wee lassie from up your way and now they want to speak to George. Were you on to something?'

'Not at all. It's a complex situation. The case continues.'

'Big George is her natural father? Get away! You didn't say that. If he's the father that's a different ballgame altogether,'

'Why?' said Angus, grinning in irritation. He had so much to ask and had not anticipated having to answer questions.

'Well, I told you the McLaughlins wouldn't kidnap a child . . . but blood, blood is a different matter. That family are tight, and if that wean is a McLaughlin, George might've taken her after all.'

'Thank you,' Angus managed, gritting his teeth in anger. 'I was calling on another matter, albeit related.'

'Fire away, wee man.'

Angus winced. 'Talking about the McLaughlins *in general*. They have been in and out of court, in and out of jail for that matter . . . Are there any links between them and the police?'

'What do you mean, links?'

'Well, do they have "friends" in the police?'

'Certainly!'

'Tell me.'

'Well, they have "friends" all over Glasgow and beyond. The police are no different, I suspect. All it takes is a gambling session gone wrong, or Maggie Thatcher and her redundancies and fifteen per cent interest rates – you go in search of whoever'll give you money. And I would *imagine* . . . be clear I'm not telling you how it works, I'm just saying how I *think* it goes . . . if you happen to work for the police and you can't pay your loan shark back, that might be . . . helpful. It could help you shave off a few bob in repayments, for a favour here or there, so to speak.'

'Do you think it's possible that there's an exchange of infor-mation, between the police and the McLaughlins?'

'Why, yes, it's possible . . . I should imagine so.'

Angus bought some mints and returned to his car. He left Scotland and continued on to the M6. He had been right to consider his journey a crusade. He was the force of goodness, of light – but the forces of darkness were journeying with him. He imagined that he, the police and the McLaughlins were all travelling down the country right now, seeking a man with a young girl in an old Allegro. It was a chase but it was also a race to victory.

If Angus had assumed correctly, then the McLaughlins would know everything that the police did about Molly and her dis-appearance, possibly more. Tam Driscoll was quite probably dead, having told the McLaughlins whatever George had told him about stealing a large amount of money. Whoever George had stolen the money from might also be heading down to Penzance. Like flatworms to darkness, Angus imagined them all drawn to the very end of the land.

After he passed Liverpool, Angus began to look for a place to stay. It was dusk and he was hungry for a real meal and a bed. He headed on to Stoke where he began to look for a small hotel. Just before dark he pulled up outside the Crown and left the car running while he asked if they had a room. They were full, but Angus decided to eat there, drive on and rest after darkness, in his car if necessary.

He tucked himself into a corner table, put a napkin on his lap and ordered minestrone soup, roast beef, and apple pie with ice cream for dessert.

He ate like he had never eaten before. It wasn't just that the food was so much better than Hazel's cooking.

The hunt gave him an appetite.

28

Big George
Wednesday 9 October, 1985

George got on to the A51, which he would follow for a while. He felt like he had been around a thousand roundabouts since he left Hanley, Stoke-on-Trent, but it seemed sensible to stay on the quieter roads. He was headed towards, but would miss, Birmingham. He had decided to bypass all the major towns; it would take him longer, but he had been lucky and now he didn't want to take risks. He could get to Penzance in under six hours, but if he avoided motorways and major towns it would take him more than eight. It wasn't just the time and the risk of being caught: the wee one couldn't sit for long hours in a car. It would've driven him crazy at her age. They had their hotel on wheels and they could take it easy now.

He put on the radio, changing stations until he found some good tunes, and then sang along as he drove. He kept to the inside lane because the van would go no faster than sixty miles an hour, but he tousled Moll's hair and encouraged her to sing along with him, as car after car overtook them.

He felt confident for the first time: full of wild optimism.

They were on the road with all their supplies, and could rest when they wanted. There was no longer any need to risk hotels or cafés and he had got rid of the stolen Glasgow car. They were untracked and free, and heading for the good life. He had the freedom and the space to look after his daughter now. He hadn't intended it to be this way. He had hoped to be a family: him and Kathleen and their wee girl. It was all he had ever wanted, but now, for whatever reason, it was just him and Moll. He had stopped believing long ago, but maybe, just maybe, it had been *meant*. They were going to disappear and no one would ever hear from him or her again.

The music was interrupted for the news.

A national manhunt continues for the kidnapper of seven-year-old Molly Henderson who was taken from the northern town of Thurso in Scotland on 2 October. Molly has long dark hair, often wears an eyepatch and was last seen wearing her school uniform.

There have been no sightings of Molly since her disappearance and police are urging members of the public to come forward if they have any information. Molly's natural father, George McLaughlin, is also wanted for questioning in relation to her disappearance. McLaughlin is six foot three, broad and of heavy build, with black hair and blue eyes.

George held the smoke in his lungs as he heard his name mentioned on the radio. The report didn't say as much – only that he was wanted for questioning – but he wondered if the police now knew that he had taken her.

The report ended with the tape of Kathleen begging for her

daughter's return. George quickly turned the radio off, in case Moll heard her mother's voice. He reached for a cigarette.

He turned to Moll, but she was in her own world, staring out of the window, as if she had not been listening.

As he smoked, a deep spasm of regret crushed him. Kathleen had meant so much to him. The thought of her suffering pained him, but she had taken his baby girl away, and now he simply could not bear to be separated from Moll. She was his child as much as Kathleen's.

After dark, he noticed that Moll was becoming restless. They were not far from Bath. They had been on the road for nearly four hours and she needed to move around.

He saw a small parking area surrounded by trees beside the road, and doubled back to park in it overnight.

It was cold and getting dark, but she did handstands on the grass as he sorted out the camper van.

The first thing he did was extend the roof, but even extended, George had to hunch as he moved around the space. The previous owners had been quirky in the furnishings they had added. The wall at the back of the van, which fronted off the engine, had been carpeted, ceiling to floor. It was a strange seventies psychedelic choice, but it made the caravan feel like a small, cosy nightclub.

He put a small step outside so that Moll could enter and leave the van with ease – it was nothing for George, but it was a large step for the bairn.

They had practised setting up the bed and table while they were in Stoke, and George now clipped the table into place. The mugs and plates were plastic, although the cutlery was real and George passed it up to her.

There was a six-kilogram bottle of Calor gas. George had bought a new one, to replace the almost empty cylinder that the previous owner had given them. He hooked up the nearly empty cylinder to the outlet so that he could power the stove and set the new cylinder by its side, ready to change when the old one was fully depleted.

'Now, my lady,' he said, on his knees in the small space of the caravanette, beside the cupboard where he had packed the groceries. 'What would madam like for her supper?' He tilted the beans towards her as if they were a bottle of fine wine. 'Could I tempt you to a spot of baked bean caviar, or indeed the delicious hoops of spaghetti, which were imported direct to our fine restaurant from Italy?'

She giggled. 'Hoops, please.'

'Indeed, my lady. Right away. And may I ask what you would like to drink? Would you like this stunning vintage of lemonade, or perhaps an orange juice while you wait?'

'Irn Bru?'

George put a hand over his chest, in mock grief and disappointment. 'Alas, I am afraid to report that we have just sold out of the fine Irn Bru, but I would strongly recommend the lemonade to madam.'

She nodded and so he poured her half a mugful, then gave a flourish with his right hand and bowed, making her scream with laughter.

There was a single gas ring that could take a pot and George cooked her hoops in it, hunched over and banging his head once or twice, despite the extended roof. He served Moll's dinner but there was not enough gas for his own, so he changed the cylinder to cook a tin of sausage and beans for himself.

It was not much of a dinner, but George ate it hungrily, washed down with warm beer. Moll ate quickly and when she was finished there was a ring of tomato sauce around her mouth. He had bought her Happy Face biscuits and she ate them as he stepped outside and smoked a cigarette. The small parking area had been empty when they pulled into it, but now there was one other car. It was pitch dark outside, apart from the orange glow of Bath in the distance, and George couldn't make out if there was someone sitting in the car or not. He listened to the hoarse whisper of the road as he finished his cigarette and then slipped back inside. There was a chill in the air and he closed the van's curtains to keep in the heat, grateful now for the psychedelic carpet on the walls.

'I need a wee-wee,' she said, and so he held the door open while she squatted next to the van.

There was no one for miles, and she was hidden from the view of the car behind, but it was dark and barren outside. 'That's right, just do it there. You're all right, no one can see you.'

He had filled up the water container at a garage while getting petrol, and so there was water for her to wash her hands at the tiny sink, and then rinse their dishes. While she waited outside, he folded the table down to make a bed, plumped up the cushions and shook travelling rugs out on top.

'We'll get up early. Soon as it's light,' he said, settling back on the bed and shaking off his boots. 'We best try and get some rest.'

'I'm not tired,' she said, and he noticed that she was shivering after being outside, pulling the sleeves of her sweater over her hands.

'C'm'ere,' he said, holding out his arm.

'Your feet smell,' she said, climbing up on to the bed beside him.

'Sorry.' He took her hand to help her. 'You're not the first woman to tell me that.'

She settled down beside him.

'It's better up this end, that's all I can say. One good thing about having long legs is your smelly feet are far enough away.'

She sat beside him, hands between her knees.

'You're cold,' he said, daring to draw her nearer.

She allowed it, putting her arm around his waist and cuddling into him. George held her close, kissing the top of her head. 'Are you warmer now?'

She nodded, one hand over his stomach and another squished into his side.

'Do you want me to sing to you again – help you go to sleep?'

He felt her elbow in his stomach as she sat up. 'We could practise your *writing* again.'

'Watch your pointy elbows. What are you trying to do to me?'

'You could write me a letter.'

'How can I write you a letter when I can barely write at all?'

'That's why you need to practise.'

Before he could say anything, she was crawling off the bed, bum in the air and one sock hanging off, and climbing into the front seat where she had her satchel. She pulled out her school exercise book, but also the stationery that she had taken from the hotel in York. She had taken all of it – even the envelopes. She crawled back on to the bed beside him, took the edge of the rug and used it to cover her knees and then his, and spread the paper on the top.

'We'll need something to lean on,' he said, reaching for one of the placemats they had used, wiping a spot of tomato sauce off it with the heel of his hand.

She started up where she had left off – marching him through the alphabet from *a* to *z*, drawing each letter for him carefully then asking him to copy it. It had been years since George had tried to write. He found that now, couried in the back of the van with the bairn, he was able to learn from her.

'It's all right,' she whispered, close to his face with sweet tomato sauce breath, when he tried to write *my name is George*. 'You don't have to write it straight. When I write it goes uphill, but you write downhill. That's OK.'

'It's easier with your left hand after all.'

'That's because *we're* left-handed,' she said, grinning at him. 'See if you can write my name.'

'I can write your name better than my own,' he said, unbuttoning his shirt to look again at the red calligraphy on his chest, the skin scarred with dye and his own blood.

The pen was still cumbersome in his hand, and he felt the strain if he held it for some time, but he wrote *Moll + George*.

'You should write *and* properly,' she said, printing the letters for him to copy, so he wrote the sentence again.

'I know!' she said, jumping up to kneel beside him. 'I'll draw pictures of things and you can write what they are underneath.' Her eyes were wide with excitement.

She drew a house, and George began with an *h* but was then uncertain. She showed him how. She drew a cat and a dog and then a van like their own, and George found that he could remember how to write those words, but she had to help him with others: tree, flower, sausage, bread.

She wrote down a list of numbers and asked him to write the

words. He got most of these wrong, but she spent time with him, patiently writing the words out for him and asking him to copy.

'It's OK,' she said, 'I used to get *twenty* wrong too, but now I think it's easy. Once you've done it a few times, you'll remember. We should try some sentences now.'

'I don't know. Maybe let's stick with the words first.'

'But words make up sentences. Words on their own are boring. We can start with an easy one.'

George sighed his assent.

'You should be able to write "My name is George and I am ..."' She stopped and opened her eyes wide as she looked into his face. 'How old are you?'

'Twenty-seven.'

'That's quite old,' she said, pushing the paper towards him, 'but not as old as my other daddy. My other daddy is forty-one. That's very old.'

George looked at her, unsure what to say.

'Write down "My name is George and I am twenty-seven years old."'

George did as she asked and found that he was able. He looked at their handwriting – his and hers side by side.

'Well done,' she said.

'Och, my letters are ugly next to yours.'

'They're not ugly,' she said, her young face suddenly solemn, and George recalled the night by the forest when he had told her she was beautiful. 'You're just learning and they're already a lot nicer than the letters you did when we were in the hotel.'

'Thank you,' he whispered, kissing her ear.

'Your face is scratchy.'

'I need to shave.'

They worked for hours and George learned hungrily from

her, without shame. Sometimes it felt as if he had been raised on shame, the way some other children were raised on love. He wanted to learn from her, so that he could be the kind of father he wanted to be. He would love her the way he had never been loved.

'If you're too stupid for school, then you can go to work with me,' said Brendan, sitting down to lace up his steel-capped boots. Since he was very small, it had been George's chore to polish the family's shoes. Brendan's boots often had rusty splatters, which came off easily apart from where they had seeped into the stitching. George had always known this was blood and he could never look at the boots without imagining his father kicking someone, the way he had seen him kick his mother.

There was no point in arguing. George knew what happened to people who contradicted his father.

'It'll toughen you up.'

George nodded and slipped his boots on, then followed his father out to the car. All he wanted was a life where he had peace to listen to music and the freedom to be himself. He didn't want to get tougher; knew he couldn't. The horrors he had seen so far had only made him feel sadder and more vulnerable. He had become somewhat accustomed to pain, but he found he could not get used to the suffering of others.

He was the baby, his mother's baby, and liked to spend as little time as possible with his father. He would have been happy with no father. Brendan had many enemies and all of them wished him dead, but, secretly, no one wished him dead more than his youngest son.

George was fifteen, nearly sixteen and already taller than his father, but he was thin: all ribs, kneecaps and joints, Adam's apple and cheekbone. He was six foot one already and a size thirteen shoe. George wondered if he would ever stop growing.

Yet with Brendan, George hunched, fearful of even physically looking down on his father, in case it was regarded as impudence. George always knew that however tall he grew (and he was already the tallest member of the McLaughlin family) he would never be as tall as his father.

His father's car was a long black Jaguar with dark windows. They sat in silence as they drove to a building site near Alexandra Parade. They could see out, but no one could see inside. The car felt like their family, with its secrets and its violence and its unwitnessed horror.

They were going to see Brian Coulston, a building contractor. He had a gambling problem and had got into debt while hoping to gamble himself out of it, but had only lost more money. Peter and Richard had called already with threats, and now it was time for consequences. George had eaten breakfast, egg and a slice of toast, before Brendan had required his company for the day and the food now lay like cement in the pit of his stomach.

The car smelled of Brendan: leather and cigars and Old Spice aftershave. It was intoxicating and George felt almost unable to breathe.

A derelict area had been fenced off with wire mesh. It was an old demolition site, and before that high-rise flats, and the ground was a beach of exploded concrete and cinder block. They got out of the car and walked side by side towards the Portakabin at the far end. There was no one working on the land, but diggers and cement mixers stood at the ready. Like volcanic ash, the rubble broke under their feet as they marched.

'What are you going to do?' said George to his father, when he saw him put on his leather gloves.

'I'm going to show you the power of the mind.'

'What do you mean?'

'What a man believes is what he manifests.'

George turned to his father, not understanding, but not having the courage to question. He curved his spine and hunched lower, as if wanting to hear more.

Brendan didn't knock at the cabin door, and George followed him inside. It was almost colder inside than it was out, and Brian jumped up from behind a desk, where he had been doing paperwork dressed in an anorak and scarf. He stood before them with hard heavy breaths that were visible in the small cold room.

'Brendan, I . . . I nearly have it . . . I only need . . .'

Brendan smiled and clasped his gloved hands.

George stood just behind his father, his hands at his sides. They felt hot and heavy – as if they might be asked to perform a deed for which they were unwilling.

'Nearly, maybe, might . . .' said Brendan, smiling.

George glanced down at his father. There was a wicked smile on Brendan's face. He smiled that way at home sometimes. Once he had smiled just like that before he broke a bottle of wine across Richard's face, when he had agreed with their mother that there were fifty-four cards in a deck. His mother had also been beaten later, so the family all agreed that in fact there were only fifty-two cards. That was the way the McLaughlin house was run. Truth was imposed, not discovered. It was fundamentalism and Brendan expected to be obeyed with religious observance. Black was white if he said so. The bottle had broken Richard's cheekbone, and given him a scar for life that he wore like a medal. His mother had been right all along, George discovered later: fifty-two cards and two jokers, and, as it only could have been, the joke was on her.

'Honestly, Mr McLaughlin, I promise you that . . .'

'Promises, wishes, beliefs . . .' said Brendan, quietly as ever: sinister, silent and slow as lava. 'This here is my youngest son,' he said, tipping his head to George.

George's mouth felt dry as Brian stared at him, lips parted, spider veins on his cheeks and bloodshot eyes. Brian licked his lips and his eyes filled, so that he seemed desperate, grief-stricken. George felt his own eyes sting, but knew that Brendan would not allow tears – he never had – and George had learned early, from his father, from the nuns, how to control his own self-pity.

'My youngest son has instructions from me to pull out one of your teeth for every hundred pounds you owe me. Now . . . I don't know exactly how many teeth you have in that ugly head of yours, but I'm reckoning that we're going to run out. So after we've pulled them all out, we're going to have to extract that unpaid debt from elsewhere. You only have ten fingernails and toes, so we'll have to move on . . . your balls, your ears, your eyes, your tongue . . .'

George stood rooted to the spot, knowing that he would be unable to hurt Brian and aware that if he didn't his father would hurt them both. He was nearly sixteen years old and already he felt that he had seen enough. At night he dreamed of running away – going somewhere where nobody knew him and where he could live his life without the dark soup of fear in his stomach. But as long as Brendan McLaughlin was alive, there could be no escape.

'What's it to be?' said Brendan, slowly taking off his gloves and removing a pair of pliers from his pocket. 'The easy way or the hard way.'

Tears spilled from Brian's eyes, fat, thick tears that fell quickly over his full cheeks and off his chin. 'I can get it. I can get it.'

'You said that last week, now it's time to pay. Now either we take our time and we see if you survive, if indeed that kind of life is worth living, or you do us all a favour and speed things along.'

'My business; I'll give it to you.'

'If memory serves we looked at that. You're making a loss. What matters now is that you learn the consequences. I'm running a business too. I can't let the message get out that I'm a charity. Now decide – the quick or the slow way.'

'Quick,' said Brian, his eyes now dry, but the colour gone from his face.

'Fine. There's a digger out there. You dig your own grave and then mix the cement.'

It was cold outside, but just as his father had told him, Brian got into the digger and began to make a hole in the rubble and dry, frozen earth. George watched him with his hands in his pockets, wondering what kind of hopelessness would cause such actions. It reminded him of the scrupulous way his mother cleaned up all her own blood after a beating, as if this had been her mess, her fault, her responsibility. The sound of metal breaking through the rocky earth seemed to scrape to the very core of George. He felt a dark, seething hatred inside him. It was as if all the ugliness in the world had a face, and it belonged to his father.

Brendan opened the boot of the Jaguar and took out a cricket bat.

'Well,' he said, smiling at George with his yellow teeth. 'Are you ready to prove yourself?'

'What do you mean?'

Brendan handed George the bat. 'I'll give you the nod and then you need to do the business. You'll be pleased to know it doesn't matter which way you hit him – with your left hand or your right.'

'I don't think I can . . .' said George, so quietly that the wind seemed louder than his words.

'I don't care what you think. You'll do it. You're useless at everything else, but anyone can swing a bat.'

Brendan turned and walked away from George, towards Brian in his digger, alone in the rubble; man and machine. The bat was heavy, the wood smooth as skin. It was a dead weight in George's sweaty hands as they walked back to Brian to find that the grave was dug and ready.

Brian turned off the engine and climbed out of the truck. He stood before Brendan, hands at his sides, shoulders down, so that he seemed less than a man, Neanderthal, base, awaiting his fate. Without being asked, Brian moved to the head of the pit he had just dug. The wind breathed coarse and chill through the exposed site, lifting up the fine hairs on Brian's scalp and causing Brendan to turn up the collar on his wool coat.

Brendan moved closer to Brian and took the back of his neck between forefinger and thumb. He forced him down on to his knees in the pit, climbing down into it with him. George watched from the lip of the grave, the cricket bat in his hands. He looked around, as if for help, but there was no one and nothing in this wasteland: no witnesses, no judge.

Still with his hand on Brian's neck, forcing it downwards, Brendan looked up at George, commanding.

The smooth cricket bat was slick in George's hand. His heart was beating so hard that it felt as if it might fall, pounding, out of his chest. All he could hear was the rush of blood in his ears.

'Are you ready, Brian?' Brendan whispered hoarsely. 'Have you said your prayers?'

Brian was still hunched, bent over, his knuckles almost touching the rubble in the pit that he had dug.

'I'm ready,' he said.

Brendan turned and put a hand on the lip of the pit to help himself out.

Brian hunched, spun and straightened, as if throwing the discus. He had a brick in his hand and smacked it into the side of Brendan's face. There was a dull thud as the brick made contact: flesh over bone. Brendan sank to his knees and stayed there, stunned, a hand to his face and then watching the blood on his palm.

Brian looked up at George. It was clear what was going to happen, but Brian had shown that he would go down fighting. The isolation of the yard crawled over George like cockroaches. It was a deed no one would witness. It would right a wrong. It would free him.

George refused to meet Brian's watery blue eyes. He swung the heavy bat, left-handed, driving it away from his body, then pulling it forward, true, athletic, murderous. It was a fluid, beautiful moment of perfect coordination and power.

There was a sound like an axe hacking into a tall tree. George drew the bat towards him and the tip was bright red with his father's blood. Brendan fell forward into the grave.

'Mother of God,' said Brian as he scrambled out.

Face to face, Brian and George looked at each other. Brian was a small man and had to raise his chin ninety degrees to meet George's gaze. George was a boy, not even sixteen years old. They were silent, looking each other in the eye, kindred in guilt.

George swung the bat again and Brian winced, but George

merely tossed it into the pit on top of his father. 'I suppose you know what to do now?' he said, looking down at his father, his hands in his pockets.

Brian said nothing but went to the cement mixer and began loading it up with cement, sand and water, while George kicked in the rubble. When the cement was ready, Brian poured it into the hole.

The way that Brendan had fallen into the hole, his wrist and hand were in the air, as if to contest a point, raise a question. A full batch of cement covered Brendan's body, but not his questioning hand. Brian mixed another batch to cover the grey hand that rose from the grave, assertive, blaming.

As the second batch of cement was poured in, George slipped into the Portakabin and came out with Brian's half-smoked pack of Silk Cut in his hand.

They stood, side by side, smoking a cigarette, silent over the grave, then let the butts fall into the slowly hardening cement.

'What happens now?' Brian asked.

'Nothing,' said George. 'I'll say we warned you and left. My father went for a pint and I went home and we never heard from him again. Who'll be sorry?'

Brian's eyes were round, all the whites showing.

'The important thing is to say nothing. My brothers might come after you for the debt, but this . . .' George kicked a quarter brick over the grave. 'This didn't happen.'

George drove the Jaguar into town where he parked on the Shettleston Road, not far from the Portland Arms where his father drank. He dropped the keys down a drain and then returned home, where his mother was making stovies.

The pot of boiling potatoes had made the kitchen windows steam up, and so George opened one as he ate. A breeze came into the kitchen and the frill of the tablecloth fluttered. His mother was smoking Woodbines by the fire, watching him.

'How did you get on?'

'It was fine.'

'Was there trouble?' she said, wincing at him, holding the smoke in her lungs.

'There was none. It was just warnings.'

'Did he say when he'd be back?'

'No, he went for a drink.'

His mother looked back at the fire.

George took another mouthful, but something flew at his head and he ducked, stabbing himself in the mouth with his fork. It was a sparrow. It darted around the kitchen, quick as a grenade, panicked, hitting off the mince pot and the stone sink before it found its way back to the window.

'Quick, George, help it.'

George threw open a second window, but the bird did not see it – could not determine glass from open window and continued to batter itself against the panes. With his large hands George tried to clasp it, but the bird only threw itself harder against the glass in panic, its small wings and beak now weapons of self-harm.

'Here, George, use this,' said his mother, handing him a tea towel.

George stood with the towel in two hands, as if waiting to receive a baby from its bath. He walked towards the window and tried to catch the bird, but it only became more fearful and agitated. It flew a loop of the kitchen and then straight into the glass before falling dead on the floor.

It was smaller than a mouse. He held it, still warm in his hands, flecks of its blood marking the white tea towel.

'The poor mite,' said his mother. 'The stupid wee thing.'

'Not so stupid,' said George. 'Birds aren't used to being in kitchens.'

The page was covered in untidy letters, blue pen on ivory hotel paper. The bairn slumped into him and he pulled the travelling rug over her.

'Are you sleepy?'

She was too tired to respond. The eyelid over one eye was closed, the other half open, watching him. The letters that he had written lay on his lap, a testament of what he could have become. Before he had been able to write his name he had killed a man: cracked his own father's skull. Now he was twenty-seven years old and trying to make a fresh start. The layers of his life were compacted already, as sand and silt turns into rock. He couldn't see clearly how to turn the violence, hurt and corruption into love and truth. He wasn't sure he would be allowed. With her small, warm, soft body next to his he felt guilty, red-handed. For a moment in the warm twilight of the caravan, he wondered if this was as far as he could go. He wondered if the dream would be for ever out of reach.

Freedom at what cost? He remembered the coconut-cracking sound of his father's head splitting to the cricket bat that George wielded. He had felt no remorse. He had felt only relief that Brendan did not rise up, as George had fully expected, and whack the bat back in his face, as he had smashed the wine bottle over Richard's cheek. Brendan had been everything that George hated and he had killed him. The act was a horror but it had filled him with secret pride, confidence. Brendan had thought that George was soft and George knew that his father was right, in that he did not possess the callousness that his father and brothers wore like aftershave. But everyone in Glasgow had feared Brendan McLaughlin, and George had killed him and got away with it.

The McLaughlins were used to people disappearing and never being found. They had *caused* several people to go missing, never to be found. But the truth was that when Brendan McLaughlin went missing, nobody asked. No one complained that he had failed to return from the pub. No one questioned the fact that his car was parked on Shettleston Road for over a week before it was either stolen or towed. Even his family hoped someone had killed him. The missing persons report was filed and after that the only people to enquire after Brendan were the Inland Revenue.

Cuddled down, ready for sleep, Moll began to cry. Her tears were silent. George lay down on the pillow next to her, watching her with his eyebrows raised.

'What's the matter, baby girl?'

'I'm just sad.'

'Why are you sad?'

'I want to see my mum.'

'I'm sorry.'

She nodded and sniffed, and another tear left her eye and splashed on to the pillow.

Almost all of George's childhood had been spent crying in bed at night, and now seeing Moll cry pained him.

'Don't cry, button,' he said, pulling her into him.

'I'm trying not to,' she sniffed. 'When do you think I can go back? When will it be time?'

'Once we find the place we're going, I promise then I'll let you go back.'

'I just miss her and I miss my other daddy.'

'I know,' said George, pulling her tight. 'But I'm so glad that

I got to meet you properly. Aren't you? This is like winning the jackpot for me.'

Moll said nothing but turned her face up to his. He looked down on her mushroom skin, long eyelashes and violet eyes, one cast away from him. Her hand was lying across his chest and he took it in his, as if preparing to waltz.

'Come close, button, cuddle down and listen to me.'

The van was warm and George tugged the travelling rug over her and gently pulled her into his arms. He ran his fingers through her hair as he began to sing. He sang the same song that he had sung to her at Bernie's:

> And I love you so,
> the people ask me how . . .

The weight of her increased as she dropped off. When she was sound asleep – wet lips and rough breaths in her nose – George lifted her off him and on to the bed, where she lay sprawled until he tucked her in, settling her arms and legs under the travelling rug.

'God bless you and God bless me,' he whispered as he kissed her forehead.

Outside, the air was sharp, threaded with exhaust fumes yet austere and fragrant from the ash trees that stretched out towards the moss and wasteland that was the beginnings of wherever-they-were near Bath. George tapped a cigarette against the packet and then lit up, inhaling and enjoying the rush of it.

He bit down on the cigarette as he focused into the distance, then took it sharply from his mouth, exhaling. He narrowed his eyes as he stared into the darkness. The car in the lay-by was still there and George was sure he saw a person behind the wheel, staring. He took another drag, wincing as smoke got in his eyes, then exhaled and looked away. He was getting paranoid, and he knew it.

29

Margaret Holloway
Thursday 26 December, 2013

It was Boxing Day and Ben had left just after breakfast to drive up to Rugby to bring her father back for lunch. She had made a roast, which she sliced and returned to the oven. Ben had called from the road to say that the M1 was clear and he was making good progress.

Most of the snow had melted and outside, on their small lawn, a snowman was folding in on himself, eroded by warm rain that bored holes into his body. His carrot nose was limp and his black pebble smile lopsided, but still grinning in decay.

The house was a mess: new toys marooned on the couch and needles from the Christmas tree scattered over the carpet. Eliot was kneeling in the middle of the floor with the controls to the Xbox in his hands, his eyes wide and unblinking, seeming possessed. Margaret rushed around the house, frowning as she vacuumed and polished the furniture. She prepared the vegetables and took the cheese out of the fridge. When everything was ready, she went upstairs to shower and stood under the jet, trying to calm herself and wash the dark thoughts from her mind.

Ben had asked her to go back and see the doctor and she had agreed to do so after the holidays.

She dressed and blow-dried her hair and then sat staring at herself in the mirror, thinking how sad and tired she looked. Her neck was still sore from the crash, which the doctor had said was mild whiplash, although part of her believed it was the tension afterwards that had caused it. She lined her upper lids with thick liquid eyeliner, lacquered her lashes and put lipstick on. She pressed her lips together as she stood looking out of the window, watching for Ben's car.

There was no sign and so she turned away and opened the door to the spare bedroom, where once again she removed the box from under the bed and lifted the lid. Each time she would kneel on the floor as she examined its contents, and each time she could look at only one or two items before she had had enough.

This time she lifted out a notebook and opened the first page. It was her mother's diary for 1986. Margaret placed the book on the bed and sat up to read it. Tucked into the fold were photographs of her when she was a child, unsmiling, looking warily at the camera.

A month has gone by and still she has not spoken a word. The doctor said that there are no physical signs of injury, but that molestation cannot be ruled out. Even writing that word hurts me. I hate to think what might have happened to her. The psychologist suggested I keep a diary, for my own mental health as well as to keep a record of her progress, but I am still not sure of the purpose of this. What is the point of writing about it? What does this change?

I have not yet sent her back to school. I am trying my

best to teach her at home. She hears and understands. She completes her exercises as instructed and almost everything is correct. She does what she is told immediately, without question, but slowly, without any kind of enthusiasm.

Yet she will not speak to me, nor will she smile, even when her father tries to tease and tickle her as he would in the past. She seems happy to be back and stays near me, cuddling into me for comfort if I sit still for any length of time, but it feels as if I have been returned half a child, half of my daughter. I don't know where the rest of her has gone. She was such a happy little girl, quick and bright and energetic, but now it is as if part of her has died, or been stolen; as if she is a changeling.

John is beside himself. He had almost not slept since she was taken, organising search party after search party, even though we were unofficially told to prepare for her body to be found. Now he seems destroyed, convinced that her innocence has been taken. He blames himself, tells me how he should have protected her. I feel the same. I think I should never have let her out of my sight. She is my only child and I should have taken more care.

Today, at lunch, I tried to fool her – asked her if she wanted toasted cheese or a boiled egg sandwich. She shrugged, as always, but this time I persisted. I told her that she would get nothing until she told me which she preferred. She looked so sad but didn't say a word, and finally got up and left the room. I was incensed. I caught her in the hall and shook her, and she went rigid with fear in my arms. Then I broke down. I held her and cried but she remained passive, allowing me to hold her but not putting her arms around me. She is still so little, but it was as if she realised that I was asking for comfort from her and despised me for it. I begged her to talk to me, to tell me what had happened to her, but she only held out her forefinger to catch my tears.

I told John, expecting him to understand, but he only blamed me.

I feel ashamed and desperate. I wonder if our family is now broken, if it will ever be the same again. If only she could tell us what happened to her. Our daughter is returned, but will she ever be with us again?

There was the sound of the front door opening and the children calling for their grandfather. Margaret closed the diary, returned it to the box and pushed it back under the bed. She took a deep breath, braced herself and then went downstairs.

Her father looked thin and grey, but his face lit up when he saw her. She stood on the bottom step as she hugged him, curling her hands around his shoulder blades.

'I'm so glad you came,' she said, looking into his face and thinking that his eyes were sad. For so long, she had thought it had been her mother's death that had caused the spores of sorrow to settle on him, but now she considered her mother's diary: *destroyed* was the word her mother had used to describe her father.

'Are you all right?' he said, leaning back and frowning at her, looking at her directly, as if he saw his pain reflected in her face.

'Of course,' said Margaret, washing a hand across her eyes.

'You look . . .'

'I'm fine, come on . . . You sit yourself down,' she said, plumping up the cushion in the big armchair near the fire. 'Dinner won't be long. Thought we'd eat about three.'

'Whisky, John?' Ben asked.

'If you'll join me.'

The children started showing off their presents. They tried to teach John how to play a computer game where he had to navigate a futuristic car over a space-scape obstacle course.

Her father looked relieved when he finally sat down at the table. Margaret's jaw ached from smiling. She was trying to do things too quickly and Ben was now in their small kitchen with her. He was so big and kept getting in her way. It was pâté to start, but they had to coordinate the vegetables for the main course.

Margaret lined up the pâté dishes while Ben mixed up the salad dressing. She missed the counter putting down a plate and it shattered on the kitchen floor. When she bent to pick it up, she nicked her forefinger.

'Mags, what are you doing?' said Ben, nudging her out of the way so that he could pick up the smashed dish.

'I've *got it*,' she said, surprised to hear anger in her voice.

'You see to your finger.' He raised his eyebrows at her as he collected the pottery into the palm of his hand.

'I'm sorry,' she said to the cold-water tap as she rinsed her finger until the bleeding stopped.

She heard the lid of the bin slap shut and then felt his arms on her shoulders.

'Are you all right?'

'How many times?'

'Just chill out. There's no rush, nobody's demanding anything.' He turned her round by her shoulders and took her face into his hands. She nodded, feeling the warmth of his palms on her cheeks.

By the time they were sitting down, Margaret felt a little better. Eliot got out of his seat to pull his Christmas cracker with his grandfather. It spilled its contents with no sound, but John, engineer that he was, insisted on re-pulling the paper sparker.

375

The bang, although expected, made Margaret's fingers tremble. She could taste the gunpowder at the back of her throat. They sat with paper hats on, trying to be jovial.

Her mouth was dry. She took a sip of wine and cleared the starter plates.

'Are you all right?' Ben asked again, noticing that the small tower of plates shook in her hand as she carried them to the kitchen. He followed her.

'Stop asking me that.'

He looked dejected.

'Just tell me what I can do.'

She breathed out, allowing her shoulders to relax. 'I'm thirsty. Could you pour me a lemonade?'

She lined up the crème brûlée dishes and sprinkled brown sugar on top, then turned on the chef's torch. She watched the blue eye of the flame for a moment and then turned it on the sugar, watching it blacken and bubble. The roar of the torch flame reached deep inside her memory. She thought about what she had read in her mother's diary earlier.

'Think that's them about done, sweetheart, don't you?' said Ben, looming over her. 'Don't worry, I'll take that burnt one. You didn't like him, did you? He got a right roasting.'

Margaret smiled despite herself and followed him through.

After pudding, the children asked to be excused, while the adults sat over the cheese and wine.

Ben was doing impressions of a politician he had interviewed recently, and telling John about the House of Commons bar. Margaret had hardly eaten anything, and realised she didn't want her wine. She was feeling quite unwell. She found herself checking her watch and thinking about hospital visiting times.

She wanted to see Maxwell, and the betrayal implied in that desire flooded her with guilt. It was Christmas and she was with her family, and yet all she wanted was to be with a man she hardly knew.

Under the table, she felt Ben's fingers find her thigh.

'You're very quiet,' said her father, raising his eyebrows as he struggled to cut a piece of Brie.

Margaret shrugged.

'You feeling any better now that you're off work? Christmas is over and done with and you'll get a few days to put your feet up.'

'I don't think that'll help,' said Margaret, rubbing her face.

There was silence for a few moments – the chink of her father's cheese knife against the plate.

Margaret swallowed. Her heart rate was increasing again. She wanted to *know* and she didn't care any more about upsetting anyone.

'You know that stuff I took from the attic?' she said to her father.

He was still smiling happily at her – relaxed after the wine and the company. She could barely breathe, but she continued. 'It was the box of things Mum collected from that time . . .' she said, looking across the table at her father. The smile began to fade on John's lips. He nodded once. He seemed to know immediately what she meant. 'I've been going through it slowly. It's hard but . . . I found Mum's diary.'

John's pale eyes narrowed. He wiped his mouth with a napkin and pushed away his plate. 'The only time she ever kept a diary. The doctor told her to . . . suggested I did as well, but I could never see the point of it.'

She met her father's sad eyes. She saw how vulnerable he was. He had always been thin, a consequence of working too hard and a disinterest in food, but the past few years he had got thinner, making him seem diminished.

'You're right,' she said. 'It was just a diary for that one year – 1986 – the year after I came back.' She felt so much love for him and did not want to confront him.

'Came back from where?' said Ben.

Margaret continued as if she had not heard her husband. 'It was hard to read. Mum wrote that you blamed yourself.'

John shifted in his seat and rolled the stem of his wine glass between his fingers. 'Of course I did,' he said, chin down but looking across the table at Margaret.

'Why?'

'Well, any father would blame himself when his young daughter is ... taken. We thought you were dead, and we were supposed to ... protect you.'

They were interrupted suddenly as Eliot burst into the room asking if they could open one of their selection boxes. Ben had turned very pale, but he answered Eliot quickly and the child left the room.

'What happened to me?' Her voice was so quiet as to be almost inaudible, yet her words made the candle flicker in the middle of the table. Shadows of the flame oscillated, magnified, on the pale walls.

'We never knew,' said her father, his voice brisk, businesslike; the way he had sounded when she was a child and the plant called him at home. 'Your mother was intent on dredging it up, finding out. For a while it seemed that was all she thought about. I thought it was better to let you forget, and you seemed to do that well ... When you started to speak again, you were back to your old self. You were so happy.' John's eyes misted with tears. 'You forgot and we all tried to do the same.'

'What is all this?' said Ben, looking at Margaret before turning to John.

John cleared his throat loudly. 'You didn't tell him?'

Margaret was looking straight at her father. 'What was I to say? Even now I wouldn't know where to start.'

'Mags?' Ben whispered, hunched down over the table, his eyes imploring.

Margaret cleared her throat, sat up straight and clasped her hands. 'When I was little, I was abducted,' she said simply, looking unblinkingly at her husband. She bit the inside of her lip, watching his face for a response.

He put a hand over his mouth while the other reached out to touch her.

'*Why now?*' her father whispered. 'Why are you thinking of it again?'

'I don't know,' said Margaret. 'I've been remembering things since the crash – bits here and there, nothing significant, but enough to . . .'

She freed her hands from Ben's.

'It was such a long time ago,' said her father. 'Maybe let it rest.'

Two tears flashed over Margaret's cheeks. She spoke very quietly. 'I remember . . . that you're not my father.'

John was silent, but seemed to shrink further into himself. Margaret's eyes filled with tears again. 'I don't mean to be cruel, but I remember that . . . I remember that you're not . . .'

'Margaret?' said Ben, his brows furrowing.

He almost never called her by her full name.

Her cheeks were burning. She got up from the table, wiped her face, turned to the dresser and picked up her car keys.

'Hang on, where are you going?' said Ben, following her into the hall where she picked up her coat and pushed her feet into her boots.

The children appeared in the hall, their eyes wide; Eliot's mouth was smeared with chocolate.

'I'll be back soon,' said Margaret, half smiling at Ben as she left.

She put on her coat, on the doorstep, and got into her car. It was cold and wet, frost glistening like dropped diamonds on the black pavements.

Ben pleaded with her through the closed car door, but she pulled out of the drive. As she merged on to the M11, she felt waves of frustration building up inside her. She knew it was madness and that Ben would be beside himself, but she just needed to be away and, inexplicable as it was, she wanted to see Maxwell.

At this time of night on Boxing Day, the traffic was light. It took her only thirty minutes to get to Whitechapel. She drove carefully, calmly, not listening to music or the radio, silent tears streaming down her cheeks.

For weeks, a chasm had been opening within her, and it felt as if, now, she was looking down clearly into it. She was realigning everything in her life: her husband, her father, her children, her work. She was putting everything in perspective; seeing it for what it truly was – seeing herself clearly for the first time.

The hospital car park was crowded but she finally found a space, then walked, hands in her parka and head down, into the hospital, mechanically following the path to Maxwell's ward, unsure why she was here, but knowing that she needed to be.

The door to the ICU was locked and she buzzed to be let in. It was warm and she shook off her coat. The stench of disinfectant and bleach was overpowering, as if to disguise the smell of the sick people.

The door clicked open. It was Harvey, the charge nurse, and Margaret's face lit up.

'Margaret, he's gone . . .'

She put a hand over her mouth and Harvey's face blurred before her.

The breath was stolen from her again. She wasn't sure if she could cope with Maxwell's death. She didn't even know him, but the loss would be unbearable. She felt Harvey's hand on her shoulder.

'Hey, calm down. Are you all right? He's been moved, is all. They took him out of his coma, and he came round. I was going to call you. He's in Ward 21. He's not saying much yet, but we have high hopes.'

'So I can go and see him?'

'Sure. Do you know where to go?'

'I . . . I . . . sure,' said Margaret, thanking him and making her way back to the lift. She was trembling all over and the muscles of her back were sore. Alone in the lift she stretched to try to loosen up.

Ward 21 was large and busy. Visitors were whispering to relatives and the windows of the ward had been rimmed in tinsel. Margaret looked left and right as she walked along the corridor, searching for Maxwell. A nurse with a large smile stopped her.

'You all right? You lost?'

'I was looking for Maxwell Brown.'

'Come w'me.'

In the last bay on the right, the nurse stopped and pointed at the faraway bed. 'That's your man. It was touch and go with him for a while and he's not out of the woods yet, but we think he's pulled through. He's yet to say a word to us, so let's see if you can make a difference.'

The nurse squeezed Margaret's arm and left her.

Margaret stood for a moment, staring at the pale face on the far side of the ward. She walked slowly forward. From this distance, with his eyes closed, he was featureless. He was now wearing a pyjama top, his hands outside the bedclothes, no longer connected to respirators and heart monitors.

At his bedside, she stared at him. His pyjama jacket was open, exposing his shiny burned chest. His eyes were closed as they had been on each of her visits, but she could tell, even from his sleeping state, that consciousness had returned to him. He seemed changed. He turned towards her, and his eyes moved around under his eyelids, as if he were dreaming.

The other patients in the ward were older. An old woman was asleep in her chair, her head back and her mouth open. Another was spitting into a cardboard bowl, and clearing her throat repeatedly. A television, fixed high up above the windows, was showing a game show, but with the sound turned down low.

Margaret took a deep breath, and just as she exhaled, Maxwell's waxy eyelids opened. His eyes were beautiful: an impossible blue. They struggled to focus for a second and then fixed on Margaret.

She smiled at him, tears filling her eyes.

His lashless lids widened.

'Hello,' Margaret began, suddenly lost for words. 'You don't know me, but I've been visiting you. You were in a coma. There was a pile-up on the motorway and you saved my life. I'm pleased to meet you, finally.'

Margaret sat down at his bedside and looked up into his face. The burns no longer fazed her and she almost did not see them. His blue eyes moved over her hair and her face and down to her hands. She smiled awkwardly, aware that she was being studied, observed. She put her hand on the edge of his bed.

'I . . . I wanted to thank you, that was all. If you need anything, you must let me know.'

The man lifted his left hand and Margaret watched it, wondering if he wanted water, but instead he took hold of her wrist and squeezed it, hard. His face flushed and the white tentacles stood out paler and more pronounced.

'Please, stop,' Margaret said, not yet loud enough for anyone else to hear. 'You're hurting me.'

30

Richard McLaughlin
Thursday 10 October, 1985

It was a ten-hour drive to Penzance. Richard had left Glasgow in the middle of the night.

Peter had wanted to send someone else, but Richard had argued that they didn't know *exactly* where George was headed. Family knew family and although Richard wasn't close to George, he felt he would have a fair idea of his movements. The plan was to get to Penzance and try to find brother George and then the Watts' money.

Peter also wanted George to be *dealt with*, and this preyed on Richard's mind as he crossed the border and joined the M6 after Carlisle. He was sure that he could find his brother, but he was not sure that he wanted to.

Richard had killed before, but he wasn't sure he would be able to kill his own brother. Killing family was entirely different to killing other people. Blood was blood, despite everything else. Richard had fantasised about killing his father, and he was sure that every one of them – every single McLaughlin, not to mention all the poor folks in the East End – had shared that fantasy.

Yet even when his father smashed a wine bottle across his face, Richard had been unable to wound him back. Even Peter had not had the courage to commit that great crime, or even get close.

George wasn't just family. George was no Brendan McLaughlin. He was the baby and, useless as he was, Richard knew that George had a heart of gold. He had stepped out of line, but violent retribution just seemed wrong. Big George with his baby blues. He was six foot three – taller than all of them – but gentle as their mother had been. Yet Peter had been adamant.

In the past few years, Peter had become as unrelenting and as cold as their father. Before his last trial, Peter had been cut by a rival gang leader. He had tried to give Peter a Glasgow smile, slicing from the corner of his mouth to his ear, but Peter had fought him off. Peter had the strength of a mule and, lying on his back in an East End side street, he had lifted the man wielding the knife right up into the air. Slashing from a distance, the man had been unable to be so accurate and had nicked Peter's jugular vein instead, covering himself in a fountain of McLaughlin blood, before he ran away from what he believed had been an accidental murder.

Yet Peter had lived, and still wore the gnarled white and red scar that blossomed from his neck like spring buds, as a mark of his infallibility. 'No one takes down Peter McLaughlin,' he would now boom with regularity. 'I can lose half my blood and still come back and take my revenge. No one can take me down.'

Richard had eaten nothing since the day before. The thought of catching up with George and doing Peter's bidding sickened him, but he also knew that if he didn't, then the Watt brothers were sure to take revenge on the McLaughlins. It was find George or be killed; kill or be killed. As he drove, Richard tried to think of ways that he could let George escape while persuading Peter that the deed had been done.

Richard was fourteen and George nearly eight. They were playing football in the street with boys Richard's age and older. Richard's mother had told him to take George with him out to play, but George wasn't as good at football as the older boys and Richard resented having to babysit him. George had been accidentally kicked twice when going in for a tackle and cried and now stood on the sidelines, his knees blue from the cold, his nose running and washing a thin, clean trail to his upper lip.

Richard was good at football. He ran fast, his hard-soled boots slipping on the tarmac, firing goal after goal between the makeshift posts, which were marked by two sweaters on the road.

A kitten approached George, who crouched down to pet it. It was blue-grey with pale blue eyes, and George took a green wooden yo-yo from his pocket and trailed it along the pavement. The little cat bounced in pursuit, reaching out to catch it with one paw and then the other. George picked the kitten up and sat on the sidelines stroking it until its purrs made its whole body vibrate.

It was teatime, and one by one the boys playing football were called inside by their mothers, who leaned out of tenement windows shouting their names. Only when the others were gone, taking the ball with them, did George and Richard make their way back home. George carried the cat in his arms.

'You can't take that in. It might belong to someone.'

'It doesn't. It's an orphan.'

'A stray, you mean.'

George nodded; he licked the drips from his runny nose with the point of his tongue.

'Well, either way you won't be allowed.'

'It can kill the mice.'

'They end up dead anyway.'

'I want to keep him. I'll keep him hidden.'

'As if you could. Cats smell. They get into everything. You'll only get into trouble.'

'I just want something to love that'll love me back.' George went on holding the kitten in his arms like a baby.

Richard said nothing as they opened the door and climbed upstairs, Richard trailing his fingers against the blue and white tiled wall. It was Tuesday and the stairs had been scrubbed with bleach. George tried to hide the kitten under his sweater but it clawed at the wool, pulling it out of shape.

As soon as they entered the lobby, the brothers saw that their father was home. He was not expected this early on a weekday, but his coat was hanging in the hall, and his tackety boots were unlaced and sitting on a sheet of newspaper, waiting to be polished. They could hear their mother in the kitchen, emitting small sighs as she chopped vegetables, and then, from the sitting room, came the heavy stink of their father's thin cigars.

When Brendan was home, it was as if he took up more than his share of air. Richard stood in the hall, feeling the pain in his lungs. He had been playing football and then climbed three sets of stairs and now he made an effort not to breathe too hard, as he pushed his brother into their bedroom.

George sniffed and set the cat down on the bed, where it arched its back and stared at them both.

'You'll never be able to hide it. You best take it outside again.'

'No. I'm going to keep it here.'

'What'll you feed it?'

'I'll save bits from my dinner. I can give it my milk.'

'Well, I'm telling you now, you'll get found out.'

'Why? Will you tell?'

Richard looked at George, his lips pressed together. The truth was that if it was Peter's cat, Richard would have told quickly, but then Peter would only have wanted to torment it.

Dinner was silent, punctuated only by the sound of Brendan demanding things from their mother: more potatoes, hot tea, a sharper knife. When their father rose from the table to go to the bathroom, Richard and George made their way back to the bedroom. They had each secreted some food in a napkin: a piece of a beef and half a sausage from the stew, a boiled potato and a sliver of apple.

As soon as they entered the room, the cat pounced on to the bed, tail up and eyes wide.

'I don't think cats eat this stuff,' said Richard. 'They like fish and milk.'

'There's some salmon in the cupboard.'

'As if you'd be able to get that.'

Nevertheless, when they opened up the napkins, the cat began to mew, pacing back and forth on the bed, looking at the napkin, which George held in his hands.

'Whssssh,' said Richard, tapping the cat's head, over the sound of the toilet flushing.

'Don't hurt him.'

'*He'll* hear.'

George let the napkin sit on the bed and the cat sniffed and pawed at it, then sat down on its haunches, looking at it. George held out a piece of meat, but it turned its face away, then continued to miaow, sitting up on the bed.

'What's going on?'

The boys turned to find their father at the door, hands on his hips. Richard stood with his back to the bed, but George turned and scooped the cat into his arms, which Richard considered nothing short of stupidity.

'No animals in this house.'

'But . . .' George began, and the rage came to Brendan's eyes, bloodshot whites showing behind his watery transparent blue. 'It's my pet,' he managed, brushing against Richard's arm, as if for support.

Richard said nothing.

'Your pet, is it?'

Brendan reached out and took the cat from George's hands, taking it by the scruff of the neck between finger and thumb. He swung his arm like a cricketer and threw the cat against the wall.

It fell to the floor, grey and limp as the string mop their mother used on the close stairs.

Brendan turned to smile at them both. 'Now get that dead cat out of here.'

Richard's eyes were hot from staring at the road and his limbs were cramping after the long drive. He had stopped twice, briefly to eat and drink coffee, but he had been staring at motorways for over nine hours and his whole body felt fatigued.

As Richard drove into Cornwall it was lunchtime and his empty stomach contracted. There was a bitter taste in his mouth, but Cornwall was a relief after the monotony of the road. As the grey flank of the English Channel came into view, he remembered how crushed George had been after the kitten died. He had been white-faced before their father, but had not shed a tear until bedtime, when Richard had heard him crying in the darkness, whispering: 'I only wanted something to love.'

Something to love. Richard slowed down as he drove past cottages with terracotta roofs and whitewashed stone walls. He pulled up and rolled down the window, taking a long breath of the sea air and listening to the peal of seagulls, as he considered where to go first in search of George. He took the map out of the glove compartment and glanced at it and the road signs around him.

Outside the newsagent's, a man was standing, spreading a map out over the bonnet of his car. There was a breeze, which lifted the scant hairs from the man's head, and also the corners of the map. The man fidgeted, smoothing the hair over his scalp only to lose control of the map, which flapped in his face.

Despite himself, Richard smiled at the man's struggle, because even from this distance he could tell the man was annoyed and his movements were funny, trying his best to control the large, unruly map with his short arms.

Finally, the man began to fold the map. In the wind, this also took some time as he made an effort to refold it along the original creases. Watching was a rare meditation for Richard: it took him out of himself.

It was only when the short man tossed the map into the car and straightened his shirt and tie that Richard realised he had seen him somewhere before. As the man climbed into his old Ford, Richard recognised the journalist Tam Driscoll had been whispering to. Richard had been on the desk when he came to pay his bill, insisting on a receipt with his twitching eyes and mouth.

As the old Ford pulled away, Richard tossed his own map on to the floor and began to follow.

31

Margaret Holloway
Thursday 26 December, 2013

Maxwell's strong hand tightened around Margaret's wrist. She pulled away from him but he was holding her fast. She looked around the ward, but the nurses had vanished.

'You really are hurting me,' she said firmly, quietly.

His perfect blue eyes were wide and she found that it was his eyes more than his scarred appearance that terrified her. He was holding her wrist at an angle, so that pain shot up her forearm. He looked straight up into Margaret's eyes and she saw that he was trying to speak. His lips were dry and cracked, and he blinked and a tear flashed over his shiny, poreless face.

'Please,' she said again, but then realised he was urging to get her to sit down or move closer to him.

There was a plastic chair near the bed and she pulled it over. As soon as she sat down, he released her.

She exhaled, holding on to the side of the bed, as he turned to face her. His mouth opened and shut.

'Would you like some water?' she asked.

He nodded, his blue eyes following her as she stood and

poured a little water into a plastic beaker. She placed the glass in his hand, but he struggled to hold it, in turn gripping too hard and then not strongly enough.

'It's all right, let me.' She raised the glass to his lips and he took a sip. When he drank again, a little water ran over his chin and down his neck. She reached for a tissue and dabbed it away.

Just the act of drinking seemed to exhaust him. His head fell back on to the pillow and he closed his eyes, his bare chest rising and falling. She watched him. The water had made his lips pink. Finally, he opened his eyes and scrutinised her again. Now that she looked at him calmly, she was once again flooded with gratitude. She felt a rare kinship towards him.

He reached for her hand again, and she hesitated but then gave it to him. He rested his palm over her fingers, patting and then stroking, his eyes closed. Margaret swallowed, unsure what to say. His hands were cool and smooth as alabaster.

'It is so good to . . . see you,' he said, speaking slowly, as if each word was an effort.

Margaret smiled. 'And you. Thank you, once again.'

'Don't you know me?' he said, turning to her slowly, the scarred skin on his neck twisting like rope. '*I* know *you*.'

Margaret said nothing, feeling a flush on her cheek. She opened her lips to speak.

'Don't you remember?' he said. 'You taught me to read.' The words came with dry choking coughs. 'You taught me how to read and write.' He rose up a little on the bed and Margaret patted his shoulder and then helped him again to more water. He drank it audibly, sucking and gulping, as a child might.

He rested back against the pillow. While he recovered, Margaret put a hand on his arm. 'I saw . . . I saw that you had my work telephone number on you. I wondered then . . . did we meet at school? You're too old to be a pupil – a parent perhaps?'

He seemed to smile. It was a garish stretching of his face, to reveal teeth that were straight but yellowed. 'I *am* your pupil,' he said, still labouring to speak. 'Maybe your first.'

As if it were a game, Margaret sat back, smiling, looking up at the ceiling as she thought back to a time when they could have met. She remembered the first classes she had taught. She had volunteered as a tutor of illiterate adults when she was applying to teacher training college.

'Was it the volunteer centre in Tower Hamlets?'

Again the face stretched into a smile. He was teasing her, she realised.

'Your name: Maxwell Brown – I would have remembered it. I don't believe I've ever known any Maxwells, until now.'

He turned to her again. His blue eyes were fierce as truth. He tried to rise, but couldn't and instead settled for twisting towards her on the bed. 'That's not my real name,' he said, licking his lips and staring at her, unblinking, so that, despite herself, she had to look away.

Margaret began to feel very hot. The person in the adjacent bed was vomiting again and the acrid scent of it drifted across to them, until nurses came and briskly drew the curtain.

She clasped her hands and leaned towards him, whispering, 'Really? The hospital has records for you going right back. You were unconscious but they must have found your wallet or something...'

He nodded, looking up at the ceiling. From the side, even though the tip of his nose had been burned, there was something about the structure of his face that resonated in her memory.

'I've been going as Maxwell, with that date of birth, for some time, for as long as I've ...' he turned to her, 'been like this.'

A second spasm of coughs racked his body.

'I like it,' he continued. 'It suits me. Maxwell is a grand-sounding name, I think, and Brown is nothing, ten a penny.' He placed one of his palms against the other. 'Put together, that's just about right. That's who I am.'

Now that he had been speaking for longer, sentences and idioms, she realised that there was a subtle but noticeable Scottish lilt in his voice, not unlike her own. She had lived down south since her late teens and had been to university, teaching college and then worked in England. Ben teased her when her old accent crept into their conversation. When she was in pure emotional states – anger, love, joy – her childhood accent was more noticeable.

'So, who are you then?' she asked, leaning towards his face.

Although the skin around his eyes was immobile, unable to wrinkle in appreciation, it seemed as if his blue eyes were smiling at her.

'You *know*,' he said, nodding, letting his eyelids close.

Margaret put a hand in her hair. She *didn't* know who he was. She was frustrated with the game now and only wanted him to tell her. She put a palm on the bedsheets covering his stomach, worried that he was about to go to sleep.

He opened his eyes.

'What do you mean? I really don't. I need you to tell me.'

He closed his eyes again, as if her chatter was tiring him. He took a deep breath – his expansive, scarred chest rising up, buoyed by it. She thought he was sighing, preparing for sleep, but then he cleared his throat and began to sing.

It was not really a song. His voice was dry and weak, and it was more of a passionate whisper.

Margaret listened, politely at first, smiling, nodding her head to an imagined beat.

Then she heard him and the words and melody assaulted her deep inside. Her nose stung, and tears flashed over her cheeks.

'*And I love you so,*' he sang.

'*The people ask me how,*' she said, louder than she had meant, but the tears in her throat made it difficult to speak.

They looked at each other.

Suddenly she knew the flames that had engulfed him, searing his skin before her very eyes. She blinked and blinked again, remembering an explosion and the sound of metal bending, breaking. She could hear his screams, so loud that they seemed to rip through the very core of her. For years afterwards, they were the only thing she could hear inside her head. It had made her unable to speak, unable to think of anything else. But she had methodically bedded the memories down, as her mother had boxed her scraps, notes and articles – storing them safely away – so that they might move forward.

'I thought you were dead,' she whispered. 'I watched you burn.'

'I burned, but I didn't die, although I felt like I was dead,' said Maxwell. 'For years to come, I wished that I had died.'

'Don't say that.'

'But for the joy of seeing you again . . .'

'You saved my life.'

'You saved mine first.'

'How did you find me?'

'It was easy. There's the internet now. I looked you up. I found out where you worked, where you lived even – your husband is Ben, he writes articles for the *New Statesman*, the *Guardian* sometimes. Your children are Paula – and she looks so like you, I think – and Eliot. You work too hard and you go home late.

It was like that the day of the crash. You shouldn't have been out at that time, driving in that weather. You should have gone home earlier or taken the train.'

'I had a meeting.'

'You always have a meeting.'

Margaret put a hand over her face. The realisation was blinding, sudden.

'I'm sorry,' he said, his wild, scarred face lifting up from the pillow. 'I was following you but I meant you no harm. I only wanted to be near you. It was all I ever wanted. I didn't want to frighten you – but I knew if I had introduced myself you would have been ... The sight of me – I terrify everyone. But then you were in danger and I had to protect you ...'

The curtains surrounding the adjacent bed sounded against the rail as the nurse dragged them open. The woman who had been vomiting was pale and impassive, raised up on three pillows. The nurse, a short woman with large hips and chest, pressed her lips together in apology as she carried two cardboard bowls of vomit out of the warm ward.

'It's really you?' Margaret whispered.

'Hold my hand.'

She took his hand with her left, then with her right touched the skin of his chest, just above where his heart should be. 'My name. It's gone.'

'Your name was gone and you were gone. It broke my heart. I let you down.'

Margaret felt a fist of pain in her stomach. Tears blurred her eyesight. 'You didn't let me down.'

'If you look closely,' said Maxwell, wiping a hand over his scarred chest, 'you can still see a bit of the red ink. You can see part of the letter M.'

He struggled to raise his head off the pillow, his neck wrinkling as he looked down at his chest. She followed his gaze and sure enough there was a red line with a tail that had once been part of her name. She palmed a tear from her cheek.

'Your eyes,' he said, gazing at her. 'They fixed your eyes. They're beautiful, but they were always beautiful.'

'And I remember you were so handsome.'

His face stretched into a smile. 'Aye, I was not bad at all.'

'Why did you take me?' said Margaret, leaning forward and swallowing as she waited on his reply. He looked away from her, at a point in the distance.

'I've had a long, long time to think about what happened – nearly thirty years to wonder what on earth I thought I was doing. I've gone over it in my mind a million times.' He turned to meet her eye. 'What can I say? I was young and stupid. I only knew that I loved you from the first moment I saw you, and your mother ... I loved her too, you know.'

Margaret pressed her lips together as she listened, a pain in her throat.

'I didn't mean to take you. It all happened so fast. You were crying and I was trying to get out of town and then that was it; we were on our own, on the run together.'

'But why come for me then? Why didn't you want me when I was a baby?'

'Want you? You were all I wanted, but your mother didn't want me. I couldn't blame her either and you had a good life. That old man she married, did he love you?'

'Yes,' Margaret whispered.

'And who wouldn't. It's hard to say this, after all that happened – not just getting burned, but how *lonely* I've been these last years – but if I had to go back, I might do it all over again.

It was the wrong thing to do, but even after all that happened, I might just do it all again . . . just for that time with you. That time with you . . . I have no regrets.'

'I'm sorry,' she said. 'I just . . . I can't . . .'

She got up, leaving her coat and bag by Maxwell's bedside, and ran out of the ward. She made it to the elevators before she had to throw up into a metal-lidded waste bin.

When she finished, she wiped her mouth and eyes with the back of her hand, then walked down the rubber-floored hall. She took the stairs instead of the lift, walking as fast as she could, thinking only of the cool winter air that would absolve her.

As she descended the stairs, her mind was a kaleidoscope of images, smells and sounds from her childhood. Her throat hurt and her legs felt weak, but with each step she took she remembered more.

She remembered the warmth of her mother's hand one morning, and the smell of her towelling dressing gown as she hugged her before she set off to school. She remembered her black patent shoes with the single buckle and the rattle of her pencils in her school satchel. She remembered the too-green grass of the park near their home. She remembered running so hard that it felt as if her lungs would burst, and hearing his weight thundering behind her, like a racehorse. She remembered skinned knees and classmates taunting her. She remembered returning home, thinner and taller than she had been when she left, and the strange way that her father embraced her, awkward and unloving, as if she had done something wrong. She remembered hospital curtain hooks sounding against the metal rail and having to spread her legs wide. She remembered her mother shaking her, as if to jolt the words from inside her, when the only words she now knew were *fire*, *burning* and *death*.

*

Outside, the winter air was a relief. She unbuttoned her shirt and put a hand to her throat, feeling it wet with sweat. There were smokers at the hospital entrance and she moved away from them. Her eyes hurt and she saw white spots. She put her hands on her knees and bent over, thinking she might faint, taking deep breaths, as if recovering from a run. After a few seconds she felt better.

She felt a hand on her shoulder and a pair of battered, red All Star baseball boots appeared next to her feet.

'Are you all right?'

It was Ben, and the sight of him was blissful, a relief hard as the sea. She folded into him, pressing herself against him and reaching up his back for his shoulder blades. She cried silently, and he squeezed her tight, as if he had forgiven her.

'What's going on?' said Ben, taking her by the shoulders and holding her far enough away from him so that he could look into her face. 'What on earth are you doing?'

'I'm sorry, I . . .'

'You're here to see this burned guy who helped you?'

She nodded, catching her breath.

'I wish you hadn't run out like that. Anything could've happened. I was worried sick.'

'I'm sorry . . .' The tears in her throat made it hard for her to speak.

'What happened? Did he . . . die?'

'I thought he had,' said Margaret, her teeth suddenly chattering. 'But he'd been moved. He's awake and . . . you remember the number in his wallet? He's been . . . following me and I know him and—'

'Slow down,' said Ben, taking off his jacket and putting it over her shoulders. 'What do you mean, he's been following you?'

There was a fine silt of rain in the air and Margaret felt it dampening her hair.

'Where are the children?' she asked.

'Your dad's watching them. I knew you'd come here. I got a taxi. I was worried you'd crash again.'

Margaret smiled as tears spilled down her cheeks. 'Thank you,' she whispered, looking at the night and the drizzling rain and the far-off oily streetlamps. She took his hand and squeezed it as she sat down on a bollard next to one of the disabled parking spaces. 'You'll get a medal for this last month. Husband of the Year badge or something . . .' She tried to smile.

Ben crouched down beside her and took her hands into his. His face was full of concern. 'Your dad and I had a chat . . . Over dinner, I had no idea what that was all about, and he told me some things. Not the whole story of course. When you're ready . . .'

She nodded and got to her feet. The rain was becoming heavier. Their hands hung at their sides, fingers interlaced, foreheads touching.

'I'm sorry,' she whispered again, into his neck.

'Let's go home,' Ben said, running two hands down her arms.

'Not yet,' Margaret said, straightening, wiping her face with her palms and smoothing her hair, tucking it behind her ears. 'Do something for me. I want you to meet him.'

He frowned, hunched, looking down at her. 'Mags . . .'

'I need you to meet him,' she said, washing two hands over her face. 'Please.'

'Sweetheart, we shouldn't leave your dad with the kids . . .'

'I know, but I need you to meet this man.' She folded her arms, nodding. She was still trying not to cry and despite Ben's jacket she was still shivering. The shoulders of Ben's shirt were wet with rain. A raindrop flashed from the hair that hung over his forehead.

Ben took a deep breath and looked away, as if preparing to disagree with her. She reached out and took his hand. 'If you want to know what happened back then, then you have to come and meet this man.'

Ben turned to her. 'What's he got to do with that?'

Margaret took a deep breath and looked up at her husband.

'He's my father.'

32

Big George
Thursday 10 October, 1985

The exhaust of the old camper van was roaring by the time they drove into Penzance and George knew that he would soon have to patch the hole. He lay on the ground and shimmied underneath to inspect it. The hole was the size of a halfpenny piece.

The engine was overheating. The temperature gauge on the dashboard had been almost into the red and he had opened up the back of the van to look at it. He had waited for the engine to cool, but still singed the knuckle of his forefinger brushing against it when he added water. He inspected again a loose wire that he had found when they were in Stoke. He wondered what Tam would have made of it.

The old van had slowed them down, but arrival had filled George with elation and he decided to drive on while he could. There would be time to look at the engine when they found the cottage. It was a fine October day. The sky was blue and blown with thin clouds. The wind was up, and it buffeted the sides of the van as they pulled into town. Everything was so much more beautiful than George had imagined it. After Glasgow, the buildings seemed tiny and clean. He rolled down the window and took a deep breath.

'Do you smell that, Moll, can you taste it?'

Moll shook her head, taking deep breaths with her mouth open.

'It's the smell of the sea. Isn't that grand?'

Moll rolled her window down and knelt with her head outside, and her tongue sticking out as they drove slowly along Alverton Road.

'What are you doing, ya daftie?'

'Trying to taste it.'

George found a parking space and told her to wait in the van. He bought her an ice cream with raspberry sauce and a Flake and a packet of cigarettes for himself.

'Here,' he said, climbing into the van and handing it to her, licking the ice cream that had melted down his wrist while he waited on his change. 'This is our celebration. We made it. One end of the country to the other. The longest adventure ever.'

Moll sat concentrating on the ice cream as he drove, yet he noticed that every time he went over a bump in the road or turned a corner she got ice cream on her nose or her cheek. He smiled and sat back in his seat, wondering if *now* he would be able to be happy.

She turned to him, her face a palette of white ice cream and pink sauce. 'Now that our adventure's over, will I go home?'

He ran a hand through his hair, keeping his eyes on the road. 'Well, I didn't say the adventure was *over*. We need to find our dream home first. We need our perfect cottage. I bet once I find it ...'

'But can I call my mummy at least?'

'I'll let you do whatever you want, button, but we need to get set up first, remember? We need to get sorted. We've only just got here. Once we're sorted, if you still want to leave me, I can let you go.'

'I don't want to leave you,' she said, crunching the wafer of her ice cream, 'but I want to see my mum too. I could see you sometimes and my mum and dad the rest.'

George winced at the sunshine that split through the windscreen. He bit his thumbnail, and then put a cigarette between his lips. 'Not sure how that would work, button,' he said, biting on the cigarette to light it and exhaling through his open window. 'I think it's going to have to be one thing or the other. Like a lot of things in life – you have to choose.'

He glanced at her, and she was looking at him, wide-eyed, her face covered in ice cream. He pulled over. He didn't have a tissue so instead used the inside of his T-shirt to wipe her face and hands.

'You have a hairy belly,' she said.

He laughed down his nose at her, but he was cleaving inside, wondering what he would do if she refused to stay with him. He remembered the scratch of the tattoo needle over his heart and the warmth of his own blood that had flowed down to his nipple.

It was too soon, but he knew that he would have to let her go, if that was what she wanted.

'I choose you for now,' she said, licking her lips, as if she could tell what he was thinking.

'That's good enough for me.'

They left town and headed along the coast, where fields were expansive and green with patches of burned heather near the cliffs. The sea was wild and the cliff edge rose higher as they drove along the road towards Land's End. George drove through a village called Mousehole and parked for a while near the circular harbour, so that they could look at the floating, moored fishing boats and yachts and see the waves crash against the breakwaters.

He took out his map and tried to work out where his mother's cottage was.

He indulged himself as he drove, dreaming about what it would look like, and how they would live there. He would find her a school and would collect her each day. And they would be happy.

They drove on, with the windows down and the volume turned up on the stereo, looking out at the wild navy-blue sea. Brotherhood of Man came on the radio, and she knew it well, and together they sang 'Save Your Kisses for Me' at the top of their voices, 'kisses for me, save all your kisses for me' – George banging on the steering wheel and Moll kneeling on the seat slapping her small palms on the dashboard.

They sang so loud and so hard that George's throat hurt when they finished. They had been following the coastal road, driving slowly at forty miles an hour, farmers ploughing fields on one side and the deafening crash of waves on the other. Despite the speed they were travelling, the van was still buffeted on its left side and George felt the gale's power in the steering wheel.

The wind was blowing in from the sea, so there was no danger, although the cliff side was becoming perilously high. The tide was in and Moll sat with her nose pressed to the side window, looking down at the ocean as it swirled, gutting the cliff sides with spectacular sprays of surf.

There were few cars on the road, but when the wind altered George's steering again, he glanced in the mirror and noticed that an old brown Ford had been behind them for a while, despite their ice-cream stops and other wanderings.

The road curved up ahead and there was a passing space by

the cliff edge. George indicated and pulled over, then sat, hands on the wheel, watching as the Ford slowed down, then accelerated to pass. George peered out of his window as the car went by, wanting a look at the driver's face, but the driver was holding a map by the side of his face.

George got out of the car and slid another cigarette from the pack. He cupped his hand against the wind and lit up, watching as the Ford slowed but then drove around the corner and disappeared behind the field ahead. Moll tried to get out of the door but he raised his hand to stop her.

'Wait a moment, poppet.'

When the brown Ford was out of sight, George opened the door for her. They stood near the edge together, hand in hand, watching the waves break far out at sea and then lap and crash against the shingle below: breaking on overhanging rock, then silently absolving the sheltered bays.

'Don't stand too close to the edge,' he said, pulling her back, before flicking his cigarette and watching it fall down towards the wild water below.

She leaned into him, one arm around his waist, and he put a hand through her hair and over her shoulders.

'We'll be needing to cut your hair again.'

'No, I want to let it grow.'

'Understood, button.'

'How high up are we?'

'I don't know. Fifty feet, maybe more. A long way to fall, that's for sure.'

He felt a darkness shift over him, which he ascribed to the brown Ford he had seen and his paranoia about being followed and caught. He wondered if the man he bought the camper from had recognised them and told the police. He tried to brush his worries aside, as the north wind rushed the clouds over the cliffs. He picked her up and spun her and placed her back in the front seat of the van, then he drove on, telling himself that he was just imagining things. The brown Ford could have been an undercover policeman, but that was ridiculous. The police had no reason to be undercover, they would just pull him over as they had outside the Peak District.

He smiled to himself: the brown Ford was nothing. If he saw one of his brothers following him, then that would be a *real* paranoid delusion.

After Porthcurno George kept following the coast. The roads were like those he had driven on in the Highlands – single track. He had to pull into passing spaces to give way to oncoming traffic; except there was little traffic and the speed on the roads was otherwise fast. The cars that did pass George were travelling at least fifty miles an hour, while he only reached forty with a clear road ahead.

Around the next corner, George saw a cottage just after the Sennen road. It was single-storey, whitewashed with a black slate roof, like a croft. George reached into his bag and took out the map and the address that he had been given by the lawyer just after his mother's funeral. There was a black and white photograph of the property attached, and now George held it up against the house ahead of them.

'Look at that, button,' he said, pulling over and pointing it out in the distance. 'What do you think about that for a house?'

'It's pretty.'

When they drove nearer it was clear that it was almost a ruin. George pulled up and got out of the car. He had a key, but he could see as he approached that it would not be needed. One of the windows was broken and he peered inside. It smelled of damp and was unfurnished but for an old school desk in the corner. The floorboards were bare but there were still strips of old damson wallpaper on the walls. The lounge contained two simple open fireplaces.

George felt Moll at his side, her arm threading through his. Together they went around the back and peered into the small kitchen and two bedrooms. The back door was rotted; he merely pushed it and it opened.

'I don't want to go in there,' she said. 'It smells funny.'

She stayed outside, sitting on the grass, splitting autumn daisies with her thumbnail and threading one through the other to make a chain.

George stepped inside and walked from room to room, smelling the dampness, stamping on the rotten floorboards and inspecting woodworm. He imagined fresh paint and carpets, the fires burning, new wood in the window frames, a room filled with toys for Moll. He put his hands on either side of the broken window and looked out to sea.

The waves were wild but comforting and George felt a peace settle on him, which he had always known he would feel when he had arrived.

He turned and she was standing at the door with a chain of daisies held out to him.

'Very pretty,' he said.

'It's for you – a necklace.'

He knelt before her and bent his head, as he had as a child at mass. She tied the necklace carefully, taking her time, her breath a balm against his neck.

He stood up and the necklace stayed in place. 'C'm'ere till I show you the rooms.'

'It's all right,' she said, turning and skipping. 'It's too dark and scary.'

'I'll be out in a minute then.'

The kitchen was old blue Formica with a stone sink, but there was no cooker. A bashed metal kettle sat on the worktop. His mother had had one just like it, and George smiled as he picked it up. She had used it to fill the bath when the hot water ran out – back and forth, lifting the kettle with two hands.

George glanced out of the window, but Moll was not there. He went into the living room and looked out of the south-facing window, but he could not see her there either. He frowned, wondering where she had gone.

Just then, he heard her scream.

33

Angus Campbell
Thursday 10 October, 1985

He approached her, his hands tight fists at his side, the wind lifting the scant hair from his head. He knew he would only have a few moments to save the child. He worried his lip as he formulated his plan. The child's safety had to be his priority. But first, he needed to confirm her identity once and for all. He had to look her in the eye.

The wind was deafening – a rush in his ears – and he felt it push against his chest as he walked towards her. She was standing still, her fingers touching, hair messy across the nape of her neck.

'Molly?' he said, louder than he might have, because of the wind.

She turned immediately. Her hair had been roughly cut but it was her: blue eyes and a pronounced squint and her front teeth missing.

'It's nice to see you,' he said, licking his lips, knowing that he did not have much time before George came out.

She said nothing, her head cocked to one side.

'Are you all right?'

She nodded.

'I've come to save you.'

He held out his hand to her, but she didn't take it. She clasped her hands and pressed them into her chest, looking towards the cottage.

'I know you're afraid, but it's all right now. Come with me. I'll take you home.'

The wind was at her back, so that she wavered like a flower in the wind. She squinted at him, wrinkling her nose, as if to see him clearly.

Angus's breath was in his throat.

'There's no time for this. You have to come with me now.'

'I don't want to,' she said, looking again towards the cottage.

'There's no time for this,' he repeated, taking her by the elbow and tugging her.

Her scream was high-pitched and sudden. It shocked Angus so much that he jolted backwards. He glanced at the cottage. They had only seconds. He knew how to deal with disobedient children, so he took her by the wrist and began to drag her towards his car, knowing that she would thank him in time.

Angus had always known that the Lord would lead him to George McLaughlin. When he reached Penzance he had taken the coastal route, making his way to the area that May Driscoll had told him about. He saw a camper van up ahead and had tailed it. He had imagined himself arriving in Penzance in similar style, and so he followed the van for fun around the snaking coastal roads. He imagined a family of believers inside, singing hymns.

The van pulled over and Angus had no choice but to pass.

414

He glanced at the driver, out of interest. It was only seconds, but one look was sufficient. Angus had been certain. Big George McLaughlin was driving that van. Angus had finally found him.

It made sense that George would have taken another car, after the news reports indicated that the police were searching for a particular vehicle.

Angus's mouth was suddenly dry with the excitement of it all. He would save Molly and return to Thurso not only a hero, but a *soon-to-be prize-winning* journalist.

He held up his map to disguise his face as he overtook the camper van. It was a straight road ahead and he was forced to keep driving until he was out of sight. He took a right off the coastal road and drove back towards town, before doubling back on himself and returning to the coast down the Sennen road. There were few cars on the country roads, and as Angus doubled back, he noticed a black sedan in his wing mirror. He was travelling fast, over fifty miles an hour, in an attempt to find George again, and so he slowed down, taking his foot off the accelerator until he was only doing forty. Instead of drawing closer, or overtaking, the car behind also slowed and maintained its distance. Angus began to feel a flicker of apprehension.

There were several bends in the road, which was flanked by fields. After the third bend, Angus looked in the mirror and found that the black car was no longer there. He breathed a sigh of relief, thinking that it must have been visiting one of the farms, and continued on his way.

It was just after three when he saw the camper van ahead, parked by a cottage near the cliff side. He pulled into the roadside, parked with his tyres on the edge of a field of rape and proceeded on foot.

Once again, the Lord was guiding him. The child was kneeling in the grass picking flowers. He only needed to get close enough to see the eyes and then he would know for sure that it was Molly Henderson.

She was a wildcat and though she was tall for her age, Angus had not known a seven-year-old girl could possess such strength. She screamed as he tried to drag her back to his car. She was hitting his arm and pulling against him when George McLaughlin came out of the cottage.

Angus looked down at the child, whose face was streaked with tears. She was screaming up at his face, shouting, '*No, no*,' as if *he* was the monster; as if *he* was the depraved animal who had taken her from her home.

He glanced behind and saw that the black sedan had parked next to his Ford. Instinctively, Angus let go of the child's hand, but she had been pulling against him so hard that they both fell over on to the grass. Angus rolled on to his knees and when he sat up the child was in George's arms. Angus was unsure whether to stand or to stay on his knees. He knew what George was capable of, although he doubted if he would do it before witnesses. Angus was now grateful for the black sedan's presence.

'Who are you?' said George.

Angus stayed on his knees. George seemed like a colossus, his large hairy arms wrapped around the child.

'You don't know me, but I know you. I know who you both are,' said Angus. He was shouting to be heard against the wind, but his voice sounded higher than normal. He swallowed, feeling his heart flail like a fist in his chest. 'You are George McLaughlin and you have abducted this child, Molly Henderson, and I am here to take her home.'

'Who *are* you?' George shouted again, backing away with the long-legged Molly in his arms.

'I'm a reporter from the *John o'Groat Journal*,' Angus said, dusting the dampness and dirt from his knees and then smoothing down his hair. 'I'm here to take Molly home.'

George frowned, and Angus thought that his assertive stance had made him weaken, but then he heard a car door slam and turned to see a tall, dark man standing beside the black sedan. Angus stared at him. He knew him. It was the man from the McLaughlin garage who had written him a receipt. Angus had suspected he was Richard McLaughlin.

George had seen the tall man too. He ran back to the van carrying Molly and drove off with sufficient acceleration to leave rubber marks on the road.

Angus had twisted something when he fell but he also ran back to his car. He glanced in the rear-view mirror as he pulled away and gave chase, and, as he expected, the black sedan also set off in pursuit. The car continued to tail Angus, but from a distance.

The camper van, which had been keeping to a leisurely pace until now, roared along the cliff-side road. Angus had to put his foot down to catch up and guessed that the van was doing sixty miles an hour or more. The exhaust was noisy but it also began to belch black smoke from the rear as the van snaked its way along the hillside. Angus was not very familiar with the Volkswagen caravanette, but he knew that the engine was at the rear and it looked as if it was on fire.

Above the sound of the exhaust and the crash of the waves, Angus heard a distant wail of sirens. The fire had come and now the police. He assumed that the police were here for George; that they had continued to track him even though he had changed vehicles. The Lord was showing his presence.

'Your time is up,' Angus proclaimed out loud as he drove. '*For the wages of sin is death* – Romans chapter six, verse twenty-three.' Angus felt his face flush in anger, and the throb of the vein on his forehead that ran from one eyebrow over his pale, freckled scalp. George McLaughlin was going to pay for his sin and Angus relished the thought of witnessing it.

The sirens were still audible but Angus could not yet see a police car, so he kept up the chase. The black sedan was small as a beetle in his mirror. Angus was focused on the camper van, as it skidded and belched black smoke four hundred yards ahead. It felt as if everything in Angus's life had been leading to this point where he, the righteous man, would root out the sinner.

Up ahead, he watched the camper van pull over next to a field. Angus drove forward one hundred yards then also pulled over to watch. The dazzle of the yellow rape field hurt Angus's eyes and he strained to see what was happening up ahead. The van's engine was still running – spewing black fumes. He wondered if he should overtake, try to slow George down; or if he should now approach McLaughlin and attempt a citizen's arrest. The police were sure to be closing in and Angus calculated whether a citizen's arrest would be possible, considering George's great size. He sat clenching his hands on the steering wheel, wondering what was going on inside the parked camper van.

Finally, Angus got out of the car and walked carefully towards the vehicle. The smoke was heavy in the air and Angus had to put a hand over his face. He looked over his shoulder and saw that the dark sedan had also stopped in the distance. As he approached the smoking vehicle, he saw that the van was shaking a little, back and forth. The wind was still high but the shaking seemed to be coming from *inside*. It occurred to Angus that George could be murdering Molly right now. He began to walk faster.

The passenger door of the van next to the field of rape flew open. Above the sound of the wind, Angus could hear Molly crying. As he drew closer, he saw she was standing on the edge of the field. 'No, no, I don't want to,' she was crying.

Just then, the van door slammed and the camper drove off, leaving the child behind. Angus ran up to Molly, only wanting to save her, but she screamed as soon as she saw him, and began to run at full pelt after the camper. There wasn't much traffic, but the child could surely come to harm. She was hysterical and running down the middle of the road. Angus was surprised how fast she ran. He got into his car and followed.

As he drew near to the child, Angus noticed that the camper started to veer off the road towards the cliff side and then back towards the field, as if George was losing control of it. The girl was still running after it and Angus could not understand why.

At first Angus thought he saw a piece of material flapping between the back wheels of the van: something that George had run over – an orange flicker of fabric between belches of smoke. It was only when George veered again towards the cliff that Angus realised the van was *on fire*. Angus pressed on his brake and watched, mouth open, wondering if the camper van was going to head straight off the cliff, but instead it stopped only a foot from the edge. Now, side on, Angus could see that the engine had caught fire and this had spread to the inside. The child was now dangerously close to the burning vehicle and Angus realised that it might explode.

When he got out of the car he looked behind him. The

black sedan was still parked half a mile up the road, and Angus listened against the wind, but thought he could no longer hear the sirens. He ran towards Molly, who was trying without success to open the van doors. Angus ran up to her and lifted her off her feet.

'You're all right now,' he told her. 'You're safe, but you have to come with me.' She was heavier than he had expected.

'No,' she screamed, kicking him in the shins so hard that the pain took the breath from Angus. He let her go and had to clench his fist to curtail his urge to hit her in retaliation. There was rebellion in her that should have been crushed early. Did she not realise that Angus was here to save her?

He took a handful of her sweater in his fist, and pulled her back as she again tried to lunge at the van. 'It's on fire. It's not safe. Don't you understand, child? You need to stay back.'

The child covered her face with her hands, and she seemed to be screaming 'Daddy,' although Angus could not be sure.

There was a sudden explosion from inside the van, and Angus covered his face with his arm and instinctively pulled the child into him to protect her. He opened his eyes to the heat of fire and the taste of smoke. Angus peered through his fingers at the van. The explosion had not come from the fuel tank. The fire raged, burning from the inside out.

As he drew closer, Angus saw that George McLaughlin was engulfed in flames and trying to get out: his large white palm pressed against the glass of the side window.

Angus moved closer still, so that he was able to stand on tiptoe and peer into the rear windows of the van. He could hear George screaming.

He walked closer, his hands heavy at his sides, immobile. It reminded him of the Sabbath day when he had watched Maisie in labour; listened to her long, low moans as she tried to push out the calf inside her.

Perhaps the locks had jammed in the heat or perhaps the door was also on fire, but George could not get out. Angus drew closer, watching the urgency in his face – teeth and staring eyes as the fire covered his body. He was shouting something, but Angus could not hear what.

'Help him!' Molly screamed.

Angus turned to glance at her, behind him, elfin, shorn, indignant.

'*Help him.*'

The smell of burning combined with the brine of the sea was intoxicating. Angus felt a rare exhilaration. He was watching justice, he realised. God's hand had reached down and delivered judgement. He moved closer, unblinking.

He watched George flailing, twisting and turning, as if the fire was an animal on his back, rampant, possessed, hungry. The fire was roaring, and above its cackle and spit was the sound of George screaming. So quick that Angus could almost not believe it, the fire consumed him, so that even the hand which now pawed at the glass was engulfed in flames.

Angus's lips moved but made no sound as he whispered the words of the Lord: 'As *for the cowardly, the faithless, the detestable, as for murderers, the sexually immoral, sorcerers, idolaters, and all liars, their portion will be in the lake that burns with fire and sulphur, which is the second death.* Revelation, chapter twenty-one, verse eight.'

Angus felt a strange relaxation seep through him. ' . . . *and they will be tormented day and night, forever, and ever.*'

Molly began to beat the sides of the van, screaming, and Angus had to use all his strength to drag her away. He heard the sirens now, throbbing, pulsating as they came closer and closer.

Just then, over the roar of the fire, Angus heard the sound of the camper van's engine, revving up. Angus held on to Molly's upper arms as she thrashed and pulled against him. He couldn't believe it, but – *on fire* – George was attempting to escape, to drive away. Angus tightened his grip on the child and smiled at George's folly.

The van screeched into reverse and Angus stared, his mouth open as he watched the burning driver. The van paused, back tyres on the edge of the field, headlights facing the ocean. It was impossible for him to drive and Angus shook his head at the man's ridiculous attempt to escape justice. Just then the back wheels spun and the smoking, burning van charged forward, right over the edge of the cliff. As it fell, there was a second, larger explosion that blew the van open.

The child screamed and then went limp in Angus's arms as together they watched it take off from the cliff at Land's End and fall, head first, into the wild waves below.

They went to the edge and watched as the van bobbed in the water, only its boot and back wheels visible. It had been blown to pieces. A tyre floated alongside kitchen items: plastic plates and cups. The police arrived: a male and a female police officer. The female officer took Molly to the police car and called the ambulance and the coastguard, while the man took Angus's statement. Angus peeked over the edge of the cliff, as the van sank from view.

Back in Thurso, Angus sat in his study, with his fingers poised over the keys of the typewriter. It was the afternoon and his eyes were hot with tiredness. He had driven up from Penzance the day before, driving overnight and sleeping for a few hours in service station car parks. He had arrived early this morning, and had bathed but not slept. He had changed all his clothes and asked Hazel to wash those he had been wearing, but he could still smell the smoke from George's burning van. The stink of McLaughlin was still on him.

Angus was annoyed that the article he now had to write was not as revelatory as he had dreamed. He had seen George McLaughlin burn to death for his sins and he had saved young Molly Henderson from a wicked, brutal criminal. Only the Bible had better stories, and Angus had wanted to write it. He knew the truth and he wanted the world to know.

But the police had been last on the scene. Molly had been taken away first by ambulance, then the coastguard had been called to dredge up the van and look for a body. Angus had enjoyed describing George's slow death to the police officers. He told of the flames engulfing his body and the two explosions that had come from inside the van.

By the time the police were ready to take statements, Richard McLaughlin was long gone. Angus emphasised to the police that it had been *George McLaughlin* driving the van, but a day later the police had failed to verify it. The owner of the camper van had recognised Molly's squint and contacted them, and then police in Cornwall had had reports of sightings, but George had been merely an unconfirmed suspect. Angus's editor forbade him to print George's name in the article. Molly Henderson cried at the scene but quickly became mute and would not say a word to either investigators or hospital staff about her kidnapper or anything else.

Chewing his lip over his typewriter as he considered what it was possible for him to write, Angus remembered with some bitterness the jibes that his colleagues had made about his obsession with George McLaughlin.

Angus was familiar with this situation: he knew the truth; he had seen the light, but he was surrounded by heathens who lacked faith.

The van was dredged from the ocean, but the police couldn't find a single usable fingerprint inside. Gas canisters were found, which explained the two explosions. The coastguards had been tasked with finding the body, in the expectation that it would be in pieces. The tide had been going out and the divers were searching a wide area. They found a burned shoe, but no remnants of the body. Back in Glasgow, all George's family and friends said that he was alive but had skipped town to see a girlfriend and would be back soon.

Angus had called Inspector Black as soon as he returned to Thurso, but the inspector had called him 'obsessed' and hung up before he was finished speaking.

Merely because Angus had been *seeking* George, his achievement in finding him was not recognised.

'Do you know George McLaughlin?' Inspector Black had asked him.

'I *know* it was George driving that van . . .'

'But do you know him really? No, you don't. How could you tell George McLaughlin from a hundred other tall, dark men? You were only in Penzance to find George and find him you would, come hell or high water.'

'Hell or high water indeed,' muttered Angus.

He placed his palms together as he prepared to write. It was not the story he had intended, but sometimes one had to deal with reality. What Angus *believed* had happened was not the accepted story and, as a journalist, he had been reminded that he was duty bound to report only accepted facts.

There was a knock on his study door and Angus turned. It was Hazel. She was wearing her coat and hat and looking different from how he remembered her. He narrowed his eyes for signs of make-up, but could not detect any. Still, she seemed smarter, cleaner and more awake than he had seen her in some time.

'What is it?' he said impatiently, turning back to his work.

'I've washed the clothes you brought back. I've made dinner and Rachael says that she will serve it. I'll be back some time this evening.'

Angus wasn't listening. He turned around to his work before she had finished speaking.

It was only when she had left the room that Hazel's words reached him.

Angus got up and bounded to the top of the stairs. He hung over the banister and called to her.

'What do you mean, Rachael will serve dinner? Where are you going?'

'I'm going out, Angus,' said Hazel, with a strange new wilfulness in her eyes that reminded him of the Henderson girl.

'But where are you going? You can't . . .'

'I'm going to a women's Bible group in town. Rachael knows what to do. I'm sure you'll be fine.'

She pushed her hands into leather gloves and started down the stairs.

He was still standing there, almost paralysed by disbelief, when Rachael came out of her room.

'Your mother's *gone out*,' Angus announced to her.

The girl's skin was red from acne, and he noticed that her

ears were still reddened and scabbed since his last punishment. Rachael always tied her hair back but he wondered why she did not wear it loose to cover the marks.

'She'll be back later,' said the girl coolly. 'I can sort dinner.'

Angus rubbed his nose and then dared, 'You should let your hair down. Your ears, they're ... not pretty to look at.'

Rachel was halfway downstairs but she turned and looked up at her father. 'Were you afraid someone saw?' she whispered to him strangely.

He pressed his lips together. He had been gone for only two days and in that time it seemed as if the spirit of the Henderson girl had taken over his wife and daughter.

Angus turned but then called down after her. 'I don't care who sees, but I thought you would. You might have put your hair down just this once.'

'I thought you would disapprove.'

'And why would that be?'

'*Women should adorn themselves . . . not with braided hair and gold or pearls or costly attire, but with good deeds.*'

'First book of Timothy, chapter two, verse nine,' said Angus.

'So Mum has gone out to do good work, and I will make your dinner.'

Angus sensed that there was dissension afoot but could not be sure, so he returned to his study.

He began to type. It was not a scoop. It would not be syndicated worldwide. It was a dull, factually accurate article about a recent unsolved crime. He knew the truth, but still no one was willing to listen.

It would not make him famous, but it was all he could write at this time.

426

The John o'Groat Journal, Friday 11 October 1985

HENDERSON CHILD SAVED AS MANHUNT ENDS IN DIVINE PUNISHMENT

By Angus Campbell

Molly Henderson, who went missing from Ravenshill Primary on 2 October, has been found and reunited with her parents.

She was abducted as she walked to school, sparking a nationwide search. Although Molly was found alive, the vehicle her abductor was driving caught fire and plunged over a cliff into the English Channel. Molly was lucky to escape the van before it caught fire and fell into the sea. As it plummeted from the Land's End cliff, there were two explosions inside the van, killing Molly's kidnapper, who burned to death.

Pieces of the van have been recovered, but the abductor's charred remains have not yet been found. Police and coastguards continue the search for the body.

The child was at the scene when her abductor died, but has not spoken since and is said to be suffering from extreme shock. Molly has been taken to the Royal Aberdeen Children's Hospital in order to ascertain the extent of her physical and psychological injuries. The identity of the kidnapper is unconfirmed but it is hoped that Molly will bear witness when she recovers.

Trained police officers and medical staff experienced in treating children who have suffered sexual abuse and psychological trauma are working with Molly and the Henderson family to try to ensure a speedy recovery.

Molly's mother, Kathleen, gave the following statement: 'I'm just so glad to have her back. I thought she was lost but to have her back in one piece is the greatest gift.'

Molly's father, John Henderson, thanked the public for its unflinching support.

34

Margaret Holloway
Thursday 26 December, 2013

Ben and Margaret walked hand in hand along the corridor in Ward 21.

'He's not pretty to look at.'

'Neither am I,' said Ben, and Margaret nudged him gently.

When they arrived at the bedside, the curtain was half drawn and the nurse was taking blood from George's arm. 'You think I'm a pincushion,' they heard him tease her.

'Doctor's orders – we need to make sure you're out of the woods.'

'Ah, you're never out of the woods. I learned that a long time ago.'

George noticed Margaret and her husband standing a few feet away. His face stretched into a smile.

When the nurse drew the curtain back, she frowned sympathetically at Margaret and Ben. 'Only a few more minutes. His blood pressure's very high.'

Since Margaret had left he had been connected to a heart monitor, which now emitted a low pulsing sound.

'My Moll,' he said, turning up his palm to ask for her hand again. 'My Moll.'

She slipped her hand into his. His fingers were still cold.

'This is Ben,' said Margaret, stepping out of the way, so that Ben could lean in to shake hands.

George kept hold of Margaret's hand while he offered Ben a free one. There was a needle taped to his arm for administering drugs.

'George McLaughlin,' he said as he took Ben's hand. He said the name carefully, breathing out as he did so, as if with relief.

'Nice to meet you.'

Ben looked weary, overcome.

'You married my little girl.'

'So I understand.'

'You better look after her.'

'It's a harder job than you think,' said Ben, raising both eyebrows at Margaret. 'Stubborn and independent.'

'You always were ... weren't you, button?' said George, turning to her.

Margaret felt her eyes prick with tears, but fought them back. She pulled up chairs for her and Ben and they sat down.

'What happened to you?' she dared to ask. '*I saw you die.*'

'A man dies more than once in his life,' said George. Margaret found that when she met his eyes and looked straight into them, the rest of his face reformed, so that she could imagine it as it had been. He was still holding her hand, coursing the back of it with his thumb, and she remembered nights leaning into him as he sang to her. 'I suppose I was trying to kill myself, but the old bastard upstairs – if there is one – had other plans for me. When the van sank, I managed to get out – I've no idea how. There was an explosion and I must have been knocked unconscious for a time – thrown out somehow. The seawater – I think it helped, with the burns ... I tried to swim for a bit as best I could, not swim as such but tried to stay afloat. I kept passing out and was sure I would drown. I had no idea how badly hurt I was. A woman walking her dog helped me when I was washed ashore. When I woke up in hospital, they told me I was in Torquay. I had floated so far along the coast. I told them I couldn't remember anything except my name and that I'd been in a boating accident. I told them my name was Maxwell Brown. I said I was born in 1955 instead of 1958. I was in hospital a long time. I expected the police, or my family, or someone ... but no one ever came. All those years I hadn't wanted to be a McLaughlin, and then there I was, erased. But ...'

The pulses of the heart machine quickened. George pressed his lips together again and again.

'Do you need more water?'

He looked away and closed his eyes. She poured some for him anyway, an inch in the plastic beaker beside of the bed. He took it into his hand but then spilled it right away. Ben leaned over and brushed the water off the top sheet.

'He's too tired,' Margaret said. 'We should go.'

'We should,' Ben whispered. 'And your dad's with the kids.'

George's eyes opened wide. '*I'm* her dad,' he said loudly, although it seemed to cost him all his strength. Ben nodded.

'They wrote such *lies* about me,' George said. The word *lies* forced open his lips, revealing his purple gums. 'They said I hurt you and I never. I never would ...'

'I know,' said Margaret, stroking the back of his hand. 'Don't let yourself get upset. It's all over now. I'm here.'

'When I got out of hospital and I got set up, I started taking classes. When I rented that first flat I was able to write Maxwell

Brown. I knew how. We . . .' he broke off to cough again, 'we are both left-handed.' He held up his left hand and Margaret put her left hand against his.

'We are,' she said.

His eyes were now half closed, and Margaret got to her feet. She was worried that he would not feel it were she to kiss the waxy skin of his forehead, so she leaned forward and kissed the palm of his hand.

'I love you so,' he was still whispering, as if trying to sing again.

Ben rubbed Margaret's shoulders and then they left him.

Walking along the corridor, Margaret felt enervated, depleted. She walked with her fingers loosely laced through Ben's.

When they got home, it was late and the children were in bed, but Margaret was in time to say good night. Her father had done all the dishes by hand and stacked them on the kitchen table. The cutlery was shining: little regiments of teaspoons, knives and forks.

'We have a dishwasher, Dad.'

'Oh, they're a waste of money. It gave me something to do.'

Margaret went to him and kissed his cheekbone. He smiled and dipped his head a little in response. She had called him while Ben was driving back, to say they were on their way.

Her father folded the tea towel he had been using. 'I told them to go to bed. I thought it best, when it was nearly ten. They gave me no argument. They're a credit to you.'

Margaret pressed her lips together in a smile. Ben had gone upstairs to kiss the children good night.

'Let's sit down for a moment,' she said, putting a hand on her father's elbow.

She sat down at the table opposite him. She was exhausted,

but there was more to say. She remembered the words that she had said to him before she ran out of the house. His face was pale, his eyes saddened. She took a deep breath.

'I need to tell you about what's been going on with me since the car crash.'

The skin on John's high forehead wrinkled.

'I don't want to upset you, I ...'

His fingers fluttered on the table, as if his feelings were of no consequence. The stacked spoons trembled audibly.

'A few weeks ago, I found the man who had pulled me out of the car on the M11. He had a head injury too, and ... he was put in a coma, so that when I found him I couldn't thank him, but I kept on visiting.' Margaret wiped a hand across her eyes. She was deeply tired, yet there was a bright, crackling wakefulness in her veins. 'I was in shock after the crash and, sitting quietly with him, I guess I did a lot of thinking. That was when all that stuff ... all that *stuff* ... started to come back to me ... or not come back to me exactly, but I couldn't stop thinking about it. I wanted to know.'

John nodded gravely.

'Mum's things ... that box of cuttings and photographs, letters ... it was *so hard* for me to go through, but I had to do it. And it was harder because she's *not here*,' her throat clotted with hurt, 'and she had *collected* all of it.'

John licked his lips, as if tasting the grief one more time.

'And tonight, when I ran out, I went to the hospital again to see the man, the man who saved me on the motorway. I didn't know when I left, but he had woken up from his coma and then I started to understand why I'd been so drawn to him.'

She paused and looked across the table at her father. He was frowning, as if anticipating what she was going to say. She swallowed, once again wondering what it had been like for John – searching for her, thinking she was dead. She had been stolen from him – the man who had always loved her, from her earliest memories.

She wasn't sure how he would react if she told him she had been visiting George McLaughlin – a gangster who had been her mother's first love, and had taken her away from home as a seven-year-old child.

He would be angry. He would be angry at the man who he thought had hurt his little girl. If he knew that the person who had taken her was her real father it might devastate him.

He was sitting waiting for her to speak. She reached over and clasped his hand in hers.

She cleared her throat and struggled to reform her thoughts. 'I was drawn to him because he saved my life and I realised that I was so glad to be alive.'

Her hands were warm inside her father's. 'I'm so sorry ... about what I said to you at dinner.'

John nodded with his eyes closed.

'I think everything suddenly came into focus. The car crash ... they said I was in shock, but it seemed like the opposite was going on. Suddenly things became clear to me – where I was from, who I was, what had happened to me and ... it made me miss Mum.'

A thin tear flashed over John's grey face.

She took a deep breath. 'You're my dad and you always will be.'

John cleared his throat. 'You were trapped and the car was burning. The fire,' her father wiped his eye with his forefinger, 'the fire ... I know what that must have meant to you.'

Margaret heard Ben's footsteps on the stairs. They got to their feet, expecting the membrane of their conversation to be broken.

'I'm sorry,' her father said, hurriedly.

'Don't be silly. It's me who should apologise for running out like that – causing a scene.'

'No, I mean, *I'm sorry*, back then . . . I could have been better. Your mother and I, we both could have been better.'

'Thanks for coming, Dad,' she said. 'That's all that matters.'

He patted her shoulder. 'I should turn in now. Early start back.'

His hand stayed on her shoulder for a moment, and then he clung to the wool, balling up her cardigan in his fist. He covered both eyes with forefinger and thumb. Margaret put her arms around his waist.

'Uh-oh,' said Ben, 'not more tears, just when I'm ready to get the party started.'

'We're fine,' said Margaret.

'An excellent bit of dishwashing, Pater,' said Ben, motioning to the table. 'You can come back.'

'I shall look forward to it,' said John, his face puckering into a smile.

Ben and Margaret sat up past midnight, with glasses of wine, talking. The fire was on, but Margaret was shivering, so much that Ben put a blanket around her shoulders. She sat with her feet in his lap as he rubbed them.

'Moll,' he said, and then again, 'Moll,' as if trying it out on her. 'Should I start to call you that?'

Margaret laughed. 'It was my baby name. Just before I started high school, I decided I wanted to be called my full name. Maybe even my name was a reminder . . .'

It was not until later, when she was in bed lying curled into Ben, that she fully remembered the very first day she met George. She remembered the smell of his aftershave and the clear sparkle in his eyes as he knelt, one knee on the pavement as he unbuttoned his shirt, showing her the name written on his chest.

Margaret blinked in the darkness of their bedroom. She could taste black smoke at the back of her throat. She could hear him screaming but she couldn't get to him.

When they took her to the hospital they had stripped her and inspected her for harm. She had deep, purple bruises on her arms, which the doctors and her parents all decided had been inflicted on her by the tall dark man who had kidnapped her. Margaret had not said a word – she had been unable, but she knew that the journalist who had arrived at the scene and tried to hold her back had made the bruises. She still remembered the pain – wanting to protect her father, sure she *could* help him, but unable to get free. It had been this shame that had so overwhelmed her later: that she had not been able to save him.

She turned again, her mind bright despite her need for rest. Ben was sound asleep, his breaths low and rhythmic. Down the hall, she could hear the intermittent long inhalation of her father's snores.

She was unaware, but at the Royal London Hospital the senior charge nurse was looking up Margaret's telephone number. George had had a stroke after a blood clot formed in his brain. He died as Maxwell Brown, at 01.25, leaving no known next of kin.

She had been drinking, and her mind was scorched with tiredness, but Margaret smelled burning in the bedroom. It wasn't a fire, or a cooking smell, and after a moment, lifting her head off the pillow, she realised that it was a cigarette. She frowned, wondering about Ben, her father or, God forbid – the kids. She turned over and inhaled again. It was unmistakable, at the back of her throat, mixed in with a briny whiff of aftershave. Margaret looked up, and George was standing at the foot of the bed. He was in his dark blue suit, like the day when he had met her after school. He was smiling at her, all clear skin and stubble and bad blue eyes. 'You go to sleep now, angel' was all he said.

Calm flooded her. She lay down and began to drift off to sleep.

The telephone rang and Ben was startled, jumping out of bed to answer it, palm pressed against the wall. He tried to turn on the light but knocked it clean off the bedside table. The lamp crashed to the floor as he answered the phone. Margaret lay, eyes wide open, as lights went on down the hall, first Paula's room and then her father's.

Ben hung up and came round to her side of the bed, smoothing her hair and taking her hand.

'Listen . . .' he said, frowning.

'It's all right,' she whispered.

'He's dead.'

'I know.'

She smiled, knowing that she was, for the first time in her life, whole again, present. She was ready to go back to work, ready to look after her family. He was with her, and he always would be.

SONGS

'And I love you so, the people ask me how', by Don McLean, 1970 debut album, *Tapestry*, writer Don McLean, label Mediarts.

'Kisses for me, save all your kisses for me', by Brotherhood of Man, 1976, *Love and Kisses from Brotherhood of Man*, writers Tony Hiller, Lee Sheriden, Martin Lee, label Pye Records.

'Sweet Caroline', by Neil Diamond, 1968, *Brother Love's Travelling Salvation Show*, writer Neil Diamond, label Uni Records.

'Song Sung Blue', by Neil Diamond, 1972, *Hot August Night*, writers Neil Diamond, Leon Russell, label MCA, Universal.

'I've Been Loving You Too Long', by Otis Redding, 1965, *Otis Blue: Otis Redding Sings Soul*, writers Otis Redding, Jerry Butler, label Volt/Atco.

Good Bad Love

Reading Guide

READING GROUP QUESTIONS

* Memory plays a significant role in this book; in what ways does it inform identity? Do you think even the things you don't remember can affect who you become?

* Big George wants desperately to change his path, and yet can't seem to stay on the right side of the law. Do you believe people can change, that they can escape the circumstances they come from?

* How do the events of the 'road trip' affect George? How do they shape Moll's future?

* Have you ever been in a bad accident? Did it change anything for you?

* The novel involves a road trip from the most northern point of the UK, to its southern tip – from John O'Groats to Lands End. How does that relate to the journey that each of the characters undertakes?

* How does the book comment on the relationship between parents and children?

* Which character did you sympathize most with, and why?

* This novel is written almost as if it were a fairy-tale or a fable. What do you think the author is trying to say?

* This book was published in the USA under the title *Everything She Forgot*. What would you have called this book, and why?

* Would you have given the story a different ending?

AUTHOR Q&A

**Both *Good Bad Love* and your first novel *The Guilty One*
deal with questions of nature vs. nurture. Do you believe
one plays a more important role than the other?**

I think the interplay between nature and nurture and free
will is endlessly fascinating and I continue to hope for the
power of human choice to overcome, but oftentimes this
proves futile. George and his family of Glaswegian gangsters came to me instinctively. I was attracted to the idea
of someone growing up amid great violence but refusing to
be inured, broken by it. George is an example of the tragic
questing hero, struggling to escape his environment and, to a
large extent, himself, but who ultimately fails. I think George
is the soul of this novel, and his failure is heartbreaking.

**What was the first creative seed for this novel? Did a
character or a storyline come to you first?**

When I first began to work on this book, I was interested in
Post Traumatic Stress Disorder (PTSD) and the mechanism
of memories from the past impacting on the present. The first
scene of the book – involving the car crash and the strange
saviour – came to me quite quickly and I knew that the
burned man who rescues Margaret would be the key to her
past. In writing the 1980s scenes, I knew I wanted to write

about a man who steals his daughter and for the journey they took to be a redemptive one, spanning the whole country. I wanted the relationship between father and daughter to gradually soften as the road trip progresses, from one of captor and captive, to one of genuine affection and love.

Did any of your initial ideas change as you wrote?

In the early beginnings of the novel, the father-abductor that I sketched was too harsh and faceless and I had trouble with the relationship between him and his stolen daughter. I started over, and concentrated on George himself, his past and what he had been through to take him to the point where he would want to steal his daughter, after all these years. It was then that Big George was born and I fell in love with him straight away.

Children play an important role in your books, why do you think that is?

In my writing, I always return to relationships between parents and children because it is such fertile ground. Families in general are a wonderful resource for novelists, but children in particular are interesting because their personalities are still developing.

I was also interested in the child, Moll, teaching her newfound father something – as all children are important teachers of adults. It was then that I hit on the idea of George being illiterate because of the institutional violence that he had experienced at school. Moll's patient teaching not only liberates George but also repairs some of the damage that was done in his past.

You grew up in the eighties like Moll. What, if anything was taken from your own memories of childhood at that time?

I enjoyed plundering my memory for the quirky details of those times, such as the insalubrious Tennent's lager cans with the underwear models on the side. The ubiquitous powder-blue Volkswagen camper van that features in the road trip was something I remembered from childhood, as close family friends used to transport their seven children around in an olive-coloured VW. It was fun for me to revisit those years, with real telephones and telephone directories, and Angel Delight desserts.

Do characters ever take you by surprise while you are writing?

The scene where the teenage George and his loan shark father visit a debtor on a building site was an interesting one to write. It was one of the rare occasions when a character takes over and I as the writer watched the scene I was writing unfold. I knew George intimately, and I knew that he couldn't do what his father was demanding of him. The outcome of the scene was George's only choice and so he made it for me.

447

Did you ever imagine the book ending another way?

It is hard for both the writer and her readers when the hero dies at the end of the book and for me I wanted to literally bring George back to life – not just as he had become, but as he had been, all those years ago, in the dark recesses of Margaret's memory. Ghosts are tricky to render if not infrequent in novels, but the ghost's manifestation at the end of *Good Bad Love* is exactly how one of my aunts described her husband appearing to her, soon after he died. It was an image that had always stayed with me and so I chose it for the ending of my novel. It seemed right that the love between my main characters would survive in some tangible way.

BOOKS ON LISA BALLANTYNE'S SHELF

Zen and the Art of Motorcycle Maintenance – Robert M. Pirsig

The Little Friend – Donna Tartt

Gilead – Marilynne Robinson

Tamburlaine Must Die – Louise Welsh

The Strange Case of Dr. Jekyll and Mr. Hyde – Robert Louis Stevenson

Dear Life – Alice Munro

The Humans – Matt Haig

The Human Stain – Philip Roth

Rapture – Carol Ann Duffy

What I Talk About When I Talk About Running – Haruki Murakami

The Complete Poems of John Donne

The Rainbow – D.H. Lawrence

Lisey's Story – Stephen King

The Rebel – Albert Camus

Have you read Lisa Ballantyne's extraordinary debut, *The Guilty One*?

A little boy is found dead in a children's playground . . .

Daniel Hunter has spent years defending lost causes as
a solicitor in London. But his life changes when he is
introduced to Sebastian, an eleven-year-old accused
of murdering an innocent young boy.

As he plunges into the muddy depths of Sebastian's troubled
home life, Daniel thinks back to his own childhood in foster
care – and to Minnie, the woman whose love saved him, until
she, too, betrayed him so badly that he cut her out of his life.

But what crime did Minnie commit? And will Daniel's
identification with a child on trial for murder make
him question everything he ever believed in?

Read on for the opening of *The Guilty One* . . .

A little boy was found dead in Barnard Park.

The air smelled of gunpowder when Daniel emerged from Angel Tube and headed for Islington Police Station. It was midsummer and airless, the moon slipping unseen into a bright, troubled sky. The day was gravid, ready to burst.

As he started up Liverpool Road, the thunder came and then thick drops of rain, reprimanding, chastening. He turned up his collar and ran past Waitrose and Sainsbury's, dodging last-minute shoppers. Daniel was a runner and so he did not feel the strain in his chest or his legs, even when the rain fell heavier, soaking the shoulders and the back of his jacket, causing him to run faster, and faster.

Inside the police station, he shook the water from his hair and wiped his face with one hand. He brushed the water off his briefcase. When he said his name, he steamed up the glass that separated him from the receptionist.

The duty officer, Sergeant Turner, was waiting for him and pressed a dry hand into his. In his office, Daniel took off his jacket and hung it over the back of the chair.

'You got here quickly,' Turner began.

Instinctively, Daniel slid his business card on to the sergeant's desk. Daniel frequented police stations in London, but had not been to this one in Islington before.

'Partner at Harvey, Hunter and Steele?' the sergeant said, smiling.

'I understand he's a juvenile?'

'Sebastian is eleven years old.'

The sergeant looked at Daniel, as if searching for a response in his face. Daniel had spent a lifetime perfecting reflection and knew that his dark brown eyes gave nothing away as he stared back at the detective.

Daniel was an experienced defender of juveniles: as a solicitor he had defended fifteen-year-olds accused of shooting fellow gang members, and several other teenagers who robbed for drugs. But never an actual child – never a little boy. In fact he had had very little contact with children at all. His own experience of being a child was his only reference point.

'He's not under arrest, is he?' Daniel asked Turner.

'Not at the moment, but there's something not right. You'll see for yourself. He knows exactly what happened to that little boy ... I can tell he does. It wasn't until after we called you that we found the mother. She arrived about twenty minutes ago. Mother says she was in all this time, but poorly, and only just got the messages. We've applied for a warrant to search the family home.'

Daniel watched as Turner's reddish cheeks sagged in emphasis.

'So he's a suspect for the actual murder?'

'You're damn right he is.'

Daniel sighed and took a pad out of his briefcase. Chilling a little in his damp clothes, he took notes as the police officer briefly described the crime and the witnesses and details of the interview with the child so far.

Sebastian was being questioned in relation to the discovery of another child's body. The little boy who had been found dead was called Ben Stokes. He appeared to have been beaten to death in a leafy corner of the adventure playground in Barnard Park on Sunday afternoon. A brick had been smashed against his face, fracturing his eye socket. This brick, and branches and leaves, had been used by the attacker to cover his broken face. His body had been hidden underneath the wooden play-house in the corner of the park, and it was here, on Monday morning, that he was found by one of the youth workers in charge of the adventure playground.

'Ben's mother reported him missing early Sunday evening,' said Turner. 'She said the boy had gone outside to ride his bike along the pavement of Richmond Crescent that afternoon. He wasn't allowed to leave the crescent, but when she looked out to check, there was no sign of him.'

'And you've taken this boy in for questioning because ... ?'

'After the body was found, we set up an incident van on the Barnsbury Road. A local man reported that he had seen two small boys fighting in Barnard Park. One of the boys matched Ben's description. He said he shouted at the boys to stop, and the other child had smiled at him – said they were only playing. When we approached Ben's mother with the description of the other boy, she named Sebastian Croll – your boy in there – who lives only a few doors down from the Stokeses' house.

'Sebastian was home alone in Richmond Crescent – or so we thought – when two officers stopped by at four o'clock this afternoon. Sebastian told the officers that his mother was out, that his father was overseas on business. We arranged an appropriate adult and took him down to the station just after that. It's been obvious since we started that he's hiding something – the social worker insisted that a solicitor be called.'

Daniel nodded and flipped his pad shut.

'I'll take you through,' said Turner.

As he was led to the interview room, Daniel felt the familiar claustrophobia of police stations engulf him. The walls were papered with public authority notices about drink driving, drugs and domestic abuse. All the blinds were closed and dirty.

The interview room was windowless. The walls were painted pale green and completely blank. Straight ahead of him sat Sebastian. The police had taken the boy's clothes and so he was dressed in a white paper suit, which crackled as he shifted in his chair. The oversized suit made the boy seem even smaller and more vulnerable – younger than eleven. He was strikingly beautiful, almost like a little girl, with a wide heart-shaped face, small red lips and large green eyes full of intelligence. His very pale skin was sprinkled with freckles over the nose. His hair was dark brown, and neatly cut. He smiled at Daniel, who smiled back. The child seemed so young that Daniel almost did not know how to speak to him and did his best to conceal his shock.

Sergeant Turner began the introductions. He was a tall man – even taller than Daniel – and seemed too large for the small room. He hunched as he introduced Daniel to Sebastian's mother, Charlotte.

'Thank you so much for coming,' said Charlotte. 'We really appreciate it.'

Daniel nodded at Charlotte and then turned towards her son.

'You must be Sebastian?' he said, sitting down and opening his briefcase.

'Yes, that's right. You can call me Seb if you like.'

Daniel was relieved that the boy seemed so open.

'All right, Seb. Pleased to meet you.'

'Pleased to meet you too. You're my solicitor, aren't you?' Sebastian grinned and Daniel raised an eyebrow. The boy would be his youngest client, yet his words made him seem more confident than teenagers he had defended. Sebastian's searching green eyes and lilting, proper voice disarmed him. The mother's jewellery seemed heavier than she was; the cut of her clothes expensive. The fine bones of her hand moved birdlike as she stroked Sebastian's leg.

This little boy must be innocent, Daniel thought as he opened his folder.